HOW MUCH I WANT

MIAMI NIGHTS SERIES, BOOK 4

MARIE FORCE

How Much I Want
Miami Nights Series, Book 4
By Marie Force

Nochebuena
Miami Nights Novella
By Marie Force

Published by HTJB, Inc.
Copyright 2022. HTJB, Inc.
Cover Design by Kristina Brinton
Print Layout: E-book Formatting Fairies
ISBN: 978-1952793813

The Miami Nights Series

Book 1: How Much I Feel *(Carmen & Jason)*
Book 2: How Much I Care *(Maria & Austin)*
Book 3: How Much I Love *(Dee & Wyatt)*
Nochebuena, A Miami Nights Novella
Book 4: How Much I Want *(Nico & Sofia)*
Book 5: How Much I Need *(Coming Feb. 2023)*

CHAPTER 1

Go to page 315 to read *Nochebuena*, the holiday novella from late 2021 that comes BEFORE *How Much I Want* in the series timeline.

SOFIA

I'm keeping careful watch over the moro after Marlene taught me how quickly the rice and beans can become mushy. After I turn down the heat on the gas stove, I stir the huge pot to keep the rice from sticking to the bottom of the pan. Marlene said it's a delicate balancing act. I had to look up the meaning of that expression and learned it means to carefully manage two or more things. Today, I'm managing the rice and beans and the attention of a man who makes my heart race when he looks at me the way he does.

Nico Giordino.

His sisters and cousin have warned me away from him.

Maria says he's toxic with women. I had to look up the meaning of the word *toxic*, too. I found out that means his behavior would add negativity and upset to my life, which is the last thing I need after what I've gone through with Mateo's father.

1

Speak of the devil… That's another phrase I learned from Livia. Anytime I hear something I don't understand, I ask for the meaning and then add it to the notebook I keep full of English words and sayings I want to remember. Since my son's medical emergency brought me to Dr. Jason Northrup and the Giordino family, I'm determined to learn as much English as I can. While I was blessed with wonderful translators who helped me navigate the medical maze, I decided I need a much better understanding of spoken English.

After spending most of my childhood in Mexico, I returned to Miami when I was in high school and worked hard to catch up to my classmates. I'm pretty good with reading and writing. It's the speaking and comprehension part I'm working on now. I like that word—*comprehension*.

Marlene, who committed to learning English after her first trip "home" to Cuba since the revolution made her realize that Miami is now her home, has been my partner in improving my English. While we'll always be proud native Spanish speakers, we're pleased with what we've learned at our ESL classes. The instructor says I'm a natural, and I'm on my way to being fluent. I had to look up that word, and the meaning made me proud of what I've accomplished. We start back to class in March, and in the meantime, I've been reading books in English to help with my comprehension. I try to learn at least ten new words a day that I keep in a notebook that I study every night before bed.

Back to the devil… He's due any minute to deliver our son to me for Nochebuena and Christmas.

Joaquín Diaz was my high school boyfriend, who, somewhere along the way, fell into the wrong crowd, got himself into trouble with drugs and petty crime and made my life a living hell for years with intense emotional abuse that later became physical. I've finally broken free of him, thanks in no small part to Marlene and Livia, who heard about our plight when Mateo was sick, offered me a job with benefits and quite simply saved my life—and my son's. Thanks to them and a friend who's a lawyer, I've filed for divorce and received a protective order that requires Joaquín to stay five hundred feet from me. The only exception to the order is when we hand off our son between visits.

Sometimes I still can't believe it's come to a need for official protection from the man I once loved.

"Sofia," Nico's cousin Domenic says. "Someone's asking for you outside."

I experience a moment of pure joy at the thought of seeing my little boy, quickly followed by the dread of having to see his father. After washing my hands, I ask Dee to keep an eye on the moro for me and go out through the garage to greet my son.

Mateo, who is five, is doing a lot better than he was, but he's still got a long way to go in his recovery from brain surgery to remove a cancerous tumor. Thankfully, Jason got it all, and he recommended a course of radiation that's now completed. But the damage to his fine motor skills, another English term that has become familiar to me, was significant, thus the ongoing physical and occupational therapy. He also has a slight sag on the right side of his face that Jason says may or may not correct itself. We're waiting to see on that.

Nico pulls up in his truck as I emerge from the garage into bright South Florida sunshine. Marlene sent him to pick up the keg from a nearby liquor store. He approaches Joaquín's old red sedan, which is parked in the driveway. "I'll take him," Nico says.

I stand back and allow Nico to intervene on my behalf, not willing to admit what a relief it is to have him deal with Joaquín so I don't have to.

"I need to speak to my wife," Joaquín says in Spanish as he tightens his hold on Mateo.

"She's not your wife any longer," Nico reminds him, also in Spanish, as he reaches for my son.

"Back off, dude."

I step forward before they get physical. I wouldn't put it past either of them. "It's okay, Nico. I've got this."

Glaring at Joaquín, Nico takes a step back but stays nearby. Just in case.

I take Mateo from Joaquín and hold him close. He smells like

3

cigarette smoke, which enrages me. How can Joaquín smoke around him—or allow anyone else to—after what he's been through? "What do you need?"

"I want you to come home for Christmas," he says in Spanish. "Where you belong."

"I'm sorry, that's not possible," I reply in English.

His scowl turns a face I once found handsome ugly. "You're so fancy now, you can't even speak your own language?"

"I'll see you on the thirtieth." I turn away from him to carry Mateo inside. He's looking forward to swimming in Marlene's pool before the party begins later this afternoon.

"Don't take another step," Nico says to Joaquín.

I keep walking as if I didn't hear that. I trust Nico to make sure Joaquín doesn't follow us inside. But the minute I'm safely in the house, I rush to the front window to look out to make sure the situation isn't escalating. Mateo snuggles into my embrace, seeming relieved, as he always is, to be back with me.

The two men are exchanging words, but that's all it is.

After Joaquín makes an obscene gesture at him, Nico walks away, his fists rolled tightly by his sides. My heart races at the sight of him, angry on my behalf. Why does that mean so much to me? Maybe it's because for years no one was ever angry on my behalf while Joaquín was bullying me into doing everything his way.

Nico comes to find me in Marlene's dining room, where the huge table is covered with serving dishes and other party items.

"Gracias," I say to him. "Lo siento." When I'm upset, I revert to my native language.

"Don't thank me or apologize to me," he says in a harsh tone that's not directed at me.

How do I know that? I couldn't say other than he's never been anything other than sweet to me, but Joaquín can make the sweetest person angry in a matter of seconds. I never saw that side of him until after we were married.

"I don't like the way that guy acts as if you still belong to him."

"He knows I don't."

Nico puts his hands on his hips, frustration apparent in his pose and expression. "Does he?"

"If he doesn't, that's not my fault. What else can I do besides file for divorce?"

"I hate the idea of you guys not being safe," he says, softly so as not to alarm Mateo.

"We're safe." The waver in my voice tells the true story. I never feel truly safe except for when I'm at work, surrounded by people like him who care about me. And Nico doesn't even work at Giordino's. He's just there a lot, especially when I'm working.

"I wish…" He stops himself and shakes his head.

"What do you wish?"

"We should talk about that sometime when we're not surrounded by people during a holiday."

My heart is beating so fast I wonder if I'm going to pass out, or something equally embarrassing, in front of the man who's become a close friend over the last few months. What does he want to talk about?

"I'm going to contact a friend who's a cop and ask him to send cars by here later, just in case your ex decides to come back and start trouble."

I swallow hard at the thought of my ex-husband causing trouble for the family that's been so good to us. "You really think that's necessary?"

"I do."

"Maybe Mateo and I should go. If we're not here, then no one will bother your family."

"You're safer here than you'd be anywhere else. The people here would kill for you."

"Would they?"

"They would."

"All of them, or just you?"

"All of them, but especially me."

"And why is that?"

"That's the thing we should maybe talk about when my entire family isn't about to arrive for Nochebuena."

5

The look he gives me when he says those words steals the breath from my lungs. Nico Giordino is the sexiest man on the planet, and I'll fight anyone who says otherwise. Right in that moment, I don't care that his sisters and cousin think he's toxic toward women.

I just want more of him and the way he makes me feel.

NICO

Nochebuena is usually my favorite night of the year, but I can't relax after the encounter with Sofia's ex. Not to mention work is busy, and I'm keeping an eye on things while my family parties all around me. My phone buzzes with constant questions that only I can answer as the owner of the car service that's running at full tilt tonight. Normally, I'd be thrilled about that, but I can't think about anything other than Sofia, Mateo and the son of a bitch who is her child's father.

I got to see him in action earlier when he dropped Mateo at Abuela's for the party. After he hassled Sofia—and me when I got involved—I asked my friend Miguel, who's a cop, to send patrols past the house in case he comes back looking for trouble. Miguel filled me in on Joaquín's background, which put me even more on edge.

He has a record a mile long and is well known to local police.

And he's still legally married to the woman I want with every fiber of my being.

My stomach tightens to the point of nausea at the thought of her or Mateo being in danger from a man who should've been the one to protect them.

They have me now, and I'd die before I'd let anything happen to either of them.

Abuela's annual Christmas Eve celebration rages all around me, with family, friends, food, music, booze and presents. Santa is due to arrive any minute, and the local Cuban band that plays every year is better than ever.

I can't bring myself to care about any of it. My entire focus is on Sofia and Mateo.

Watching them playing in Abuela's heated pool with my sister Maria and her fiancé's daughter, Everly, I can't help but smile at Mateo's pleasure at being in the water. The poor little guy has been through a rough ordeal since Carmen's now-husband Jason discovered the tumor and removed it in an emergency surgery. The cancer is gone, but the child is still fighting his way back to full health after months of rigorous physical and occupational therapy.

In time, he's expected to make a complete recovery, but he may always have deficiencies to overcome. We don't know yet what the future holds for him, and we won't know for a while yet, but I want to be there for them both.

That's a first for me.

I've never felt that way about anyone else, but for some reason, the minute I met Sofia, I wanted her in a way I've never wanted anyone else.

My sisters and cousin have told her to stay away from me. They say I'm "toxic" with women, and sure, that's probably been true in the past. But everything about her is different, and I'm determined to be different, too. I understand the stakes. She's a single mom of a child with special needs and is in the middle of a contentious divorce from a potentially dangerous man.

The last thing she needs is bullshit of any kind, which is why I'm determined to be a much better version of myself with her.

If only I can convince her to give me a chance to prove that to her.

So far, we've been all about the flirtation, but nothing has come of it.

Yet.

My cousin Domenic, home from New York for the holidays, brings me another beer.

I take the icy bottle from him. "Thanks."

"What's up with you, hombre? You're wound tighter than a drum today."

"Nothing. Just busy at work. I probably ought to be there, but I didn't want to miss Nochebuena."

"Try telling that to someone who doesn't know you better than just about anyone. Work doesn't stress you out like this."

"It's my first Christmas as the owner. It is stressing me out. Every car is booked through New Year's."

"That's great, primo. Congratulations."

I shrug. If you want to know how far gone I am over Sofia, the fact that I don't care that my new business is killing it is a pretty good indication.

Dom sits on the barstool next to mine. "What's going on, Nico? And tell me the truth this time."

"Sofia."

"Sofia-from-the-restaurant Sofia?"

"Yeah."

"What about her?"

I hesitate to say words that can never be taken back, even to my cousin and close friend. However, I'm clearly doing a piss-poor job of hiding my torment if Dom picked up on it. "Everything about her."

He goes still, his expression completely blank. "Seriously?"

"As serious as it gets."

"Are you… like… seeing her?"

"Not officially, but I'd like to be."

"*Dude…*"

"What?"

"It's just… you know… not like you to be into a single mom."

I keep my gaze fixed on her and Mateo. If she's anywhere near me, I can't help but look at her. "She's special."

"How so?"

"I can't explain it. She does it for me."

"What does she think of you?"

"She likes me, but the girls told her to stay away from me. The word 'toxic' was used."

Domenic cracks up at that. "I bet it was."

"You're supposed to be on my side."

8

He holds up his free hand. "I am. Always. But, Nico... A single mom? Really? You can't do what you do with her."

The comment pisses me off. "I know that."

"Isn't her son sick, too?"

"He was. He's better now, but he has a long way to go before he's fully recovered. I like him as much as I like her. He's the sweetest kid."

Domenic places his hand on my forehead. "No fever."

I push his hand away. "You can fuck off if you're going to be a jackass about it."

"Wow, this is more serious than I thought."

"I don't know how to convince her I'm for real."

"I suppose you just show up for her—and her son—consistently with no games, no bullshit, no nonsense."

"I can do that."

"Maybe some romance, too." He gives me a side-eye look. "You know what that is?"

"Fuck *off*, will you please?"

Dom loses it laughing, which doesn't surprise me.

"She's checking you out, too."

"What? She is?"

"Jesus Christmas." Dom rolls his eyes. "You've barely looked away from her. You can see as well as I can that she's watching you."

That information makes my heart do this weird flipping thing that leaves me light-headed for a second, until I see Miguel step onto Abuela's patio with a concerned expression on his face. When he finds me in the crowd, he tilts his head, asking me to come to him.

"What's up?" Dom asks.

"I don't know, but I'm going to find out."

9

CHAPTER 2

SOFIA

*M*y stomach hurts as I watch Nico cross the pool deck to speak to a uniformed police officer. His presence here can mean only one thing—trouble caused by my ex-husband. He's not technically my ex yet. I'm counting the days until he is.

"Are you okay?" Maria asks.

I force myself to look away from what's happening with Nico and the cop. "My ex has been causing some problems. Nico asked his friend to keep an eye on things here in case he tried to come back. It's probably not a good thing that he's come in."

The thought of bringing any trouble into the lives of people who've been so good to me makes me sick.

"Go see what's going on," Maria says. "I've got Mateo."

"Are you sure?"

"Yes, of course. Go."

"Thank you, Maria."

I get out of the pool and grab a towel on my way to join Nico and the police officer.

"This is my friend, Sergeant Miguel Silva with the Miami Police," Nico says. "Miguel, this is Sofia Diaz, Joaquín's ex-wife."

Miguel found him lurking outside and arrested him for violating the protective order. He wanted to let us know."

My stomach hurts even worse as I hear that Joaquín will spend Christmas in jail, which means his family and friends will blame me for that. Nothing is ever his fault with them. No, all his troubles are because of me, according to them.

Nico puts his arm around me like that's something he does all the time, but it's the first time he's ever touched me.

I can't help but lean into his warm, solid body as tremors shake me. Just when things with Joaquín have started to settle down... There hasn't been any trouble between us in weeks, since the judge approved the protective order after an altercation got physical, and he left bruises on my arms and shoulders.

He apologized to me for that via text and said the order wasn't necessary.

I didn't respond to the text. The protective order has given me some badly needed peace of mind. "What will happen to him?"

"He'll be arraigned on new charges the day after Christmas," Miguel says, confirming my fears.

"His family and friends won't be happy with me."

"You aren't the one who violated the protective order," Nico says.

"Still..."

"We can assign some people to keep an eye on your place, too," Miguel says.

"I'll be with her and Mateo tonight."

Gasping, I look up at Nico.

"I won't let anything happen to them," he says to Miguel.

"I'll still send some patrol cars by. What's the address?"

While still processing that Nico plans to come home with me and Mateo, I recite my address for Miguel.

"Try not to worry," he says. "We'll be keeping an eye out. You folks have a Merry Christmas."

"You do the same," Nico says, releasing his hold on me to shake hands with his friend. "Thanks again."

"You got it, brother."

"Are you okay?" Nico asks me after the officer goes into the house on the way out.

"I, um… What do you suppose Joaquín was doing here? He knows better than to come here or be near me unless we're exchanging Mateo."

"He was looking for trouble, and he found it." Nico's voice has a hard edge to it, but Joaquín does that to people. "I don't want you to worry about anything. You and your little boy are going to have a wonderful Christmas."

"You don't have to come home with us."

"I won't sleep for a second if I'm worried about you guys. Besides, you probably need help putting together Mateo's toys."

"I was going to do that when I get home."

"Now you have help. If you want it, that is. I can stay in my car outside if you'd prefer that."

"Why would you do that for me?"

He runs a fingertip over my face, a touch so fleeting, it might as well have never happened, but I feel it *everywhere*. "Because I *care*, Sofia. I care about both of you, and I don't want anything to happen, especially not at Christmas."

I'm breathless and speechless and every other "less" I can think of.

"If you don't want me there, I can keep an eye on things from outside. It's no big deal."

"Sure. No big deal to sleep in your car on Christmas Eve."

"I'd do it for you."

"Why?"

His gaze shifts from my eyes to my lips, lingering for a second before he looks up again. "Because."

"Okay," I say with a nervous laugh.

"Are you ready to get Mateo home?"

"The party is just getting started. You don't want to leave yet."

"Yes, I do."

"If you're sure, I'll get him out of the pool." I hope Mateo doesn't throw a fit. He doesn't do transitions well. We're working on that. I return to the edge of the pool where Maria is playing with him and

Everly. When she sees me coming, she deftly lifts Mateo out of the pool and into my arms.

I speak to him in Spanish when I tell him it's time to go home so Santa can come and bring presents. Only because he's excited for Christmas does he go along with me when I change him into dry clothes and remind him to thank Marlene when we say goodbye. I want him to be bilingual, so I'm teaching him the English I'm learning and switch back and forth between the two languages with him.

In one of the few times we've seen her in recent years, my mother told me I'm going to confuse him. So far, he seems to be getting it. If you ask me, he has much more of a natural affinity for English than I ever will. When Mateo is dressed in Christmas pajamas, I grab my backpack and shove my feet into flip-flops. I zip sweatshirts onto both of us, as the night has grown cooler, like it does this time of year. Then I pick him up to find Marlene among the sea of family members and friends enjoying the music. She's turned her backyard into a wonderland of white lights woven through palms and strung along the fence. Chairs and tables brought in from a rental company are scattered throughout the pool area along with high-tops and barstools.

I've never seen more food in my life than what was prepared for this party, and that's saying something since the weekly Sunday brunch at the restaurant is no joke.

Marlene, who is seated with her gentleman friend, Mr. Muñoz, her daughter, Vivian, and Vivian's husband, Vincent, jumps up when she sees us coming. "Are you heading home?"

"We are. This little guy needs to get to bed so Santa can come."

"Yes, you do," Marlene says, tickling his feet.

Mateo's laugh makes everyone smile, as always.

"But guess what? Santa already came to my house, and he left something for you. Do you want to see, my love?"

Mateo nods and goes willingly into her outstretched arms, which is rare for him. If I'm anywhere near him, he wants me and only me. But Marlene has a way with him, as does Vincent's mother, Livia, who joins us as we head inside to see what Santa brought for Mateo. They've told him to call them Abuela and Nona, which is such a lovely honor since his maternal grandmother couldn't care less about him—or me—and he sees Joaquín's mother only occasionally.

Nico gives his cousin Domenic a bro hug, punches his brother, Milo, on the arm and follows us inside to the family room, where a stack of gifts is piled next to the tree.

"These are for Mateo." Marlene gestures to a huge pile. "From me and Livia."

"*What? No…*" Tears fill my eyes so rapidly, it's like someone has turned on a faucet.

"We had the *best* time shopping for him," Marlene says. "Don't spoil our fun."

"It was fun," Livia adds. "Been a while since we had any babies to spoil, so we went a little nuts over him and Everly."

"You guys… You've already been so good to us. It's too much."

Marlene puts Mateo down on the carpeted floor. "Do you want to open your presents, love?"

He looks up at me, his big brown eyes huge with the wonder of it all.

"Go ahead, sweetheart." My eyes are so flooded with tears, I can barely see through them as Mateo rips into the brightly wrapped packages that are full of trucks and trains and even a Clifford the Big Red Dog, who is his absolute favorite.

Their generosity never fails to astound me. I've never in my life known people like them, who wrap their arms around a perfect stranger and make her—and her son—part of their family like that's no big deal.

"What do you say to Abuela and Nona?" I ask him.

"Muchas gracias," he says softly as he struggles to his feet and walks to each of them with his crooked gait to hug them. "Thank you."

"You are very welcome, mi amor," Abuela says. "I hope you have a very Merry Christmas."

"Feliz Navidad," he says. "That means Merry Christmas en Español."

"Yes, it does," Nona replies. "Aren't you just the smartest boy?" She kisses him on the cheek and then sends him back to me while the two of them pack up his presents in a bag one of them produces out of nowhere.

That's how they are—anticipating every need before you even have it. I want to be them when I grow up. I hug them both and blink back more tears as I thank them again. "I don't know where we'd be without you and your family," I tell them.

"We love you both," Nona says. "You'll always have a family with us."

"We love you, too."

Nico hugs them. "You guys never fail to amaze me. Love you so much."

"Love you, too, sweetheart," Nona tells her grandson. "Are you going to see them home?"

"I am," Nico says.

"Good," Abuela says as she crooks her finger to bring him down close enough for her to kiss his cheek. "Take good care of them. They're very precious to us."

"Yes, ma'am." He carries Mateo's gifts in a bag big enough to be Santa's.

"Mama, play toys?"

"In the morning, love. First you must go to sleep so Santa can come to our house, too."

"Don't wanna sleep. Wanna play."

"I know."

As I buckle him into his car seat, Nico stashes the bag of toys in my trunk. "I'll be right behind you."

I straighten and turn to face him. "You really don't have to."

"We've already had that argument. I won. Don't lose me."

Smiling, I say, "I'll try not to."

CHAPTER 3

NICO

I have no idea what the hell I'm doing with her. Domenic is right. She's so far from my type as to be a whole other species from what I'm accustomed to, but as I follow her home to a rough part of town near Little Haiti, I'm more determined than ever to make her—and her son—mine. I don't care what it takes or what I have to do to achieve my goal of having her in my life, in my arms and in my bed.

I can't even think about that last one, or I'll be hard as a rock in two seconds flat. No other woman in the history of women has had this kind of immediate effect on me. Sure, other women have turned me on and gotten me fired up, but not like this. Sofia is unique in every possible way, which is why it's so important for me to keep her and her son safe and as close to me as possible.

They're coming with me to my parents' house tomorrow, too, not that she knows that yet. I'll talk her into it, or I won't go.

My cell rings with a call from Angelo, my right hand at work. "What's up?"

"Dude, we're getting *killed* over here with last-minute requests for rides. We could really use you and one more car if you can break free."

"I can't."

"Nico... We'll have to turn people away."

"Let me call my brother. I'll get right back to you."

I use the Bluetooth in my car to call Milo.

"Yo. I thought you left?"

"I did. I need a favor."

"What's that?"

"Can you drive for us tonight? Just for a couple of hours?"

Milo's groan tells me he feels the same way I do about working on Christmas Eve.

"I know it's a lot to ask, but I've got a situation, and I need one more driver right away." Milo rarely has more than one drink per event, so I'm not worried about him being impaired.

"Is your situation named Sofia?"

"So what if it is?"

"Let me get this straight—you want me to leave my family on Christmas Eve so you can be with your girlfriend or whatever she is?"

"Did you see Miguel there earlier?"

"Yeah, I was going to ask you what was up with that."

"He arrested her ex-husband, or soon-to-be ex, lurking outside Abuela's and probably looking for some trouble. She has a protective order against him. Now he's in jail for Christmas, and she's worried about his friends and family coming for her, so I'm following her home and planning to stick around."

"I've got you covered at work, bro. Tell Angelo I'm on my way."

I breathe out a sigh of relief. "Thanks, Milo. Seriously. I owe you."

"One of these days, I'm going to cash in on all those IOUs."

"Any time, brother."

"Call me if you need backup at Sofia's."

"I will. Thanks again."

"Will we see you tomorrow at Mom's?"

"I'll be there."

"See you then."

I call Angelo back. "My brother is on his way."

"Great, thanks."

"Let me know if anything else comes up."

"You'll be the first to know."

Angelo abruptly ends the call, which is fine. He's busy. No need for formalities between us when we spend hours together or on the phone every day.

As always, I give thanks for Milo. He's the best of the best, and everyone knows it. Milo would be perfect for Sofia and her little boy. He's the sort of upstanding man she needs in her life.

That's a depressing thought, but it's the truth.

As I take a left turn and follow her into the parking lot at her apartment complex, I'm fully aware that my little brother is a far superior man. But I'm determined to be better for Sofia and for her son, even if that means changing everything about the life I've led up to now.

My gut clenches with concern for her living alone with her little boy in such a rough neighborhood. I haven't been anywhere near here in years, and I liked it better when I didn't know where she lives. Calling this place run-down would be generous.

I take a good look around as I park in a visitor spot and follow her up a flight of outdoor stairs to the second floor, toting the big bag of gifts from my grandmothers. Paint is chipping, one of the stairs sags under my weight, and I doubt the banister would stop anyone from taking a bad fall.

She juggles Mateo, who's half asleep on her shoulder, and her purse as she uses her key in the door. She'd be incredibly vulnerable if someone wanted to harm her in the unlit corridor.

Is this place even up to code? Doubtful. Maybe I'll make a call to the building inspector at city hall tomorrow and get them over here to do their freaking jobs. But then I remember it's Christmas tomorrow, and no one will answer the phone at city hall. I'll save that call for another day.

Sofia flips on a light inside the door and steps aside for me to go by her into a warm, cheerful, cozy space. I marvel at how she's made the most of every square inch of the place to create a home for herself and her son.

"This is so nice." She's asked me to speak to her in English so she can continue to learn.

"Oh, thanks. If you can ignore the outside, it's not so bad."

It's really bad outside, but she doesn't need me to tell her that.

She turns the dead bolt and applies the chain lock. Both look sturdy, which is a relief. "Let me just get him down."

"Take your time."

"His gifts are in that closet." She uses her chin to gesture to a door. "If you want to get started."

I wish I'd thought to bring tools. "Sure. I can do that."

"I have a few tools in the drawer by the fridge."

"You read my mind."

Her smile lights up her gorgeous face and makes my heart skip a beat, which is another thing that never happened to me until she happened to me.

"Be right back."

As my Nona would say, there's not a pin out of place in the apartment, which is clean and ruthlessly organized. A poster on the wall lists the seven rules of life: Smile, Be Kind, Don't Give Up, Don't Compare, Avoid Negativity, Make Peace with Your Past, Take Care of Your Body and Mind.

Words to live by, for sure.

Another poster has a quote from Maya Angelou: "People will forget what you said, people will forget what you did, but people will never forget how you made them feel."

That one makes me feel guilty over the broken hearts I've left in my wake. I'm not proud of my track record with women, but the one thing I'll say in my own defense is I've never made any kind of promise to a woman. If they read more into casual encounters than I did, how is that my fault?

It's not, but I could've been less of a dick in my dealings with them. That much is for certain.

I find the tools right where she told me they'd be and get busy unloading the boxes of toys from the well-organized closet. Everything in her home has a place, and nothing is left lying around. She'd hate my house, which is in bad need of some of her organizational skills. I also don't own a single Christmas decoration, except the tree my sisters insisted I needed. I spend the holidays with my parents and grandmothers, who have the market cornered on that stuff. What do I need with it?

Sofia, on the other hand, has an adorable little tree on a tabletop in a corner. It's decorated with colored lights and ornaments made from Mateo's art projects. Everything about her home is cozy, warm and sweet, like her.

"The pool really wore him out," Sofia says when she returns to the living room. "Usually, I have to read *The Night Before Christmas* book and put out the cookies and milk for Santa, but he didn't ask about any of that tonight."

"I'm glad he had fun in the pool."

"Swimming is so good for him. None of his problems bother him when he's swimming. He's just like a regular kid."

I turn so I can see her. "He's doing great, Sofia. You can see that, can't you?"

She shrugs. "Sometimes all I can see are the things he *can't* do."

"That list is getting shorter all the time. He's bouncing back, and soon the whole thing will be like a bad memory that happened years ago."

She links her index fingers as if she needs to do something with her hands. "He might always have some limitations."

"He'll find a way to work around them."

"I hope so." I can see her trying to shake off her worries about her son to focus on what I'm doing with the toys. "Let me help."

"I've got this if you have other things to do."

"I can't let you do all that!"

"I don't mind at all. I like doing it."

"No one likes spending Christmas Eve putting together toys, but I sure appreciate your help. Usually, it's me doing it myself until three in the morning, and then I'm a wreck the next day."

"Joaquín didn't help?" I ask as casually as I can, wanting to know more about the man who's caused her such heartache.

"God, no," she says, laughing. "He can't change a lightbulb without help, but he can fix anything on a car. I think it was mostly he didn't care about helping me."

"My dad was adamant that we all learn the basics of how to survive in this world, as he put it. If something happened to the water heater, for example, he'd march the four of us to the utility closet for a lesson on what to do."

"That's so smart." She sits on the floor next to me. "He gave you invaluable life skills."

Her appealing scent surrounds me like a cloud of sweetness. "Yes, he did, even if we had zero interest at the time. Although, I was more interested than the others. He identified a mechanical ability in me early and nurtured that as I was growing up. There's not much I can't fix as a result."

"That's an incredibly useful skill to have. Your dad is amazing. You were lucky."

"Yes, we were, and we know it."

"How's your mom doing?"

The reminder of my mom's battle with breast cancer is like a fist to the gut, the same as it's been since I first heard of her diagnosis. "She's doing well. Her treatment is due to end in January, and then I guess we'll see. It's stressful to think it could come back."

"You have to stay positive and hope for the best."

"I'm trying."

"I didn't even offer you a drink! How about some of the coquito that my neighbor made for me?"

The Spanish eggnog spiked with rum is one of my favorites. "I wouldn't say no to that."

She jumps up from the floor and goes into the kitchen, returning a few minutes later with the drinks. "It's the rum that Mr. Muñoz gave me for Christmas—along with a huge tip. He's so lovely."

I take a sip of the drink, and the rum sends warmth all the way through me. "Mmm, that's good, and yes, he is."

"Do you think he and Marlene will get married?"

"I'm not sure. She's fiercely independent after being a widow for decades. I'm not sure she'd want to give that up."

"He's so crazy about her that she wouldn't have to give up anything to marry him. He'd give her the world."

I can't help but note the wistful tone of her voice. Without looking up from the train station I'm assembling, I ask her, "Is that what you want? A man who'll give you the world?"

"In part. I also want someone who doesn't want to change me or keep me from pursuing my dreams."

"Is that what Joaquín did?"

"That was the least of what he did. He wanted to control my every thought, movement, emotion. He isolated me from my friends, who tried to tell me he was no good. I wish I'd listened to them, but then I wouldn't have Mateo. He was worth it all."

"I'm so glad you left him. For many reasons, but mostly because you deserve so much better than that."

She eyes me over the rim of her glass. "What other reasons?"

"What do you mean?" I know full well what she's asking but need to buy myself a minute to figure out what to say.

Apparently, I'm not fooling her if the look she gives me is any indication. "What are the other reasons you're glad I left him?"

"Oh, so you want an actual list?"

Smiling, she says, "A list would be good."

That smile does it for me, big-time. "Hmm, well… Of course, the fact that you're single is good news for me."

"How so?"

My gaze shoots to her, and I find her hiding a smile. "You're messing with me and enjoying it."

"I am enjoying it. It's so rare to see Nico Giordino unsettled. You're usually very confident."

"Not around you, I'm not."

"What do you mean?"

"I'm always nervous and off my game with you."

"Your game… Is that why your sisters and cousin told me to stay away from you?"

I tighten a screw into a train station toy that I would've loved as a kid. "I guess."

"What's your usual game?"

How can I answer her question without making her think I'm a total asshole? "It's not a game. At least that's not the intention."

"What's the intention?"

If I tell her my goal has been to remain free of complications and anything that smelled like commitment, I'll never see her again. Not like this, anyway. Not in her home with her little boy sleeping in the next room. "I've just kind of tried to, you know, keep things casual. In the past, that is."

"Ah, I see."

I look up to find her watching me closely, a hint of amusement remaining in her gorgeous brown eyes. "Look, I know how that must sound to you, but the truth is... I want to be different with you."

"Different how?"

"You and your probing questions," I reply with the hint of a grin.

She shrugs. "When a girl hears a guy is toxic, it makes sense to try to get to the bottom of what that means before she decides whether she wants to spend more time with him."

"Yeah, I suppose it does," I say with a sigh. "I promise not to be toxic with you."

"Have you promised other women that?"

"I've never promised anyone anything, which is how I got the toxic title. From the outside, I must look like an asshole, but I never make promises I can't keep. So, usually, I make no promises."

"But you're promising not to be toxic with me."

"You noticed that, huh?" I place the train station on the carpet so I can install the tower piece that goes on top.

"I've noticed a lot of things where you're concerned."

"Like what?"

"You're very handsome, for one thing."

"Am I?"

She rolls her eyes. "As if you haven't heard that your whole damned life."

I laugh harder than I have in a long time. It's been a rough year with my mom's illness and getting a new business off the ground. Sofia has been a bright spot, and she's getting brighter by the second. "I might've heard that a few times."

"Whatever. It's the cause of all your problems."

"I didn't know I had problems."

"With *women*. You attract them too easily and discard them just as easily."

"Ouch. That hurts."

"Truth hurts."

"Can I tell you the truth?"

"I wish you would."

I put down the screwdriver and look at her—really look at her. "I like you. I want to spend time with you and Mateo. I want to be a better man for you so you can have everything you want and deserve. But the thing is... I've never really done this before."

"Done what?"

"I think it's called a relationship?"

She loses it laughing. She laughs so hard, tears fill her eyes.

"You think that's funny, huh?"

Nodding, she wipes away tears. "Hysterical."

I shake my head in pretend despair. "I'm baring my soul to you, and all you do is laugh at me."

"Is that what you're doing? Baring your soul?"

"This is as bare as my soul gets. I don't have these conversations with women. Well, usually I don't."

"Right, because you're too busy taking whatever they'll give before you move on to the next one."

I wince at how close to the mark she strikes with that comment.

"I don't want to be one of your conquests, Nico. I learned that word in a romance novel about a guy like you."

"I want to do better for you, Sofia. And for Mateo."

"We've been through a lot, he and I." All hints of amusement are now gone. "Between his illness and everything with his father... It's been a lot."

"I know."

"You don't know the half of it." The sharp tone of her voice catches me by surprise. "I've been through hell, and the last thing I need is another man in my life."

And here I thought we were getting somewhere... "I understand if it's not the right time for you."

"I'm not saying that. Exactly."

"Then what are you saying?"

She takes a second and seems to choose her words carefully. "If we're going to do this thing you refer to as a relationship, we're going to do it very, very, *very* slowly or not at all."

"I can do slow. Isn't that what we've been doing all along?"

"I suppose we have."

I glance at her. "We've both got a lot going on, and neither of us was looking for what this has become."

"What's it become?"

"Something special and important to me. I wasn't expecting that."

"Neither was I."

I venture a glance her way. "So it's important to you, too?"

"If it wasn't, you wouldn't be here."

CHAPTER 4

SOFIA

*W*hat the hell am I doing with this guy? He's too sexy, too slick, too everything, and yet, I can't seem to help myself when it comes to him. It's been this way since I met him during one of my first shifts at Giordino's, after the family swooped in to help us after Mateo's diagnosis. Livia and Marlene raised money for us, offered me a job and generally made me part of their family.

I'm so incredibly grateful to them, which is why I've felt guilty for secretly crushing on Livia's sexy grandson. No matter how many times I tell myself I have no space in my life for a man, anytime he's around, he's all I see or think about.

While dealing with a difficult divorce and custody battle and nursing my son back to health after a hellish ordeal, the last thing I need is more drama in my life.

Nico Giordino is drama personified, or at least he has been in the past if the warnings from his family members are to be believed. And I do believe them. Carmen, Maria and Dee were pained telling me to watch out for him, as if it hurt them to be disloyal to their cousin and brother. But their concern for me was truly touching. I've missed having girlfriends, and each of them has become a good friend over the last year.

Maybe I'm a fool, but I believe him when he says he wants to be a better man for me and Mateo. The only way I can find out for certain is to let him try, to let him in. I hate feeling like I'm starting something that won't end well, especially after having already been down that road with my ex. In the back of my mind, I knew from the beginning that probably wouldn't end well, and I did it anyway because I wanted out of my mother's home so badly. I went all in with him and ended up pregnant and married to a man who wasn't worthy of either of us. I don't regret anything with him, though, because I got my Mateo out of it. He's worth any hell or heartache I had to go through.

But I'd like to think I can learn from past mistakes, and falling into this thing with Nico has heartache written all over it.

"What're you guys doing tomorrow?" he asks.

"Nothing much." I haven't spoken to my mother in months. "We're going to have a nice quiet day, just the two of us."

Without looking up from what he's doing, he says, "Do you want to come with me to my mom's?"

As if that sort of thing is no big deal.

"You can't just invite people to someone else's house on Christmas."

"It's my parents, and yes, I can. They'd be mad if I didn't invite you."

I give him a skeptical look. "Your mom has enough people to feed without adding more."

"My mom loves to feed people, and she'd love to have you two. But only if you want to. No pressure. I can hang here with you guys."

"You're not doing that. You need to be with your family on Christmas."

"I need to be sure you guys are safe. I didn't like the vibe I got from *him* today. He's looking for trouble, and with him locked up, there might be others looking for trouble."

"That's nothing new. It's just how it is."

"Was he always that way?"

"Not like he is now. He's changed a lot in the last few years. I barely recognize him anymore."

He sits back against the sofa and takes a sip from his glass. "What happened?"

"I wish I knew. I suspect it might be mental health issues, but don't try to suggest that to him. He doesn't want to hear it. He was always difficult and moody. The cruelty started after we were married a year or so. At first, it was just verbal abuse that escalated to emotional and physical abuse. I'd only just recently worked up the courage to leave when Mateo got sick. I almost went back when I couldn't pay my rent."

"I'm glad you didn't."

"I would've had to if it hadn't been for your grandmothers and the Giordino family."

"Thank goodness for them."

"I say that every single day. I have no idea what would've become of me and Mateo without their generosity and the job that allows me to live independent of him and my mother, who's almost as bad as he is. Not quite, but close." It's all I can do not to shudder thinking of her. She made my life a living hell before I traded one hell for another.

My goal now is to make good decisions for myself and my son.

"So tomorrow... What do you think?"

"Are you sure your mom won't mind?"

"I'm positive, but I could text her if that would make you feel better."

"It's too late to text her now."

He glances at the clock on the wall. "They're just getting out of Midnight Mass."

"How come you didn't go?"

"Because I had something better to do." He types the text and no sooner puts his phone down than it dings with a text. "She says to 'please tell Sofia and Mateo we'd love to have them.'"

"You're all so kind. I've never known people like your family."

"They are pretty great."

"Since your mom doesn't mind, I'd like to go tomorrow, but only if you tell me what I can bring."

"You don't need to bring a thing."

"I can't go empty-handed."

"A bottle of wine, then."

"I can do that."

He pushes the tricycle across the carpet, eyeing the wheels he just installed. "How does that look?"

"Perfect. The PT said he was still too unsteady for a big-boy bike and suggested the trike to help strengthen his legs."

"He'll love it. I think that's everything."

"Thank you so much. This would've taken me all night."

"Now you can get a good night's sleep."

"You don't have to stay."

"Yes, I do, but act like I'm not here. Do your thing. I'll be here just in case."

"Right." I roll my eyes. "Pretend like you're not here. As if that's possible."

"Does that mean you might like me, too?"

"A little. Maybe."

His smile is lethal. "Well, that's good to know."

"Don't get all full of yourself."

"According to my loving family, I was born full of myself."

That makes me laugh. "They keep you humble."

"They try." His smile fades, and he becomes more serious. "I want you to know... It's important to me that you know..."

"What, Nico?"

"That I really like you—and Mateo. And it's super important to me that you know I'd never do anything to hurt either of you. I know my sisters and cousin gave you an earful about me, and trust me, I deserve everything they said about me. But I'm very determined to be different with you."

"That means a lot to me. I've had a really hard time for a very long time, and the last thing I need is more trouble. I'm exhausted, Nico. Mentally, physically and emotionally."

"I want to be the one who brings you some relief, not more problems."

"I wish you knew how badly I want to let you be that person for me."

"What's stopping you?"

"I've made some big mistakes. I don't want to make another."

"What if I could promise you that I won't be a mistake?"

"You can't do that."

"I can do that. I can look you in the eye right here and right now and swear to you that I won't be a mistake." He takes hold of my hand, and I let him while trying not to notice the jolt of electricity that travels through me when he touches me. "I swear to you, Sofia. You can have faith in me."

Reluctantly, I pull back my hand. "I need to think about it some more before I decide anything."

"I completely respect that, but will you give me the chance to show you how it might be with us while you do your thinking?"

"How would you show me?"

"One hour at a time. One day at a time. One week at a time. However long it takes to prove to you that you can put your faith in me."

"Can I ask you something?"

"Anything."

"Why me?"

NICO

I've never worked so hard to convince a woman to date me. Sofia has been unique that way from the beginning, and now I have to find a way to tell her how and why she's special. "Have you ever had something—a toy, a car, a friend, anything—that made you feel better when you were around that thing or person?"

"I have that with Mateo."

"That's how it is for me with you. When you're around, I feel better. I feel lighter, happier, excited. It's like the best kind of natural high. I felt it when we got our first dog and when I bought

30

my first car and when I started my business. But I'd never felt that with a woman until I met you. Every time I see you or talk to you, I can't wait until I can do it again. I never want to leave wherever you are, and it absolutely *kills* me to see your ex giving you a hard time and making you feel unsafe. I want to fix every problem you have or will ever have, and I just want to take care of you and Mateo." I feel like an idiot for going on for so long. "To answer your question, that's why."

She surprises the fuck out of me when she rises to her knees and comes toward me, stopping when she's an inch from me. Then she nearly stops my heart when she curls her arms around my neck and presses her lips to mine. I'm afraid to move or breathe or do anything that'll spook her.

"Are you going to kiss me back?"

"Do you want me to?"

Before she finishes nodding, I'm up on my knees, with my arms around her and my lips sliding over hers, while reminding myself to go slow, to take it easy, to let her set the pace. I quickly discover that her pace is all in, right now, much to my astonishment. When her tongue caresses my bottom lip, I almost come in my pants for the first time since my nightmare teenage years when it seemed to happen every time a girl looked at me.

Christ have mercy, she's sexy and sweet and curvy in all the right places. I'm not sure what I'm allowed to touch, so I keep my hands on her back even though they're dying to wander and explore. But the last thing I want to do is startle her or remind her that she wanted to think about this as recently as ten seconds ago, and now she's kissing me like she's done thinking.

I wish my mind would shut off and let me fully enjoy the feeling of her tongue rubbing up against mine, her full breasts smashed against my chest and the extremely tempting ass that's located just below my hands. But I want to do this right. I've never been less inclined to end a kiss, but that's what I do, withdrawing gradually as she whimpers.

"Easy, love." With my hands on her face, I compel her to look at me while I try to ignore the sexy pout on her swollen lips. "A minute ago, you said you didn't want to rush into anything, and if you keep kissing me like that, things are gonna get real."

"What if that's what I want?"

"I'd love it if that's what you wanted, but I want to do this right. I want us to date and for you to totally trust me before we take this any further."

"What you said..." She's staring at my lips, which makes it hard for me to think about anything other than kissing her again. Being honorable truly sucks sometimes.

"What did I say?"

"About how you feel when I'm around and how you want to keep us safe..." She tips her gaze up to meet mine. "No one has ever said things like that to me before."

I take her hand and place it on my chest. "Feel that?"

My heart is hammering so hard, I can hear it fluttering in my ears.

She licks her lips and nods.

I'm so hard, I ache for her. "That's what being with you like this does to me. That's what happens when you look at me or smile at me or walk into a room. Every. Fucking. Time."

She turns our hands so mine is now flat against her chest. Her heart is doing the same dance as mine. As she releases a shuddering, deep breath, I realize she wants me every bit as much as I want her.

But with so much at stake, I refuse to let our hormones overtake common sense. She has very real concerns about me, and before we take this any further, I want to prove myself to her. For whatever reason, that feels much more critical than satisfying the powerful desire I feel for her.

Let me just say—this is a first for me. Never have I had a woman in my arms who was obviously willing to take this all the way, only to have me call a stop to it. Who in their right mind would walk away from an invitation as blatant as the one coming from her?

I must not be in my right mind. All that matters to me is doing this right—for once. And I know in my pounding heart that having sex with her now would fuck things up.

So I regretfully and painfully move away from her, settling back on my heels.

Her gaze travels over me, coming to a halt at my groin, which is throbbing.

"You don't want to…"

"Hell yes, I want to, but more than anything, I want you to trust me, Sofia. And us getting naked right now might screw things up when you wake up tomorrow and realize you did something you weren't ready for. I heard what you said earlier about how it's been for you. I want to prove to you that I can give you something better. And the last thing I'd ever want you to think is I only want this from you." I use my hand to gesture between us. "I want *everything* from you, which is why we're going to do this right."

She takes a deep breath and releases it slowly. "I didn't mean to kiss you."

Smiling, I say, "I'm so glad you did."

"So am I." She bites her bottom lip as she stares at my mouth with those eyes that just ruin me.

"You should get some rest. Mateo will be up early looking for Santa."

"Yes, he will."

"Go ahead. I'll be here to make sure you're safe." I lean in to kiss her forehead and then her lips one more time. "Rest easy."

She gets up from the floor and takes a second, seemingly to shake off what just happened between us. I get that. It's going to take me all night to shake that off because all I'll be thinking about is how soon we can do it again.

We work together to arrange Mateo's toys next to the tiny tree that sparkles with multicolored lights and handmade ornaments. Again, I admire the way she makes a cozy, loving home for her son using the resources she has available.

"I'll get you a pillow and blanket."

"Thank you."

She goes into the bedroom and returns a minute later with a pillow and a crocheted afghan that reminds me of my late great-grandmother's home. "This was my abuela's. It's my favorite."

33

"My great-grandmother had one just like it that she made."

"I have so many sweet memories of watching TV with my abuela under that blanket."

"I'll take good care of it."

She hands me an unopened toothbrush. "Thought you might want that, too."

"I do. Thanks. Go ahead and use the bathroom. I'll go after you."

"Thank you again for your help with the toys. I really appreciate it."

I flash her my dirtiest grin. "It was entirely my pleasure."

Her face turns bright red in the second before she turns away from me and goes into the bathroom, closing the door behind her with a loud whack that makes me laugh.

It's nice to know I'm not the only one thrown completely off my game by this situation.

When I'm settled in for the night on the sofa, I check my phone for the first time in hours. Angelo has texted a couple of times. *Your brother saved our asses tonight. You owe him big.*

Thanks, I'll spot him some cash for filling in.

Not like you to disappear when we're busy. What's going on?

Just some personal stuff that came up. Sorry to leave you hanging.

No worries. I'm going home. Will be back on it tomorrow afternoon.

Thanks for working during the holidays.

Thanks for paying me double time to do it.

LOL. You got it.

I wanted to be free to spend as much time with my family as I could this Christmas. We're all so thankful to see my mom heading toward the end of her cancer treatment—we hope—and I was hoping for the chance to be with Sofia and Mateo as much as she'd let me be. I never expected to be crashed on her sofa on Christmas Eve.

I send a text to Miguel. *Are you hearing anything from Joaquin's crew that I need to worry about?*

Miguel responds ten minutes later. *Just some smack talk, but nothing concrete. We're keeping an eye on her place. R u there?*

Yeah.

34

If there's any trouble, call me. Don't get into it with them.

I hear you.

I'll check in tomorrow.

Thanks for this.

You got it.

The thought of anyone coming after her because of her asshole ex fills me with anxiety. I can't be with her and Mateo all the time, as much as I wish I could. After tomorrow, I'm back to work driving customers and tending to my fledgling business. I've got everything riding on its success, and I can't afford to check out.

Between maintenance, insurance and staffing, it'll be a while before we're fully profitable, but I can see the light at the end of the tunnel coming in the next few years.

Like most small-business owners, I work part-time—twelve hours a day most days. I heard that joke at a meeting I attended to network with other business owners. I handed out a hundred business cards that day and landed at least ten new regulars. The parking at the airport is obscenely expensive. By undercutting prices offered by ride-sharing services, we get a lot of that business.

People told me I was crazy to get into the car service business in the age of Uber and Lyft, but we're finding that customers like doing business with a local company. It hasn't hurt that my uncle Vincent lets me put business cards in every check delivered at Giordino's. We've gotten a ton of new customers from that outreach and from word of mouth.

I'm enjoying the challenge of building something from the bottom up. We started with two cars and now have fifteen. I hope to have thirty by the end of next year. The more cars we have, the more money we can make, but the key is to keep them all running at least seven hours a day. We're getting closer all the time to that goal, but we're not quite there yet. Once we surpass that milestone, I'll start adding more cars to the fleet.

My father, the accountant, and my mother, the lawyer, have been instrumental in helping to get my business up and running. But all the risk is mine, and I intend to make a success of it.

CHAPTER 5

NICO

I receive a text from my cousin Dom. *Where you at, playa? Looking for the afterparty.*

I'm at Sofia's making sure her ex's friends don't bother her when they find out he's spending Christmas in jail.

Oh damn. Everything ok?

So far so good, and I intend to keep it that way.

The girls say you really like this one.

I do.

I need a minute. My cousin Nico is talking serious about a woman for the second time today. I'm worried the aliens are gonna land next. He adds laughing emojis that make me smile.

I'm glad everyone is so entertained by my serious interest in Sofia—and her son.

Shut up.

More laughing emojis. *What makes this one so special? Serious question.*

Everything. She's sweet and sexy and kind and a wonderful mother. Her life has been hard. I want to make it better.

Never thought I'd see the day that the stud named Nico G fell in love.

36

I'm told it happens to the best of us. What about you and the GF in NY?

That's over. Ended badly when I told her I didn't want to get married.

Ouch.

It's for the best if that's how she behaves when she doesn't get what she wants, you know?

Hell yes. I know all too well.

Thinking about moving home. My lease is up at the end of Jan. Not as much fun since Dee left. Applied for a couple of jobs here. We'll see if anything pops.

That'd be awesome! You can come to work for me until you find something. If you want to, that is. You still have a driver's license, right? It's a reasonable question since he's spent the better part of a decade living in New York City without a car.

Yep.

Job is yours if you want it. The money is decent, and the tips are great.

Uncle V told me I can wait tables, too, so between those two things, I could make it work until I find something. Thanks for helping me make the decision. I'm moving home!

YES! Dom is not only my first cousin. He's also one of my life-long best friends, and I've missed him since he moved north.

Got some extra rooms at my place. All yours if you want.

Seriously? The thought of moving back with my parents is unbearable.

I gotchu covered.

You're the best, Nico. Thanks for the job and the room.

Can't wait to get you back here. Let me know if you need help moving. I'm getting rid of a bunch of stuff and shipping the rest to keep it easy.

Sounds good.

I guess I'll go to bed since you're being all domestic and Milo went out with some girl he knows from school. The girls are super boring these days. No one to play with. He adds frown emojis that make me laugh out loud.

Everyone went and grew up while you were gone.

I know! It's ridiculous. I'm never going to grow up if it's this boring.

I recall kissing Sofia earlier, easily one of the most exciting things to ever happen to me. *It's not all boring, primo. You'll see.*

I'll take your word for it. I'd rather be single than put up with the bull-shit that was happening recently.

When it's the right one, there won't be bullshit.

That's what Carmen said, too. She said everything was different from the beginning with Jason.

And now she's having a baby. So happy for her. Our sweet cousin went through hell years ago when she lost her young police officer husband on the job.

Me, too. Well, get some sleep. I'll see you tomorrow?

We'll be there. Everyone usually ends up at my parents' house on Christmas Day. It's one of the many traditions we all take for granted after so many years of the same routines. I can't wait to bring Sofia and Mateo. I've never brought a woman to anything with my family, so it'll be a big deal to show up with them tomorrow.

Even knowing that, I don't care. I want her with me for the holiday—and not just because I'm concerned about her safety. Mostly, it's because at some point over the last few months, she's become the most important person in the world to me. Not that long ago, a realization like that would've had me running for my life, changing my name and living in exile to avoid anything that resembled commitment.

Now? I want to be committed to her and Mateo. I want to be wherever they are as much as I possibly can. The thought of being with anyone but her is revolting to me. There's only her. I've got to bring my A game with her, to show her what life with me might be like. I just need to figure out what an A game looks like, and I need to do it soon.

SOFIA

Riding in Nico's truck the next day, I'm still replaying the events of last night. I can't believe I kissed him like that, but how could I not after he said what he did to me? I want to have those words tattooed onto my arm so I can see them every day and never forget them. Not that there's any chance I'll forget.

"I've got to run by my place to shower and change. Is that okay?"

"Of course. We're along for the ride." Mateo is in his booster seat in the back, with his tricycle strapped into the seat next to him because he refused to leave it at home. It'd been Nico's idea to seat-belt it in next to Mateo, which delighted my little boy. "My parents have the perfect driveway for riding a trike," he said, promising to move all the cars out so Mateo could ride.

Who is this man who makes everything so much better for both of us? I ought to be scared senseless of the way he makes me feel, but I'm like an addict wanting my next fix as soon as I can get it. He was great with Mateo, playing on the floor with him and his new toys all morning while I made us coffee and breakfast. It was the nicest Christmas morning I've ever had, and it was all thanks to him.

I can hear my mother's nasty voice in my head telling me I'm doing it again. I'm getting carried away by a man who'll treat me like shit and leave me with bigger problems than I already have when it ends. Because it always ends. That's been her experience— and mine, much to her delight. I've never understood why my own mother would want my life to be a mess like hers has been. Why wouldn't she want the best for me? That's a question I've been asking for as long as I can remember. Anytime something good happened for me, she'd find a way to undercut it.

Like when I was offered a scholarship to the University of Florida, and she told me I'd never cut it there even though I got mostly A's in high school. She overdosed for the first time three weeks before I was supposed to leave, and since she doesn't have anyone else, I had no choice but to stay home to take care of her. I can still recall her smug smile when I told her I deferred my scholarship. She got exactly what she wanted—me under her control indefinitely.

Breaking free of her was my first act of independence. Unfortunately, I relied on Joaquín to get me out of her house, trading one bad situation for another. I didn't see it that way at first because I thought I was in love with him and he with me, but what we had wasn't love. I don't even know what love is. I just know that wasn't it, not when he thought he could control everything I said and did and every dime I spent and isolated me from the few friends I still had in the area after most of my friends went to college out of state.

I could only look on with envy as they lived the life I wanted for myself. I still dream of going to college, even though that dream is so far out of reach now as to be laughable. It'll take the rest of my life to pay off the medical bills incurred from Mateo's emergency surgery. Jason deferred his charges for the surgery, but there were so many other expenses. I've never had health insurance, and Joaquín refuses to pay for anything since I left him and took his son, so it's all on me until I can hopefully get a court to eventually make him pay his share.

I try not to care about any of that as long as Mateo is on the road to recovery. Jason said it will take another year or two, and he may always have some deficiencies due to the location of the tumor, but he ought to live a relatively normal life if the cancer doesn't return. So, while I live in fear of that happening, I work diligently with him on his physical and occupational therapy while hoping the nerve in his face that was impacted by the surgery will eventually recover to rid him of the sag on the right side that makes him look like a sad little clown. Jason told me that nerve healing is a very slow process, but since there's been some improvement since the surgery, we're hopeful it might eventually heal completely.

I wish I could afford more actual therapy for him. Since I can't, I took what we learned from the therapists and work with him to the best of my ability. I've spent hours on YouTube watching videos about the best therapies for his condition. I think he's making good progress, but it's hard to tell. I'm no expert, just a mom who loves her kid more than anything in this world.

"Everything okay over there?"

Nico's deep voice brings me out of the rabbit hole my thoughts have dragged me into.

"Everything is great. Thanks for playing with Mateo this morning. He loved it."

"He's adorable. I had a blast."

A short time later, we drive up to a gatehouse where the guard smiles and waves us through.

"*This* is where you live?" I eye the gorgeous homes and lush landscaping with disbelief.

"I bought a foreclosure about six years ago. Got a great deal."

The road winds through the kind of neighborhood I can only dream of living in.

"How old were you when you bought it?"

"Twenty-six."

"You bought a house in this neighborhood at twenty-six." I can't fathom that. Also, now I know he's thirty-two—six years older than me.

"I got it for about half what they go for normally. The bank was eager to unload it."

"That's amazing."

"It's also now mortgaged again to get my business off the ground, so don't be too impressed. I'm in debt up to my eyeballs."

"What does that expression mean—'up to your eyeballs'?"

"'It means I'm in deep."

"Ah, I see, and I'm impressed. You own a home and a business at thirty-two."

"I've been lucky, and I know it. My uncle gave me an awesome job when I was sixteen that allowed me to make and save the money I needed for the down payment, and my dad helped me navigate the process to bid on a foreclosure."

"It's more than luck. It's also hard work and... What's the word..."

"Determination?"

"Yes, that's it. Determination." I make a mental note to add that one to my list of new words.

"Your English is fantastic."

"I don't know about that, but it's getting better. I try to learn new words and expressions every day. I hope you don't mind when I ask what something means."

"Of course not. Ask me anything you want." He pulls into the driveway of a two-story home painted white with gorgeous land-scaping that includes palm trees.

I *love* palm trees and always have. Looking at them makes me happy. "*This* is your house?"

"Yep. Come on in. I just need to grab a quick shower and the gifts for my family." He's out of the car and unbuckling Mateo from his car seat while I'm still processing the fact that he lives in a palace. At least that's what it looks like to me. I experience an odd twinge of anxiety as I follow him into the house after he punches in a code on the front door.

My mouth falls open as I take in high ceilings, an open floor plan, a grand staircase and a pool in the backyard that I can see through French doors to the patio. I can't believe he actually lives here.

"Sofia?"

I realize I'm still standing just inside the door.

"Do you want to come in?"

Nico's holding my son and looking at me as if he's wondering what's the matter with me. I'm wondering the same thing. What the hell am I even doing in a house like this with a man like him? But I can't be rude, so I step forward and take my son from him.

"I'll be quick. Make yourselves at home."

Mateo wants to get down, so I lower him to the tile floor and hold his hand when he leads me to check out Nico's huge Christmas tree.

"My sisters did that for us," he says from the kitchen, where he's downing a beverage. "They can't bear that I don't own a single Christmas decoration. Can I get you anything? Coffee, water, tea, soda?"

"I'm good, thank you."

"How about Mateo?"

"I've got his cup. Thanks."

I can barely breathe around the huge lump that settled in my throat the second I walked into this incredible house. I'm not sure what I pictured when I imagined where he lived, but it wasn't anything like this. I'm further surprised when his brother Milo

42

walks into the room, wearing only a pair of basketball shorts, his muscular chest on full display.

"Oh, hey, Sofia," he says. "I was wondering who was out here."

"Did we wake you?" Nico asks him.

"Nope. I was up and getting ready to go to Mom's. Merry Christmas."

"Same to you. We're headed there, too. I just need to shower. I heard you saved our asses last night. Thank you."

"No problem. It got me out of Mass, so…"

Nico laughs at the face his brother makes.

Milo waves to my son. "Hi there, Mateo."

"Santa came," Mateo says with Christmas Day excitement.

"What did he bring?"

"I got a bike!"

"His new tricycle is his favorite thing," Nico says. "We're going to try it out in Mom's driveway."

"That sounds fun."

"Ride soon," Mateo says.

"I hear you, little buddy," Nico says. "I'll be quick. Be right back."

After Nico leaves the kitchen, Milo pours a cup of coffee and asks if I'd like some.

"Sure, thanks."

"Cream and sugar?"

"Just a little cream, please." I scoop up Mateo and bring him with me to take a seat at the kitchen table that looks out over the beautiful pool.

"Swim, Mama."

"Not today, sweetie."

"Mama. Swim!"

"Can he put his feet in?" Milo asks.

"Sure. Why not?"

He brings his coffee and mine to the pool deck as I follow with Mateo. I sit on a sectional sofa and remove his sandals.

Milo puts a mug of coffee on the table next to me and holds out his hand to Mateo. "Want to put your feet in, buddy?"

"Feet, Mama."

"Just your feet. Don't get your clothes wet."

While I sip my coffee, Milo sits with Mateo on the edge of the pool and puts his feet in to show Mateo what to do.

Mateo follows suit and then giggles as he kicks and splashes. Good thing I packed a change of clothes for him, just in case, because he's going to get wet.

With dark hair and black-framed glasses, Milo is every bit as handsome as Nico. I've noticed before that he's all sweetness and lacks his older brother's rough edges. He's the sort of man I ought to be attracted to, not the one described as "toxic" by his own family members.

"So you live here, too?"

"Yep. My big brother is good to me."

For some reason, hearing that makes me feel a tiny bit better about what I seem to be getting into with Nico. "What do you do?"

"Computer stuff."

"He's a nerd," Nico says when he steps onto the pool deck, freshly shaved and showered, dressed in khaki shorts and a Cuban guayabera shirt. He smells good. Really, *really* good.

"You wish you were a nerd like me," Milo responds.

"I'll pass on that."

"And yet, you're more than happy to get my free services for your business."

"And you're more than happy to have free rent at my house."

Despite the back-and-forth, I can tell they're close, and I like seeing the devoted-older-brother side of Nico.

"Don't listen to him," Milo says. "I'm the only one who ever cleans around here. If it wasn't for me, this place would be a pigsty."

"That is not true," Nico says.

"It's absolutely true, and you know it."

"Whatever you say, bro." He rolls his eyes at me. "You guys ready to go?"

"I am, but we might have trouble getting Mateo to leave the pool."

"Hey, buddy, want to go ride the bike?"

"Bike!" He struggles to stand, but Milo is right there to help him up and onto the pool deck.

Before I have a chance to stand, Nico has picked him up and smoothly grabbed the sandals. I can tell Milo is as impressed as I am by the way Nico tends to Mateo.

"See you over there," Nico says to Milo as he heads inside.

"I'm right behind you."

"Thanks for playing with Mateo," I say to Milo.

"No problem. He's a cutie."

"I think so, too."

"See you at my mom's."

"It's okay that I'm going with Nico, right?"

"You should know by now that everyone is welcome with our family."

"Your family is very special."

"It is. We're blessed, and we know it."

Nico returns to the door. "You coming, Sofia?"

"I'm coming. Thanks again for the coffee and for playing with Mateo."

"Sure thing."

His warm smile ought to make my heart flutter, but it does nothing other than fill me with a sweet feeling of friendship. When I look at Nico, however, his expression has grown stormy. Is he annoyed? And if so, why?

CHAPTER 6

SOFIA

"What's wrong?" I ask as I follow him out the front door. He's still carrying Mateo, who's watching me over Nico's shoulder. He's comfortable with Nico, but wants to be certain I'm coming, too.

"Nothing." He straps Mateo into the car seat and puts the sandals back on his feet before getting into the driver's side.

"Why are you saying nothing when it's obvious that something has upset you?"

Sighing, he says, "You were having a good time with my brother."

"I was drinking coffee while he played in the pool with Mateo."

"You were laughing and stuff."

"Because Mateo was being cute. Are you jealous of your own brother? What is this, Nico?"

"I'm an a-hole because it made me crazy to see you laughing and talking with him, even though I know he'd never go near you because he knows I like you."

"I wouldn't go near him either. That's not how I am. Although, he's the one I should like."

Oh, he doesn't like that, but what's interesting is that I felt comfortable enough saying something to Nico that might've gotten me a backhand from Joaquín.

"What the hell does that mean?"

I give him the side-eye. "I bet no one has ever described him as toxic."

"Nope. He's too good to be true. And you're right. You'd be way better off with him."

"And yet, here I am with you."

"You don't have to be if you'd prefer him."

"Is that right? You'd just turn me over to your brother and be fine with that?"

He tightens his grip on the steering wheel and stares straight ahead, a muscle in his face twitching. "I wouldn't be fine with that at all. But if it was what you wanted..."

"It's not. For some reason, I want you, the toxic one, which is probably the last thing I ought to want."

He glances over at me, his dark eyes as serious as I've ever seen them. "I said you don't have to worry about that crap."

"I know."

"You don't believe me?"

"I want to."

"Give me the chance to prove it to you."

"How will you do that?"

"Like I said, one day at a time. Today, it's Christmas, and we're going to my mom's, where you're going to have a nice, worry-free day with your little boy."

"That's a good start."

"We'll see what we can do to make it an awesome start." He pushes the button to turn on the engine and backs out of the driveway.

"I like your brother. He's a very nice guy."

"Yes, he is."

"I wasn't trying to make you jealous by talking to him."

"I know. I'm just being ridiculous, and you should know I've never been jealous over a woman in my life. I probably didn't handle that as well as I could have."

"Do you think?"

His grunt of laughter fills me with relief that whatever that was, it's over now, and it happened without an ugly argument, raised voices or the dreaded backhand. It's going to take me time to get used to being with someone who doesn't behave that way.

"Could I tell you something else?" I ask him.

"Anything you want."

"I appreciate that we talked about it and got through it without an ugly incident."

He reaches over and takes my hand. "No ugly incidents with me. I promise."

"That's another promise that might be hard to keep."

He raises my hand to his lips and sends shivers down my spine with the tender kiss he places on my hand. "That'll be the easiest promise I'll ever keep. I will never, *ever* be ugly or violent with you or your son. I swear to God and on the lives of everyone I love that you can count on that promise."

"You can't imagine what that means to me."

"I want to kill him for hurting you."

"Don't do that, okay?"

"I won't as long as you know I want to." He continues to kiss my hand and the inside of my wrist and has every pleasure point in my body humming with awareness of him in a matter of seconds.

"I wanna ride my bike!"

Nico smiles as he glances in the rearview mirror. "Almost there, buddy. A few more minutes."

"In case I forget to tell you later, this is the nicest Christmas I've ever had."

NICO

I'm falling so hard for both of them, it's not even funny. When she said this was the nicest Christmas she'd ever had before we'd even done anything… My heart felt like it was being squeezed inside the tightest vise, and I could barely breathe. After moving all the cars out, I've been chasing Mateo around in the driveway for at least an hour while Sofia sits on the front steps, clapping and cheering him on.

Watching Mateo laugh and smile and work his tiny legs on the pedals has been the most fun I've had in a long time. After the ordeal he's been through, to see him playing like a healthy child is super rewarding, and I can tell it's making his mom happy, too.

"You want to take a break and get a snack?" I ask him.

When he nods, I pluck him off the bike and plop him onto my shoulders. "Let's go see what Mrs. Elena has cooked up."

"Mama!"

"I'm coming."

I lead the way into the house through the garage. My mother is bustling around the kitchen, barking out orders to my sisters, Maria and Dee, like a drill sergeant.

"My buddy Mateo is getting hungry, Mom. How much longer until dinner?"

"Thirty minutes."

"Can I do anything to help?" Sofia asks.

Mom smiles at her. "Absolutely not. You're our guest. You should relax and enjoy."

"Technically, I'm a guest, too," Maria says. "Since I don't live here anymore."

"You hush and keep stirring."

Dee snorts out a laugh. "Nice try, sis."

"You be quiet, too. If that rice is sticky, I'll have your head."

I lift the lid on a pot to peek inside. "She told you, DeeDee."

Mom smacks my hand away. "Get out of here, and get our guests settled in the family room with drinks."

"Yes, ma'am," I say as Dee returns my snort.

"I guess she told *you*," Dee retorts.

"I'm going to tell you all if you don't quit the bickering," Mom says.

"You're still hoping that's gonna happen, Ma?" Milo asks when he comes in from the garage carrying a big bag of presents and flowers for Mom.

"Suck-up," Maria says.

Mom holds her arms out to Milo, who gives me, Dee and Maria a smug smile as he goes to her. "Come here and give me a hug, my sweet boy."

"Mama's boy," I say on a cough.

"You wish you were her favorite," Milo says.

"You're all my favorites," Mom says. "Especially when you're not talking."

"Right," Maria says, her tone dripping with sarcasm. "Milo is your favorite, and we all know it."

"Lord save me from these children," Mom says to the ceiling.

We used to make mad fun of her for talking to the ceiling, as if God could hear her through the roof.

"What are they doing now?" Dad asks when he joins us in the kitchen.

"They won't shut up and quit bickering."

"Nothing new there, my love. Kids, get out of here, and let your mother spin her magic."

Maria's fiancé, Austin, walks in with Everly in his arms and his parents trailing behind them.

"Perfect timing," Maria says as she goes to hug them. "I just got kicked out of the kitchen."

SOFIA

"Swim, Rie!" Everly says, reaching for Maria.

"Not until we go home, Pooh. Let's play with Mateo until then."

"Bike," Mateo says.

"You can stay in here with me if you'd like," Elena says to me from her post at the stove. "Let Nico take him back outside for a bit."

"Do you mind?" I ask him.

"Not at all." He takes Mateo from me, and I marvel at how easily he goes to Nico when he usually wants me and only me. That drives Joaquín crazy. He says Mateo cries for Mama the whole time he's with him. Secretly, I love that, even though it breaks my heart to know Mateo is so unhappy when he's away from me.

I love watching Nico's family interact. They're like a TV show with the banter and the one-liners, the insults and the love. There's so much love, even when they're picking on one another. I'd never known a family like them until I started working at the restaurant and saw them together. There're so many of them, too. It took me a while to figure out who goes with who, but now I've got it down.

"You did such a good job with the moro yesterday that you can have that job again, if you'd like," Elena says.

"Sure." I take the wooden spoon she offers me. "Thank you again for having us today."

"We're delighted to have you and your little boy." She glances at the door to the garage that the others closed behind them when they went outside. "It may be premature for me to say anything, but it does my heart good to see my son with your son in his arms."

"He's very good with him."

"You have to understand…" Her gaze shifts again to the door. "It's not like him… I've never seen him with a little one in his arms."

"Mateo adores him."

"You should know he's also never brought a woman to a family holiday or dinner."

She adds this so casually, as if it's not a major disclosure. "Is that right?"

"Uh-huh. He must really like you."

"I really like him. He's a very nice man."

"He can be."

"I'm aware of his sharper edges, Mrs. Giordino. Maria, Dee and Carmen have filled me in."

She smiles. "You should call me Elena, and I'm sure they did. They'd take a bullet for him, but they wouldn't let him hurt you, not after all you've been through with your little boy."

"He promised he wouldn't hurt me. I've decided to give him a chance to prove that."

Elena puts her hand over her heart, her eyes filling with the start of tears. "That makes me *so* happy. You have no idea. He's the one I've been the most concerned about since my illness. Maria and Dee have settled down with Austin and Wyatt, men I would've hand-picked for them, and my Milo, he'll find a nice, sweet girl when he's ready. But my Nico… He's the one I've lain awake at night worrying about what'll become of him, especially if I don't make it."

"You're doing well, though, right?"

"I am, thank the Lord, but a serious illness makes you think about all the worst-case scenarios."

"What does that word mean? 'Scenarios'?"

"It means the various things that could happen."

"Ah, okay. Thank you."

"Anyway, as a mother, you think the worst. And add the potentially fatal illness to the mix, and you start planning their lives without you. Nico was the one I was most concerned about, but knowing he'd have you and your little boy makes me feel so much better."

"It's all very new still."

"I know, and I don't mean to put pressure on you. It just does my heart good to see him making a real effort."

"He's very special."

"I think so, too, and I prayed he'd find someone who can see that."

Nico comes bursting through the door from the garage, looking spooked.

I'm immediately panicked. "What's wrong? Is it Mateo?"

"No, I realized I left you alone with my mother."

"Oh, for goodness' sake, Nico," Elena says while I try not to howl with laughter at the expression on his face. "Don't be ridiculous."

He holds out a hand to me. "Come with me. I can't leave you

alone with her. She'll be planning our wedding. I don't know what I was thinking."

He'd probably lose it completely if he'd heard our conversation.

"Go ahead with my idiot son," Elena says. "I can take it from here."

I hand her the spoon and take Nico's hand, noting the way he relaxes the instant my fingers link with his. "Sorry about him," I say to her.

"No problem, love. Enjoy the sunshine."

When we're in the garage, Nico stops and turns to me. "Tell me everything she said from the second I left you with her."

"She didn't say anything. Oh, wait, she did ask if I'm willing to have more children and how many I'd be willing to have and if I know what a terribly naughty boy you are."

His face goes completely flat. "She did not."

Laughter explodes out of my chest. I laugh so hard that tears fill my eyes.

"Did she ask those things?"

Shaking my head, I wipe tears from my eyes.

"That was mean, Sofia."

"I'm sorry," I say between gasps of laughter that stop only when he puts his arms around me and kisses me the way he did last night.

In a single second, I go from laughter to intense desire in a blast of heat that threatens to consume me and everything around me.

"Cripes," Milo says when he comes upon us. "There're children present."

"Shut up or die," Nico says while continuing to kiss me as if we're alone and not surrounded by his family.

The hard press of his erection against my belly makes me wish we were alone. I haven't had sex in so long, I've almost forgotten what it's like. Not that it was very good with Joaquín the last few years.

"Break it up, lovers," Dee says.

My face burns with embarrassment.

"To be continued later," Nico whispers when he finally releases me.

Mateo's laughter snaps me out of the sex coma kissing Nico put me into. I venture outside to find him riding the tricycle with Everly standing on the back, her hands on his shoulders while Austin takes video of them.

My heart does that tightening thing again when I realize my little boy has made a friend. He's craved the company of other children, and to see him laughing and playing with Everly is the best thing ever. I love that she doesn't see anything wrong with him. She just sees a friend.

"He looks so happy," Nico says when he comes up behind me, putting his hands on my shoulders and pressing against my back to let me know he's still aroused.

"I've never seen him as happy as he's been today." I glance back at him. "Thank you."

"You don't have to thank me. By having you guys here, I'm happy, too."

I give myself permission to lean back against him, to let him wrap his arms around me and to fully enjoy this perfect moment. This sort of contentment has been missing in my life. My earliest memories are full of angst, drama, pain and disappointment. The Giordinos are showing me something different. Something better.

Carmen and Jason arrive with her parents, Vincent and Vivian.

Jason stops to give Mateo a high five and marvels at how good he is at pedaling.

"Watch me go, Doc," Mateo says as he takes off with Everly riding shotgun again.

I learned that term, *riding shotgun*, from a movie.

Mateo adores Jason, who told me months ago to call him that when I want to still call him Dr. Northrup. The man saved my son's life, and I'll be forever thankful to him and to Carmen, who had the idea for him to volunteer at the free clinic where Maria is a nurse. Jason immediately realized Mateo was seriously ill and in need of immediate emergency surgery. I found out later that he donated his services.

When he approaches us, I step out of Nico's arms to hug Jason.

"Merry Christmas," he says.

"Feliz Navidad."

"Our little friend is doing fantastically well, it seems," Jason says as he shakes hands with Nico.

"He's having a wonderful day."

"I love seeing him on the trike. That's great for his fine motor skills."

"The therapist told me it would be."

Carmen hugs us both. "Mateo is adorable on that bike!"

"I'm afraid he's going to want to sleep with it."

"We can put it right next to his bed," Nico says.

Vincent and Vivian hug me like I'm one of the family, as do Livia, Marlene and Mr. Muñoz when they arrive a few minutes later.

"So glad you and Mateo could join us, honey," Livia says.

"Thank you for having us."

I love these people. I love their warmth, their generosity, their kindness and the way they make me feel like I belong with them even if we all know I don't. Not really. That doesn't matter to them. I have no idea where Mateo and I would be without them, which is part of the reason things with Joaquín have gotten so bad. He hates the way I've been taken in by them and how I consider them like family.

"They're *not* your *family*," he once said, practically spitting the words at me. "You're just a charity case to them."

I know better. I might've started off as a charity case, but I've been on the receiving end of their love and generosity for too long now not to appreciate how deeply their affection for me and Mateo runs. Without the job at Giordino's, I would've had no choice but to go back to him when I lost the first job I'd had in years and would've soon lost my apartment, too. I'd probably be dead by now if I'd gone back to him.

Christmas Day with Nico's family will be remembered as one of the best days of my life. Not only do they make us feel like part of their family, but they have thoughtful gifts for me and for Mateo, and they didn't even know we were coming until last night.

I receive bath gel, a candle, a gorgeous silk scarf and a gift certificate from Nico for a massage at a local spa. "I'll babysit," he adds after I thank him for the thoughtful gift. He loves the watch I bought for him, hoping it would be something he'd like.

Mateo receives more toys and games, including a matching game from Jason and Carmen that Jason says will help with his occupational therapy.

I'm overwhelmed and deeply grateful as well as stuffed from the delicious prime rib dinner Elena served. I'm sent home with a massive bag of leftovers.

Mateo is exhausted and falls asleep minutes into the ride.

"This was such a wonderful day. Thank you again for inviting me. I've never had a Christmas like this one."

"I'm glad you enjoyed it. My family is crazy, but I love them."

"You're so lucky to have them."

"I know. I didn't always appreciate them the way I do now. It took seeing the crap some of my friends have dealt with to understand how lucky I am. And when my mom got sick, all I cared about was doing whatever it took to get her through it."

"She seems to be doing well now."

"She is. It's just the fear of it coming back that I can't handle."

"What do the doctors say about that?"

"They don't make predictions. But the kind of cancer she had recurs pretty frequently. Often when it does, it's considered stage four, which is terminal."

"What does that word mean?"

"That you're going to die."

"God. That's scary."

"I can't even think about it without feeling like I'm going to lose my shit. She's one of the best people I know. She'd do anything for anyone. Seeing her suffer has been hell."

I reach across the console for his hand. "I'm so sorry you've been through that."

"I'm sorry for her."

"I'm sorry for *you*."

"Thanks. I keep telling myself that she's doing great now, but it's going to be a long five years until they consider her cured."

"Five years is a long time. Same for Mateo."

"Yep. Regular scans and bloodwork and then sweating the results every time. It sucks."

As he brings the truck to a stop at a red light, he glances over at me just as someone slams into the back of the truck.

CHAPTER 7

SOFIA

"*W*hat the fuck?" Nico growls as he glances at the rearview mirror. He puts the truck in Park. "Call 911." He releases his seat belt.

I grab his arm while juggling the phone to make the call and checking on Mateo, who's still asleep. "What're you doing?"

"Someone just hit us. I need to check the damage."

I recoil from the face in the car next to us. "Wait. It's Joaquín's cousins. They probably have guns." I no sooner say those words than one is pointed at us from the next car over. Diego points to me and crooks his finger. If I go with him, he'll kill me. I have no doubt about that, but if I stay, he's apt to kill Nico and Mateo, and I can't risk that.

I release my seat belt.

"Don't move," Nico says in a low, scary tone I've never heard from him before.

"911, state your emergency."

Thankfully, Nico does the talking for us, because I'm so scared, I can hardly breathe.

Diego gets out of his car and uses the gun to bang on the window.

Nico ignores him while holding my hand as tightly as he ever has before.

The scream of sirens is the best sound I've ever heard.

Diego glances in the direction of the sirens and then gives me a menacing glare. He stares at me, makes a gun of his fingers and points it at me and Mateo in the backseat. With his message delivered, he gets into his car and takes off before the police arrive.

My hands are shaking so hard that I push my free hand between my legs to try to make it stop.

The police arrive, and Nico gets out to talk to them.

I need to end this with him right now. This is the last thing he needs in his life, even though leaving him will be the most heartbreaking thing that's happened since Mateo's illness. I'm sick to my stomach and everywhere else by the time Nico returns, bringing a police officer with him.

"We'll need to get your statement, Ms. Diaz," the officer says.

"There's not much to say. They hit us, pulled a gun on us and threatened me and my son."

"Can you give me the names of the people you recognized?"

I feel like I'm risking my life as well as Mateo's when I recite the names and tell him where they're most likely to find them.

"Do you have somewhere safe you can stay while we sort this out?" the officer asks.

"She and her son will be at my house in a gated community."

"No," I say. "We'll be at home."

"No, you won't," Nico says, his expression unyielding. "You're not safe there."

"I'm not safe anywhere, and there's no way I'm endangering you with my mess."

"I can take care of myself." To the officer, he says, "They'll be at my place." He gives the address and his phone number to the officer.

"We'll be in touch."

After he walks away, I look over at Nico. "Please take us home and go on with your life. You don't need this."

"Maybe not, but I do need *you*, and there's no way I'm taking you somewhere that you can be easily found and possibly harmed. We'll go get what you need, and then you guys can stay with me for as long as you need to. No one is getting in my neighborhood who doesn't belong there."

"I don't want to involve you in this."

"Too late. I'm already involved."

"I don't want you to be. This is my problem, not yours."

"Do you honestly think I'm going to leave you on your own to deal with men who threatened to kill you?"

"I'm afraid you'll get hurt."

"I'm afraid you will. Or, God forbid, Mateo will. Let me keep you both safe, Sofia. Please."

That last word gets to me. He said *please*. I'm so used to being told what to do, to not being given a choice, to not being asked nicely. And what he said about Mateo getting hurt also matters.

"Your family will hate me if anything happens to you because of me."

"They'd be furious with me if I let anything happen to you guys. They love you."

I can't stop the tears that spill down my cheeks.

Nico reaches over to wipe them away. "Everything's going to be okay. I promise."

"You can't promise that."

"I can promise you'll be safe. Now let's go pack up what you need and get Mateo home to bed at my place."

I still don't like his plan, because it puts him in danger with us, but I'm so afraid of Diego and the others that I go along with it. They wouldn't hesitate to kill me to get me out of the way, and the thought of my son being raised by Joaquín and his band of thugs is revolting to me. For Mateo's sake, I decide to let Nico help us.

But I'm terrified of the man I've come to care about being harmed in any way.

NICO

My heart is still beating so fast, it's a wonder I don't hyperventilate. Seeing that scumbag threaten Sofia made me want to kill him right then and there. As I follow her up the stairs to her place with Mateo asleep in my arms, I keep a vigilant eye on our surroundings. While I don't see anyone, I'm sure we're being watched.

They blame Sofia for the fact that Joaquín is in jail, but he's the one who violated the protective order in the first place.

All I want is to get her and Mateo out of here and back to my place as fast as possible. So I put Mateo carefully on the sofa, cover him with his blanket and go to see what I can do to expedite matters.

In the bedroom, Sofia is sitting on one of two twin beds, both of which are pushed against walls. The other has a rail on it, probably to keep Mateo from falling out of bed. She looks so defeated that I can't bear it. I go to her, sit next to her and put an arm around her. "None of this is your fault."

"I chose a bad man to father my son."

"Did you know he was a bad man when you chose him?"

She shakes her head. "He was so sweet and kind until about four years ago. I don't know what happened, but everything changed, and he made my life a living hell. One of my friends said it's because he was jealous of Mateo and all the attention I gave him."

"What do you think of that?"

"I suspect it's something much more involved, not that he'll ever admit to such a thing. That would be a sign of weakness, and he'd rather be dead than show weakness."

"What can I do to help you pack?"

"Maybe grab some of the toys from this morning?"

"I can do that. Let's be quick so we can get out of here before anyone knows we're here."

"You're sure I can't talk you out of making my problem your problem?"

I kiss the top of her head. "One hundred percent positive."

"What about the damage to your truck?"

"Dom has a buddy from high school who does body work. He'll fix it for me. Don't worry about that."

I'm working on nervous energy as I quickly collect some of the toys Mateo liked the best this morning and put them in one of the boxes that's still piled in the living room from last night. "I'm going to take this stuff down," I say to Sofia. "Come lock the door."

"Please be careful."

I can't stand the sick, worried tone of her voice. What kind of monster—and his family and friends—would threaten a mother and her child? I head down the stairs, carrying an armload of Mateo's new toys, and scan the parking lot, looking for trouble. I don't see anything concerning, but I'm not deluding myself that they won't be back for her. When they come, they won't be able to find her.

I glance at the back of my truck and see a small dent that'll be easily fixed. Messing up my truck wasn't the point of this mission for them.

I'm worried about her going back to work, but I'll talk to Uncle Vin about that and figure something out. I'll do whatever it takes to keep her and Mateo safe. I make several trips to bring toys and the bags she packed for them before I carry him down and strap him into his seat. The little guy never stirs, having worn himself out playing earlier.

On the ride to my house, Sofia doesn't say a word as she stares out the passenger window.

I don't try to make conversation with her because I understand she's processing everything that's happened and is fearful for herself, her son and me. I also get that she'd much rather I not be involved in her problems, but it's too late for that. I'm involved, and I plan to stay that way.

When we arrive, Milo is on the sofa watching a movie and drinking a beer. "Hey," he says, his eyes widening with surprise when he sees that Sofia and Mateo are with me.

"Hey. Sofia and Mateo are going to stay with us for a while."

"You want me to make the bed in the guest room?"

I'd much rather have her in my bed, but that's probably not

going to happen. Not tonight, anyway. "That'd be great. Thanks, M." Once I tell him why Sofia is here, he'll be fully on board with helping to keep her and Mateo safe.

"Sure. No problem."

Sofia stands next to me, seeming as if she doesn't know what to do with herself.

With my finger under her chin, I tip up her face and gaze into her eyes. "Mi casa es su casa."

"Gracias."

"Make yourself completely at home, okay?"

She nods, but I still sense her reluctance. She doesn't want to be here, doesn't want me involved in her problems, but what am I supposed to do? Let her fend for herself against people who'd threaten her life and Mateo's?

I've never been so agitated as I show her to the guest room, where Milo is finishing making the bed, and help her get Mateo settled in the queen-sized bed. "We can set him up with something separate tomorrow, if you'd like," I tell her after my brother has left the room.

"This is fine. Thank you." Her words are stilted and the distance between us vast. Gone is all the warmth from last night when she put her arms around me and changed my life forever with one kiss.

It'll take time to get back to that, but I'm in it for the long haul. I want her. I want Mateo. I'll do whatever it takes to make them mine, including protect them, whether she wants me to or not.

"There're towels in the bathroom closet. If you need anything at all, just let me know."

She sits on the edge of the mattress, seemingly riddled with anxiety. "Thank you."

"I'll check on you before I go to bed."

She gives a brief nod but doesn't say anything.

I ache for the sweet, sexy, happy woman she was last night, which was one of the best nights of my entire life and certainly the best night I've had with any woman. All I want is more of what we had then, and if I have to be patient to get back to that, then so be it.

"My room is right there," I say, pointing across the hall.

"Okay."

I leave her to get settled and go to the kitchen to pour myself a drink. I've never needed one more than I do right now.

"What's going on?" Milo asks as he leans against the counter, beer in hand.

I fill him in on what happened earlier.

"No way. Jeez."

"She doesn't want me involved."

"Too late for that, huh?"

"Way too late. I had to talk her into coming here."

My phone rings, and I take the call from my friend Miguel. "Hey."

"Hey, I thought you'd want to know we picked up Diego and the others. They had unregistered weapons on them that'll allow us to hold them until they can be arraigned."

"Can we request a protective order that covers them, too?"

"Already in the works, but you know… Sometimes they're not worth the paper they're written on."

"It's making me crazy that she and her son are in danger from these people when she hasn't done anything but leave a man who was abusive toward her. He's the one who violated the protective order and got himself arrested."

"Logic doesn't work in these situations," Miguel says, promising to call me with an update in the morning.

I update my brother on what Miguel said. "I feel like I'm coming out of my skin. Is that normal?" Milo may be six years younger than me, but he's what Nona calls an "old soul." He's wiser than his years, and I often turn to him for advice.

"It's because you care about them."

"I really do. I'm crazy about them."

"Damn," Milo says with a teasing glint in his eyes. "I need a minute to wrap my head around this development."

"I'm not joking about this."

"That doesn't mean the rest of us can't joke about it."

"I'm trying to be serious here, M."

"I know, and that's what's so amazing. You're never serious

about women. They're serious about you—not the other way around."

"Is it normal to feel like your head and everything else is going to explode?"

Milo laughs, that bastard. "I think it's normal to feel like your whole world has been turned upside down."

"Yeah, that's it exactly."

"It's a good feeling, though, right?"

"It's the best feeling ever, but I can't stand that these guys are blaming her for what her ex did. They threatened her life and Mateo's. It's unbearable."

"You've got them in the best possible place. Doug and the other security people won't let anyone in here who doesn't belong."

"I probably ought to text him, so he knows what's going on."

"Not a bad idea."

"She doesn't want me involved. She told me to go home and let her deal with it."

"Because she's afraid for you. Not because she doesn't care about you. She probably cares too much."

"You think she does?"

Milo snorts out another laugh. "For some strange reason, she digs you."

"You really think so?" I can't believe how needy I sound, but that's what she's done to me.

"*Everyone* thinks so. We can't for the life of us figure out *why*."

"Very funny."

"No, really. She's a very sweet woman who's had a rough time of it. You don't seem like the kind of guy she'd be drawn to after that."

Milo articulates all my greatest fears with one sentence that hits me in the chest like a fist. "Why do you say that?"

"I'd think she'd want someone low-key and easygoing. That's not you."

"No, that's *you*, which is why I hated seeing you talking to her earlier."

His friendly expression immediately hardens. "What the fuck? I wasn't making a move. I know you like her. I'd never do that."

"I know," I say with a sigh. "But it bugged me anyway, because you'd be better for her than I'll ever be."

"That's not true. You've got everything she needs. You just haven't had to tap into that stuff before."

"What stuff in particular?"

"Concern for someone other than yourself or your family."

"Do you have to be so fucking blunt?"

"Do you want me to blow smoke up your ass or tell you the truth?"

"The truth. I guess."

"The truth is, brother, you're not exactly a prince among men when it comes to women. But that doesn't mean you can't change to meet the moment."

"I want to be everything she needs."

"That's a good start. Bringing her here was the right move. She might not want you involved, but she needs the protection you and the rest of us can offer her."

"She doesn't have anyone, M. She and Mateo were going to spend Christmas alone."

"You and I... We can't imagine that with our huge family all around us."

"Yeah, for sure. The family used to drive me mad when we were younger, always up in my business. But since Mom got sick, I have a whole new appreciation for how lucky we are." Our extended family has rallied around us with love and food and comfort and anything we needed before we even knew we needed it. "I want her to know she's not alone anymore."

"You're showing her that. Just give her time to get her head around it and don't be overbearing. She's used to taking care of herself and her son. She won't take kindly to you telling her what to do."

"That's true."

"You can be protective without being a dick."

"How do you always know the right thing to do?"

Milo shrugs. "I pay attention to people."

"Whereas I only pay attention to myself."

"You said that, not me."

"If you laugh, I'm gonna fucking punch you."

"Truth hurts, huh?"

Before I can fire back with a cutting reply, Sofia comes into the kitchen carrying something that looks like a small radio, and the debate with Milo is forgotten.

"Baby monitor," she says when she sees me looking at it. "I got it for a gift when I had Mateo, but I've never needed it in my small place. Sometimes he wakes up in pain at night."

"Ah, that's good to have here."

"Yes, it is. Could I please have a glass of water?"

"Of course." I grab a glass, fill it with ice and water and hand it to her. "You want to watch a movie or something?" Anything to keep her out here with us.

"I don't think I could concentrate."

"How about a swim in the pool, then? It's warm enough, and the pool is heated."

She eyes the pool through the kitchen window, and I'm thankful for the weekend Milo and I spent installing the lighting in the gardens, which make the pool look inviting. "You wouldn't mind?"

"I told you my house is your house. Whatever you want, whenever you want it."

"That might be relaxing."

I'm glad I reminded her to bring a swimsuit. "Go get changed. I'll meet you out there."

She looks at Milo. "Sorry to invade your house with my kid and my troubles."

"We're very happy to have you," he says in the sweet, gentle way that's so him. "Don't worry about a thing, okay?"

She puts the glass on the counter and crosses her arms. "You're all so kind."

"We care about you, Sofia," I say before Milo can beat me to it. "And Mateo. We want to be there for you both."

"Thank you." Her sweet smile fills me with hope and the kind of happiness that turns men into fools over women. I've managed to avoid that until now, but all I want is to make a complete fool of myself over her. "I'll, ah, be out there in a minute."

"You're welcome to join us," I tell Milo after she takes her water and leaves the room.

"Thanks, but you don't need your little brother in the middle of this." He finishes his beer, tosses the bottle in the recycling and gives me a salute as he heads for the doorway.

"I always need my little brother."

Milo shoots a smile over his shoulder. "Likewise, bro, only change 'little' to 'big.'"

The two of us have always been close, despite the years between us and the vast differences in our personalities. Maria says we're the yin to the other's yang, whatever that means. He drove me crazy until he was about seventeen and started making himself useful to me in more ways than I can count. Now I don't know what I'd do without his calming influence in my life. He's truly my best friend, along with our cousin Dom.

I need to hit up Dom to see when he's going back to New York. I'll do that later. Right now, I need all my wits about me to deal with Sofia in a bikini. She has a cloth thing tied around her waist, but I'm not looking at her waist. All I can see is a stunning face and gorgeous breasts. I also see uncertainty, anxiety and discomfort.

I want her to be more comfortable with me than with anyone else in the world, so I go to her, extend my hand and hope she'll take hold and never let go. After she grasps my hand, I realize I was holding my breath waiting for her to decide.

"The water is nice. Let's swim."

CHAPTER 8

NICO

Sofia unties the skirt around her waist before we go down the stairs to the shallow end. I don't let go of her hand even when we're fully submerged.

"This is why I love Miami. Swimming in December."

"It's really nice. I still can't believe you live in a house like this."

"Where did you think I lived?"

"I don't know, but I didn't picture this."

"It's just a building."

"Right," she says with a laugh. "Just a building. It's like a palace to me. My apartment would fit in your guest room."

"I want you to be comfortable here."

"Anyone would be comfortable here, Nico."

"I want *you* to be."

"I am, thank you."

"You're welcome to stay for as long as you want or need to." Forever would be good, but I don't dare say that to her. Not yet, anyway.

"I'll figure something out tomorrow."

"I won't want you to leave tomorrow or the next day or the day after that." As I say that, I move closer to her, hoping I'll still be welcome to put my arms around her, to hold her close, to offer comfort and protection and anything else she needs.

"It's not up to you to solve my problems."

"I know that, but why can't I help you? I thought, maybe, we were starting something here."

"We are. Or we were. I don't want you involved in this crap with Joaquín and his band of thugs. If something ever happened to you, I don't know what I'd do."

"That's how I feel about something happening to you—or Mateo." I smooth the hair back from her face. "My friend Miguel called and said they've arrested Diego and the men with him. They're charging them since they hit us with their car on purpose and threatened us with unregistered guns."

"They'll make bail and be out in a day or two. That's how it always works."

"He said they're going to be under a protective order, too, and they're facing some pretty significant charges. They'd be crazy to come anywhere near you."

"That won't stop them. They think I've done him wrong, and they won't leave me alone no matter what. They'll find a way to harass me endlessly. I've seen them in action for years. Diego's ex-girlfriend ended up in a mental hospital when she tried to leave him and take their children. Now he has custody of them, and she never sees them."

"That's not going to happen to you. I won't let it."

"Is there anything I can say that would convince you to let me handle this on my own?"

I shake my head. "Not a single thing."

Her deep sigh says it all.

"Hold on to me. Let me help." I kiss her neck until she shivers in my arms. "I care so much about you and Mateo. I'd go insane if you didn't let me help keep you safe."

"You have enough going on in your own life. You don't need my stuff, too."

"Yes, I really do. How am I supposed to concentrate on anything if I'm worried about whether you guys are safe?"

"I have to work tomorrow—or I guess it's tonight now."

"I'll take you and watch Mateo while you're there."

"You don't have to do that! I have someone who watches him while I'm at work."

"Where?"

"In my building."

"You can't go back there right now, Sofia, and you can't leave Mateo there either. I assume Joaquín knows what you do with him while you're working. What if he makes bail, and you come home to find Mateo gone?"

"He... He can't do that. We have a custody agreement. He only gets him one night a week."

"And he's been so great about following the rules and the law. He's in jail for violating the protective order. I imagine he's pretty angry to be locked up, and who's he going to blame for putting him there? Himself? I highly doubt that."

She rolls her bottom lip between her teeth. "Maybe I shouldn't go to work if there's a chance of trouble."

"We'll talk to my uncle Vin and tell him what's going on so he can be aware."

"He's not going to want me there if I bring trouble with me."

I tip her chin up. "You're *family* to us, Sofia. Your troubles are our troubles. That's how it works in a family."

"But I'm not really family. This might be too much for them."

"My family doesn't only care about me when things are going well for me. They care about me all the time. They feel the same way about you and Mateo. Abuela and Nona would beat the shit out of anyone who tried to hassle you."

That draws the first hint of a smile I've seen since Diego and his buddies smashed into us in traffic.

"I wouldn't want to mess with them," Sofia says of my grandmothers.

"They're a formidable team, and they protect their own. They've made you and Mateo part of our family, and that extends to bad times as well as good."

71

"They've done so much for me. The last thing I'd ever want is to bring trouble into their lives."

"You're not the one bringing the trouble."

"You know what I mean. There'd be no trouble to worry about if I wasn't here."

"Maybe not, but we'd worry about you if you weren't here." I put my arms around her and hold her close under the water. "I'll talk to Vin in the morning, tell him what's going on, and we'll see what he has to say. All right?"

"I guess so. I just hate that this is happening and that I have to involve him. It's the best job I've ever had. I love everything about it."

"I've heard everyone say how great you are with the customers and how much they love having you on the team."

"They say that?"

"All the time. Giordino's is a very special place. They don't let just anyone work there. If you weren't a good fit, they would've helped you find another job somewhere else. They wouldn't have kept you on. One of my dad and Vin's cousin's daughters lasted two weeks before he showed her the door. She was a terrible waitress, which is bad for business. Vin apologized to his cousin and said it wasn't going to work out. End of story."

"Wow, that must've been awkward."

"It was, but he's very unapologetic about doing what's best for the business that supports a lot of families, not just his. He takes that obligation very seriously."

"I've learned so much working there, not just about the restaurant business, but about life and people, too."

"I know what you mean. Every day, I apply some lesson I learned working there in my own business."

"Thank you for everything you're doing for me."

"You don't have to thank me. I'm so glad you're here. You and Mateo are welcome for as long as you'd like to be here."

"You and your brother don't need me and my kid in your... What's it called..."

"Bachelor pad?"

"Yes, that's it. I heard Livia call it that."

"In case you haven't noticed, I've been actively trying to change my status from 'bachelor' to 'in a relationship.'"

"You could find someone less complicated than I am."

"Maybe so, but I've never found anyone who I wanted to be with the way I want to be with you. I look at you, and I just want you. It's been that way since the first time I saw you at the restaurant and I asked my uncle who you were. He told me you were our new waitress, Sofia, and that I'd better watch myself with you because Nona and Abuela had appointed themselves your guardians and would kneecap me if I stepped out of line with you."

"He did not say that!"

"He did, and they'd do it, too, which is yet another reason why you have nothing to fear from me. I'm terrified of them."

That makes her giggle, which utterly transforms her and makes me realize how serious and anxious she is most of the time. I vow right then and there to make her laugh as often as I possibly can. I told myself I'd keep my distance tonight, knowing she's upset, but damn if I can be this close to her and not want to kiss and touch her.

I move in slowly, giving her time to say no. She doesn't say no. Instead, she runs her fingers through my hair and sends a jolt of need straight down my spine. As my lips connect with hers, I feel light-headed as all the blood in my body seems to gather in one central location. I try to pull back a bit so she won't feel what she does to me, but she wraps her arms and legs around me, nearly making me whimper from the surge of desire.

Christ have mercy, she's so hot and sexy and sweet and everything I'll ever want or need. I know that without a shadow of a doubt only twenty-four hours after we kissed for the first time. She just does it for me, and as my hands slide over soft, wet skin, I'm completely lost to her. We end up reclined on the stairs, her under me, her arms and legs keeping me trapped in the sweetest web ever.

My hard cock presses against the heat between her legs as I slide a hand up to cover her breast. I'm starting to wonder if we're going to get busy right here in the pool when my phone rings with the tone I assigned to Angelo. Groaning, I withdraw from the kiss with the greatest reluctance of my life. "I've got to take that. It's work."

She looks as shell-shocked as I feel as we disentangle, and I stumble out of the pool to find the phone I left on a table.

"What's up?"

"Dude… Someone just hit one of our cars when it was stopped at a light and then took off."

My heart sinks at this news. How can it not be related to what happened earlier? "Anyone hurt?"

"The passenger complained of neck pain, so Rudy called 911. They took her to the hospital to get checked out."

"And Rudy is okay?"

"Yeah, just pissed. He said the other car came racing up behind him, smashed into the car and was gone before he could react. Happened fast."

"How bad is the damage to the car?"

"The whole back end is smashed in."

"Did he get a description of the car that hit him?"

"He did, and the police have the info."

"Thanks, Angelo. I'll be in tomorrow. Appreciate you covering me this weekend."

"No problem, boss."

I put down the phone, my heart heavy with the realization that this shit is only going to intensify if I'm with Sofia. I'm undeterred. They can come for me any way they want, and I'll deal with it as long as she and Mateo are safe.

Sofia gets out of the pool and takes the towel I hand her. "What happened?"

SOFIA

I'm sick to my stomach after hearing about the hit-and-run with one of Nico's cars. Knowing how hard he's working to build his business, the certainty that the "accident" is related to me is devastating. For a minute there in the pool, I was able to forget the chaos swirling around us.

Even as my entire body continues to hum with desire so intense it took my breath away, I'm fully aware that I can't do this to him.

Tomorrow, I'll figure out a way to distance myself from him.

It's the right thing to do, but it kills me to think of being separated from him after having experienced a small taste of what might be possible for us.

"I can see your wheels turning…"

"What does that mean?"

"That you're thinking of a way to get free of me, so your trouble won't spill over onto me."

It's a little scary how he knows exactly what I was thinking.

"Cut it out," he says. "We're in this together."

"How would you feel if something in your life was putting me in danger?"

"I'd feel very determined to protect you from it, but I wouldn't push you away." He puts his arms around me and draws me in close to him. "I'd hold you like this through all the storms that come our way until we're free to fully enjoy the good stuff." His lips are warm against my neck, and just that quickly, the fire between us reignites. "Don't push me away."

My fingers dig into the dense muscles that cover his hips, even as I tell myself to let him go. I don't want to, which makes me feel totally selfish. I'm not good for him or his family. I've brought trouble into his life that he doesn't need.

However, I can't deny that we fit together like two pieces of a puzzle, his chin resting on my head and his erection hot against my belly.

"Let's go to bed and get some rest. Tomorrow, we'll figure out what we need to do about the nonsense."

"I should just drive away from here with Mateo and go somewhere that no one can find us."

"I'd find you."

"You're not making it easy for me to do the right thing."

"The right thing is for you to be here with me, surrounded by everyone who cares about you and can help keep you and your son safe."

"While I bring turmoil into their lives." I loved that word until it applied to this situation.

"You're not the one bringing the turmoil."

"It's related to me."

"It's not your fault. None of this is your fault."

"It feels like it is. Two of your cars are damaged because of me."

"No, it's because of Joaquín and how he can't accept that you don't want to be with him anymore. Everything that's happened stems from that simple truth."

He releases my hair from the clip that held it up while we were in the pool and runs his fingers through it, making my scalp tingle with sensation. I'm not sure why my body reacts to his every touch this way, but I'm quickly becoming addicted to the way I feel when I'm close to him.

"If we let him drive us apart with his bullshit, then he gets what he wants and succeeds in keeping you afraid of him. We can't let him have that."

"I am afraid of him. Not just for me and Mateo, but for you and your family, too."

"I'll text Uncle Vin to let him know what's going on and what we're doing about it. That way, he'll know to be vigilant on your behalf and their own. Joaquín will regret the day he crossed the Giordino family. I promise you that."

His sisters and cousin warned me to stay away from him, but all I see is a man who'd do anything for me and my son and who's proven that numerous times today alone. I still believe he'd be better off without me, but he's made it clear he's not going to let me go easily.

I follow him inside and watch him set the alarm.

"The code is 1215, which is also the code to the keyless entry on the front door and the garage. If you need to turn the alarm off, you just press in that code. To set it, you hit Armed Stay, which means you can move around in the house without setting it off. Armed Away sets the motion detectors, too."

"Will you write that down for me?"

"Yep. I'll text it to you. Let me see your phone. I'll put the app on it so you can control it from anywhere."

As I hand over my phone to him, I'm astounded by the trust he's placing in me by giving me access to his home.

A minute later, he returns the phone to me. "There you go." He shows me how to use the app for the security system. "I realized I never showed you my room. Come see."

The look he gives me is all heat. I take the hand he offers me and follow him to the first-floor main bedroom, which is huge even with a king-sized bed taking up a big chunk of the space. "You have a fireplace!"

"Yeah, it's pretty nice on the four or five days it gets really cold in the winter."

"I *love* fireplaces."

"I'd be happy to light it—and turn down the AC so it doesn't sweat us out—if you'd like."

"You don't have to do that."

"I know I don't. I want to. Go get comfy and come back."

"You're like the devil." Although this devil is nothing like the one I was married to. Nico is a different kind of devil—the best kind.

His brow furrows. "How so?"

"I keep telling myself I need to walk away from you—for your own good—but you keep giving me reasons to stay."

"Please don't walk away from me. You're what's good for me."

"We both know that's not true."

"Yes, it is."

"Everyone was warning me away from you, but they should've been warning you away from me."

"All the warnings in the world wouldn't change the fact that I want you like I've never wanted anyone else."

I fan my face. "It's getting warm in here, and you haven't lit the fireplace yet."

His smile is the sexiest thing I've ever seen. "You haven't seen hot yet, baby."

"Oh boy. Be right back."

"I'll be here."

CHAPTER 9

SOFIA

I go into the guestroom, check on Mateo, who hasn't moved since I put him down, and rush through a shower. As I rub lotion all over and dress in a tank and boy shorts, I ignore the many alarms blaring in my mind that tell me I need to slow this down, to proceed with caution, to protect myself and Mateo—and even Nico. But I don't care about any of that. All I want is more of him and the way he makes me feel when I'm in his arms.

This is madness.

I don't do things like this.

I work and take care of my son and study English and keep my head down since I left Joaquín, promising myself I was done with men forever.

That was before Nico Giordino walked into his aunt and uncle's restaurant one night and blew all my promises to bits. I didn't even try to hide my fascination with him. I happened to be working with his cousin Carmen, who'd gotten me the job in the first place and noticed me staring at him like a lovesick teenager.

"Don't go there," she said. "He's nothing but trouble for women."

After what I've been through, those words should've been more than enough to end my fascination right then and there. But it only grew every time I saw him, which was often once I realized the fascination was two-sided. He seemed to come in every time I was working, which of course Carmen and the others noticed. She and Jason come in for dinner most Saturday nights, which is one of my usual nights.

"He's never here this much," Luisa, one of the other waitresses, told me.

I got the feeling she was pissed that he was obviously coming to see me and not her. The more I saw him, the more I wanted him. I even dreamed about him—more than once—and the dreams were R-rated. I'd wake up sweating and throbbing and wanting him with every part of me, even if I'd been told that wanting him wasn't a good idea.

I didn't care.

I just wanted.

And now… Now I can have him, and I'm terrified I'm going to be the one to screw things up for him rather than the other way around. If I had an ounce of decency in me, I'd take Mateo and leave Nico's home to go somewhere else that Joaquín and his friends couldn't find us. But where?

Where could I go on my limited resources? I make very decent money at the restaurant—the most money I've ever made in my life —but it barely covers the rent, utilities, food, clothing, transportation, childcare and small monthly payments on the staggering medical bills from Mateo's illness. That's why I had to stop most of the PT and OT for now. There's nothing left for the co-pays when the other bills are paid.

Vincent added me and Mateo to the restaurant's health insurance as soon as he possibly could, and that's been a lifesaver. In between occasional therapy appointments, I work with Mateo as much as I can on the things we learn.

Leaving the area isn't an option with Mateo's doctors and therapists here, not to mention my job.

I hate feeling like I have no choice but to accept the help Nico has offered, even though I worry about what his generosity toward us will cost him. Now two of his vehicles are damaged, the second one most likely done by another friend or family member of Joaquín's looking for revenge by hassling the new guy in my life.

It's all so ridiculous.

Our marriage was in trouble long before our son got sick, and Joaquín was nowhere to be found during those dreadful first days. And when he finally decided to show his face, he was angry with me for incurring hundreds of thousands in medical bills to save our son. "It'll take the rest of our lives to pay down that debt," he screamed, his face red and his fists raised to me.

When I look back at it all, that was the moment when I truly began to hate him. It wasn't when he failed to show up or be there for us during the crisis. It was when he put money ahead of our son's life.

Only when I was offered the job at Giordino's, along with the friendship of Marlene and Livia, did I have the courage and the resources to file for divorce, thanks to a regular customer at the restaurant who offered to help me for free.

That's when Joaquín got *really* angry.

A soft knock on the door drags me out of the rabbit hole I've fallen into. I go to the door to open it to a shirtless Nico, which is a thing of beauty. "You didn't come back."

"I… I was thinking."

"Don't do that."

He makes me forget every problem I have the second he touches me in any way. He places his hand on my face and runs his thumb gently over my cheek. "Don't think. Just feel."

That quickly, I've forgotten why this could be a terrible idea, and I'm right back to wanting him with everything I am.

"I lit the fire for you. Want to come see?"

I nod. "Let me just grab the monitor for Mateo."

A minute later, he leads me into his room across the hall and closes the door. The fire has cast a cozy glow in the room that makes it look so inviting. I try to imagine what it would be like to live in a house like this one, and I just can't.

"What do you think?" he asks from behind me, his hands on my shoulders.

"It's beautiful. The most beautiful bedroom I've ever seen."

"You really think so? I haven't done much with it."

"I really think so." I turn to face him. "You should put some fun wallpaper on the wall behind the bed."

He looks over my shoulder at the wall in question. "Maybe you could do that for me?"

"If you want me to."

"I'd love to see what you'd do."

"And you wouldn't care what it looks like?"

"If you like it, I'll like it."

I give him a playful side-eye. "How do you know that?"

"Because whatever you do will be better than what's there now, which is nothing. And besides, I'm curious to see what you have in mind."

"I love to decorate. My teachers used to say I could make something out of nothing."

"I can tell you're good at it. Your place is awesome."

"It's all just junk."

"You'd never know that to look at it. You made something amazing from it."

"I'm glad you think so. Decorating on a budget has always been fun for me. If I could do anything I wanted, that's what I'd want to do for work. Decorate and organize people's homes."

"You can start right here. Do whatever you want to this place. Take before-and-after photos you can use for a website later."

My heart begins to beat faster at the thought of what he's suggesting. "Sure. I should just completely redecorate your house like that's no big deal."

Smiling, he says, "In order to redecorate, you have to decorate—and I've never done that. I've lived here for years with basic furniture and nothing else. My sisters have been after me for ages to do something with the place, but I have no idea what to do. So have at it."

"You're serious."

"Completely. I can't spend a ton of money, because most of what I have is invested in the business."

"I'm at my best on a budget."

"Your eyes are glittering right now."

"It's exciting to think about decorating a house like this."

He takes hold of my hand and leads me to his bed. "I like the way excitement looks on you."

I'm not sure if being in a bed together will lead to the logical conclusion, but either way, I'm here for whatever he wants. "I must look excited a lot when you're around." I can't believe I said that, but oh well. It's true.

His grin is the sexiest thing ever as he pulls a light blanket over us and brings me in close to him.

I breathe in the scent of his skin. "You smell so good."

"Dee gave me new body wash and cologne for Christmas. I decided to break it out."

"I like it."

"Then I'll use it every day." His hands move over me with gentle reverence that has everything female in me wanting to be as close to him as I can get. "Tell me more about your life. I want to know everything. Were you born here in Miami?"

"Yep. My mom had me when she was nineteen. My father was a one-night stand, a navy guy from Minnesota, of all places. He never knew about me."

"Have you ever tried to find him?"

"Nah. What would be the point?"

"You could have your father in your life."

"I wouldn't even know how to go about that."

"You could do one of those DNA kits and see if you match with anyone. A friend of mine from high school connected with his birth parents by doing that, although a lawyer friend of ours says it's not a good idea to put your DNA out there to be found by law enforcement."

"If you don't plan to be a criminal, that shouldn't be an issue."

"That's what I said, too. But his point was that someone related to you could be caught."

"Mateo isn't going to be a criminal either, so I suppose I could try it. I've always wondered about my father."

"You could try social media, too. Imagine his shock at finding out he has a twentysomething daughter he never knew existed."

"I'm twenty-six. What if he had an affair with my mother and hearing about me sets off a bomb in his life?"

"Yeah, that'd suck, but it would be cool to know, wouldn't it?"

"I suppose. I doubt it would change my life in any meaningful way."

"You never know." He never stops playing with my hair. "Tell me more. Were you a good student?"

"I was. I got mostly A's all through school. I even got a scholarship to UF."

"Why didn't you go?"

"My mom OD'd for the first time three weeks before I was supposed to leave. I'm her only family, so I couldn't go. I soon realized she'd done it on purpose because she didn't want me to have that opportunity."

"Why in the hell would she not want that for you?"

"She was jealous of me my whole life. She hated the attention her boyfriends paid to me—and I hated that, too. I was two when she drove us to Mexico, following yet another loser guy, who ditched us shortly after we arrived. It took until I was almost fifteen to get back to Miami, which is why my English isn't as good as it should be."

"Ah, I see. Your mom didn't speak English at all?"

"God, no. She was raised in Puerto Rico, came here when she was seventeen and basically refused to learn English. She hates that I know it and she doesn't, though. All my life, she hated when people would comment on how smart or pretty or talented I was. It infuriated her, and she took that out on me. She'd treat me like shit and tell me I thought I was better than her when I was nothing but a one-night-stand bastard who never should've been born."

"Jesus," he whispers. "She actually said that to you?"

"More times than I can count. If you wonder why she's no longer in my life, that's why, although she didn't go quietly either.

I keep thinking I should block her so she can't bother me anymore, but I still hope that maybe someday, she might act like a mother."

"I'm so sorry she treated you that way and that you had to give up your scholarship. Maybe you can still go to school somehow."

"I'd probably suck at it now. It's been so long since I had to really study, I've forgotten how."

"You'd still be a great student. Look at how well you're doing with ESL classes."

"I guess." He's quiet for a long time, which leads me to ask, "What're you thinking?"

"That you've had an incredibly difficult life, and all I want to do is make things better for you."

"It's not up to you to make things better for me."

"I know that, but I still want to."

For the longest time, we simply stare at each other, breathing the same air, which crackles with an electric energy that I've never experienced with anyone else. When he reaches for me, I go willingly, my mouth fusing with his, our bodies aligning as arms and legs intertwine. During the hottest kiss of my life, I'm aware enough to know that everything is changing, and I'm allowing it—and loving it.

NICO

She's the sweetest person I've ever known, and I meant what I said about wanting to make things better for her. I hate that her life has been such a struggle up to now. I hate the way her mother treated her, the way Joaquín abused her, that she lost her scholarship and how everything has been so difficult from the start. She never stood a chance with her only parent working against her.

As one kiss spins into another, I'm desperate to show her how much I care about her. But I don't want her to think this is all I want, even if I want it with a fiery desire I didn't know I was capable of until I felt it for her. I remember wondering, as recently as when Carmen fell for Jason and Maria fell for Austin, why people limit themselves to one person for the rest of their lives when there are so many people to meet and experience.

Now I get it. If this is what Carmen feels for Jason or Maria feels for Austin or Dee for Wyatt, I understand why they'd go all in with one person. It's a feeling like nothing else, the highest of highs, and all I want is as much of it as I can get for as long as I can have it. Pulling back from the kiss pains me.

Her eyes open slowly, and she blinks me into focus. "Why did you stop?"

"I don't want you to think this is all I want."

"I want it, too, or I wouldn't be in your bed."

"I don't want to rush you into something you might not be ready for."

"We've been leading up to this for months."

"Yeah, I suppose we have. I want you to know…" I cup her face as she looks up at me with big brown eyes that seem to see right through to the very heart of me.

"What do you want me to know?"

"That I really, really, *really* care about you. More than I've ever cared about anyone."

"I feel that, Nico. I see it in the way you look at me, how you touch me, how you care for Mateo. And I feel the same way about you, even if I still think it would be better for you not to be involved with me when my life is such a mess."

"No, it wouldn't be better, and your life isn't a mess. Your ex-husband's life is a mess, but I don't want to talk about him."

"What do you want to talk about?" she asks with the biggest smile I've ever seen from her.

"You and me and us."

"What about us?"

"This." I kiss her neck and down to her chest while tugging on her tank. "Can we lose this?"

"Uh-huh." She sits up and draws the garment up and over her head, leaving full, gorgeous breasts on full display.

With my hands on her hips, I lean over her as she lies back and puts her arms around my neck. "You're so fucking sexy. You have no idea how crazy you've made me from the first time I ever saw you."

"All that time?"

"Mmm." My lips can't get enough of her soft skin. "I haven't been with anyone else since I met you. I also wanted you to know that."

With her fingers buried in my hair, she directs me to the hard tip of her left breast.

I have a whole new appreciation for the expression *died and gone to heaven*, because that's exactly what this is like. I'm so fucking hard, I feel like my cock is going to burst from wanting her so desperately. I could live right here, with my face buried in her perfect breasts, for the rest of my life and be happy. I want to make her feel so good, she won't ever need anyone but me forever.

Though I'm desperate for her, I take my time and kiss her everywhere. I bury my tongue and fingers inside her and make her come twice, one right after the other, leaving her gasping and panting and begging me to give her what we both want more than anything. I grab a condom from the bedside table drawer and roll it on as she watches me, her face flushed, her lips swollen, her body ready for me.

I want to ask her again if she's sure about this, but I don't. She knows she can tell me to stop at any time, and I would, even if it'd kill me to stop.

She runs her hands down my back and pulls me toward her, wrapping her legs around my hips as I sink into her heat.

Holy. *Shit.*

The sound she makes as I fill her completely goes straight to the base of my spine. It takes everything I have not to lose it within the first two seconds inside her. "Christ, Sofia."

"Feels so good. Don't stop."

I grunt out a laugh. "Not going to stop." I'm never going to stop wanting her or this. One minute inside her, and I'm addicted for life.

She moves with me like she was made to love me.

I pick up the pace, and we go at it like it's the first time after years without. It's like the first time all over again because it's her and me and us.

Her fingers dig into my back, and the desperate sounds coming from her as she comes again are my undoing. I press into her and let go in the most intense release of my life. Nothing has ever been like this or her, although I've known from the start it would be this way with her.

Epic.

Life changing.

It's all I can do not to tell her I love her. Maybe I should so she knows. It feels too soon and not soon enough all at the same time. I've never said those words to a woman, so I have no idea what the proper timing would be. All I know is that what I feel for her is something I've never felt for anyone else.

I raise my head off her chest and kiss her. "Are you okay?"

"Mmm, so okay."

"That was incredible."

"Knew it would be."

"Did you?"

She smiles and nods, but keeps her eyes closed. "I've had some pretty vivid dreams about you and this."

"Really? Do tell."

"I'd rather show you."

Four little words are all it takes to get my blood boiling all over again. "I'm down with that."

"I just need a little nap first. You wore me out."

"It was the other way around." I can't stop kissing and touching her now that I'm allowed to. I want to turn her over, kiss her back and fuck her from behind, but I'll save that for next time.

I withdraw from her and leave the bed to get rid of the condom. After I put on shorts, I cross the hall to check on Mateo. He's sleeping right where we left him in the guest bed.

Then I return to Sofia. She's on her side, sound asleep, one bare shoulder peeking out from under the covers. I place a kiss on her shoulder and smooth the hair back from her face as I watch her sleep. Another thing I never do is sleep with women. It conveys intimacy and commitment, which are two things I never wanted anything to do with until now.

Until her.

She's sweet perfection, and I love having her sleeping in my bed, which is also a first. I never bring women to my home.

I've played by a set of rules that worked for me. What my sisters and cousin call toxic was hardly that. I was honest with every woman I ever dated about what I wanted and what I didn't. Was it my fault that every one of them thought they would be the one to change my mind about the things I didn't want?

Yes, I broke some hearts, but I didn't do it intentionally. I was honest when I told them not to fall in love with me. Is it my fault that they did anyway?

I hate thinking about this shit or having to feel guilty for choices other people made even after being told not to go there. I'm filled with nervous energy after the best sex of my life. I get up to grab a glass of water and find Milo doing the same in the kitchen. He's glistening with sweat after a workout in our basement gym.

I prefer the kind of workout I just had with Sofia, a thought that nearly makes me laugh as I drop ice into a glass and get water from the dispenser on the door of the fridge.

"Are your guests asleep?"

"Yep. They're out cold."

"I was just thinking this is the first time I've ever seen you bring a woman here."

"Funny, I was thinking the same thing. Not my usual routine, but nothing about this is usual or normal."

"She seems really great."

"She is, and she's been through so fucking much, it's not even funny—and it's not over."

"I heard about one of the cars getting hit. You think that's related?"

"A hundred percent related. He's refusing to let her go even months after she left him and filed for divorce. He's got his friends and cousins and who knows who else hassling her even when he's locked up."

"I hate to think of her or Mateo being in that kind of danger."

"I do, too. Makes me crazy."

Milo gives me a serious look. "It makes *me* crazy worrying that they're going to come after you."

"I can take care of myself."

"You don't carry a weapon, Nico. You're no match for a gun."

"With the cops already all over them, they'd be crazy to take it to that level."

"They've already run cars into your truck and now one of your work cars. It doesn't seem like the cops are deterring them."

"I'll talk to Miguel tomorrow. Try not to worry, and don't say anything about this to the family. I'm going to tell Uncle Vin what's going on so he can help to keep Sofia safe at work, but I don't want Mom and Dad all over me about it."

"I won't say anything, but you have to promise me you'll be careful. Out of curiosity, I did a search online for Sofia's ex, and he's got a long rap sheet, as do his known associates. It doesn't seem to me that he and his pals are all that worried about the cops."

"When I talk to Miguel in the morning, I'll ask him what can be done about a repeat offender who can't accept that his wife doesn't want to be married to him any longer."

"I know you care about her, but I want you to look out for yourself in this, too."

"I hear you, and I do care about her. I think I might even love her."

Milo's eyes bug behind his black-framed glasses. "Seriously?"

"As seriously as it gets."

"Well, this is definitely a first."

"Yeah, for sure. I kinda get it now."

"Get what?"

"Why other guys make fools of themselves over one woman."

Milo loses it laughing. "Oh, how the mighty fall."

"I guess it happens eventually to the best of us."

"I gotta be honest, bro. I never thought I'd see the day with you, but the first time I saw you with Sofia, I thought something was different about you with her."

"That's how it's felt from the beginning. I've wanted her since the first time I saw her. The thought of this guy hassling her because she doesn't want to be with him anymore is making me nuts."

"Happens all the time, unfortunately."

"I hate this for her. I just want her to be free of him so we can make some plans." I mess up Milo's hair as I walk past him. "Thanks for having my back."

"Always."

I return to my room and crawl into bed next to Sofia, putting an arm around her to keep her close to me while she sleeps. I'm determined that no harm will come to her or her little boy on my watch. I'd die myself before I'd let that happen.

CHAPTER 10

MARIA

I wake from a deep sleep to a kiss from my beloved.

"Are you alive in there?" Austin asks, smiling down at me as the scent of freshly brewed coffee fills my senses and turns my stomach.

If I'm looking for proof that I'm sick, sleeping like a dead woman and recoiling from coffee is all the evidence I need. "Barely," I say in reply to his question. "I think I have the flu or something. All I want is sleep. Thank God I'm off this week."

"I thought we might go do something fun, like hit the beach."

"I don't think I can, but you and Everly should go."

"She won't want to go without her Rie."

"Rie is a drag."

"No, she isn't. Don't talk that way about my beautiful fiancée."

"Your fiancée is a drag." Soon he'll be reporting to spring training in Jupiter, a thought that only exhausts me further. His parents live with us, but I'll be the primary caregiver for his daughter, Everly, while he's at camp. Most of the games are in Jupiter or West Palm Beach, so we'll go up to watch him play on the weekends, but Austin is going to be staying up there most nights.

With his season looming, we've looked forward to this week off together, and now I'm sleeping through it. Determined to power through, I force myself to sit up and get my shit together. Except this shit isn't having it. My head spins with dizziness that immediately makes me nauseated.

"Jeez, babe. You're green."

"I feel awful. Maybe it's an inner ear thing. I've had that before."

"Can you get it checked today?"

"I suppose I can go to the clinic. Miranda will check me out."

"I'll drive you."

"I'd tell you I can drive myself, but I honestly don't think I should."

"Of course you shouldn't drive when you feel this shitty. I'll ask my mom if she can watch Ev for a few hours."

"Sounds good, thanks."

After I call the clinic where I work to ask if I can pop in for a quick ear check, I struggle through a shower that leaves me completely drained and dying to go back to bed. When Austin returns to the bedroom, he finds me right where he left me—sitting on the side of the bed, trying to stay awake.

Whatever this is, it sucks. I started feeling like crap on Christmas Eve after we got home from Nochebuena at Abuela's, and it's been all downhill since then. I got through Christmas Day at my parents', but I've been asleep since we got home from there.

Thank goodness for Austin, because he keeps his arm tight around me on the way to the new Mercedes G-Wagon he bought me for Christmas that I've ridden in only twice. This will be the third time, but I'm too exhausted to enjoy the new-car smell or the smooth ride or anything other than more sleep in the time it takes Austin to drive us to the clinic.

Because I texted my boss, she's waiting for us when we arrive.

"Ah, chica, you don't look good."

"Thanks, amiga."

Miranda laughs. "Well, you always look good, you bitch, but today, not so great."

"I feel like absolute shit."

"Let's take a look." To Austin, she says, "Are you coming, or would you rather wait out here?"

"I'll come if Maria doesn't mind."

"I don't." I always want him with me, even when I feel like shit.

In the exam room, Miranda begins the exam with a look inside my ears. "Everything looks fine in there. Why do you think it's an ear thing?"

"I'm super dizzy and exhausted. I've had ear infections before that've been like that."

"Your ears look great. Lie back and let me check the rest of you."

It says a lot about how lousy I feel that I nearly doze off while a friend is palpating my abdomen.

"Is there any chance you could be pregnant?"

Suddenly, I'm wide awake. "No. There's no chance of that."

She grins at me and glances at Austin. "None at all?"

"I'm on birth control. I get the shot."

Miranda moves away from me and types something into the computer. "I show you overdue for a shot by six weeks."

"What? No way. That's not possible. I get alerts on my phone."

"Unless you get the shots somewhere else, you're overdue. Our system is fully automated to alert patients, but as you know, we don't have the staff to follow up with people who don't show up."

"You will when we open the new place," Austin says, though his face has been flat with shock since Miranda said the word 'pregnant'. As the clinic's primary benefactor, he's tuned in to the many improvements that will come with the new clinic that's under construction.

"How about we do a quick test?"

After she helps me sit up, I begin to cry at the sheer preposterousness of me forgetting about my birth control shot and getting pregnant. I'm a nurse, for crying out loud. Who knows better than me not to let things like that slide?

Austin puts his arms around me. "Shhhh. If you're pregnant, we'll have a beautiful baby to love. It's no biggie."

"But our wedding and your season and everything… I'm not ready for this."

"Let's make sure that's what it is before you worry about all that, okay?" Miranda asks.

Nodding, I wipe the tears from my face, fully aware that an accidental pregnancy in my blessed life hardly counts as a crisis. Austin and I have the resources and the ability to handle anything that comes our way, and as someone who works with people who have serious needs, I never forget the privilege that comes with that reality. But damn it, I'm not ready to have a baby.

"We're not even married yet." We've been planning our wedding for November, after his upcoming season.

"We can fix that anytime you'd like."

"We're supposed to have a wedding, not a shotgun thing."

Laughing, Austin says, "No one's holding a gun to my head, sweetheart. You know I can't wait to marry you and have more babies with you and everything else with you." He kisses away my tears. "We can get married and have our baby and then throw a big party to celebrate our marriage when the season is over. It'll all be fine."

Miranda returns with the items needed to take the test.

Austin helps me down from the table. "You got this?"

"I got this. You don't need to help me pee."

"I would if you needed me to."

"It hasn't quite come to that. Not yet, anyway."

"I'm here for it, babe. I'm here for it all."

"We'll be right back," Miranda tells Austin. She walks with me to the bathroom that's reserved for staff. "Whatever happens, you've got a great guy who'd do anything for you. It's all going to be fine."

"I'm fully aware that I have no business reacting this way to the possibility of being pregnant."

"You're allowed to react any way you wish to."

"We see plenty of people here for whom this would be a certified crisis. For me, it's not even close to that."

"Pregnancy is always a shock when it's not planned." Miranda pats my arm with the maternal affection she's always given me and the others who work with us.

"Suddenly, it all makes sense, though. The over-the-top exhaustion, the sore boobs, the ravenous appetite, the missing period. Jeez, Miranda. What kind of nurse am I if I can't put those pieces together on my own?"

"You're one of the best nurses I've ever worked with, and you've been crazy busy working, taking care of your parents during your mom's treatment, settling into a new relationship and becoming a mother to your fiancé's child, with the holidays on top of everything. That's a lot for anyone."

"I suppose that's true."

"It is true. We've all been amazed at how you've kept it all together when you had so much going on."

"We all have a lot going on."

"You've had more than most, so please be kind to yourself, amiga. Go take the test and confirm what you already know so you and your Austin can have some answers."

I take the test kit from her, give her a grateful smile and go into the bathroom to take care of business. I swear the freaking thing pops positive the second my pee touches the wand. I break down into tears all over again.

Holy shit. We're having a baby.

A streak of excitement goes through me. Carmen is pregnant, too, and now our babies will grow up together the way we did. That's definitely a silver lining in this unexpected situation. I'll have to figure out my due date, but we'll probably have to postpone our November wedding to give me time to recover from having a baby.

Ugh.

I can't believe this.

Miranda knocks on the door. "Everything all right in there?"

I wash my hands and then open the door. "As positive as it gets."

"I had a feeling it would be. Am I allowed to say congratulations?"

"You are."

She hugs me. "I'm thrilled for you both and for your sweet Everly. She'll be a wonderful big sister."

"Yes, she will." The thought of that has me sobbing again.

Austin comes out of the exam room, sees me crying and comes to me. "Are these good-news tears or bad-news tears?"

"What counts as good news in this situation?"

He gives me an exasperated look that's adorable on him, but then again, everything is.

"Good news."

"Whoop!" He picks me up and twirls me around before I can tell him that might not be a good idea. "I know we didn't plan this, babe, but this is one of the best days of my whole life. We're gonna have a *baby!*"

"Everly is going to be a big sister."

"She'll be the best big sister ever."

"Miranda just said that, and it made me cry."

"Those are the best kind of tears." He tips my chin up and kisses me right there in the hallway where anyone might see us. "I know we didn't plan this, but it's going to be great. I promise."

"I know. I just freaked out for a second there."

He leads me into the exam room and closes the door. "Take a deep breath. It's all good." He bends his knees so he can look into my eyes. "We made a *baby!*"

"This is what happens when I play with fire."

His grin is the sexiest thing in this universe and the next. I continue to wonder what I did to get so lucky as to find him in this world. Well, I donated the bone marrow that saved his daughter's life, but the rest of the story, our story, is one that continues to amaze me all the time. "You're hot like fire, and I can't get enough of you. I love that we made a baby. I can't wait."

"It takes a few months, you know."

"Really? How long?"

I roll my eyes at his silliness. "You know because you've already had a baby."

"When can we tell everyone we know?"

"Not until at least three months along. We want to make sure nothing goes wrong."

"Nothing will go wrong. I won't let it."

"Unfortunately, not even you can control that, and besides, you won't be here for most of it."

His grin falters for the first time. "I hate that I'll be gone so much. Maybe I should just retire so I can stay home and rub your belly and your feet and any other part of you that needs rubbed."

"You just signed a new contract, so stop that nonsense right now."

He hugs me tightly. "I don't want to be away from you."

I breathe in the clean, citrusy scent of my love. "I don't want you to be away from me either, but your career is important, and you need to stay focused on that during your season."

"We've got a few more weeks to spend together, and I'm going to take such good care of you before I have to go." He smooths the hair back from my face. "Don't worry about anything, okay?"

"I'll try not to. As long as I have you and Everly and now our baby on the way, I have nothing to worry about."

Austin's eyes brighten for a second. "You know how my brothers are coming this weekend to hang out before the season starts?"

"Sure, what about it?"

"I have the *perfect* idea."

"What idea is that?"

"Let me see if I can pull it off, and then I'll let you know." Austin kisses my forehead and hugs me again. "In the meantime, don't worry about a thing. You'll always have us. Forever and ever."

"That's all I need."

CHAPTER 11

NICO

a s I wait for Sofia to get ready for work, I feel like the proverbial cat on a hot tin roof. I can't stop pacing, moving, worrying. I'm not able to be at the restaurant for her full shift, and the thought of her being unsafe for even a minute is more than I can handle. However, I have my own work to see to, and we're booked solid tonight.

With a driver out sick, I have to be there.

We've arranged for Mateo's usual sitter to come to my house to watch him while Sofia and I are at work. I sent one of my guys to pick her up, and she should be here any minute. I'll drive Sofia to the restaurant and pick her up after her shift. I'm doing everything I can to keep her safe, but it doesn't feel like enough, and that's what is making me crazy as the clock ticks down to four o'clock.

We had a fun, relaxing day by the pool with Mateo, followed by two amazing hours in bed while he napped. It took about ten minutes in bed with Sofia to become completely addicted to her. I love everything about her, from her soft skin to her silky hair to her sweet curves and the way she responds to my touch. I wish we had nothing else to do but spend days in bed together, but that's not an option.

She comes out of the bathroom with her hair up in the sexy bun she wears to work, her crisp white shirt tucked into a short black skirt that puts her killer legs on full display. As she ties her apron in a bow behind her back, she glances at me. "Why are you staring at me?"

"Because you're the sexiest woman I've ever seen."

"You've already gotten what you wanted from me, so you don't need to say that stuff."

I get up and go to her, putting my hands on her hips as I look into her eyes. "I've only *begun* to get what I want from you, which is everything, and you are, without any doubt, the sexiest woman I've ever seen. Please don't think for one second that the only thing I want from you is sex. That's one-tenth of it, although it's a very nice tenth."

"I didn't mean to offend you."

"You didn't, but this isn't just about sex. I'd hate if you thought that."

"I don't. I know it's more than that, which makes it kind of scary."

"Why?"

"I promised myself I'd never again give a man the power to hurt me."

"I'd rather die than hurt you."

"I believe that, and it's why I'm here."

"I mean it, Sofia. I'll never do anything to hurt you."

"Yes, you will." She looks up at me with those big eyes. "I'll probably hurt you, too. But it won't be intentional, and that makes all the difference."

"You have no idea how much I care about you."

"I think maybe I do, and I care about you, too. Just as much. I wish I didn't have to work tonight so we could spend more time together."

"I wish that, too."

"This was the best Christmas of my whole life, and I'll never forget it."

"Same goes."

"Let's go to work so we can have more time together afterward."

I hold her close for another moment. "Do you promise you'll be vigilant and let Vin know if you see anything concerning?"

"I will. I promise. I'm scared of bringing trouble there."

"You aren't bringing the trouble. They are, and we all know it."

"My stomach hurts from worrying about it."

"Don't make yourself sick over it. Joaquín and his boys are still locked up for now."

"Not all of them. He has a lot of friends and more cousins than I can count. His parents both came from big families, and he's tight with a lot of them."

"I'd think the fact that he and several others are locked up after messing with you would send a message to the rest of them."

"That would be giving them far too much credit."

"Miguel said he'd make sure patrol cars are in the area. We're doing everything we can, so try not to worry." A chime sounds, indicating a door opening in another part of the house. "That'll be Gladys."

She's a former neighbor from when Sofia was a kid. She said Gladys was always kind to her. They kept in touch over the years, and when Sofia decided to leave Joaquín, Gladys helped her get an apartment in her building. Sofia says Gladys has been a godsend to her by helping with Mateo while she's at work. Gladys treats him like a grandchild, which is the sweetest thing.

"Thanks again for having all this at your house."

"Mi casa es su casa." I'll keep saying that until she believes me.

"Muchas gracias."

She goes to meet Gladys while I stand rooted in place, fearing the trouble she's worried about and wondering how I'll concentrate on anything else while we're apart.

In the kitchen, I'm surprised to see Milo dressed in his Big G Car Service shirt. "What're you doing home already?"

"I was done at work, so I thought I'd cover your rides tonight. I figured you'd want to keep an eye on things at the restaurant.

His kindness and thoughtfulness overwhelm me. "I... I can't afford to pay you very much."

"I don't care about the money. I care about Sofia being safe. Make sure she is, okay?"

I hug him tighter than I have in years. "I don't know what I ever did to deserve a little brother and best friend as great as you, but whatever it is, I'm goddamned thankful for it and you."

"You'd do the same for me."

I pull back from him but keep my hands on his shoulders. "I'm not sure I would. I probably wouldn't think of it."

"You don't give yourself enough credit. You'd do anything for me, the same way I'd do anything for you."

"I wish I was more like you."

"You're just fine the way you are."

Sofia comes into the kitchen with an older woman. "Nico and Milo, I wanted to introduce you to Gladys."

She greets us in Spanish, so we reply in kind. I thank her for coming to care for Mateo. She compliments my home and says she's thrilled to see her little friend. He's clearly just as happy as he hovers next to Gladys, waiting for her to play with him.

"I made pasta and chicken for your dinner," Sofia tells her. "It's in the fridge, and there's ice cream for dessert."

I told her to use anything she needed in the house, but she insisted on having groceries delivered earlier.

While she talks to Gladys, I hang on her every word, enjoying seeing her in mom mode. She has a moment with Mateo before he scampers off to play, and then I lead her to the garage. "Guess what?"

"What?"

"Milo is taking my rides so I can hang with you at the restaurant tonight."

I help her up into the cab of my truck. "Did you ask him to do that?"

"Nope, he volunteered."

"Wow. That's so sweet of him."

"He's the best person I know."

"You're pretty great yourself." She hooks a hand around my neck. "Interrupting your own life to keep me safe."

"I'd do anything to keep you safe."

When she kisses me, my knees nearly buckle. I wish we had nowhere to be. I'll be counting the hours until we get home later.

"Thank you for everything, Nico. I don't know what I'd be doing if you hadn't made it your goal to keep me safe."

"That's not my only goal, you know."

"I'd like to hear more about them. But for right now, I need to get to work."

"Then you have to let me go so I can drive."

Smiling, she kisses me one more time before she releases me, seeming as reluctant as I feel. Soon enough, I hope we'll have every Saturday night to spend together, but for now, duty calls.

I drive her to the restaurant and walk her in through the back door, keeping a watchful eye out as we go. I breathe a little easier once we're inside, surrounded by people who care about us both.

Nona greets us with hugs. "What're you doing here, Button?"

"Don't call me that in front of Sofia, Nona. She doesn't need to know the bad stuff about me."

Sofia's eyes light up with interest. "Yes, I do. Why do you call him that, Livia?"

"Because he's our button pusher. Always starting something with someone and causing trouble."

"I *used* to be that way. I'm not anymore." I'm desperate for Sofia to see only the good things in me and not the stuff that drives people crazy.

Nona raises a brow that calls me out on my bullshit. "And when did this miraculous transformation take place?"

"Recently."

My grandmother howls with laughter. "I see how it is."

I kiss Sofia's cheek. "Go on to work, and don't listen to anything they say about me."

"Oh, I'll be listening," she says with a sexy grin.

It's going to be a very long night.

After she walks away, Nona's hand on my arm keeps me from following her. Having Sofia out of my line of sight makes me itchy.

"What's going on?"

"With Sofia?"

"With all of it, and don't say it's nothing. Vin told us you asked for security for her."

I give her a brief rundown of what's happened—enough so she'll be aware, but not so much that she'll be afraid.

She listens with her usual sharp focus. "Is that why you're here rather than at work where you belong on a busy Saturday night?"

"Milo offered to cover for me so I can be here with her."

"That's good of him."

"Very good of him, and I told him so. He's the best."

"So are you."

I give her the side-eye. "What's with the sudden compliments?"

"We give you a hard time because you can take it." She draws me out of the fray into a quiet alcove near the back door. "You've always been a good sport about the family razzing you. But sometimes I worry that you don't see the many ways we also respect and admire you."

This is unprecedented. I have no idea how to respond.

"You've grown a successful business from nothing while working a second job until recently to pay the bills. You've taken beautiful care of your parents during your mother's illness, including doing all the yard work for your dad, bringing meals, visiting and doing anything else you could to make life easier for them. You're a wonderful brother, cousin and friend, and now you've decided to be a protector to Sofia and her little boy. I'm not sure what you see when you look in the mirror, but I see a young man anyone would be proud of."

"Jeez, Nona, you're gonna make me bawl over here."

She smiles as she hugs me. "I see a man coming into his own and perhaps having found the love of his life."

"I think maybe I have."

"That makes me so, so happy. She's a lovely young woman,

strong and brave and hardworking. And she's a wonderful mother. I couldn't love her more if she was actually family."

"She loves you and Abuela, too. She's so thankful for everything the family has done for her."

"She and her little boy are delightful."

"Yes, they are."

"Her situation is complicated."

"In many, many ways." I step back to look out to the hallway, but I can't see her, and that makes me anxious.

"You've never been serious about a woman."

"No, not like this."

"Which is why you need to be careful, Nico. I know the girls have warned her about you, but you need to look out for yourself, too. She's not officially divorced, her son is facing serious health challenges for years to come, and she doesn't need any more drama or nonsense in her life."

"I know that, Nona. I just want to make things better for her."

"And I applaud you for that, but what I'm saying is she might need more than you have to give."

The thought of that sends an arrow of fear straight to my gut. "I'd give her anything. Everything. And she knows that."

"Still… Everything might not be enough. Be careful, my love. Guard your heart even as you give it to her. That's all I'm saying."

She's rocked my world by suggesting that everything I have might not be enough for Sofia. How is that possible?

"I've upset you. I'm sorry. That wasn't my intention. I'm just a worried old granny butting into things that're none of my business."

"You're not old, and since when is my business not your business?"

I love her bark of laughter. "True."

I hug her and kiss her cheek. "I heard what you said, and even if I didn't like some of it, I appreciate that you care so much about me —and about Sofia and Mateo. In case I haven't told you lately, you're the best Nona in the whole world, even when you're calling me that stupid Button name."

Her smile is positively wicked. "That's the best nickname I've ever given anyone."

"If you say so."

"Oh, I do. I say so."

I roll my eyes and leave her to go find Sofia. She's chatting with Abuela and her gentleman friend, Mr. Muñoz. I'm so relieved to see her that I feel light-headed for a second from the rush of air that leaves my lungs. It occurs to me that I've never experienced fear this potent, not even when my mom was diagnosed. I've believed from the start that she would beat the cancer. But this... This is something else altogether, and the fear is palpable.

"Come have a drink, Nico," Vin calls from the bar.

I force myself to pull my gaze off Sofia. She has her back to me, so she can't see me staring at her. I head to the bar and take a seat on one of the barstools.

My uncle puts a Tanqueray and tonic in front of me and twists a lime on top. "Drink."

"Do I look like I need it?"

"Yep."

Vin, who is my father's brother, has been a giant in my life, a second dad to me and my siblings. "Miguel is here."

"He came himself?"

"He did." When I would've gotten up to go find him, Vin stops me with a hand across the bar. "He's pretending to be a customer, so don't blow his cover."

I relax into my seat, or at least I try to. "Yeah, right, okay."

"Take a breath, Nico, before you have a stroke or a heart attack or something else that'll make a mess of my restaurant."

I give him a small grin and take a deep gulp of my drink. "Thanks for looking out for Sofia—and me."

"Always."

All my life, I've known our family is special, but I appreciate them more than ever tonight when my girlfriend and I have possibly brought trouble to their doorstep.

Rather than telling us to stay away, they've closed the circle around us both. I pity the fool who messes with the Giordinos or their friends. For the first time in hours, I exhale ever so slightly. My chest still feels tight with anxiety, but at least I can breathe a bit easier and enjoy watching Sofia work.

She's a natural with the customers, laughing and talking with them in Spanish and English, which makes me ridiculously proud of her after knowing how hard she's worked to perfect her English. She did that primarily to communicate more easily with English-speaking medical personnel when her son first became ill, but it comes in handy here, too, as Giordino's attracts tourists from all over the country as well as locals who are more apt to speak Spanish.

Abuela has told me Sofia is a natural when it comes to learning English, whereas she's an old bird who can't be taught new tricks. But that's not true. Abuela's English is much better than it used to be, and I told her she needs to be proud of her accomplishments.

I love this place all the time, but especially on Saturday nights when the regulars come in, and on Sundays when the family gathers for brunch. I need to ask Sofia and Mateo to come with me tomorrow, although that would be another coming-out party for us as a couple. Not that I care about that, but she might not be ready.

I want so badly to talk to her about that and a million other things that'll have to wait until later.

I check my watch. Five thirty.

This night is going to crawl by.

CHAPTER 12

SOFIA

I feel him watching me during my shift. He never moves from his post at the bar where he can see the Italian side of the house where I'm working tonight. I wonder if they put me here because it's more sealed off than the Cuban side.

I wouldn't be surprised.

I spotted Nico's friend Miguel squatting at one of the tables in my section, but Livia told me to ignore him so he could do his job.

It makes me a little sick to think that Vin and Viv might be paying a cop to keep an eye on things while I'm working. I wonder how much that's costing them. Perhaps I should offer to have them take it out of my pay.

"What's wrong?" Livia asks when she finds me stewing in front of the soda machine.

"Nothing." I straighten up to head back to work.

She shifts to block my exit path. "What is wrong, Sofia?"

"How much is it costing to have the police officer here?"

"I don't know. Why?"

"I should pay for it since he's here to protect you from people in my life."

"They're not people in your life. They're people in your soon-to-be ex-husband's life."

"What is the English word for when something means the same thing or something similar? We learned it in school."

"Semantics."

"Yes, you're using semantics. They wouldn't be of concern to you or your family if it wasn't for me."

"Let me tell you something about how things work in this family. You are one of us. We protect our own. Period. The end."

I'm mortified when tears fill my eyes. "You're far too kind."

"This isn't kindness. It's *family*, Sofia. We'd do this for anyone in our family who was in danger. I know I speak for Vin and Viv when I tell you not to give another thought to the cost of having Miguel here. They don't care, and you shouldn't either."

"I do care. I hate that this is happening."

"We hate it for you."

"He… He wasn't always this way. He used to be sweet and kind and…" My chin wobbles. "He wasn't like this."

Livia looks around to make sure the early customers have drinks and bread. "Once upon a time, before I met my husband, I had a boyfriend like your Joaquín. Oh, he was so sweet and funny and handsome as all get-out. I was madly in love with him. So madly in love that I didn't notice for the longest time that he didn't like it when I disagreed with him or wanted to do things with my friends that didn't include him. Every time I went anywhere, he asked where I'd been, who I'd talked to and if I was interested in other men. He controlled my money, my mind, my body and made me afraid to tell him the truth and just as afraid to lie to him. He made me afraid of everything, and that was before he started hitting me."

A sob erupts from the deepest part of me as Livia wraps her arms around me.

"Shhh. It's all right now. You're free of him, even if he hasn't realized it yet. He will. Eventually. And in the meantime, you must stay firm in your resolve to move on without him."

"I'll never go back to him."

"You may be tempted to before all is said and done."

"I won't be."

"No matter what happens from here on out, we've got your back. We're here for you and your son. You're not alone with it. Not anymore."

"Thank you so much. For everything. For the job and the family and for letting me know you understand how I found myself in this situation."

"I understand all too well. I saw it in you from the beginning. You looked stunned, the way I did when I finally came out of the fog and saw what he'd done to me. I get it, and I'm here for you and Nico. Whatever you need. I'm here. We're all here."

I hug her this time. "I love you all so much. I'd die before I'd bring any trouble into your lives."

"We love you, too, and we know that." She kisses the top of my head. "Now take five, dry your eyes and go on back to work. Mr. Andruzzi doesn't like to wait for his gnocchi."

"No, he doesn't," I say, laughing as I dab at my eyes with a napkin.

"What's wrong?" Nico asks from behind Livia.

She turns to him. "Nothing is wrong. Just some girl talk."

"Why has Sofia been crying?"

"Because your Nona was exceptionally kind to me."

"I'll never understand the things women cry over."

Livia bops him on the head. "You don't need to understand. You only need to make her cry with happiness and nothing else, you got me?"

"I got you."

"Good, now I'm going back to work."

After she walks away, Nico puts his arms around me. "Are you really okay?"

"I am."

"Then I'll let you get back to work, too."

I hold him tighter so he can't get away. "One more minute of this first."

"Gladly."

We're still there a full minute later when Mario, one of the busboys, comes to find me. "Delivery for you, Sofia."

"For me?"

"Yep, and you're gonna want to see this."

I glance at Nico, who shrugs as he follows me to the restaurant's main entrance, which is full of white roses. There are dozens of them, and the scent is so overwhelming, it drowns out the usual smell of Cuban and Italian food. "What the heck?"

Marlene hands me a card. "For you."

I turn to Nico. "Is this you?"

"No," he says, his face tight with tension.

My hands tremble as I open the card that says, *I'm so sorry for everything. I love you and Mateo more than my own life. I'd give you anything, do anything to have our life back. Everything would be different this time. I swear on my mother's life. I love you. Please come home. J*

I feel like I'm going to be sick. This must mean he's made bail, which has the bile rising to burn my throat. Thank God Mateo is at Nico's in that secure, gated community while I'm at work. "Is the delivery truck still here?"

Mario looks out the front door. "It is."

"Tell them to take them back. Take all of them back."

"I, uh…"

I push by him and go outside, waving to the delivery driver parked at the curb. He puts down the passenger side window. "You need to take those flowers back. I don't want them."

"Take them back?"

"You heard me. Come get them out of here."

"I'm going to have to check with my boss."

"Why? I'm not asking for a refund. I'm just returning the flowers."

"I've never had anyone return flowers before."

"Then I guess this is the first time. Come. Get. Them. *Now.*"

The young man swallows hard, making his Adam's apple bob. "Y-yes, ma'am."

It's the first time I've been called "ma'am," but whatever. I just want the flowers and everything they stand for gone. While I stand on the sidewalk, watching and hoping someone is taking care of my tables inside, he makes multiple trips to return the vases of flowers to the truck. I count twelve dozen.

Idiot.

As if that's going to fix everything that's so wrong between us.

I recall my birthday two years ago and how he made a big deal out of it with flowers and gifts and a cake that had me on edge all day because he hadn't remembered my birthday in years. He was so proud of himself for the effort he expended and expected me to be proud of him, too. What he didn't get was how sick I felt at the realization that I expected so little of him that when he did come through for me, I was shocked.

"Can you, uh, sign here to say you don't want the flowers?"

"Sure." I sign my name and write REJECTED next to the signature. "Ask your boss to inform the customer that the flowers were returned."

"Yes, ma'am."

I head back inside, but over my shoulder I say, "And don't call me ma'am."

Marlene, Livia, Nico and Vivian are in the reception area when I enter through the front door.

"Everything all right?" Vivian asks.

"It is now. Sorry for the disruption."

"Don't be," Marlene says. "You didn't cause it."

"Still... I'm sorry." I glance toward the Italian dining room. "I'll get back to work now."

As I walk away, I feel their eyes on me, probably filled with sympathy I don't want. I hate feeling like a charity case who can't handle her own life. I'm tired of my life being a chaotic mess. I want some peace and quiet, like what I've found with Nico.

As I go through the motions of picking up where I left off with my early-bird customers, I tell myself I'm not trading one man for another. I've lived separately of Joaquín for months now, and during that time, there hasn't been anyone else. Thanks in large part to this job, I'm able to provide a clean, loving, stable home for my son, even if it's not in the best part of town.

I'm not trading one man for another. I've begun a new relationship with a hardworking man from a wonderful, loving family. What I have with Nico is nothing like what I had with Joaquín. For one thing, Nico would never tell me what to do or how to feel or who I can talk to. He'd never isolate me from my friends or weaponize the love I feel for my son against me.

All he wants is to care for me and Mateo, not control us. That makes him as different from Joaquín as night is from day. I learned that expression from a TV show and looked it up on Google to make sure I understood the meaning. I added it to my notebook full of English words and expressions so I won't forget it.

I love to learn. I always have. That was another thing my mother hated about me—how easily I pick up new things and how well I did in school. What Nico said about me going to college now has been on my mind since he mentioned it. God, I'd love to go back to school, get a degree and have a profession that could support me and my son. That kind of safety net under us would change our lives forever.

But for now, I need to be checking on Mr. Ricci's chicken marsala and picking up house salads for Mr. and Mrs. Marino. All of them are regulars and order the same things every week.

"We're in such a rut," Mrs. Marino says every Saturday. "But I look forward to Giordino's chicken parm all week long."

The routine comforts me. Same people, same food, same conversations and generous tips at the end before the second wave arrives at six thirty. That's when we get really busy, and I have no time to think about anything other than cocktails, salads, appetizers, entrées, dessert, coffee, check, rinse and repeat.

On a regular Saturday night, I clock about twelve thousand steps. I was shocked when one of the other waitresses showed me how to find the counter on my phone. I never would've guessed the number would be that high, but Saturday nights are the craziest—and most lucrative—nights of the week. Mateo and I can almost live on what I make on Saturdays alone, which is such a blessing.

Livia and Marlene have probably told the customers about my son's illness, which is why they're so good to me. The generosity of strangers has been overwhelming, to say the least.

We've reached the busiest part of the evening when I see Miguel suddenly stand and rush toward the main door.

My heart is in my throat, and I'm frozen in place as I notice numerous other officers standing just outside the door. Something has happened, and I'm terrified it has to do with me.

Nico appears by my side.

"Wh-what's wrong?"

"I don't know."

"But something..."

Vincent lets out a sound that's a cross between a wail and a howl.

Nico leaves me to go to his uncle.

I follow him, even though I'm afraid to hear whatever this might be.

"What's wrong?" Nico asks Vincent, who's now in tears.

"Milo."

Every muscle in Nico's body goes rigid. "What about him?"

"He was shot while stopped at a light on Coral Way. They're taking him to Miami-Dade, but they said it's bad. I... I need to go tell your parents."

Dee, who's come out of the office to see what's going on, let's out a scream I'll never forget when she hears Milo's been shot.

I can't breathe or think or do anything other than silently shriek at the possibility that people related to me have harmed Nico's beloved brother. I can't bear it.

And then Marlene is there with her hands on my shoulders and tears in her eyes. "Go with him, cariño. He's going to need you."

"My... My tables. I can't... Oh God, Marlene. This is because of me. They thought he was Nico."

"Unless you were the one to point a gun at our Milo and shoot it, this is *not* because of you. Go with Nico. He needs you. I'll finish your shift and collect your tips for you."

I want to tell her I don't care about the money, but I don't have that luxury.

Marlene squeezes my arm. "Breathe, Sofia."

Nodding to her, I take the hand that Nico extends to me and follow him out to the back door, practically running to keep up. Just before we reach the door, Carmen and Jason come in, all smiles until they see us rushing toward them.

"What's wrong?" Carmen asks.

"Milo's been shot. They're taking him to Miami-Dade."

"We'll be right behind you," Jason says. He's on the medical staff there, and having him with us will help tremendously.

"Thank you," Nico says, his voice wavering with emotion.

We jump into his truck and peel out of the parking lot seconds later.

Nico is so tense I fear he might explode. I wouldn't blame him. I don't know what to say or do or think. My skin feels too small and tight to contain the emotional storm raging inside me. If he loses his beautiful brother because of me, I'll die. I'll simply cease to exist in any meaningful form.

It takes thirty grueling minutes of tense silence to get to the hospital. We park in the emergency lot and run for the doors. I'm aware of Carmen and Jason behind us, as well as Vincent, Vivian and Livia. We're there a few minutes, waiting for information, when Nico's distraught parents and sisters arrive with Austin and Wyatt.

Everyone is so upset.

I want to disappear.

Jason goes through the double doors to the trauma unit to find out what he can.

Miguel comes in a few minutes later and signals for Nico. "We've got the whole thing on video. We'll get them."

"Could I see it?" I ask, my voice wavering from the storm of emotions rushing through me.

Miguel calls it up on his phone and shows it to us.

Nico moans at the sight of his brother being shot while stopped at a red light in one of Nico's black cars.

I gasp at the red '69 Pontiac GTO that Joaquín helped his cousin Diego restore. They worked on it over an entire winter four years ago. "The car belongs to Diego Garcia, Joaquín's first cousin on his mother's side. He's the one who threatened us in traffic." As I rattle off his address, a place I visited many times while they were working on the car, I'm completely dead inside from the confirmation that the shooting is, in fact, tied to me.

"This is good information," Miguel says. "Thank you."

"Don't thank me. None of this would be happening if it wasn't for me."

Nico puts his arm around me, but I shake him off. I can't bear to be touched.

Jason comes out from the back, his expression grim. Everyone surrounds him, desperate for any information they can get. "He was shot in the neck, and the bullet is lodged next to his spine."

Elena would've fallen to the floor if Lorenzo and Vincent hadn't grabbed her.

"He needs emergency surgery," Jason says. "I'll do it. I'm his best chance for a full recovery, and I'll do everything I can to make sure that's what he gets."

"Jason," Elena says, wailing. "*Please save my baby. Please.*"

"I'll do everything I can, Elena, but his condition is grave. I need to be honest with you. The surgery could result in anything from death to paralysis to complete recovery. I won't know for sure until we get in there and see how bad the damage is."

"Oh my God," Maria whispers.

Dee weeps silently next to me as Wyatt keeps an arm around her.

"We'll pray for you," Carmen tells her husband. "And for Milo. Go save him." She hugs him, tells him she loves him and lets him go to do what he does best. "Let's pray," she says to the rest of us.

Since the day I met this amazing, generous, loving family, they've wrapped their arms around me and made me—and my son —a part of their family. This is the first time I've felt that I don't belong with them. As they gather into a tight circle to pray for

Milo, I take a step back. I feel sick to the depths of my soul that I brought this horror to them, even if inadvertently.

If Milo dies or is paralyzed, they'll never forgive me. I'll never forgive myself. He's the sweetest guy, and to think of either of those fates befalling him is crushing, to say the least.

CHAPTER 13

SOFIA

For the first time since Miguel suddenly stood and ran for the front door of the restaurant, I think of Mateo at Nico's with Gladys.

I step outside into the humid night and pull my phone from the pocket of my apron. My hands are shaking so badly, I can barely put through the call.

"Hi there," Gladys says. "All is well here. He went down nice and easy and has been asleep for more than an hour."

"Gladys."

"What, honey? What's wrong?"

I can't get the words past the massive lump in my throat.

"Are you all right?"

"Nico's brother, Milo, was shot. He's in surgery. It's bad."

"Oh God. Oh no."

"It was Joaquín. They must have thought he was Nico. They shot him because of me."

"Oh, honey. My Lord."

"He was shot in the neck. The doctor said he could die or be paralyzed."

"And you're blaming yourself for what that son of a bitch and his friends did. Am I right?"

"They wouldn't be targeting Nico or his brother if it wasn't for me."

"This is about *them*, not you. How long have I been telling you that man was trouble?"

"As long as I can remember."

"I was so thankful when you finally listened to me and left him, chica."

"I don't know what to do. The Giordinos have been so good to me and Mateo, and this is the thanks they get? One of their beloved family members fighting for his life because of me?"

"It's because of *him*, not you."

"I didn't pull the trigger, but dear God, Gladys. Milo could *die* because of my ex-husband. And Nico… He's blaming himself. He let Milo take his rides tonight knowing Joaquín and his boys were harassing us. We just never imagined they'd go this far." And then another thought occurs to me. "Oh my God. The flowers. I sent back his flowers."

"What flowers?"

"He sent dozens of roses to me at work with a note apologizing for everything and promising it would be different if I gave him another chance. I sent them back." I slide down the stucco wall to sit on the sidewalk as sobs shake my entire body. "I made him mad, Gladys, and he took it out on poor Milo."

"He's a sociopath, Sofia, who should've been locked up *forever* years ago. This is not your fault!"

"I didn't even know he'd made bail until the flowers arrived."

"What did he think sending flowers was going to do? Change your mind about leaving him? He's insane. We knew that before he shot Nico's brother. The best thing you ever did was get yourself and your son away from him. If there's any good news in all of this, perhaps the court will ban him now from seeing Mateo."

That's a speck of good news in a sea of despair.

"I'll be here for as long as you need me. Don't worry about me or Mateo. Take care of Nico and do what you can for the family."

"Are you sure I should be here? Maybe I should go back to my place—"

"No! Do not go near there, do you hear me? Stay with Nico. You're safer with him."

"But is he safer with me?"

Gladys's deep sigh says it all.

"I need to get away from him."

"That's not happening." His deep voice from above startles me. "You're not going anywhere."

"I, uh, Gladys, I need to go. I'll keep you posted."

"Don't worry about a thing here. Mateo and I are fine."

"Thank you for that. It means the world."

"Love you, chica. Stay strong."

"Love you, too."

Nico sits next to me. "You're not leaving me. Unless you don't care about me anymore, and then, of course, you're free to do whatever you want. But if you *do* still care, please don't leave me."

"Of course I still care about you, but this is my fault, Nico," I say in a whisper. "Your brother is fighting for his life because of me and us."

"That isn't why. It's because of people who can't take no for an answer and who think they can do something like this to an inno- cent person who has nothing to do with anything." His voice catches on a sob. "If anything, it's *my* fault. I knew they were coming for me, and I let him take my rides. I never should've done that."

I reach for him, put my arms around him and cradle his head on my chest as he breaks down.

"I'm so sorry I brought this hell into your life."

"No one blames you, Sofia."

"They will if he's paralyzed or… God forbid…"

"Don't say it. He can't die. And we all know this isn't your fault. If anything, we're more thankful than ever that you left him if this is what he's capable of."

I use my sleeve to wipe tears from my face. "It's because I sent back the flowers. I shouldn't have done that. It made him mad."

119

"Him being mad or jealous doesn't give him the right to shoot at me or my brother. That's on *him*, not you. Please tell me you can see that."

"What I see, once again, is the incredible grace and generosity of a family that took me in and is now paying for that in the worst possible way."

"I thought I might find you two out here blaming yourselves for things you had nothing to do with," Livia says.

We look up at her, staring down at us, hands on hips and her expression conveying devastation and determination.

"Don't do that," she says. "You can't change what's happened. We know who did it, and they're going to pay. Milo is young and strong and has the best neurosurgeon in Florida operating on him. We must believe he's going to be all right. And if he isn't… We'll cross that bridge when we come to it, but you two sitting out here gnashing your teeth over blame isn't helping anyone. Especially you."

"How can you be so kind to me when this is tied to me?" I ask her.

"It's tied to your ex-husband. Not you. You, my darling girl, had every right to leave him, to divorce him, to make a new life for yourself that includes a new love if you so choose. You've done *nothing* wrong and certainly nothing to warrant what he's done to you and others." Her glance shifts to Nico. "And it's not your fault for letting your brother take your rides tonight. You were doing what you thought was best by keeping an eye on Sofia."

"He's my little brother," Nico says softly as tears slide down his face. "My best friend."

"Which is why he stepped up to help when you needed him, the same way you would've done for him if the situation was reversed. Taking the blame for someone else's violent behavior is pointless. No one in there blames you for this, Sofia. They know exactly who is responsible for putting Milo in this hospital, and it is *not* you."

Livia's grace toward me at a time like this amazes me. Though I can see she's completely wrecked by what's happened to Milo, her voice never wavers as she exonerates us from responsibility. I want to be her when I grow up. I want to always do the right thing and be there for people when they need me and shine light on darkness the way she does.

A man comes rushing up to us, someone I don't recognize. "Livia! I got here as soon as I could. How's your grandson?" He's ruggedly handsome, with brown eyes and wavy dark hair shot through with hints of silver. He's deeply tanned in the way of someone who spends most of his time outdoors.

She seems stunned to see him, whoever he is. "Uh, Chris... You didn't have to come."

He gives her a perplexed look. "Of course I came to support you."

"Um, this is my grandson Nico and his girlfriend, Sofia. This is, uh, Chris, my flight instructor."

"Ohhhh," I say on a deep exhale. I've heard a rumor that Livia may have a crush on the man who's been teaching her to fly. "You're Chris, the flight instructor."

Nico stands, offers me a hand up and then shakes the other man's hand. "Good to meet you."

"You as well. How is your grandson, Livia?"

"He's in surgery. We don't know anything more than what I told you in the text."

"What can I do for you?"

"Nothing, really. It's going to be a long night."

"Then I'll wait with you and get you anything you might need."

Is it my imagination, or does the formidable Livia Giordino *blush* when he says that? "You don't have to do that."

"I insist."

Before she lets him guide her inside, where his arrival will give everyone something else to think about other than the dread we all feel over Milo, she looks at both of us again. "Are we clear on the whole blame thing?"

"Yes, ma'am." Nico kisses her cheek. "Thank you."

"Sofia?"

"Yes, thank you." I still feel responsible, but I'll keep that thought to myself for now.

"Good. Come back inside."

"We will," Nico says. "In a minute."

Livia nods to Chris, and they go in through automatic doors that release a whoosh of chilled air as they open.

Nico puts his arms around me. "Please stay with me. I need you."

I hold him close. "I'm not going anywhere."

NICO

This is a fucking nightmare sent straight from hell. As the hours crawl by with only sporadic updates from the operating room that tell us nothing more than Milo is still alive, I feel like my head is going to explode as I wait to hear if he's going to survive. If he's going to be paralyzed from the neck down, God help me, but I cannot bear to think about that possibility.

I can't stop the tears that keep coming despite my desperate desire to be strong for my parents, grandmothers and Sofia, who still blames herself, despite what Nona and I have told her.

Sofia's head is on my shoulder, her hand wrapped tightly around mine. She hasn't left my side for a minute.

Abuela and Mr. Muñoz arrived after they closed the restaurant early. My cousin Domenic is sitting next to me. His parents are on the other side of him. All of us are receiving relentless texts from concerned friends, extended family and longtime customers of the restaurant hoping for news about Milo, but there's nothing to tell them yet.

The sun has risen by the time Jason finally comes into the waiting room, wearing navy blue scrubs and looking as exhausted as the rest of us.

"He's in recovery, which is good news. He survived a very difficult surgery."

"And the paralysis?" my dad asks as he fights back tears.

"We won't know anything on that for a while yet. There was a lot of bruising, bone fragments, etc. Our initial check of his reflexes was encouraging, but we won't know anything for sure until he can tell us what he feels. I wish I had a more definitive answer on that, but we're in wait-and-see mode while the swelling subsides and gives us a better sense of what he'll be left with."

My dad's shoulders sag as he absorbs that news. *What he'll be left with*... As if he'll have less than he did before. I can't hear that.

"The best thing you all can do for Milo now is go home and get some rest. It's going to be a long, arduous recovery, and he'll need you guys to be strong for him."

"I'm staying," my mom declares.

"There's nothing you can do for him, Elena," Jason says gently. "He'll be in recovery for hours yet and then in the ICU, where he'll be allowed one visitor at a time, but not until much later today. I'll be with him, and I'll call you if anything changes. I promise."

Dad hugs Jason. "Thank you for saving my son's life. We'll never forget what you've done for him and us."

"I'm glad I was here when it happened. He's not completely out of the woods yet, Lo. I wish I could tell you he is, but I promise to tell you the truth the minute I know anything new."

"We understand," Dad says tearfully. "Elena, everyone, let's go home for a while. You heard what Jason said. Our boy is going to need us, so we should rest up for him. Thank you all for being here with us and getting us through the longest night of our lives."

As I hug my parents, sisters, cousins and grandmothers, I feel like a robot going through the motions. It should be me in that hospital bed fighting for my life and my mobility, not sweet Milo, who's never had a bad word to say about anyone. I'm the one who's been a dick to half the people I've met in my life. Where's the justice in this?

Sofia and I walk out to my truck.

"Do you want me to drive?" she asks.

I look at her, almost as if I've never seen her before. Everything about my life seems unfamiliar to me this morning after a night in hell waiting to hear if my little brother was going to live or die. "No. I'll drive."

Out of habit, I hold the door for her, help her up into the truck and wait for her to get settled before I close the door and walk around to the driver's side. Every step I take feels wrong now that it's possible Milo may never walk again.

Because he was covering for me.

I knew they were watching me, and I sent him out to be nearly murdered.

I sit behind the wheel, staring straight ahead for a long time before I remember what I'm supposed to do. Turn the key. Put the truck in Reverse. Back out. Drive. Move forward. Go on with my life as if everything is normal when nothing is.

We're parked in my driveway when I glance over at Sofia for the first time since I got in the truck and see tears rolling down her cheeks that she silently brushes away with the back of her hand. Her tears break me.

"Don't." My voice is gruffer and harsher than I intend. "Don't cry."

"Can't seem to make it stop. I feel sick to my soul over this."

"I'm right there with you."

"I really think Mateo and I should go home to our place so you can give your family your full attention."

"No."

She turns to me, her eyes shooting fire. "You aren't telling me what to do, are you? Because I'll never again allow a man to decide *anything* for me."

"I don't want to decide for you. I just want to keep you and Mateo safe, which is easier to do here than at your place."

All the fight seems to go out of her on one long exhale as she sags into her seat. "I'm sorry. That's just an issue after what it took me to leave him."

"I understand. I have no desire to control you. I just want you safe."

"I don't know what to do or say or feel. Every part of me aches for Milo and you and your family. Everyone has been so kind to me and Mateo, and now we've brought this to your sweet brother. I appreciate that you don't blame me, but I'm sick over it."

"I know you are, and of course we don't blame you. Miguel and his people are going to arrest them and throw them in jail for the rest of their lives. If there's any upside to this, that's it. You won't have to deal with him anymore, and he'll be out of Mateo's life, too."

"The only thing that matters is Milo and his full recovery."

"You matter, too. And so does Mateo."

"I'm so, *so* sorry, Nico."

"You don't have to apologize to me."

"Yes, I do. I'm sorry this happened to your precious Milo."

"Thank you, but please, let's stick together through this rather than going our separate ways. That's not going to fix anything. It'll just give them what they want. I need you with me to get through it."

"I'm here."

"And you'll stay?"

She glances at the house and then back at me. "Yes, I'll stay."

"Thank you."

"Don't thank me for letting you keep me safe."

"I'm deeply appreciative that I won't have to be out of my mind with worry for you and Mateo while I'm dealing with everything else."

Her small smile is like the sun emerging from behind the darkest of clouds. It gives me the tiny bit of hope I need to press forward. "Wait for me."

I get out of the truck and go around to help her down, keeping my arms around her longer than necessary out of a desperate need for comfort only she can provide.

She hugs me tightly. "I'm here for you, Nico. For anything you need. All you have to do is ask."

"I don't know what I need, but this feels pretty damned good."

I'm not sure how long we stand there, taking and giving comfort, before my neighbor Josh interrupts us.

"Nico. I heard about Milo. Is he... Is he okay?"

I release Sofia and turn to Josh while keeping an arm around her. "He made it through surgery. We're not sure about anything else yet."

"God. It's so awful. Did the cops get the guy who shot him?"

"I haven't heard yet, but they know who they're looking for."

When he glances at Sofia, I say, "This is my girlfriend, Sofia. Sofia, this is Josh. He lives next door."

"Nice to meet you," she says.

"You, too. Let me know if I can do anything. I'll cut your grass and clean the pool. Whatever you need."

I release her to give him a bro hug. "Thanks, man."

"Milo is the best," Josh says, his voice breaking. "We all love him around here."

"Everyone loves him."

"Yeah, for sure. Text me if I can do anything, okay?"

"I will. Thanks again." I guide Sofia inside through the garage and into the kitchen, where Gladys and Mateo are having breakfast.

Mateo gets up and comes to his mother, his gait crooked and unsteady, but his determination to get to her fierce.

She hugs him tightly. "How's my best guy today?"

"Good, Mama. Gladys says I can swim after breakfast if I eat all my pancakes."

"You'd better get back to it, then."

"I made enough for you guys, too," Gladys says, gesturing to the stove.

"I don't think I can eat," Sofia says.

"Me either," I add. "But thank you."

"I'll put them in the fridge for later if you're hungry. How is he?"

"In recovery from successful surgery," I tell her. "We're not sure about anything else yet."

"I've got my entire church praying for him, and we'll continue to pray for as long as he needs it."

"Thank you," I whisper, overwhelmed by the idea of people Milo has never met praying for him. We'll take whatever we can get.

"I can stay to keep an eye on Mateo if you guys want to get some rest," Gladys says. "If it would help, I can run home, pack a bag and come back to stay with him for as long as you need me."

I glance at Sofia. She bites her bottom lip as she considers it.

"What do you think?" she asks me.

"It couldn't hurt, if Gladys doesn't mind."

"I don't mind at all."

"I'll take you to your place," I offer.

"That would be great. Let me just grab my purse, and then we can go."

Mateo holds up his empty plate. "Mama, can we swim now?"

"We sure can. Bring your plate to the sink and then change into your suit."

"Mateo."

He turns to me, his face serious and solemn.

"What's the rule about the pool?"

"I can't go out there unless someone is with me."

"That's right, and that's *always* the rule. Understand?"

He nods. "Yes, sir."

"Okay, go get changed, then."

He takes off as fast as he's able to, which is pretty fast considering his impairments.

"Swimming is so good for him," Gladys says as she returns with her purse.

"Do you think we should let Miguel know you're planning to take Gladys to our building?" Sofia asks.

"Yeah, I suppose I should." I kiss the spot between her brows where all her stress has landed. "Have some fun with your boy, and when we get back, we'll get some sleep."

Not that I think either of us will sleep until we know Milo is going to be okay.

"Please be careful."

"I will. I promise."

CHAPTER 14

DEE

I can't stop crying no matter how hard I try. The possibility of losing Milo is so horrifying as to be impossible to accept. Sitting in bed, I wipe my face for the thousandth time since last night.

Wyatt comes in with a cup of the lemon tea I often drink at night that he hands to me. "Try this. Maybe it'll help you get some rest."

"Thank you." I take a sip and then another, surprised when they stay down. I've been viciously nauseated all night from nerves.

He gets in bed next to me and puts an arm across my abdomen.

"Tell me the truth. Will he be paralyzed?" I can barely say the words without wanting to wail.

"I don't know, sweetheart. I'm sure Jason did everything he possibly could to give him the best chance, but anything to do with the spine is dicey."

"What will we do if he is?"

"We'll support him every way we can and get through it one day at a time. I have no doubt your amazing family will rally around him."

Tears continue to rain down my face like a waterfall with no end. "I hate this so much. He's the best of us."

Wyatt wipes away my tears the way he did all night. "I know, honey. I hate it, too."

"Can I tell you something you can't repeat to anyone?" I ask him.

"Of course."

"Part of me wants to be angry with Sofia, but I can't quite seem to get there."

"She didn't shoot him, and she certainly didn't think her ex would go this far."

"They thought he was Nico." I'm equally undone by the thought of my older brother being harmed. "He's the one they wanted to kill."

"Imagine how Nico and Sofia must feel. It's so awful."

"I try to put myself in the mindset of a person who'd shoot someone he doesn't even know, thinking that will somehow get his ex-wife to come back to him."

"You could never pull off that mindset, so don't even try."

"I want to understand it."

"We'll never understand this."

"I feel so bad for my parents. They've been through so much with my mom's illness and now this."

"Your parents are the strongest people I know. I'd want them— and all of you—on my side if something like this ever happened to me."

"Don't even say that. Nothing can ever happen to you."

Smiling, he takes the mug from me and puts it on the bedside table. "Let me hold you."

Because there's nothing better than being held by him, I snuggle into his warm embrace.

"I wish there was something more I could do for you."

"This helps, and your medical knowledge helped us during the night."

"My knowledge is all yours for the bargain-basement price of one kiss."

I pull back from him, smile for the first time in twelve hours and kiss him.

"I should've charged more."

I would've thought it impossible to laugh until he showed me otherwise. "I don't know what I'd ever do without you."

"You'll never have to find out." He kisses me again and then again, until I'm clinging to him and desperate for him to take my mind off the trauma the way only he can.

When my phone chimes with a text, I pull back from Wyatt in case there's news about Milo.

"Marcus texted to say he and Tara are thinking about Milo and my family."

"That's nice of him," Wyatt says, nonplussed by the mention of my ex-fiancé, because he knows he has nothing to worry about where Marcus or any other man is concerned. "They're doing well?"

"He said it's going great with her, and he's been sober for almost sixty days. I guess they aren't defining their relationship because his sobriety is still so new, but he said she's been amazing and he's crazy about her. He said he's praying for Milo and all of us."

"Glad to hear he's doing well," Wyatt says. "I need a shower."

I love how Wyatt is glad to hear Marcus is doing well and isn't the slightest bit threatened by him texting me. "Me, too."

"Care to save water with me?"

"I'd love to."

We get up and go into the bathroom, pulling off clothes as we go. The sight of his bare ass gets my attention, the way it always does. When he turns to me, he catches me gawking at him.

"Don't objectify me. It's unseemly."

He makes me snort with laughter. "How do you do that?"

After he checks the water temperature, he turns to help me with my bra. "Do what?"

"Make me laugh at a time like this."

"Sorry. I don't mean to be disrespectful."

"You're not. I'm saying it's just what I need. *You* are just what I need."

He puts his arms around me, and the feel of his skin against mine has the same effect on me as usual. If he's near me, I want him. Hell, I want him even when he's nowhere near me. "I always want to be what you need."

In the shower, he washes my hair and body with the sort of reverence I've come to expect from him. He never touches me with anything but love and the utmost gentleness. Even when we get carried away, he's careful with me. But when he lifts me against the wall of the shower, I start to object. There's never a time when I'm not concerned about his fragile heart.

"Shhh," he says as he joins our bodies. "I'm fine. You're fine. Milo will be fine. I feel it in my bones."

That's all it takes to restart the tears. "God, I hope so." I've never prayed harder for anything in my entire life than I have for my brother since I stepped out of my office into a nightmare at the restaurant last night. At first, I feared my mother had died, but hearing what'd happened to Milo was worse than even that would've been.

"Hold on to me, love," Wyatt says. "I've got you."

I tighten my arms around his neck and close my eyes, letting him take me on the sweetest ride ever. Half an hour ago, I wouldn't have thought it possible to be on the verge of an orgasm, but leave it to Wyatt. I know I shouldn't be surprised that he's capable of this even at the worst of times, but it's just further proof that he's the one for me.

"I love you so much," I whisper as I come back down from the highest of highs.

"I love you more, and I'm so sorry you're hurting."

"You make it bearable."

He buries his face in my neck and kisses me there, sending a tingle of sensation through me.

But even as I luxuriate in the arms of my love, I fear that Milo might never have what I've found with Wyatt.

MARIA

I've never felt like this. Not when my mom was diagnosed. Not when we thought Everly might have relapsed. Not when my ex cheated on me. Nothing can compare to the bone-deep fear of losing Milo or him losing his mobility. I can't stand it. We're supposed to be resting, but that's not going to happen.

I sit up in bed, listening to Austin's deep voice as he talks to Everly and his parents. They offered to take her on an outing so we can get some sleep, but we want her with us.

Austin comes into the bedroom with her in his arms.

"Rie," she says.

"Come see me, Pooh."

Austin puts her on the bed, and she crawls into my arms, as much my child now as his. I love her so, so much, and the sweet scent of her clean hair comforts me.

"I sorry about your brudder," she says in a tiny voice.

"Thank you, love."

"Is he okay?"

"We hope he will be, but we don't know yet."

We told her only that Uncle Milo got hurt. We didn't tell her how bad it is, although she must be able to tell from the way everyone is behaving.

Austin stretches out on the bed, turns on his side and puts an arm around us.

Rarely will Everly stay still and silent for long, but she seems to sense that's what I need right now. Wrapped up in the two of them, I finally doze for a bit. When I awake sometime later, I'm alone in the bed. I wonder if Austin got any rest at all.

He comes into the room with a tray and closes the door. "Mom made what she calls comfort food. Grilled cheese and tomato soup."

"That sounds good." The sleep helped, and I'm not as nauseated as I was during the endless night when the thought of eating anything made me want to vomit. I push myself up in bed and gather my hair in a ponytail that I twist into a bun secured by a clip I grab from the bedside table. "Is there any news?"

"Not that I've heard."

I reach for my phone, looking for texts from my parents or

Jason in a sea of texts from friends and extended family expressing their concern for Milo and the rest of us. There's nothing from the people I most want to hear from.

Austin puts the tray on my lap.

"Tell your mom thanks for me."

"I will."

I take a tentative bite of the sandwich and then another when the first one goes down easy.

"You look a little better," Austin says.

"I won't feel better until I know he's going to be all right. I keep thinking about how he could be a quadriplegic."

"I can't let my mind go there. It's unfathomable."

"But it's very possible. A bullet that close to his spine…" I shudder, and my stomach starts to ache like it did all night, during the dreadfully long hours he was in surgery.

"We have to keep praying and never stop hoping for the best," Austin says. "It's not the same, but that's how I got through the days when Ev was sick. I just prayed as much as I possibly could for her to get well and took every day one minute at time, trying not to get too far ahead of myself. That's how I stayed sane."

"It's a good strategy. Thanks for sharing that with me. Do you think we should cancel our plans?"

"Not yet. Let's wait and see what happens. My brothers are still planning to come, so…" He shrugs. "One minute at a time."

"Right. Thanks for the reminder."

"I wish there was more I could do for you and your parents."

"Just being here with us helps. We should go over there and be with them."

"I was thinking the same thing. I doubt they're sleeping."

"I'm sure they aren't."

"Eat your lunch, and then we'll go."

I feel slightly more alive after lunch and a shower, and by the time we pull up to my parents' home an hour later, I'm ready to be strong for them. At least I think I am. We left Everly with Austin's parents so we can focus on mine.

"Hey," I say to Austin before he gets out of the G-Wagon.

"Yes, dear?"

"Thank you for being here for me and my family."

"Of course, sweetheart. They're my family now, too. You're my family. Milo is my family. I hate that this has happened to him and to all of you."

"I hate it, too, but I'm coping with it better than I would be without you here to support me."

He takes hold of my hand. "The best thing about this, about you and me, is we never have to go through anything alone ever again." Bringing my hand to his lips, he kisses the back of it. "We're in this together."

"I'm very thankful for that every day, but especially today—and yesterday."

"I got you, baby. Let's go see what we can do for your parents."

The first thing I notice when I step inside is that the counters are laden with food of all kinds, which doesn't surprise me. That's what our community does when someone experiences a tragedy. But we can't let it sit out to spoil, so I get busy organizing and labeling the trays before storing them in the fridges in the kitchen and garage. With Austin's help, we get everything put away while making a list of what we have and who sent it so my mother can send thank-you notes later.

People are so incredibly generous. There's a wide variety of main dishes that run the same rich gamut as our neighborhood, with everything from Cuban to Italian to Caribbean to Puerto Rican and Brazilian. The scents that would normally have my mouth watering in anticipation have the opposite effect thanks to my pregnancy, and by the time we're done, I'm in a cold sweat from trying not to be sick.

Austin hands me a glass of water and a handful of crackers. "Drink and eat. It'll help."

While I know that's true, it's nearly impossible to swallow the crackers. I try anyway.

"Your folks are in the family room."

Nodding, I take another drink of the water and prepare myself to stay strong for them as I go in to see them.

They look terrible, and it's obvious they haven't slept at all.

Mom holds out her arms to me, and I go to her, hugging her tightly.

"We got a text from Jason that he's doing well, resting comfortably," Dad says. "They're hoping to move him to the ICU in a few hours. We can see him then."

"That's good news." I need to watch every word and expression. As a nurse, they'll be looking to me to interpret things for them, and I want to keep them optimistic even as I shatter on the inside while considering the possible outcomes for Milo. "We put all the food away."

"Oh, thank you. People have been coming all morning. Everyone is so kind."

"You'd do the same for them."

"Yes, I suppose so."

Nico comes in looking like the walking dead. I can tell he's ravaged by guilt and remorse and the same bone-deep fear that's gripped the rest of us. Only it's a million times worse for him because he feels responsible for Milo being hurt in the first place.

My heart goes out to him as I hug him. "How're you holding up?"

"Not well. I just went to look at the car…" He shakes his head. "It's a wonder he survived at all."

"Why'd you do that?"

He shrugs. "I needed to see it."

"Any word from the police?"

Shaking his head, he says, "Miguel says they're still looking for them."

"They'll find them."

"I hope so."

"How's Sofia?"

"Terrible. She feels responsible."

"I feel so badly for her. Of course she's not responsible."

"Try telling her that." He glances at our parents in their side-by-side recliners. "How're they doing?"

"Hanging in there. They're very anxious to see him."

135

"All I want to hear is that he's going to fully recover. I don't know what I'll do if he doesn't."

"He's young and strong, and we have to hope and pray for the best. That's all we can do."

My dad's cell phone rings, and we all freeze as a combination of dread and hope fills the room.

"It's Jason." Dad takes the call and puts it on speaker. "Hi, Jason. Everyone is here."

"Great. I wanted to tell you that Milo is awake and alert and responding to pain stimuli in all his extremities."

"Oh, thank you, Jesus," Dad says as he breaks down into sobs. "And thank you, Jason."

"We still have a very long way to go, but this is very good news."

"It's the best news we've ever gotten. Thank you so much, Jason. From the bottom of my heart… I'll never have the words."

"I'm glad I was there when he needed me. If you want to come in around four, he should be settled in the ICU by then, but let's keep it only to immediate family for now. We don't want to overwhelm him."

"I understand. We'll see you then." After he ends the call, he looks over at my mom. "Our prayers have been answered."

"I, uh, I have to go," Nico says, leaving the room before anyone can stop him.

As I watch him go, I'm almost as worried about him as I am about Milo.

136

CHAPTER 15

NICO

*I*t sounds like Milo is going to be okay. At least that's the word right now. Who knows what an hour or two hours or two days will bring? I need to get home to Sofia, to share the good news with her in person. I'm almost to the gatehouse for my neighborhood when Miguel calls.

"We got them. They were hiding out in one of those shipping containers people convert into houses on Diego's property. They had the car in there with them."

"That's great news." I'm filled with relief over all the recent developments. "Tell me they're not going to be back out on bail in ten minutes."

"We're charging them with attempted murder. They'll be held without bail. How's your brother?"

"Awake, alert and responding to pain stimuli."

"I'm so glad to hear that, Nico. Milo is such a good guy. I hate that this happened to him."

"You and me both. He was doing me a favor... He could've been killed..." My throat closes around a lump so huge, it's a wonder I can still breathe.

"These guys have been nothing but trouble for years now. Your girlfriend is better off without her ex in her life."

"She knew that before all this. What about the rest of them? Do I need to be worried about their friends coming after us now that Joaquín and Diego are locked up?"

"We've got eyes on them, but I'd stay vigilant for a while longer."

"Will do. Thanks for everything, man. I owe you."

"Just doing my job. I'll be in touch."

I take the time to call my dad to let them know the shooters have been caught.

"Well, that's more good news. Thanks for letting us know, son."

Since we're not on speaker, I say, "Dad…"

"What is it, Nico?"

I can't hold in the sobs that burst from my chest. "I'm so sorry I let this happen to Milo."

"Aw, son, you didn't let it happen. You'd take a bullet for him yourself. It's always been that way with you two, since the first day we brought him home from the hospital. You said he was yours, and he has been ever since. As awful and upsetting as all of this has been, you know what I said to your mom last night?"

I wipe my face with my shirt sleeve. "What?"

"How wonderful it is that our kids are so there for each other. Milo saw what you were trying to do for Sofia and stepped up to help like you did for him when he wanted to move out of here and couldn't afford his own place."

Thinking of my little brother, I'm so blinded by tears that I pull over before I crash into something. After I put the truck in Park, I wipe away more tears with the back of my hand. "I love him so much. I had no idea how much until I thought we might lose him."

"You knew before then how much you love him. Even when he was little and driving you mad wanting to be with you all the time, you always loved him."

"Yeah." I wipe away more tears. "I'd give anything for it to have been me instead of him."

"Don't say that, son. It would've been just as devastating for us if it'd been you."

"He's so much better than me."

"That's not true."

"It is, Dad. He's just a better person."

"You have some rougher edges, to be sure, but you're just as good of a person as he is."

"I don't volunteer to play dominoes with old guys at the nursing home or drive for Meals on Wheels one day a week or cut the Millers' grass since Mr. Miller broke his hip. He's way better than I'll ever be."

"Don't be so hard on yourself, son. You're good in your own way, and he's good in his. There's nothing you wouldn't do for your family or friends. You're always there when we need you. I tell Mommy every day that I don't know what we ever would've done without you kids during her illness. Look at what you're doing for Sofia and her little boy. You're a good person, Nico, and I'm proud of you."

"I'm so sorry, Dad." Sobs rack me as I think about what could've happened if Joaquín and his cousin had better aim. "I'm going to make this up to him and you and the family. If it's the last thing I do."

"Nico, I want you to hear me on this. You have nothing to make up to any of us. A terrible thing happened, but you had no way to predict it or stop it."

"They'd been coming at me and Sofia. I knew they were out there and blaming her for Joaquín being locked up. I didn't know he'd made bail until later, or I never would've let Milo take my rides last night."

"Which would've left Sofia at the restaurant without you there to keep an eye on things."

"Miguel was there. I should've gone to work."

"And then you'd be lying in that hospital bed instead of Milo."

"I wish it was me. It should've been me. I was the one they were angry with because I'm with Sofia."

"In situations like this, it's easy to play the what-if game, but you know I believe everything is preordained by a higher power. Milo was the one who was supposed to be shot. Not you. We may not immediately understand the why of it, but eventually, it'll make sense to us."

"This will never make sense to me."

"Where are you, son? Maria said you left."

"I'm on my way home to tell Sofia the latest news about Milo."

"That's good. That's what you should do. Go be with her and take comfort in each other. The two of you are as much victims of this senselessness as Milo is."

"No, we're not."

"You are because you're blaming yourselves when both of you would've given your own lives to keep this from happening to him."

I shudder at the thought of Sofia giving her life to save Milo's or mine. God forbid.

"The good news," Dad adds, "is Milo is doing better, and the men who hurt him are locked up. If we can stay focused on the positives, we'll get through this. You will get through this."

"I'm going to be better. I'll be better for Milo."

"You're more than enough already, but you do what you need to, son. You know you'll always have my love and support."

"I love you so much. All of you."

"We know that, and we love you, too. Go be with your lady. She'll make everything better for you."

"I love her, Dad."

"I know, son. We can all see that."

"I'm so afraid I'm going to mess it up."

"Then don't let that happen. Be there for her and her boy every day. Show her what she means to you and never let her wonder how you feel about her."

"I will."

"Are you going to be okay?"

"Yeah. Eventually. Don't worry about me."

"That's like telling me not to breathe."

"You've got enough to worry about. I'm okay. I'll see you at the hospital later."

"See you then."

I end the call feeling slightly better than I did before I talked to my dad.

I'm going to be better for my family, too. I've missed more Sunday brunches than I've attended, skipped birthday parties I didn't feel like going to and have been generally lackluster in my devotion to my family. Yes, I stepped up for my parents over these last few months while my mom was going through treatment, but I can do better. Be better.

That starts today.

SOFIA

I'm so tired, I can't see straight, but I play in the pool with Mateo for more than an hour, encouraging him to practice his swimming. The first therapist we worked with said swimming would be very good for his muscle development and fine motor skills, but I haven't had regular access to a pool until now. I can already see how swimming will be excellent therapy for him, but I still feel like we shouldn't be here.

Gladys sits by the side of the pool, sipping from a tall glass of lemonade and reading a magazine she brought from home. She told me to go lie down, but my mind is racing too much for sleep.

"Are you ready for some lunch?" I ask Mateo when I see him starting to tire.

"Yes, Mama. I'm hungry."

It's such a relief to hear him say that, as his lack of appetite has been another concern since his illness. Some days, I've relied on chocolate-flavored protein shakes to keep him nourished.

We get out of the pool and dry off before going inside, where I make him a peanut butter and jelly sandwich that I serve with carrot sticks. He eats them first, laughing at the crunchy sound they make.

After lunch, he agrees to some quiet time before we swim again later. I have him change into a dry bathing suit and set him up with some books in his bed. I remind him again that he's not to go anywhere near the pool without an adult with him.

"I know, Mama. I won't."

"Thank you for being Mama's good boy." I kiss his forehead and leave him with his books.

"Mama?"

I turn back to him. "Yes, honey?"

"Are we going to live here now?"

"No, we're just staying for a little while."

"Oh. Okay."

I can see the disappointment in his expression. He likes it here. Of course he does. Nico's house is a mansion compared to our tiny apartment—and he has a pool. But this isn't our home, and I can't let Mateo get too comfortable here.

"Mama's going to take a shower. Come get me if you need anything."

"I will."

I cross the hall into Nico's room and head for the shower to wash off the horror of the last eighteen hours. When I think of Milo in the ICU, fighting for his life and mobility because of my ex-husband... I begin to tremble so violently I fear I'm going to come apart. How will Nico ever again see me as anything other than the woman who nearly got his precious younger brother killed?

Just when things between us were moving in a wonderful direction, Joaquín ruined it for me. I should be used to it by now, but this... This feels like too much on top of the things he's already taken from me. I was finally getting back to feeling like myself, the self I was before he decided who and what I was going to be for seven endless years, when he struck again, making me feel like I'll never be free of him.

I'm wrapped in a towel, standing before the mirror, staring at the face that is at once the most familiar to me and at the same time looks like a stranger. Who is this woman? What does she want? I was on my way to answering those questions when Joaquín pulled the rug out from under me once again.

Nico comes in through the door I left open so I'd hear Mateo and stands behind me, putting an arm around my waist and his chin on my shoulder.

With one quick look, I can see that he's been crying, and my knees want to buckle under me. "Milo."

"Is awake, alert and responding to pain stimuli in all his extremities."

My English fails me with *stimuli* and *extremities*. "Wait, so that means…"

"He can feel things in his arms and legs. We don't know any more than that right now, but Jason says that's very positive news. And Miguel called. They found Joaquín and Diego hiding with the car in a shipping container on Diego's property. They're in custody and will be held without bail on attempted murder charges."

I release a deep, rattling sigh. "Thank God on all of it."

"Yes."

I cover his hands with mine. "Why have you been crying?"

"I was talking to my dad about Milo, and it all sort of hit me."

"Are you okay now?"

"I'm better than I was since hearing Milo is improving and Joaquín is in custody. Again."

"Mateo and I should go home to our place."

"Miguel said we need to continue to be vigilant. Just because Joaquín and Diego are locked up doesn't mean their friends and family aren't still blaming you."

"I've brought enough chaos to you and your family."

"We're not doing that, remember?" His hand works its way inside my towel and up to cup my breast. He runs his thumb over the tight nub of my nipple, and just that quickly, I want him.

"Don't try to distract me. It's time for us to go home."

"No, it isn't." He rolls my nipple between his fingers, and I push back against his hard cock even as I realize I'm saying one thing and doing another. "This is your home for as long as you'd like it to be. In fact, forever would be perfect."

"Nico, stop. Don't say things you don't mean."

"I'll never say anything to you that I don't mean. I swear to God, Sofia. You can believe me when I say I want you both here with me. I love coming home and knowing you're here. I love touching you and kissing you." He kicks the door closed and uses his free hand to lock it. "I love everything about you."

My towel falls to the floor. In the mirror, I watch as he unbuttons his shorts and frees his cock from his clothes. It's hard against my back as his hands come around to cup both my breasts. I'm as aroused by his words as I am by the way he touches me, making me believe what he says with the way he looks at me in the mirror.

"Tell me you want me." He presses his cock between my cheeks. "Tell me you feel the same crazy need for me that I feel for you."

"I do. I want you even when I'm sure I shouldn't."

"You should." With his hand in the middle of my back, he tips me forward and slides into me from behind.

He's so much bigger than I'm used to that it takes me a second to relax enough to let him in.

"Shit, I forgot the condom," he says gruffly.

"It's okay. I'm on birth control."

A low groan tells me what he thinks of that news. "God, you feel so good." His breath against my ear gives me goose bumps, and when he reaches around to press his fingers to my clit, I nearly explode.

"Not yet."

I feel like I've been plugged into an electrical outlet as I vibrate from the overwhelming need to come. I grasp his wrist as his fingers continue to stroke me. "Nico."

"What, honey?"

"I need to…"

"Tell me what you need."

I look up and meet his intense gaze in the mirror, and what I see reflected there is everything I've ever wanted for myself and my son—a man who loves us with his whole heart and soul. "I need you. I need this."

My words spark something primal in him. He holds my hips in place as he pounds into me.

I bite my lip to keep from screaming when I come the first time, and then when it happens again, this time with him, the effort to stay quiet is nearly painful.

Nico drops his forehead to my shoulder. "Is it too soon or too much to tell you I'm falling hard for you?" After a second in which I try to absorb that, he adds, "No, wait. That's not true. I've already fallen for you."

"Let me up."

He withdraws from me and helps me to stand.

I turn to face him, wrapping my arms around his neck and pressing my naked body to his. "I've fallen for you, too."

The smile that lights up his sinfully handsome face is the first one I've seen from him since we heard his brother had been shot. "I want you guys to officially move in here with us."

I'm shaking my head before he finishes the sentence. "I don't want to do that."

His smile fades that quickly. "Why not?"

I reach around him for the robe I hung on a hook on the back of the door. After I tie it around my waist, Nico gathers my hair from inside the robe and lets it slide between his fingers. "I want to try to explain this in a way that makes sense."

He pulls his shorts up, zips them, but leaves the button undone as he follows me into the bedroom and sits next to me on the bed.

I appreciate that he gives me a second to get my thoughts together and isn't immediately trying to talk me into going along with what he wants. "It took me a long time to work up the courage and to save the money to leave Joaquín. I know our apartment doesn't look like much when you live in a house like this one, but it's the first real home I've ever had, and I'm not ready to leave it yet."

"I understand that. I just want us to be together all the time now."

"We can be, but I'm not moving."

"What about the safety issue? Joaquín and Diego are locked up for now, but we were having problems with his friends and family even when he was in jail. That threat won't go away. If anything, it's apt to be worse now that they're facing even more serious charges."

"I know, and it is important to me that Mateo and I are safe. We feel safe here, and he's addicted to your pool."

"My pool is his pool no matter where you call home."

"Thank you. I'll never forget your kindness to us or your family's kindness. It's meant everything to me."

"You say that like this is some temporary infatuation or something."

I'm sure the look I give him is full of world-weary reality. "You and I live in the real world, Nico. Things like this fall apart all the time, regardless of how much we might wish otherwise. I can't rebuild my entire life a second time. The first time almost killed me."

"I know you've been through some difficult stuff and that my life has been abundantly blessed by comparison. I heard my Nona tell someone once that most of the luck you get in life comes from being born into a good family. If that's true, then I was one hundred percent lucky from the day I was born."

"I'm glad you see that."

"I do. The older I get and the more people I meet, the more I see how very lucky I am. Nearly losing my brother is a reminder to be thankful for everything I have. And more than anything, I want you and Mateo in my life. I want you living here where we can be together as much as possible. I want to make your life easier, more comfortable, safer. But I respect that you're not ready for that stuff. Just know it's on the table indefinitely."

"What does that mean? 'On the table'?"

He kisses me softly on the lips. "It means my home is your home forever even if you keep your place, too. No expiration date."

"That's very generous of you, but you should probably talk to Milo about that. This is his home, too, and he might not want us here after what happened to him because of me."

"I can speak for him without hesitation. He'd want you guys here and would never blame you for what someone else did."

"Still, you should ask him."

He kisses me again. "I will, but right now, I need to go cut Mr. Miller's grass."

"You have to do that today when you haven't had any sleep?"

"Milo does it every Sunday after brunch. So yeah, I have to do it. I'll catch a nap before work."

"It's good of you to do that."

"Milo is the good one. I'm just filling in for him."

I grab his hand before he can escape. "You're a good one, too."

"I'm not good like him."

"You're good like *you*, and that's more than enough for me."

He gazes at me for a long moment. "That might be the nicest thing anyone has ever said to me."

CHAPTER 16

NICO

I'm crazy about her. Not only is she sweet and sexy as hell, but I love that she's so fiercely independent. Even though I want them to move in with me and stay forever, I have tremendous respect for her desire to keep the home she established for herself and Mateo after leaving her husband.

As I roll the riding mower out of the garage and check to make sure it has gas, Mrs. Alvarez from across the street comes over, carrying a tote bag.

I stop what I'm doing to say hello to her.

"We heard about Milo, and we're simply heartbroken for him and all of you."

"Thank you."

"How is he?"

"The latest report was that he's awake and alert and doing as well as can be expected. We won't know anything for certain for a few days. They said we can see him later today."

"Thank God he's still with us."

"Yes, for sure." Contemplating the alternative still has the power to reduce me to tears.

"I made a casserole and some brownies for you."

"That's very kind of you. Thank you so much."

"Will you please give Milo our love?" she asks tearfully. "Everyone in the neighborhood thinks the world of him."

"I'll do that."

Before she can walk away, Mrs. Sanchez from two doors down arrives with another casserole and the apple pie that Milo supposedly loves. She has the same message for my brother and is on the verge of tears as she lets me know her entire church is praying for him.

I thank them profusely before carrying the food inside to put in the fridge. When I come back out, I move quickly to start the mower and head for the Millers' home three doors down so I can get the job done and grab a nap before work. I can't drive people without sleep.

I'm about halfway through the cutting of the Millers' front yard when they pull into the driveway in their new Buick. Mrs. Miller helps her husband from the car and then waves me down.

I cut the power to the mower.

"You don't have to do that!" she says.

"Milo would want me to."

"But you should be with him, Nico," Mr. Miller says as he leans on a walker. "Not here cutting our grass."

"We can't see him until later, so it was something to keep me busy."

"If you're sure that it's no problem."

"I'm sure."

"How is he?"

I give them the latest info, feeling like I'm on autopilot as I say the same words for the third or fourth time now.

"Please tell him we love him, and we're praying for him."

"I will."

"Thank you, Nico. Your parents raised good men."

They raised one good man and one who could use some improvement. "That's nice of you to say."

"Let us know if we can do anything for you or your family."

"Will do. Thanks. I'd better get this finished."

Mrs. Miller surprises me when she walks over to hug me. "God bless you and your brother."

I've had a funky relationship with God. My siblings and I were raised in the Catholic Church, but ever since I had a choice, I haven't spent much time there. I used to go crazy during weekly Mass, trying to sit still while wishing to be anywhere but there, and don't get me started on CCD classes and the like. I was outta there the minute my parents weren't telling me what to do anymore. I've got to say, though, I'm appreciative of the prayers people are saying for Milo and our family—as well as the many we've received for my mother during her illness.

As I lose myself in the back-and-forth rhythm of mowing the grass, I dust off my faith and say a prayer to the Almighty that He will allow Milo to regain all the things he had before last night and that, before long, he'll be back to cutting the Millers' grass and spreading joy everywhere he goes. "I know I have no right to ask You for anything after not coming around You in years, but please let Milo make a full recovery. He's the best person I know and deserves only good things."

I wipe away a tear that slides down my face and make another turn, taking the mower along the edging of the front garden. I hear Sofia's voice telling me I'm a good guy, too, but there's a lot of room for improvement.

By the time I finish the Millers' lawn, I'm in bad need of a nap. My own lawn needs to be cut, too, but I'm not doing that today. After the mower is back in the garage, I check my phone for the first time in an hour and find nothing new, which is a relief.

Inside, the house is quiet. Gladys is asleep on the sofa, Mateo is sacked out in his bed, and Sofia is curled up on her side in my bed, sound asleep. I take a quick shower, set the alarm on my phone for four thirty and stretch out next to her, hoping I can quiet my mind enough to sleep for a few hours.

Before I doze off, I go back to that prayer from before and say it all over again, adding an Our Father and Hail Mary for old times' sake.

Whatever it takes.

LIVIA

Chris insisted on driving me home from the hospital and asked if he could come in and cook me breakfast. I was shocked when he came to the hospital and then when he stayed, talking to each member of my family like it was no big deal for me to have a man show up in my time of need.

If things had been normal, that would've been the story of the decade. I'm sure I'll hear all about it from everyone after we get our precious Milo through this crisis.

Dear God, I love that boy. A grandmother isn't supposed to play favorites, and I try very hard not to do that, but I defy anyone who knows Milo not to call him one of their favorite people. He's been an angel from the minute he was born, the youngest of my Lorenzo's four children and the light of all our lives.

When I think about how close we came to losing him... My hands begin to shake, and my heart feels like it's going to explode. I've been through a lot in my life, losing my young husband far too soon and having to finish raising my kids as a single mother. But having to face the possible loss of my beloved grandson was too much for me to handle.

Somehow, Chris knew that from a few texts when I said I was at the hospital with my grandson. He'd asked which one and then come there like that wouldn't be the story of the century in my family.

Truth be told, I've never been so happy to see anyone as I was to see him last night.

As he places a plate with a cheese omelet and wheat toast on the table in front of me, my stomach growls.

"Bon appétit, my sweet," he says, kissing the top of my head.

Let me back up a bit to say that, up until last night, our friendship was made up of him teaching me how to fly along with some subtle flirtation and a bit of innuendo. I was not "his sweet," and he wasn't kissing me on the top of my head (or anywhere else, for that matter) or visiting my home like it was no big deal for him to be here.

I see him once a week for two hours of lessons. One hour on the ground and the other in the air. It's the most fun I've had in ages, and if I've developed a massive crush on my much-younger instructor, well, call me Cougar.

"Thank you," I tell him as I take a bite of tasty eggs. "This is very good."

"That's high praise coming from a Giordino."

"We're known more for our pasta than our eggs."

He pours coffees for both of us and sits with me at the table while I eat. "You're known for extraordinary cuisine and a welcoming atmosphere."

"You didn't make any for yourself."

"I'm not hungry."

All at once, it occurs to me. Today is Sunday. "You should be at work! Today's your busiest day at the flight school."

He waves away my concerns with a sweep of his hand. "I cleared my schedule for the day right after I heard how serious your grandson's condition was."

I'm unreasonably touched by that information. "This is all very much above and beyond the call of friendship."

"Is that what we are?" He flashes the slow, sexy smile that sparked the first crush I've had on a man in more years than I care to count. "*Friends?*"

I'm so out of practice that I can't tell if he's flirting with me or seriously asking if we're friends. "I'd like to think we're friends."

"We are."

The time we've spent together has been a dream come true in more ways than one. Not only am I following in my late father's footsteps by finally learning to fly, but I've loved the conversations I've had with my handsome instructor about life and growing older and family and so many other things. We bonded immediately over our affection for dogs after I met his golden retriever, Jet, who comes to work with him.

"Who's taking care of Jet?"

"My neighbor."

"Oh, good."

He props his head on an upturned hand as he studies me.

I must look frightful after being up all night and ravaged with worry about my sweet Milo. All at once, I feel wildly self-conscious, which is rare for me. At my age, what the hell do I care about how I look? Except when Chris is around, I care. I run my fingers through my hair, hoping it's not standing on end.

"I know this isn't the time or the place with your grandson in the hospital and all, but I'd like to be more than friends."

He no sooner says those life-changing words than someone knocks at my door.

Chris jumps up before I can tell him not to. "I'll get it."

I'm sure a family member has come to check on me, and them seeing him here will raise questions I'm not prepared to answer.

I hear Marlene's voice and want to groan. She'll take one look at this cozy situation and jump to all kinds of conclusions.

She comes into my kitchen with Alfredo behind her carrying a platter of treats. "I brought the pastelitos you like with the cheese."

Alfredo puts the platter on the counter. "Can I get you one, Livia?"

"Sure, thanks."

"And for you, too, young man?"

I want to die when Alfredo calls Chris that. Dear God... *What am I doing?*

"I'd love one," Chris says. "Thanks." He makes more coffee and brings it to the table with mugs for Marlene and Alfredo.

"What are you hearing from the hospital?" Marlene asks.

"Jason called Lo and said Milo was awake and aware and responding to pain."

"That's very good news," Marlene says on a long exhale. "My heart's been in my throat since the minute we heard."

"Mine, too."

"I knew you wouldn't be sleeping like you ought to be."

"Too hopped up on anxiety and caffeine. I don't think I'll sleep until I see with my own eyes that he's okay."

"I came because I didn't want you to be alone, but I see that you're not," she says, her devilish eyes twinkling.

I want to smack her. "Chris was good enough to drive me home and make me breakfast."

"I see that."

Her gaze dances between me and Chris, questions burning on the tip of her sharp little tongue.

"How do you two know each other?"

"Chris is my flight instructor."

"Ohhhhh. How is she doing?"

"She's an excellent student. A natural pilot."

I'm shocked to hear him say that. "You really think so?"

"Absolutely. You're one of my best students ever. You study hard and listen to what I tell you, and you take a cautious approach, unlike some of the kids I teach who want to skip to the flying right away. They don't take the time to learn the fundamentals."

Like the fool I am, I soak up every word of praise.

"We worry about her getting hurt," Marlene says as if I'm not there.

"She's in very good hands." Chris unleashes his sexiest smile on me. "Don't worry."

Desperate to change the subject and regain some equilibrium, I glance at Marlene. "Have you spoken to Nico or Sofia? They were in rough shape last night."

"I haven't, but I heard they're back at his house."

"I'm glad she's there, with those lunatics shooting innocent people."

"I am, too," she says, "but they're blaming themselves. I hope this doesn't drive a wedge between them. I like them together."

"I do, too, which is surprising because I wasn't at all in favor of it at first."

"Why not?" Chris asks.

"My Nico… He's too handsome for his own good and has had women flocking around him since he was a teenager."

"Poor guy," Chris says with a twinkle in his eye.

Alfredo laughs. "A terrible burden, I'm sure."

The four of us share a laugh.

"The attention has come too easily to him, and as a result, he hasn't always been as honorable in his dealings with women as we'd like him to be."

"He's different with Sofia, though," Marlene adds. "I think he's in love."

"I think so, too, which is why I'm feeling better about it than I was." For Chris's sake, I add, "Sofia came into our lives when Jason diagnosed her son with a cancerous brain tumor that he removed. We took her under our wings, gave her a job and a family. She's been through a lot with her son and leaving an abusive marriage. We care for her very much. The last thing we wanted was our grandson causing her any more heartache."

"I can understand that," Chris says.

"When he's at the restaurant while she's working, he never takes his eyes off her," Alfredo says. "It's like he can't help but watch her."

"I've noticed that, too," Marlene says with a warm smile for her partner.

The two of them are so damn cute together. She told me over Christmas that he wants to get married, but she isn't sure that's what she wants. I get that. The two of us have been widowed longer than we were married and are set in our ways.

"Nico hasn't spent this much time at the restaurant since he was a waiter," I tell Chris. "He's there all the time these days, but only when Sofia is there, too."

"It sounds like your grandson has met his match," Chris says.

"I sure hope so." I take a sip of coffee and a bite of the delicious Cuban pastry Marlene brought. "She's good for him. She won't put up with any of his crap."

"I doubt she's going to see that side of him," Marlene says. "She brings out his softer side. In other news, when do you suppose Maria is going to tell us she's expecting?"

"Wait. What? How did I miss that?"

Marlene shrugs her petite shoulders. "I noticed last night her cheeks look fuller, and she gets queasy over every smell, like Carmen does."

"How dare these kids do this to us?" I ask on a moan. "I'm so not ready to be a *great*-grandmother. Nothing says *old* quite like that does."

"You are not *old*, Livia," Chris says emphatically. "You're *magnificent*."

Marlene's busybody eyes nearly pop out of her head when he says that.

I'd die of mortification on the spot if I wasn't on fire with curiosity about what might happen next. I can't die right when things are getting so interesting.

"I couldn't agree more, Chris," Marlene says with her sweet-as-sugar smile.

Again, I want to smack her. That impulse happens a lot when she's around.

"Livia is magnificent," Marlene says. "She and I love to bicker."

Alfredo's snort of laughter sets us off. "That's putting it mildly. The two of them are like angry cats half the time, but they'd cut you if you said a bad word about the other one."

"That about sums us up." I grin at my best friend. "It's been like that between us from the minute her Vivian met my Vincent more than thirty years ago now."

"We started poking at each other the first time we met," Marlene says with a smile, "and we've never stopped."

"It's all in good fun," Alfredo tells Chris.

"Most of the time, anyway," Marlene says.

"There's no one I'd rather have at my kitchen table after the night from hell," I tell her.

"Likewise, my dear friend." She glances at Chris and then to me. "Now that I know you're in good hands, we're going to go and let you get some rest." With a sly grin, she says, "You should come to brunch next Sunday, Chris. I'm sure we'll be back to normal by then."

"I'd love to. Thank you, Marlene."

I'm in for a grilling about him the next time we have two minutes alone, but I can handle her.

"Thank you for coming by to check on me." I walk her and Alfredo to the door and hug them. "Means a lot to me."

"We'll be right here for you and your Milo," Alfredo tells me.

"He's *our* Milo. Mine and Marlene's."

Her eyes fill with tears as she hugs me a second time. "Yes, he is."

We've shared everything over the years, including our grand-children.

"We'll see you later at the hospital," Marlene says.

"See you then."

My belly flutters with nerves as I return to the kitchen, where my much-younger, sexy flight instructor waits to further define our relationship. They say there's no fool like an old fool, a thought that nearly makes me laugh out loud.

"What's so funny?" he asks.

"I am. I'm funny."

"I've noticed that."

We laugh a lot when we're together, which is another thing to like about him. The list of things I like about him is long and includes the way he speaks of his daughter with such affection and obvious love. He was never married to her mother but has been in her life from the beginning. He taught her to fly when she was sixteen, and now she works with him teaching others.

"Why are you funny now?"

"Because I'm an old fool acting like a teenager in the throes of a first crush."

"This crush works both ways, then?"

"Apparently so." I glance at him. "Could I ask you something?"

"Anything you'd like."

"How old are you?"

"Sixty-one."

I wince. "Ouch."

"Age is just a number. You, my friend, could be fifty for all your youthful vitality."

"Oh," I say, hooting with laughter, "you're a charmer, aren't you? Did you hear what Marlene said? We're going to be *great-grand-*

mothers before this year is out! You don't even have grandchildren yet!"

He tosses his head back and laughs, and Lord have mercy, the man is sexy when he laughs.

Hell, he's sexy when he breathes.

Then he ups the ante when he puts his hands on my shoulders and gazes down at me with the look men have been giving women since the beginning of time. It hasn't been so long for me that I don't know what that look means.

I take a step back. I'm not ready for whatever he's thinking. Not when I'm exhausted, overwrought and probably have the world's worst coffee breath after drinking gallons of it during the night.

"I'm sorry. This is certainly not the time for this conversation. But I'd like to have it one of these days. When your grandson is on the road to recovery. Would that be okay?"

As I look up at him, handsome and kind and far too young for me, I realize this is a moment of truth. Am I willing to explore this attraction between us, or should I put a stop to it while I still can? I no sooner ask myself that question than I'm silently screaming NO! He and the flight lessons are the most exciting thing that's happened to me in years.

"Yes." I sound much calmer than I feel. "That would be okay."

CHAPTER 17

MARLENE

"*I* think our girl has a boyfriend!" I wait until we're in the car before I say a word, but I'm busting to get it out from the second we leave Livia's home.

"Looks that way," Alfredo says with a chuckle as he drives us to my house.

"How old do you think he is?"

"Sixties?"

"Yeah, I'd say probably early sixties. Girlfriend is a... What do to they call it?"

"A cougar?"

"Yes! She's a *cougar*!"

"You might want to refrain from saying that to her. She's apt to punch your lights out."

"True." I rub my hands together, thinking of all the many ways I can push her buttons about this. I love that expression—push her buttons. I learned it from Livia calling Nico Button. When I asked her why, she told me how he pushes everyone's buttons and what that means.

If you ask me, Nico comes by his button-pushing naturally, straight from his grandmother, the master button pusher.

"Thank you for driving me around and taking care of me today," I tell Alfredo. He's been a rock since we got the news about Milo last night.

"It's my pleasure to drive you around and take care of you."

I look over at him, handsome and immaculate even after a night without sleep. How does he do that when I feel like a wreck? "I'd forgotten what it was like to have someone to lean on at times like this."

"I'm happy to be the one you lean on in good times and in bad."

"What you said... On Nochebuena..."

"About getting married?"

"Yes. That."

"What about it?"

"I, uh, I've been thinking a lot about it."

"I'm very happy to hear that. I think about it all the time."

"You do? Really?"

At a stoplight, he looks over at me with so much love and affection. "All the time."

The surge of emotion that comes over me takes me by surprise, but I'm not sure why. It happens a lot when he's around and saying sweet things to me and anticipating my every need. He's been a gift to me, and to deny that would be foolish and pointless.

"I'd understand if you wanted to hold out for a young, handsome fella like Livia has found for herself."

The comment has me sputtering with outrage. "I'm not holding out for anyone else."

His laughter lets me know he was teasing, and I fell right into his trap. I laugh, too. I've laughed more with him than I have in years.

"I've got all I can handle with you."

He pulls the car into my driveway and shuts off the engine before turning in his seat to look at me. "I love you, Marlene. You know that, right?"

"Yes, I do, and I love you, too. I'm so sorry I held out for so long on accepting your dinner invitation. I was a fool."

"That's all right. All that matters is that you eventually said yes."

"Still. I wasted time that we can never get back."

He brings my hand to his lips and kisses the back of it. "We can spend the rest of our lives making up for lost time. Will you marry me, Marlene?"

"Ah, jeez, you're really asking, huh?"

"I really am. And just so you know, I asked Vivian for your hand in marriage weeks ago, and after she finished crying, she said we have her blessing."

"You... You asked her?"

"Of course." He seems offended I'd question such a thing. "I knew her support would matter to you."

"Yes, it does."

"Vincent overheard our conversation, and he said to tell you he approves, too."

I'm laughing and crying at the same time. "I'm sure he does. He probably begged you to get me out of his hair."

"He never mentioned the word 'hair.'" He links his fingers with mine. "What do you say? Shall we spend the rest of our lives together?"

I once visited the Grand Canyon with my late husband and stood on the edge, looking down into the abyss and trying to imagine what it might be like to fall in. This feels like that, like freefalling into the unknown, only with my Alfredo, I know the landing will be soft and safe. "Y-yes, Alfredo. I'll marry you."

"Are you sure?" he asks with that twinkle in his eyes that I adore so much.

"I'm sure."

"Open the glove box."

I take a second to translate the word *glove*.

He points to the box he means, and I open it to find a blue velvet box inside.

I lean forward for a closer look. "Is that... Is it Tiffany?"

"Nothing but the best for my fiancée."

"When... How long..." I look over at him, stunned.

"Two months ago. I wanted to be ready if I ever got you to say yes." After a pause, he adds, "Go ahead and open it."

I reach out to touch the small box with the same careful reverence I would a stick of dynamite. The soft velvet against my hand sends a shiver of excitement through me. I still wear the wedding rings from my beloved Jorge, but on my right hand, as I couldn't bear to put them away after he died. I hold the small blue box in the palm of my hand for a few seconds before I take the next step to open it, gasping at the sight of a huge square-cut diamond surrounded by smaller stones. "Oh, Alfredo. My goodness!"

"Is it too much? I wanted something as extraordinary as you are."

It's far too much, but I'd never tell him that. My fingers are like sausages as I try to work the ring free of the box.

He stops me and does it for me, sliding the ring onto my left hand.

"It's… My goodness, it's exquisite."

"As are you. I hope you know how happy you've made me, not just today, but every day that we've spent together."

I can't stop staring at the ring. "You've made me just as happy," I say when I finally tear my eyes off the ring and look up at him. "I feel the same way I did when Jorge asked me to marry him, full of butterflies and excitement and anticipation."

"Yes, I know that feeling, and it's the same this time for me, too. I think your Jorge and my Diana are looking down at us, pleased with how we've honored their memories, but also happy for us to have this second chance."

"You really think so?"

"I know so. They loved us. They'd want the best for us." He leans across to kiss me. "Thank you for saying yes."

"Thank you for asking, for talking to Vivian—and Vincent—and for this beautiful ring."

"You're welcome. Now I want you to go inside and get some rest before you have to be back at the hospital. I'll come get you around four thirty."

"Why don't you come in and rest with me?"

His brows rise in an expression of total surprise that I haven't seen before now. I love that I shocked him. "Are you sure?"

"Yes, Alfredo. I'm sure."

MILO

I'm super confused about where I am and what's happening. There's this thing around my head that reminds me of an erector set. Just as I start to panic, a young woman appears by my bed. She's got big brown eyes, shiny dark hair in a ponytail and is wearing pink scrubs.

"Take it easy, Mr. Giordino. You need to remain still."

"Why?"

"Do you remember what happened?"

I'd shake my head, but I can't. "No."

"You were shot in the neck. Dr. Northrup performed emergency surgery that saved your life."

"Jason did?"

"Yes."

"My family…"

"They were all here during the night, but he sent them home to get some rest. They'll be back in a few hours."

"I was shot."

"Yes, while sitting in traffic."

"I don't remember."

"That's not uncommon. My name is Gianna, and I'll be your nurse today. Is there anything I can get for you?"

"I'm thirsty."

"I'll grab some ice chips until Dr. Northrup says you can have water."

I stare up at the ceiling, desperately trying to remember what happened. But the last thing I recall is dropping passengers off at the airport. They were on their way home to Boston. After I left them at Departures, I was headed back to Little Havana to pick up a bachelorette party. Everything after leaving the airport is a blank. Considering what Gianna told me, I suppose that's for the best.

Gianna returns with the ice chips, which are the best thing ever in my dry mouth.

"Do you have a cell phone by any chance?"

"I do."

"Could you call my parents for me?"

"Sure."

I recite my dad's number, since he's the one more likely to have his phone on him. My mom never knows where hers is.

Gianna puts the call on speaker, and it rings several times.

I hope he takes the call from the unknown number.

"Hello?" he says, sounding uncertain and nervous.

"Dad? It's me, Milo."

"Oh God, son." He's immediately sobbing. "It's so good to hear your voice. You scared the hell out of us."

"Sorry about that."

"Don't be sorry. How do you feel?"

"Um, good, I guess? Jason has me wearing some sort of device to keep my head still."

"Can you move your hands and feet?"

I wiggle my fingers and toes. "Yeah, why?"

For a long, long moment, my dad is completely silent until more sobs echo through the phone. "We weren't sure you'd be able to."

"Oh." The implications of that are almost too big for me to handle. "Really?"

"It was a very, *very* long night, my boy. Everyone was there. The entire family."

I can picture what a mob scene that must've been.

"Everyone who knows you and the rest of us has brought food. The outpouring has been incredible. You're very loved, my dear Milo."

"That's nice of them."

"We don't want you to get too tired," Gianna whispers.

"Dad, I have to go, but I'll see you later?"

"We'll be there. Jason told us he'll call the minute we can see you."

"Okay."

"We love you so much," he says, barely able to get the words out. "So damned much."

"Love you, too."

Gianna ends the call and uses a tissue to wipe tears off my face that I didn't know were there. "Sounds like you have a very nice family."

"Yeah, they're amazing. You know the restaurant Giordino's?"

"Of course. Who doesn't? It's one of my favorites."

"My aunt and uncle own it. We've all worked there at one time or another."

"I wondered if you were related."

"My dad's brother, Vincent, and his wife are the owners. Which do you prefer? Italian or Cuban?"

"I love them both, but I'm partial to the Italian side."

"Me, too, but don't tell anyone I said that. We can't play favorites."

Her smile is beautiful. "I understand, and your secret is safe with me."

I close my eyes, just for a second. The next thing I know, my parents and Jason are there.

My mom is stroking my arm, and based on what they told me earlier, I understand I'm lucky I can feel it. "There's my sweet boy," she whispers as tears slide down her cheeks. "Don't ever scare me like that again."

"I'll try not to." I want to ask where Gianna is, which is odd, but I'd like to know.

Jason asks me a bunch of questions and does a series of tests, asking me what I can feel. At the end of it, he smiles. "You passed with flying colors."

"Thank God," Dad says, weeping. "Thank You, God."

"That said, you're looking at a long recovery, Milo. We need to keep you very still for a few days to give the surgical site time to heal. The downside to keeping you still is that it can cause secondary concerns such as blood clots, which is why you have these pressure stockings massaging your legs. We'll be monitoring you very closely over the next week or so."

"So I have to lie here and look up at the ceiling for days?"

"Pretty much, but we'll sit you up a little more every day."

"Well, that kinda sucks."

"It beats the alternative," Dad says. "We'll be here to keep you entertained. Don't worry."

"Did someone call my work?"

"Not yet, but we will. I'm sure they've heard about it. It's been all over the news."

I'm not sure how I feel about being all over the news.

Gianna appears by the side of my bed, and I experience a profound sense of relief. I wonder what that's about. "How are you feeling?"

"Okay, I guess. Can I have some water?"

"Small sips," Jason says. "We don't want you to aspirate."

"How will I eat?"

"Carefully. We're giving you everything you need via IV but will introduce some soft foods tomorrow probably."

"So, no cheeseburgers for a while?"

Jason smiles. "Sorry. Not until we can get you moving. We want your surgical site to be stable before we move you."

Over the next few hours, every member of my family cycles through. Because Jason is family to us, they break the rules and allow two visitors at a time. Maria and Austin are standing by my bed when he gets a text that makes him frown.

"What's up?" I ask him. I'm jonesing for my own phone, but I'll save that request for tomorrow.

"The media has connected me with the shooting of a Giordino. 'Future Brother-in-Law of Marlins' Superstar Austin Jacobs Injured in Drive-By Shooting.'"

"Sorry to drag you into it."

"No worries, bro. I don't care what they say as long as you're okay."

Maria can't stop weeping as she stands next to my bed, pretending she's not weeping.

"What's with the waterworks, sis? I'm fine."

"You're not fine, and I can't make it stop no matter how hard I try."

"She's been like this since last night," Austin adds. "We've gone through an entire box of tissues."

"Quit being a drama queen," I tell my sister.

Maria laughs. "You're the one wearing the crown."

"Exactly. How long will I have this contraption anyway?"

"Six weeks at the very least," Jason says from his perch behind a rolling computer stand.

"Ugh, I'm sorry I asked."

"We need to keep your neck as still as possible until we're certain you've healed properly."

"Is he always this much of a drag?" I ask Carmen, who's swapped out with Austin.

"Not usually, but he knows what he's doing around here, so you need to listen to him."

"Yes, Mom. How are you feeling?" She was sick during Nochebuena and still doesn't look quite right in the eyes.

"I'm fine."

"Are you knocked up?" Maria asks her.

"Maybe. Maybe not. Are you?"

"Maybe. Maybe not."

"Wait a minute." My eyes, the one part of my head I can move without a problem, dart between them. "What gives?"

"If I tell you," Carmen says, "will you keep it between us? We were waiting until after the three-month mark to tell people."

"We were, too," Maria adds.

They go into a girly squealing thing as they hug each other, for a second seemingly mindless of the fact that they're in an ICU hospital room.

"That explains the nonstop crying," Carmen says.

"And here I thought it was concern for me," I say.

Maria's eyes fill again with tears. "Of course it was."

"Stop. I'm joking."

My older sister wipes her face with the back of her hand. "It's not funny. You have no idea what an ordeal we went through last night."

"Sorry to do that to you."

Maria runs her hand over my arm. "I've decided to forgive you, but only because you lived through it."

"Gee, thanks."

I enjoy visits with Vincent, Vivian, Abuela, Nona, Domenic, his parents and several close friends before Gianna says it's nap time, ushering my visitors to the waiting room for now. I'll never admit to being relieved to hear her say that, because I'm so tired, I feel like I could sleep for a week.

"You're a popular guy," she says.

"Tell me the truth. Have they completely overtaken the ICU waiting room and set out a buffet for everyone?"

"How'd you guess?"

"I know how they roll. It's all about quantity in my family— people and food."

"You're lucky to have that."

"And I know it, most of the time, anyway. When they're all up in my business, I'm a little less thankful than I probably should be."

She's a natural beauty with flawless light brown skin that needs no makeup or embellishments. Her smile is electrifying, but her eyes are the showstopper. I wish I could see more of her, but I can see only her top half, which is pretty great. "You should be thankful all the time."

"What's your family like?"

"I have no family to speak of, other than close friends who are like family."

"Oh. I'm sorry to hear that."

"It's for the best."

I have so many questions, but she pats me on the arm and tells me she'll check on me later. "Get some rest while you can." Before she leaves the room, Gianna dims the lights, but I can still see the hustle and bustle of the ICU through the big windows. The beeping of the machines I'm attached to is going to drive me crazy, but my eyes are so heavy, I can't keep them open.

I wonder if I'll see Gianna again.

I hope so.

CHAPTER 18

NICO

*M*ilo is sitting up awkwardly in bed, attached to the halo thing that's screwed into his head and a million other machines. It's completely overwhelming to see him that way. I got only a minute with him while my mom was there, too, so it wasn't the right time to apologize for being partially responsible for putting him in the ICU. I'm trying to stay focused on the positives. Jason expects him to make a full recovery, but it'll take time and physical therapy. It could take as long as six months for him to get back to where he was before he volunteered to take my rides.

Six fucking months.

They say no good deed goes unpunished. If that ain't the truth.

I wish I had some way to deal with the white-hot anger I feel toward the men who put my brother in the hospital. I want them to suffer the way he is, but I keep those thoughts to myself, as the last thing my family needs is more trouble brought to them through me.

But I'm fuming just the same, strung so tightly that vengeance is almost all I can think about even as I go through the motions at work. We're down a car after the shooting, so I've doubled up on rides, which keeps me so busy, I don't have much time to plot revenge that I won't get to pursue.

I need to keep my eye on the things I can control, including my relationships with Sofia and Mateo, my brother and his needs, my parents and their needs, my business, my home, my extended family and the wide circle of friends who've been checking in, bringing food and offering whatever help we need.

I like that Sofia is seeing the way our family and friends come together at difficult times. In a way, the outpouring reminds me of the days that followed the death of Carmen's first husband, Tony, a police officer gunned down on the job. That was one of the worst things that ever happened to us, if not the very worst thing. We were devastated to lose a young man who'd been one of us for years.

Thinking about the dreadful weeks that followed Tony's death makes me even more thankful my brother survived. As bad as this is, I'm well aware of how much worse it could've been.

My phone rings, and I take the call from my dad on Bluetooth. "Hey, what's up? Is Milo okay?"

"Yeah, he's good. He's been asleep for a couple of hours. We sent everyone else home, but Mommy and I are waiting to see him again before we go."

"Don't wear yourselves out. It's going to be a long haul."

"As long as he's okay, we're okay. But we're worried about you."

"About me? What the heck for? I'm not the one who got shot."

"No, but you're the one thinking it should've been you."

"Well, it should've been me. Why didn't I think about how they'd already come at me once before?"

"Are you beating yourself up for not thinking like a criminal?"

"No, I'm beating myself up because my little brother took a bullet that was meant for me. We almost lost him, Dad. If Jason hadn't been there…"

"I know, son. We got very lucky. And I understand why you feel the way you do. Hell, I'd feel the same way if Vincent took a bullet that was meant for me. I'd probably never forgive myself."

"I'll never forgive myself for letting this happen to him."

"What good will that do, though? Will it change what's happened?"

"No, but—"

"No buts, son. Your rage, your thirst for revenge, your regrets... None of that will change what happened, but I can promise you all those things will make it worse, and not just for you, but for everyone who cares about you."

I'm momentarily stunned by how he's zoomed right in on what I'm thinking and feeling. I let out a huff of laughter. "Are there *any* secrets in this family?"

"Not too many. I could see the rage simmering in you one second after you walked into the ICU waiting room today. I got to thinking how I'd feel if I were you and Vincent were Milo. I really, really do understand. I'd want to kill the people who hurt him."

"Yeah." I use my sleeve to brush away tears that infuriate me. I'm not one to sit in my car and cry over anything, but this... I could've *lost* Milo. I can't imagine life without him.

"I truly get it, son, but vengeance won't fix anything. It sure as hell won't help Milo."

"It would make me feel better."

"For a minute or two, but your brother would still be in the hospital staring down a long recovery and needing you there with him, like you have been since the day he was born. Mommy and I were talking about that earlier, the day we brought him home and how you wouldn't let anyone else hold him. You told the girls they had each other and Milo was yours and to get away from him."

A sob escapes through my tightly clenched jaw. I remember that day vividly as one of the best days of my life. After two sisters, I finally had a brother.

"After the girls, we tried for one more because you wanted a brother so badly. Did you know that?"

I wipe away more tears that won't stop. "No, you never told me that."

"You asked so many times when you were going to have a brother that we decided to try to get you one."

"Thank God he wasn't another sister."

Dad laughs. "Aw, come on now. You love them, too."

"Yes, I do, but I'm so, so thankful for Milo. I have been every day of his life."

"Even when he was pestering the living crap out of you, following you around, getting into your stuff, borrowing your clothes, teasing your girlfriends?"

"Even then."

"Remember the time that kid was bullying him in school?"

"That was one of my finest moments as a big brother."

"Tell me that story. I never get tired of hearing it."

We've gone over this a thousand times, but I indulge him once more because I know he's trying to help me with this walk down memory lane. "Milo was coming home from school every day and acting super weird. Wouldn't talk to anyone, wouldn't eat dinner, wasn't sleeping. I finally got him to tell me about this kid who was picking on him, calling him fatso and trying to steal his glasses. I wanted to go beat the shit out of the fucking bastard."

"Just like now, right?"

"Yeah."

"So, what'd you do about the bully?"

"We found out he worked at McDonald's, so Milo and I went there one Saturday for lunch, and I stared at the kid the whole time we were there. I never blinked."

"And he got the message?"

"Oh, hell yeah," I say on a laugh. "He nearly shit himself when he realized he had my full attention."

"I remember being so, so proud of how you handled that. It was perfect. You didn't say a word to him, but you put him on notice that Milo wasn't to be messed with."

"That didn't mean I wasn't dying to pound his ass into the pavement."

Dad laughs. "I was right there with you when I found out what that little punk had been saying to Milo, but the point is, you handled it with tremendous maturity and showed your brother he will always have an advocate in you."

"No one ever bothered him again after that."

"Because they were scared shitless of his menacing big brother."

"Damned straight."

"You're the best big brother those three ever could've asked for. You're always there for them when they need you, and so of course it kills you that you couldn't have been there for Milo last night. But I want you to be thinking about all the times you *have* been there for him and try to let that balance out the one time you weren't. Can you do that?"

"I can try."

"Try hard. Don't bring any more problems down on yourself or Sofia or the people who love you both by doing something stupid. You're too smart for that, Nico."

"Sometimes I wonder if I am."

"You are. Keep the big picture in mind."

"I will, thank you, Dad. Not sure how you can see so much with one look at me, but I appreciate you talking me off the cliff."

"Someday, you'll be a father, and you'll see the same things I do when I look at my kids. I told your mother that Maria is pregnant."

"Is she?"

"No confirmation yet. Just speculation on my part."

"Interesting. I wonder what that means for their wedding in November."

"I guess we'll see. Are you going to be okay, son?"

"Yeah, don't worry about me. Keep your eye on Milo."

"I've got my eye on all of you, and I always will. Call me if you need to talk. Anytime. Day or night."

"I will. Love you, Dad."

"Love you, too, son."

I end that call and sit there for a long time, thinking about the things he said. I haven't thought of that bullying thing with Milo in years, but the memory makes me smile. That was one of my finest hours if I do say so myself. Milo kept asking me why I didn't say something to him. I told him no words were necessary. It was enough for me to stare at him for so long, he got the message not to mess with my brother.

Thirteen-year-old Milo was skeptical.

Nineteen-year-old Nico was certain it would work, and besides, I couldn't very well get into it with a kid unless I wanted to find myself locked up. Thus, the staring contest, which I won by a mile. The kid was shaking in his boots by the time we left, and he never bothered Milo again.

In fact, no one ever bothered Milo again, which meant the word got out about his badass older brother. No one messes with my siblings. I had words with Marcus after he *married* someone else while he was still dating Dee. I ran into the douchebag who cheated on Maria more than a year after it happened, and I advised him to give me a wide berth unless he wanted to end up in the hospital. The asshole ran off like the limp dick he is.

Maybe that's why this thing with Milo is so hard for me to take. I've spent my whole life trying to keep my siblings safe, and to be responsible, even from a distance, for something like this happening to one of them is unbearable.

It's well after two a.m. by the time I pull into my driveway, still driving the black Cadillac CT4 from work. I try not to bring work cars home, but sometimes it's easier to go straight home after my last run than go back to the yard and switch out the cars. My drivers aren't allowed to take the cars home, but I can do what I want. They're my cars, after all.

When I tiptoe into the bedroom where Sofia is asleep in my bed, I notice her bags are packed and sitting by the door.

Shit.

I heard what she said earlier about wanting to go home, but I can't handle the thought of her being vulnerable or accessible to people who'd hurt her simply because she dumped that asshole Joaquín. Since when is wanting out of a marriage grounds for attempted murder? I no sooner ask myself that question than I realize that sort of thing is far more common than I'd like to think. I just hate that it's happening to her.

I'll take her home if that's what she wants, but I'm going with her, and I'll stay there with her every night and do what I can to help keep her safe.

When I get in bed, I snuggle up to her warm body and put my arm around her.

She sighs in her sleep and relaxes into my embrace as I breathe in the fresh, clean scent of her hair.

For the first time since I heard Milo was shot, I feel myself settle a bit as the ache in my chest seems to subside somewhat. Being close to her this way is all it takes to calm the storm that's been raging inside me all day. As I close my eyes and try to sleep, I vow to keep her close to me for as long as I possibly can.

SOFIA

I'm awake early the next morning, but I stay still and quiet, hoping Nico will sleep for a while longer. I have no idea what time he got home, but I know it was late, since I stayed awake until well after one, hoping to see him. He texted to tell me Milo was in good spirts when he saw him but didn't say much more than that.

I hope maybe I'll get to see him myself at some point, although I won't blame Milo if he doesn't want me there.

The sick feeling I've had in my stomach since Saturday night is still there on Monday morning. That Nico's sweet, kind, younger brother could've been harmed by the monster I was married to is just too much for me to handle. I keep thinking I should walk away from Nico and his family, but I can't bring myself to leave the best people I've ever known, even if it would be better for them.

I love them all so much.

Especially Nico, who's been nothing but kind and supportive of me for as long as I've known him.

I wish I was a stronger person who could do what was best for him and his family, but the thought of returning to any semblance of the life I was leading before I knew them breaks my heart.

"Whatever you're thinking, knock it off," he says in a gruff, early-morning voice as he draws me closer to him.

"How do you know I'm thinking about anything?"

"Every muscle in your body is tight with tension."

I'm shocked by how well he knows me in such a short amount

of time together. But then again, no one has ever paid closer attention to me—the real me—than he has. "Is it?"

"Uh-huh."

The next thing I know, I'm on my back, looking up at him gazing down at me with an intense expression on his face.

"Um, hello?"

When he smiles, his entire demeanor changes. "Morning. Why are you so tense?"

"Gee, I wonder."

"I told you. He's going to be fine."

"I'm very, *very* glad about that, but I still feel sick over it."

"I know, baby." He closes his eyes and rests his forehead on mine. "I do, too." After a full minute of silence, he says, "I saw that you packed to leave."

"I need to go home today. It's my day to get everything done before the work week starts again on Tuesday."

"And there's nothing I can do to convince you to stay here for a little while longer?"

"I know it's not what you want me to do, but… I'd really like to go home."

"Okay, then, we'll go to your place."

"You don't have to come with us."

"Yes, I do, Sofia. How do you expect me to have a moment of peace knowing you guys are unprotected?"

"And what will you do if they come for me? Put yourself between us and them?"

"Yeah," he says as if that's no big deal.

"So your mother will have another son in the hospital, or worse?"

"If you were to stay here until things calm down, then we wouldn't have to worry about them being able to get at you or me."

"Except for when I'm at work or driving to work or at the grocery store or the drugstore or Mateo's school or any of the dozens of other places I am during a given week."

"Hearing that list sends my anxiety into the red zone."

"That's bad, right?"

"Very bad." He rolls off me onto his back, taking his body heat and the start of a promising erection with him.

I look over at him staring up at the ceiling as if he might find the answers there. His obvious distress hurts me.

"I'll stay."

He turns to me. "Really?"

Nodding, I say, "I'm not trying to make this harder on you than it already is."

On his side now, he puts his hand on my belly. "*This*, as you put it, is the sweetest thing I've ever had in my entire life. The stuff that's happened outside of *this* can't touch *us* unless we let it. I respect your desire to return to your own home, but the truth is, I can keep you safer here in this gated community. You can get groceries and anything else you need delivered. I can go with you when you take Mateo to school and pick him up. If we reduce the opportunities for them to get at you, we keep you safer until things settle down."

"I know, and I agree. I hope you don't think I'm being foolish by wanting to go home. It's just that I worked so hard to have that place and to establish a routine for us that it's hard for me to be removed from it."

"We'll get you back there as soon as it's safe. I promise. I'll talk to Miguel today to get an idea of what the cops are hearing from Joaquín's crew. Maybe having him and Diego charged with serious felonies will scare them enough to stand down."

"I wish I believed they were that smart."

"Yeah, me, too." He links his fingers with mine. "Tell me about your Monday routine, and let's see what we can do to get everything done."

"Don't you have work?"

"Not until later on."

"You must be tired. You got home late."

"I'm fine with five or six hours of sleep. I've always been that way."

"You're lucky. If I don't get at least seven, I'm cranky."

"I can't imagine you cranky."

"Just wait… It's not pretty."

"There's never a time when you're not pretty. I refuse to hear otherwise."

He makes me smile and laugh when I'd think neither was possible. "Mateo will be happy to hear we're staying awhile longer. He cried last night when I told him we were going home and couldn't bring the pool with us."

"I told you he can swim in my pool anytime he wants, regardless of where you guys are staying."

"That's very sweet of you. It's so good for his therapy. After just a few days of swimming, I can already see him getting stronger."

"Then he needs to be swimming every day."

"He'd love that."

"We'll make it happen."

"Can we go to my place today to pick up mail and a few other things we need?"

"Of course. We'll go after we get Mateo to school."

I glance at the clock on the bedside table. "I've got to get him up in fifteen minutes."

"Fifteen whole minutes? Do you know what we can do in fifteen minutes?"

"Take a shower? Cook breakfast? Start some laundry—"

His kiss is filled with laughter as he sets out to show me a much better use of that time. "Come here."

"Let me pee first."

"Hurry. We only have fifteen minutes."

After I quickly use the bathroom and brush my teeth, I get back in bed and curl up to him. He effortlessly moves me so I'm on top of him, with his erection throbbing against my belly.

His hands slide down my back to cup my ass as he presses against me. "You feel so good. So, so good."

"You do, too."

"This," he says, "with you… I want you to know… You're the best thing to ever happen to me."

"You really think so? Even after everything else that's happened?"

"God, yes. From the first minute I ever saw you, I wanted you more than I've ever wanted anything, even the train set I begged for when I was ten."

Smiling, I place my hands on his chest and push myself up so I'm straddling him. "More than the train set, huh?"

"Way more, and I wanted that train set like I've never wanted *anything.*"

I press my core against his erection, and he groans as he tugs at my tank. I pull it up and over my head.

His eyes go hot when my breasts spring free of the top, and his hands are there a second later, his thumbs stroking my nipples.

My head falls back in surrender.

He sits up and replaces his hands with his lips, tongue and teeth.

I can't sit still. "Nico."

"What, baby?"

"I want you."

"Best words I've ever heard from anyone."

We disentangle long enough to remove my panties and his boxers, and then I'm back on top, taking him in slowly and carefully, moaning the whole way as I struggle to take him in. I've never had that problem before, which is another thing that makes him different.

"Easy, sweetheart. Nice and easy."

I can't believe this is all it takes to bring me right to the brink of orgasm. He hasn't even moved yet. Toward the end, I was faking it with Joaquín, which I now realize was part of a much larger problem. I was afraid of him when we weren't having sex, so how was I supposed to relax and let go when we were?

"Why the tension?" Nico asks. "Does something hurt?"

"No," I say on a long exhale, not wanting him to know Joaquín is on my mind, especially right now. "It's the good kind of tension."

"Ah, we like that kind of tension."

"Yes, we like it very much."

"Do we like this even better?" He presses his fingers to my clit as he pinches my nipple with his other hand. I come so hard I see stars, and when I recover from the incredible high, I realize I'm the only one who saw stars. "You ready for some more?"

Nodding, I pivot my hips and love his sharp gasp.

"Do it again."

I do it again and again until he's pushing back with every thrust, taking me up again. I can't believe he's going to make me come twice in less than fifteen minutes.

We broke our own record.

CHAPTER 19

NICO

I love this routine with Sofia that includes early-morning sex, breakfast with Mateo, dropping him at school and doing errands. I keep a watchful eye on the rearview mirror and am always acutely aware of our surroundings. After we drop Mateo at school, I breathe a little easier with one less person to worry about for a few hours.

My dad sent a text saying he checked in with the nurses and Milo had a restful night and is doing well, which is a relief. We can see him later this afternoon.

When we park outside Sofia's apartment, my anxiety spikes all over again. If they're watching us, they'll be looking for my truck, so the fact that we're still in my car from last night might help, except the shiny black Cadillac stands out like a sore thumb in a parking lot full of regular cars.

After she grabs her mail from a box in the lobby, I usher her up the stairs to her place while I scan the area again. Everything is quiet, but that doesn't mean they aren't watching us. Maybe they have to work like normal people and don't have time to be stalking Joaquín's ex-wife this morning.

"We should put together a full list of all the people he associates with so I can pass it on to Miguel." I wish someone had thought of that before my brother was nearly killed. "Is that something you can do?"

"Yes, I'll do it right now. You want some coffee?"

"Always."

She puts a pot on to brew and then sits at the kitchen counter with a pad and pen, using her phone contacts to compile a list. "I'm including phone numbers for significant others in some cases, because that's all I have."

"Whatever we can give him will be helpful. I suspect the reason he hasn't asked us for this info is because they already know these guys. But it can't hurt to give him your list. Include anyone peripheral, too."

Her brows knit with confusion over the word *peripheral*.

"People who hang out sometimes, but maybe aren't part of the main group."

"Ah, right. Okay. I need to add that new word to my list."

By the time she finishes, she's covered three list-size notebook pages with names and phone numbers.

"This is great, babe." I take photos of it and compose a text to Miguel.

Hey, so Sofia compiled this list of people who associate with Joaquín. We're at her place now for a short time, but she and her son will be staying with me until we're sure it's safe for her to go home. We're all a bit on edge, as you can imagine.

Miguel replied immediately. *Thanks for this. It'll help. We know this crew, but it's good to have all the info we can get. We're keeping an eye on them and have put them on notice that we're watching and prepared to charge anyone who thinks they can finish what Joaquín and Diego started. How's your brother?*

He's doing ok. In ICU and facing a long recovery, but we're thankful he's still with us and isn't paralyzed.

Thank God for both those things. I saw the incident report this morning, and the responding officers initially thought he was DOA.

My stomach drops when I see that. Jesus. *We got very lucky, and we know it.*

Yeah, for sure.

Sofia goes back to work tomorrow night.

We'll have eyes on the restaurant while she's there.

How long will that be necessary?

Until we're sure that no one is going to pick up where they left off. I like to think seeing Joaquín and Diego in serious trouble might put a scare into the rest of them, but it doesn't always work that way, so we'll remain vigilant for now.

I'm worried about my extended family. They came for me because I'm with her, and then they shot Milo because they thought he was me, but what if they go after my parents or my sisters, looking to hurt me enough that I leave her? (Which isn't going to happen.)

I understand the fear. All I can say is we're watching the ones most likely to be looking for retribution. I'm glad your lady got away from Joaquín Diaz. He's bad news. Has been for years.

After everything she went thru to break free of him and leave, I hate to see her living in fear for herself, her son, for me and my family.

I hear you, brother, and we're doing everything we can. Will keep you posted on any developments.

Appreciate it.

"What'd he say?" Sofia asks with the pinched, anxious expression that makes me want to go to the city jail and beat the shit out of her ex-husband.

I give her the gist without saying anything that'll make her more afraid than she already is. "He said your list will be very helpful."

"Glad I could do something, although if they find out I gave the cops their names, that could make everything worse."

"They won't find out it was you. Miguel would never let that happen, and besides, he said they're very well known to the police, long before now." I go to her and put my arms around her. "Try not to worry. We're doing everything we can."

She relaxes into my embrace and loops her arms around my back. "It's hard not to worry. Never in my life would I have expected him to do the things he's already done."

"Miguel said he's been bad news for a long time. I think maybe he's gotten lucky evading serious trouble before now, but he's been on their radar for years."

"I had no idea. I guess that makes me naïve, but I really didn't know. When we were first together, we had so many plans and dreams. He wanted to open an auto body repair shop, and we were going to buy a house and have more kids. I was going to take some classes and work toward my degree and maybe help him run the business. None of it happened. It just became this daily struggle to get by, and the harder things got, the meaner he was to me, as if it was my fault that nothing was working out the way we thought it would."

"I'm sorry you went through that."

"I should've left him years ago when I started noticing long absences that he couldn't explain. I thought he had another woman, but now I see he was probably doing stuff with his cousins and friends that could've gotten him into big trouble if he'd gotten caught." She straightens suddenly. "There was one time, about two years ago, when he disappeared for a whole week. No one knew where he was. I was convinced he was probably dead. I bet he was in jail."

"We could find out."

She ponders that for a second. "I think I'd like to know."

I send a text to Miguel, who writes back quickly.

He was locked up for eight days two years ago for suspected auto theft. We held him due to outstanding warrants while we investigated the car thing. We suspected he and his boys were running a chop shop, but in the end, we couldn't prove it and had to let him go. But he was on probation for failing to appear on several other misdemeanor charges.

I read Miguel's response to Sofia.

"I knew nothing about any of that. He came back home after the week he was missing like it was no big deal and said he'd gone out of town to pick up some parts he needed for a job he was doing. I didn't believe him, but I wasn't about to ask any questions. After that… That's when I started seriously saving up to leave. It took almost a year to save enough for my own place and then another six months to work up the courage to leave."

"What happened when he figured out you guys were gone?"

"He lost his mind. I had friends who kept me in the loop. They told me he went crazy trying to find me and called the police to say I'd taken off with his kid. Now I get why they didn't take him seriously. They already knew who and what he was and probably thought it was a good thing that I'd gotten his son away from him. But I was so scared he was going to find me and kill me for taking Mateo."

"God, I hate that you went through that alone."

"I wasn't entirely alone. I had Gladys, who's been like a mother to me and a grandmother to Mateo, and some good friends who still took my call even years after I'd last talked to them. Some of them had been with guys like Joaquín and knew how they operated, isolating us from our support networks so they could control everything we said and did."

"I'm glad Gladys and your friends were there for you."

"They did what they could, but I was still afraid all the time. And then he took me to court, trying to get custody of Mateo. That's when I really got scared that he might win. But it didn't really go anywhere, and I couldn't figure out why, but now I know it was because he'd been in jail and was on probation. However, the judge gave him one overnight with Mateo a week, which forced me to have to see him. That was terrifying. I worried all the time whether he was going to take off with Mateo, and I'd never see him again."

I lead her to the sofa and sit next to her, continuing to hold her hand. "I can't imagine how scary that must've been."

"It was horrible, and then Mateo got sick. That was the scariest thing of all."

"Tell me about that." I want to hear all her secrets, all her stories, all her dreams. I've never wanted to *know* another person the way I do her.

"I thought he had the flu. He was lethargic and didn't want to do anything but lie around and watch TV, which was so not like him. He was always begging me to go to the park to play on the swings, to play chase with him or to ride the Big Wheel we got him for Christmas one year. But for like two weeks, he was just so tired all the time. It just got worse and worse, and I was so, so scared that something terrible was wrong with him."

"You knew."

"I think I did, even before Jason said it was something bad. That day at the clinic… I'll never forget how scared Jason was. I could see it in his face even though he was calm for me. Everything happened so fast. They took us by ambulance to Miami-Dade. Jason did some tests, found the tumor and operated all within an hour or two of us first seeing him. That sense of… What do you call it?"

"Urgency?"

"Yes, urgency… It was very scary. My hands… They were shaking so bad, I could barely fill out the forms. I was terrified for Mateo and wondering how I'd ever pay for him to have surgery." Her eyes shine with tears when she looks up at me. "Jason… He donated his services. We owe him everything."

"He's incredibly talented."

"Later, he told me that the tumor Mateo had is the one he'd been studying for years and that there was no one in the country better prepared to operate on that particular tumor than he was. God was really looking out for us that day."

"I'd say so, and He's been looking out for you ever since. Look at how well Mateo is doing now."

"He's so much better than he was, but there's still a long way to go. Sometimes the other kids at school ask him why he walks funny or why his face is 'frowny.' He tells them because he had cancer, and now he doesn't."

"I love that. He's such a great kid."

"Yes, he is. Somehow, he's come through all the craziness still as sweet as he was before."

"That's thanks to you. You're so good with him."

"He's the most precious thing in my life."

"Do you want more kids?"

The question seems to take her by surprise. "I certainly didn't want them with Joaquín. He barely noticed Mateo until I left with him, and then he was more interested in him than he'd ever been. I have no idea where he was the day Mateo had surgery. I texted him several times, but never heard from him."

"Every new thing I learn about him makes me hate him more than I already do."

"Believe me, I get that. I was very careful to make sure there wouldn't be any more kids with him. I got birth control injections at the clinic so he wouldn't find pills in the house. He wanted more kids, but what I think he wanted more than anything was more reasons to tie me to him. It wasn't about the children. It was about controlling me."

"Well, if there's one bit of good news in all the chaos of the last few days, it's that he's locked up, and he's going to stay that way for a long time."

"What'll I tell Mateo about his father when he asks?"

"He's old enough to hear the truth."

"Yeah, I guess so," she says with a deep sigh. "He probably won't be surprised. He's seen Joaquín in action enough to be afraid of him. He hated having to go with him for overnights."

"Thankfully, he won't have to do that anymore."

"I suppose that's one... What's the term for when something good comes of something bad?"

"Silver lining?"

"Yes, that's a silver lining." She glances at me with a hopeful look in her eyes that I haven't seen before. "I've been thinking about what you said about maybe trying to find my father."

"Really?"

Nodding, she says, "My mother always said he seemed like a good man, although she only met him that one time, so I'm thinking maybe that good man would want to know he has a daughter and a grandson."

"I'm sure he would. What else do you know about him?"

"That his name was Jon, he was from Minnesota, and he was stationed at Homestead while he was in the navy during the mid-nineties."

"Sofia... That's probably enough to find him. Do you have a Facebook account?"

"Yes, and Instagram."

"You should post that you're looking for a man named Jon from Minnesota who was stationed at Homestead in the Miami area in the mid-nineties and knew a woman named… What's your mother's name?"

"Mildred, but she goes by Millie."

"A woman named Millie. Say that anyone who knows who this might be can contact you by direct message. And ask people to share it."

"You really think that might work?"

"It can't hurt. Social media is very powerful, and when people start sharing, you never know what'll happen."

She holds up her arm. "I have goose bumps when I think about finding him."

"Do you want me to do the post for you?"

"No, that's okay. I'll do it." She picks up her phone, opens the Facebook app and starts typing. "I just remembered something else. My mother told me about meeting his sister, Jessica, who was visiting when they met."

"Add that. Every detail helps."

"I can't believe I'm actually doing this," she says with a nervous laugh.

"I think it's awesome. I hope you find him and that he's thrilled to know he has a daughter and grandson. Anyone would be thrilled to have you two in their lives."

"Thank you for that and for encouraging me to do this. It's something I've wanted to do for a long time, but life got in the way." She types up the post and then hands the phone to me. "Did I spell everything right?"

I read through the post, which is almost exactly what I suggested she write. "Looks perfect to me." I hand the phone back to her.

She holds it for a long moment before she moves her thumb to press the Post button. Then she blows out a deep breath. "Well, here we go."

"Here we go. Post it to Instagram and Twitter, too, if you have that."

"I do."

She makes the other posts and then tosses her phone aside. "How am I supposed to function with that out there?"

Smiling, I lean in to kiss her. "Let social media do its thing while you do yours. If nothing comes of the posts, I have a friend who does some private investigation work for lawyers here in town. I'll ask him to look into it for you."

"In case I haven't told you, you're the best."

"You really think so?"

"I really do. Your first thoughts are always, 'How can I make things easier for Sofia and Mateo? How can I keep them safe? How can I help them?' I've never known anyone like you, except for your grandmothers and the rest of your family. That's where you get it."

"I'm not sure anyone has ever looked at me that way before."

"I see *you*. I see your character. I see the guy who mowed his neighbors' lawn after being up all night worrying about his brother. I see that guy, and I like what I see."

"Thank you."

"Please don't thank me. You've done so much for me."

"We've done a lot for each other."

"If you say so."

"I do. What you just said... You have no idea how much that means to me. Most people see the less flattering parts of my personality. And I admit I deserve criticism for how I've behaved in the past. Being with you and Mateo... You make me want to be worthy of you."

"You're incredibly worthy of us."

Her gaze shifts to my lips, and just that quickly, I'm hard for her. "About those things you need to do today..."

She continues to stare at my mouth. "What about them?"

"Will they keep for a little while?"

"I suppose. I just need to pack some more clothes and then do laundry at your house. Why?"

"I was thinking we've got the place all to ourselves and nowhere to be until it's time to pick up Mateo."

"And what would you like to do with all this time we have before we pick up Mateo?"

"How about I show you rather than tell you?"

"Okay…"

When I might've swooped in, picked her up and tossed her over my shoulder to take her to bed, I resist that urge out of respect for what she's been through in the past. The last thing I'd ever want to do is scare her. Instead, I stand and give her hand a gentle tug, bringing her to her feet. Then I put my arms around her and lift her, drawing a surprised gasp from her.

"Is this okay?" I ask as I walk toward the apartment's only bedroom.

She nods and smiles before she kisses me. "It's okay."

When her phone rings, she glances back at where she left it. "I've got to get that in case it's the school."

I put her down, and she goes to get the phone, freezing when she sees the screen.

"Who is it?"

"My mother."

"Do you want to take it?"

"No."

"Then don't. You're not obligated to talk to her."

"She hasn't called me in more than a year."

"Is it possible she saw the post on Facebook?"

"Yes, I suppose it is."

"Put the phone down, Sofia, and come here."

She places the phone on the coffee table and crosses the room to me.

I rest my hands on her shoulders. "Are you okay?"

"Yeah, it's just strange to have her call me." Her phone chimes with a voicemail message. "That'll be from her. She's probably angry that I'm looking for him."

"Why would she care?"

"She never wanted to talk about it when I'd ask her why she

190

didn't tell him about me. Once, when she was drinking, she said the stuff about him being a good man and seemed kind of sad, as if she wished that maybe she'd tried harder to see him again. But most of the time when I asked about him, she'd say, 'He had his life, and I had mine.' That would be the end of the conversation, except she'd sometimes add that I wasn't the only kid growing up without a father, and I'd survive. I think all the time about how my life might've been different if my dad had been around."

"He might've kept her from being so hard on you."

"I'd like to think so, but who knows? He might've been even worse."

"I don't think so, and she probably knew you'd like him better, which was why she kept him away from you." I continue to massage the tension from her shoulders. "Do you want to listen to her voicemail?"

She shakes her head. "I'd like to go back to what we were going to do before she called."

I put my arms around her and lift her again. "You mean this?"

Her smile again reminds me of what sunshine looks like when it emerges from behind the clouds. "Yes, that's what I mean."

CHAPTER 20

SOFIA

*L*ying naked in Nico's arms is about the best thing I've ever experienced, second only to the way he loves me. He's so gentle and sweet, yet also hot and passionate. I never knew it could be this way, that I could feel so safe with a man and let myself fully experience the act of love the way I do with him.

He's got me tucked up against him, my leg between his as his hand strokes my back and bottom, making me want him all over again. I'm not sure how he does that so effortlessly. He's got me so relaxed that I'm not thinking about my long list of things I need to get done while Mateo is at school. I've even forgotten about the social media posts that might lead me to my father at long last.

No, all I'm thinking about is this man and the love I feel for him that seems to grow stronger by the day. I kiss his chest and breathe in the scent that drives me crazy. I'm not sure if it's soap or cologne or just him, but I love it.

I love him. So, so much. It sort of scares me how much I love him, because when you give someone that kind of power over you, it can be terrifying.

My phone rings again. "I've got to get that."

Nico releases me, and I get up, grab his T-shirt from the floor and put it on before I go to get my phone.

It's my mother again.

Ugh.

I listen to her voicemail. "What the hell are you doing posting about Jon without even talking to me first? You have no idea what you're starting with that. Take it down. Now." She ends the message without even asking how I am or how Mateo is. When I called to tell her he was sick, she said she told me not to have him in the first place. I haven't called her since then.

I'm not taking down the posts. I want to know the man who fathered me. I have a right to that information, regardless of what she says.

My phone chimes with a text that says basically the same thing the voicemail did. Without taking the time to even think about it, I block her. I should've done that a long time ago. Next, I block her on Facebook and the other platforms so she can't see what I'm posting. My life is none of her business. That's how she wanted it.

"Everything okay?" Nico asks.

"Yep." His phone rings, so I bring it with me when I return to the bedroom and hand it to him.

"Thanks. Hey, Maria, what's up?" He listens for a minute and then looks up at me. "Sure, we can do that. Sounds like fun. What can I bring?" After another second, he says, "Yes, can do. See you then." After he ends the call, he reaches for me and brings me back into his arms. "Maria and Austin are having everyone over for dinner. They thought it might help to be together after the last few days."

"You don't have to work?"

"Not until later. My first ride is at eight."

"Are you sure they want us there?"

"My sister said, 'We'd like to invite you, Sofia and Mateo to join us.' Those were her exact words."

"If you're sure it's okay."

He holds out a hand to me, and when I take hold of it, he guides me back into bed, covering me with the down comforter I saved for weeks to buy. "I'm sure it's okay. As much as we may be blaming ourselves for what happened to Milo, no one else is."

"I'm not sure I'd have that kind of grace if this had happened to my son."

"My family loves you. They *know* you. They'd never blame you for what your ex-husband did, Sofia."

"We got so lucky, Nico. Milo got so lucky. An inch or two either way, and he'd be dead or paralyzed. I keep thinking about what we would've done if that had happened."

"We need to thank God every day for the rest of our lives that it didn't happen."

"But it could have, and that will always be tied to me, even if indirectly."

"I understand why you feel that way, and I would, too, if the roles were reversed. Just like I feel responsible for letting Milo take my rides when they'd already come for me and one of my work cars. That said, we're not the ones who hurt him, and everyone knows that. My dad reminded me earlier of how much I've always loved him. From the day they brought him home, I said he was mine, and that was that."

"That's very sweet."

"One time, this kid was bullying him. We went to the McDonald's where the kid worked, and I stared him down the entire time we were there. He never bothered Milo again—and no one else did either. My dad reminded me of that story. I'd forgotten about it."

"I'll bet Milo never forgot it."

"I guess not."

"You're a wonderful big brother, Nico."

"Not always, but I'm going to be from now on. I've taken my sisters and brother for granted, that they're always going to be there. Now I know that's not necessarily true."

"You're lucky to have them. I used to yearn for siblings."

"I'm happy to share mine with you—and all my cousins."

"How many cousins do you have?"

"Like thirty-two, I think. Nona has sixteen, and my mother's side has sixteen, plus ten more honorary cousins from Abuela's side."

Her eyes bug at that number. "Are you close to them all?"

"Not all of them, but I certainly know them all. There are tons of family weddings, graduation parties, reunions. It's always something in one family or the other, although we're closer to my dad's side since most of them live here."

"I can't imagine being part of a family like yours."

"You *are* part of a family like mine. My family is your family. No matter what happens between us, once Nona and Abuela adopt you, there's no getting out."

Her smile doesn't quite reach her eyes the way her real smiles do. "You wouldn't mind if your family keeps me around even if you don't?"

"I have every intention of keeping you around for as long as I possibly can. In fact, forever would be perfect."

"You really mean that?"

"I really do. I'm in this for keeps, Sofia. With you and with Mateo. I don't want you to ever think otherwise."

"That makes me feel very lucky."

"I'm the lucky one. Don't worry about anything, okay? Everything is going to be great from here on out. I know it."

I hope that's a promise he can keep.

Two hours after I posted on social media, the posts have been shared more than a thousand times, and I have a message from a young woman named Janelle. *I think the Jon you are looking for is my uncle. I'm Jessica's daughter. Why are you looking for him?*

"What should I say?" I ask Nico. "Should I tell her the truth?"

"Why not? You're going to have to say why at some point. Why not now?"

"What if she doesn't tell him? Maybe I should just say I need to discuss a private matter with him and would appreciate his contact info if she's willing to give it."

"I suppose that might be better than putting the choice in her hands to tell him what you want to ask him."

"Okay."

Thank you so much for replying to my post. I have a personal matter I'd like to discuss with Jon and would appreciate his contact info if you're willing to share it. I include my phone number and email address, while realizing she could be my first cousin. After hearing about Nico's cousins, I wonder how many I have. I press Send on the message, hoping she passes it on to him.

"What if she doesn't tell him?"

"We can find Jessica through her and go from there. It won't be hard to find him now that we have a family member to work with."

"You sound like you've done this before."

"Not like this, but my friend does this sort of stuff all the time and has shared some stories over the years. He could find your dad in half an hour with what we know so far."

Twenty minutes later, I'm gathering laundry to take to Nico's when my phone chimes with a text. I grab the phone off the counter.

This is Jon Baxter. I was told you're trying to reach me? My niece told me you referred to Millie in Miami??

His name is Jon Baxter.

My hands are shaking as I reply. *Thank you for getting in touch. Millie is my mother. I know this might be shocking to you, but I think you might possibly be my father.*

I hold my breath, waiting to see if he'll reply.

When the phone rings with an out-of-state number, I nearly die of shock. How could it be this easy to find him?

Nico puts his hands on my shoulders. "Take a breath, babe. You got this."

I take the breath he suggested and press the green button. "Hello?"

"This is Jon. I… I don't know what to say. I had no idea. She never told me."

"I'm so sorry to drop this on you, but I've been trying to figure out a way to find you for years. A friend suggested I try social media, and it was remarkably easy."

"How old are you?"

"I'll be twenty-seven in June," I say, adding the date of my birth.

"That adds up to when your mom and I were together. I'm speechless. Truly. All this time, I've had a *daughter* out there I didn't know about. Why didn't she tell me?"

"I don't know. She and I are basically estranged, and it's better that way for me."

"I'm sorry to hear that. Your name is Sofia?"

"Yes, Sofia Diaz, which is my married name, but I'm getting divorced. I have a five-year-old son named Mateo."

"So not only do I have a daughter I didn't know about, but I also have a grandson. Wow. I'm going to need a minute to wrap my head around this."

"I understand. I'm not getting in touch because I want anything other than to know you. I've wondered about you all my life."

"It's unreal to me that Millie wouldn't have reached out to me. She knew I was going home to the Minneapolis area after I got out of the navy."

"I wish I knew what she was thinking, but I've never been able to read her. That was part of our problem. Do you… Are you married?"

"I am, and we have four children. The oldest is eighteen, and the youngest is eleven."

I gasp at hearing I have *siblings* as well as cousins. "Wow."

"Do you have other siblings?"

"No," I say softly. "But I've always wanted them."

"This is unreal, Sofia. All this time… I'm just stunned."

"I'm sorry to do this to you. Like I said, I just wanted to know you. I'd understand if this is all you're able to do."

"Don't be ridiculous. Now that I know you're out there, of course I'm going to want to see you and your son and… Well, God, Sofia… You're my *daughter*."

I blink back tears at how emphatically he says that while sensing my entire life is about to change in ways I never could've imagined before today.

"I need to speak to my wife, but can you come to Minneapolis? I'll send plane tickets for you and your son."

"I, uh, you should talk to your family first."

"What's there to say? This happened long before I met my wife, and I had no idea you existed until today. They'll be as surprised as I am, but it's not going to be a problem."

Glancing at Nico, I say, "I… I'd love to meet you and your family. I just need to figure out when I can do it with work and Mateo's school."

"Call me when you know, and we'll make it happen. I'm so glad you got in touch, Sofia. I only wish I'd known about you before now. I… I would've been there for you."

My throat is so clogged with tears and regret that I can barely speak. "That means a lot. Thank you."

"You have my number. Call me anytime."

"I will. You can call me, too."

"Oh, you'll be hearing from me. That much you can count on. You may get sick of me."

Laughing through my tears, I shake my head. "I doubt that."

"We'll talk again soon, okay?"

"Yes. Okay. Thank you for calling."

"It was my pleasure."

We end the call with more promises to talk again soon.

I fall into Nico's waiting arms, sobbing my heart out. "That was my *dad*."

"So I heard."

"I have *four* siblings!"

"That's more than I have."

"He wants me to come there."

"I heard that, too."

"He said he would've been here for me. Why did she keep him from me?"

"I don't know, honey, but you have to find a way to not let that matter now that you know who he is and where he is and are in touch with him."

"I suppose so, but it's just another reason to have nothing more to do with her."

He kisses my forehead, the tip of my nose, both of my cheeks and then my lips. "I'm so happy for you, sweetheart."

"Will you go to Minneapolis with me?"

"I wish I could. More than anything. But I can't leave work and Milo, and my mom is about to finish treatment. The family will do something to celebrate the end of that nightmare."

"Right. I know. I just wish you could be there with me."

"I do, too, and I would if I could. I hope you know that."

"Of course I do. It's no big deal."

"It's a very big deal, Sofia. Don't play it down. You're going to meet your *father* for the first time in your life."

"My stomach hurts."

"Why, honey?"

"What if he doesn't like me or—"

He stares at me in astonishment. "Doesn't *like* you? He's going to *love* you. How can he not? Anyone would love you. I love you."

I'm shocked to hear him come right out and say that, even if I've suspected he might feel that way for a while now. "I love you, too."

"Really?"

"Yes, really," I say, laughing. "You know I do."

"I sorta hoped you might."

"After everything that's happened, I wouldn't have blamed you if you never wanted to see me again."

"That won't ever happen."

"Still. I wouldn't have blamed you. Instead, you wrapped your strong arms around me and Mateo and did everything you could to protect us and care for us, even when my problems were causing a tragedy for your family. So yes, I love you, Nico. I love you very much."

He wraps his arms around me, and we hold each other for a long time. We're interrupted by my phone chiming with a new text.

Nico releases me so I can check my phone.

"It's my dad." I look up at him, smiling. "That's the first time I've ever said those words."

"I'm so happy for you, babe."

"He says he spoke with his wife and children, and while they're as surprised as he was to hear about me, they'd love to meet me and Mateo as soon as possible. He said he'll send me tickets for whenever I can go."

"You should go now. This week."

"I can't. I have to work. I'll ask Dee if I can go Sunday to Tuesday next week, so I only have to take one day off."

"I wish I could cover your shifts for you so you could go sooner."

"It's nice of you to want to, but Sunday is soon enough." I type in a response to my dad. I have a dad! *Let me check with work about when I can take time off. I'll get back to you later today or first thing tomorrow.*

Sounds good, he replies. *Looking forward to seeing you both.*

Me, too! Thank you so much for being so cool about this. I know it's got to be a shock.

It is, but that's not your fault. I'm glad you reached out.

I realize I'm going to have to tell him about Mateo's cancer surgery and the lingering effects so they aren't wondering about his crooked walk, droopy face or struggles with simple tasks. And I'll have to explain to Mateo who these people are to us.

I think about that as Nico drives me to Mateo's school to pick him up. I bring our laundry to do at Nico's along with some more of Mateo's toys and clothes. I'm aware that we're slowly but surely moving most of our belongings to Nico's despite my desire to keep my own home and independence.

That's so important to me, but the longer I'm with Nico, the more I see that he has no desire to take anything away from me. Rather, he wants to give me things I've never had before, such as safety, security, love and the kind of family I used to dream of for myself before I knew I had one of my own out there somewhere.

Everything about this relationship is different from what I had with Joaquín. My world was very small when I was with him. We saw only his friends and family, never mine. After a while, my friends stopped trying to get through to me. More than one of them told me what he was doing wasn't healthy, but by then, I had a child and no way to support us without Joaquín. With my mother mostly out of the picture, I was well and truly trapped in a situation that more resembled a prison than a marriage.

He wouldn't even allow me to work because he wanted me completely dependent upon him. I see that now. At the time, I was too close to see how completely he overtook my life. I kept all my focus and attention on Mateo, who was the one bright spot in an otherwise dismal existence.

I take a deep breath to fight back the anxiety that comes with reliving that time and then exhale slowly.

Nico gives my hand a squeeze. I love how he always needs to be touching me, even when he's driving me somewhere. "Why the deep sigh?"

CHAPTER 21

SOFIA

"I'm thinking about things that are better forgotten."

"Why are you doing that?"

"Trying not to repeat past mistakes."

"Like what?"

"Getting in so deep with a man that I lose sight of myself."

"I'd never let that happen. I love yourself and the sight of you."

Smiling, I look over at him. "You're nothing like him, and I know that."

"Gee, thanks."

"I'm serious," I say with a laugh. "You're not going to suddenly turn into a control freak, are you?" I learned that expression from a friend who was married to a man like Joaquín.

"Nope."

"But the thing is, I didn't expect him to either. He wasn't like that when we first got together. The changes happened slowly, and I was so caught up in Mateo and motherhood and everything that comes with it that I missed the signs. By the time I figured out what'd happened, I was completely isolated from everyone in my life, had no access to money or resources and was stuck in a nightmare."

He tightens the grip he has on the steering wheel as his jaw pulses with tension. "I hate that he did that you."

"I let him do it."

"No, you didn't," he says in a harsh tone. "Do not blame yourself."

"I appreciate that you're always on my side, Nico, but I *did* let it happen. I put up with his bullshit for so long that he didn't see any limits to what he could do. If I had fought back, he might not have gone so far with it."

"Or he might've killed you and/or Mateo. You did what you had to do to survive. Don't ever second-guess what you might've done to appease a guy who'd do what he did to Milo."

"I guess, but I still wish I'd been less of a doormat with him."

"You were afraid for yourself and your child. Maybe you didn't see it as fear at the time, but deep inside, you knew you needed to be careful with him. And he worked that fear to get what he wanted."

I think that over for a second or two. "I guess that's true."

"It *is* true. You were afraid of him long before he gave you actual reasons to be, or you never would've put up with his crap."

"I'm different now than I was then."

"How so?"

"Since Mateo got sick, my life has changed in every possible way. After that day at the clinic, Maria went home and told your family about us. Your grandmothers came swooping in with money and a job and food and everything we needed. They completely changed my life. They gave me the resources and the confidence to file for divorce through a lawyer who comes into the restaurant every week and to be truly independent for the first time. I'm nothing like I was before that. I hate to think I have Mateo's illness to thank for changing things for the better, but it did that for us. It woke me up to what I'd been allowing in my marriage, and thanks to your grandmothers, I was able to do something about it."

"What happened when you told him you were leaving?"

"I never told him. I just did it. I had only just secured a job and an apartment when Mateo got sick, and I was so afraid I was going to lose it all. Then your grandmothers showed up with everything we needed, including an even better job than the one I'd found for myself. One of our regular customers is a lawyer and had Joaquín served with divorce papers. The protective order came later, when he kept showing up at my place without being invited or having visitation with Mateo. And I couldn't believe when the court said he could have him one night a week. He never did a thing for him and had no business having him. I was terrified the first few times, especially because of how fragile Mateo was after his surgery. Joaquín had no interest in his condition except to say that whatever they did to him fucked him up and we ought to sue."

"What an idiot."

"You have no idea what an idiot he is. He ranted to every doctor, including Jason, about what was done to his kid. I'll never forget what Jason said to him. 'I saved your child's life. If you want to sue me for that, feel free.'"

Nico's laugh rings through the truck cab and makes me smile. "That's awesome. Good for him."

"It was all I could do not to laugh in Joaquín's face. He made such a fool of himself. I was so embarrassed after everything Jason had done for us—for free, too. I made sure he knew Joaquín didn't speak for both of us."

"I'm sure Jason knew that. He's one of the smartest guys I've ever met."

"He told me not to worry about it. I guess he sees this a lot with parents who expect their kids to come out of brain surgery the same as they were before, with no deficiencies." I look over at him. "Is that the right word?"

"Yep."

"I had to look it up the first time he used it so I could understand what he meant. I cried a lot after I saw that it meant Mateo might have problems for the rest of his life."

"But at least he'll *have* a life, right?"

"Yes. I've tried to tell myself that's what matters but watching him struggle to get back what's been lost has been hard."

"I know. It's been hard for me to see him struggle, and I'm not his parent."

"I wanted him to have a better life than I had."

"He does because he has you. You're making his life better every day just by being there for him. He knows how lucky he is. His eyes follow you around the room. He always wants to know where you are."

"I've seen that, too. Ever since the judge made him spend time with Joaquín, he's been more anxious than ever. I was so afraid that Joaquín would take off with him or worse... That first night he was over there, I was so scared. Joaquín has cousins in Panama and Mexico. I imagined him taking Mateo and going somewhere that I could never find him."

"God, that's awful, Sofia. I'm so sorry you went through that."

"I cried for hours after Mateo got home, which only scared him more than he already was."

"Who could blame you?"

"I hate what Joaquín did to Milo, but I'm glad he's not getting out of jail anytime soon."

"Milo will tell you it was worth getting shot if it makes things better for you and Mateo."

"That's insane. Don't say that!"

"That's how he is."

"Do you think I could see him?"

"Sure. You can come with me when I go in this afternoon. I'm sure there'll be someone in the waiting room who can keep an eye on Mateo for a minute."

"If there isn't, we'll wait there for you."

"I'll go in and see him, and then you can."

"Okay." Despite what Nico says, I'm nervous about seeing Milo. The rest of the family has been kind to me after the shooting, but I wouldn't blame him if he hates me for it. He nearly lost everything because of my ex-husband.

When we get to Mateo's school, I'm shocked to see Joaquín's mother standing next to her car in the parking lot.

"What?" Nico asks, tuning in to my discomfort.

"Joaquín's mother."

"Is it weird for her to be here?"

"She's never once been here to pick up Mateo."

"Is there any chance she's armed?"

"I don't think so."

"But you're not sure?"

"I'd be very surprised if she is. She doesn't approve of her son's choices."

"Should I call Miguel?"

"No, I'll talk to her if you watch for Mateo. He comes out with his aide, Lauren."

"I'll watch for him, but if you need me, scream your head off."

"What does that mean? 'Scream my head off'?"

He does an impression of screaming with his head bobbing all around that makes me laugh.

"Got it."

"Be careful."

"I will."

I get out of his truck and walk over to talk to Marisol, who has always been a friend to me even in the worst of times with Joaquín. "What're you doing here?" I ask her in Spanish.

"I was hoping to see you and wasn't sure where else I could find you. I heard you're not staying at home."

"I'm not, because it isn't safe for me to be there with your son and his family shooting at people I care about."

"Joaquín says they didn't shoot anyone," she says tearfully. "He would never do something like that."

"The police have it on video, Marisol. They can prove it was them."

She breaks down into quiet sobs. "You drove him to it! You left him and took his child!"

"I left him because he was cruel to me, and you know that. You saw it and even criticized him for the way he treated me. Imagine what it was like when you *weren't* there. I saved myself and my son by leaving him."

"This isn't him. He's not someone who would shoot someone."

I don't reply to that because what can I say? What mother wants to be told her son is a psychopath who'd shoot an innocent person?

"Who is this man you're with?"

"His name is Nico. His brother is the one who was shot. They thought Milo was Nico. They were trying to kill him because I'm happy with him."

"You're still married. Maybe that's why he was upset."

"I've filed for divorce, which will be final anytime now. I'm free to see other people, as he is as well."

"He doesn't want anyone but you!"

"I'm no longer available to him, Marisol. He treated me badly, and you know it!"

"Is everything all right?" Nico asks.

I turn to find him there, his hand on Mateo's shoulder.

"Abuela!" Mateo rushes into his grandmother's outstretched arms.

"Hola, mi niño. ¿Como esta?"

"Bien."

"Let's go home, Mateo," I say.

"Where are you staying?" Marisol asks as she kisses the top of Mateo's head and releases him.

"They're staying with me until it's safe for them to go home," Nico says.

"My son is locked up for God knows how long."

"It's not just him, Marisol," I say. "You know how the rest of them are. They think I caused all this when all I did was decide I no longer wanted to be married to your son, which was my right. If you care at all about me or your grandson, you should spread the word for them to leave us alone."

"They won't listen to me."

"You could at least try, unless you want their next bullet to hit someone you care about." Over Mateo's head, I point to him and give her a pleading look. "Please. Tell them to leave us alone."

"I'll do what I can. Will you let me see him?"

"Of course I will. You're his abuela. You can see him anytime you want to if you respect me and my choices."

"I told him…" Tears run down her pretty face, which is marred by dark circles under her brown eyes. "I told him for years to treat you better, but he never listened to me. I hope you know…" Her gaze darts between me and Nico and then back to me. "The boy I raised never would've done something like this."

"No one blames you, Marisol."

She pushes her fist into her chest. "*I* blame me. He's my son. His father was never in his life. He had no one to teach him how to be a good husband and father. I tried…"

I step toward her and give her a hug. "I know you did. He made his own choices, and now he must pay for them."

"Lo siento mucho, cariño."

"Gracias. Te llamaré pronto." Her apology means a lot to me. I promise to call her soon.

She hugs and kisses Mateo and tells him to be a good boy. "Te amo."

"Te amo, Abuela."

Nico puts his arm around me as we walk to his truck.

"Mama, why is Abuela sad?"

"She misses us." I help him up and into the truck, buckling him into his booster seat. "Did you have a good day?"

He nods. "Can we swim today?"

"Absolutely," Nico says, smiling at us from the front seat.

Mateo's smile lights up my world. All I want is for him to be happy and safe, and I'm extremely thankful to Nico for giving us both those things.

NICO

I love playing in the pool with Mateo. He's so happy to be swimming that he doesn't care that I make him do exercises, like holding on to the side and kicking his legs or doing jumping jacks in the water. He's up for whatever I suggest and seems to soak up my attention like an eager little sponge.

He's the cutest little guy, and I love every minute I spend with him.

When I go underwater and come up with him on my shoulders, he screams with laughter.

He grips my hair and holds on for dear life.

"Don't make me bald!"

That has him laughing again. Suddenly, I drop us both underwater, and we come up sputtering. I realize he's laughing even as he coughs.

"Again!"

I do it no less than a hundred times. It's better than any workout at the gym. By the time I deposit him on the side of the pool, we're both exhausted, but in a good way. "We have to get ready to go see my brother, Milo, at the hospital."

"Why is he in the hospital?"

"He got shot."

His cute little eyebrows come together as he thinks about that. "How come?"

"We're not sure. It was an accident, but he's getting better."

"Are you scared?"

"Not as much as I was before we knew he was going to be okay."

"I'm glad he's going to be okay. He's nice."

"Yes, he is. He's the nicest person I know."

"You're nice, too."

The compliment means the world to me. "Thanks, buddy. Let's go get dressed so we can go to the hospital."

"Can we swim again later?"

"Maybe." Maria has a pool, but I don't want to make promises I might not be able to keep. "We'll see what happens."

Forty minutes later, the three of us arrive at the hospital and make our way to the ICU, where Maria, my parents, grandmothers, aunt and uncle are gathered.

"There's my pal Mateo," Nona says, reaching a hand out to him.

Mateo crosses the room to her and gives her a hug.

I always love my Nona, but I appreciate her more all the time when I witness the way she and Abuela have opened their hearts to Sofia and Mateo.

"How is he today?" I ask my dad.

"He's good but starting to get sick of being stuck in bed. Jason says a couple more days, and then he can start to move around a bit."

I feel for my brother. That would drive me crazy, too. "Could Mateo stay with you guys for a few minutes?" I ask. "Sofia would like to see Milo."

"Of course," Nona says. "He's fine with us. Dee is in with him now, but they've been letting us go in bunches now that he's doing better."

"Okay, thanks." I take hold of Sofia's hand and lead her toward Milo's room.

From the hallway, we hear laughter coming from him and Dee.

"What's so funny?" I ask them.

"Dee is making me laugh even when I told her not to."

"She never has done what she's told," I reply.

"Look who's talking," Dee retorts.

I glance at Sofia and catch her eyes going wide at the sight of the halo surrounding Milo's head and realize I should've prepared her for what she was going to see. "Jason says that's so he can't move his neck while it's healing. He says it looks much worse than it is."

"Easy for him to say," Milo says. "He's never been imprisoned in one of these contraptions."

"Milo," Sofia says softly, her voice wavering with emotion. "I'm so, *so* sorry this happened to you."

He raises his hand.

She puts her hand in his as I try not to bawl like a baby.

"I don't blame you, sweetheart," Milo says in the kind way that's so him. "You had nothing to do with this. I blame my brother."

That hits me like a punch to the gut. "*What?*"

"Haha, gotcha. You should've seen your face." Milo's laugh sounds different since he can't let loose like usual. "Stop looking so mopey, you guys, and stop blaming yourselves. You didn't do this.

I'm gonna be fine, and the guys who did it are locked up. That's all that matters, right?"

Sofia nods, but I can see the torment that remains in her expressive eyes.

I put my arm around her. "We'll let you get some rest, bro."

"I'll be there to help you with anything you need when you get home," Sofia adds. "For as long as you need help."

"Thank you. That's very nice of you. Take care of him until I get home. He needs constant supervision."

That makes me laugh and roll my eyes, even as I'm thrilled to hear Sofia say she plans to help with Milo when he gets home. That means she'll be sticking around, which, other than Milo making a full recovery, is all I want. "Whatever you say."

"Don't worry," Sofia says in a grave tone. "I'm keeping a close eye on him."

Milo flashes a dirty grin. "I'll bet you are."

"A *very* close eye," I add.

"That was unnecessary," Milo says.

"We'll be back tomorrow."

"I'll be here."

Sofia places a kiss on the back of Milo's hand. "Thank you for not dying and not being paralyzed."

"You're welcome. And stop feeling guilty right now, or we're going to be in the biggest fight ever. You hear me?"

Smiling even as tears fill her eyes, she nods. "I hear you."

"Good. Now go away. The nurses will be in soon to give me a sponge bath. It's the highlight of my day."

"Perv."

"Hey, Nico?"

"Go talk to him," Sofia says. "I'll meet you in the waiting room."

"All right." I turn back to him. "Yeah?"

"What I said to her goes for you, too. Quit blaming yourself. I was glad to help you out the other night, and even knowing what was going to happen, I'd still do it, because I'd hate to have anything happen to you."

211

"Then you know how I feel seeing you in the hospital because of me."

"It isn't because of you, and unless you want to be in a big fight with me, too, cut that shit out. Okay?"

"Yeah, sure. Whatever you want."

"That's what I want."

"You got it."

"Say it like you mean it."

"I mean it. Now shut it and have your sponge bath."

"Dude, it's the best. You ought to try it sometime."

"I'll take your word for it. See you tomorrow."

"Later."

I walk into the waiting room where the family is gathered. "Yeah, he's totally fine."

"Busting balls and giving orders," Maria says. "The baby of the family thinks he's the boss of us. We'll put him back in his place when he gets out of here."

"Yes, we will," Dee says.

"Now I gotta go home and get ready to feed you all," Maria says. "See you at the house in a bit?"

I give my sister a hug as she goes by me. "See you then."

"If we get a minute later, can I talk to you about something?" Sofia asks Dee.

"I'm free right now."

Sofia's eyes dart around the room as if she's not sure she should tell everyone her news.

"They'd want to know, sweetheart."

"Is something wrong?" Mom asks.

"No, nothing is wrong," Sofia says. "In fact, it's good news. I found my father after wondering about him all my life." She tells them about posting on Facebook and how easy it was to find him. "He lives in Minnesota and wants me and Mateo to visit him as soon as possible."

"Are we going on a plane, Mama?" Mateo asks.

"We are. Doesn't that sound like fun?"

"When can we go?"

"That's what I wanted to ask Dee."

As the general manager of Giordino's, Dee makes the schedule, among many other duties that will eventually free up Vincent and Vivian to spend more time traveling and doing things other than working.

"That's amazing news, Sofia," Dee says. "You have to go as soon as possible."

"I have to work this week, but I was hoping to maybe go Sunday to Tuesday of next week and only take Tuesday off."

"I'll take your shifts and give you the tips," Dee says. "You need to meet your dad. Is there other family, too?"

"He's married with four other kids."

"You have *four* siblings!" Nona says. "How exciting. I agree with Dee. Don't wait. Go as soon as you can. We'll cover for you and make sure you get paid."

"Who are you people?" Sofia asks softly. "The way you always put others first... I've never known anyone like you."

"You're one of us now, cariño," Abuela says. "And I agree with Dee and Livia. This is such amazing news. You need to go right away and meet your family. We'll cover your shifts."

"Thank you all so much. Not just for this, but for everything. I wouldn't have blamed you if... Well..."

"We know who shot Milo, honey," Dad says. "And we know who *didn't* shoot him. I'm sure I speak for my entire family when I tell you we're deeply grateful that you and Mateo are no longer with him. Oh, and one other thing. Everyone is right. You should go meet your dad as soon as possible."

I've never loved my dad more than I do in that moment, when he says exactly what Sofia needed to hear. "We'll see you guys at Maria's?"

"We'll be along after a bit," Dad says. "We want to spend more time with Milo first."

"Can you give me a ride?" Dee asks me. "I took an Uber here so Wyatt and I would only have one car at Maria's later."

"Sure. Let's go."

CHAPTER 22

SOFIA

Once again, the Giordino family has amazed me with their generosity. What must it have been like to grow up in a family that loves and supports one another the way they do? I can only imagine. But I'm thankful to have them in my life—and Mateo's—now. It's weird to think about how the day I found out he had a brain tumor was in some ways the luckiest day of our lives because it brought us to the Giordinos.

Life is funny that way. That out of something so dreadful could've come so much good is simply amazing.

When we're in Nico's truck on the way to Maria's, I send a text to my father. I still can't believe I can text my *father. Hi again. My employers want me to come see you as soon as possible. Mateo could miss a little school, so maybe Friday to Monday? If that doesn't work for you, we can do it another time.*

At a red light, I pass my phone to Nico. "Did I get everything right?"

"You sure did. A-plus."

"Thank you." I take the phone from him and send the text, holding my breath as I wait to hear back from him.

He responds two minutes later. *Let me see what I can do for flights and get back to you. Send me your full names and birthdates (with the year). And you can come anytime on Friday?*

Yes, we can, and here's our info.

After I send everything to him, he sends back a thumbs-up emoji.

"All good?" Nico asks me.

"So far. He's finding flights. I've never been on an airplane."

"No? You'll love it. I wish I could go with you."

"Why can't you?" Dee asks from the backseat.

"Work, Milo, Mom, Dad, etcetera."

"You should go with them. Wyatt, Austin and Dom would cover your rides. I know they would."

"I can't ask them to do that."

"You're not asking them. I am."

"Dee! Don't. It's too much to ask."

"No, it isn't, and I already did. Wyatt responded right away. He said, 'Tell me when and where, and I'm there.' Austin said he loves to drive and would be happy to do it. Just give him the deets."

I can see that Nico is overwhelmed by their willingness to help, as am I. "What about Milo?" he asks his sister, glancing at her in the mirror.

"In case you haven't noticed, there are a lot of people around who can help with him," Dee says. "You're going to Minnesota with Sofia and Mateo."

"This family," I say again, because they'll never stop amazing me.

"It's what we do," Dee says. "It's what family does for family." After a pause, Dee says, "Dom's in, too. There you go. Three volunteers to cover your rides. You're all set."

"Are you okay with this?" Nico asks when we're stopped at another red light.

"Yes, of course. I want you to come."

He releases a deep breath. "I want to go. You shouldn't be alone for this. I mean, other than Mateo, of course."

"I know what you mean, and I'm so glad you're coming. Let me just text my dad."

"Tell him I'll get my own ticket on the same flights."

I type the message conveying the update, debating for a second as to how I should refer to Nico. In the end, I call him my boyfriend.

I've got it, my dad replies. *Send me his full name and birthdate.*

"He says he's got it and asked for your full name and birthdate."

Nico gives me the info, and I pass it on to my dad.

"Your dad sounds like a good guy." Dee reaches forward to squeeze my shoulder. "I'm so happy for you, Sofia."

"Thank you. I still can't believe all this."

"It's very exciting."

"We're going on an airplane!" Mateo adds.

"That's all he cares about. The grandfather, aunts and uncles are secondary."

"He'll be glad to meet them when you get there," Dee says.

We're almost to Maria's house when my dad texts again asking for an email address to send the tickets to. I give him my Gmail account.

Who should I list in case of an emergency? Probably shouldn't be me since I don't know any of your other people.

When I voice the question to Nico and Dee, she says, "Put me down." She recites her phone number, which I pass along to my dad, telling him she's Nico's sister.

Got it, thanks. Watch for the tickets coming to your email. Can't wait to see you on Friday!

Same. I can't believe this is happening. Thank you for the tickets.

Least I could do. I'll pick you up in Minneapolis. Send me a picture of you guys so I have it, and here's mine.

I send him a recent picture of us and then look at the message he sent. I'll never forget the first time I see his face. I stare at it for so long, I don't even realize that Nico has pulled the truck into Maria's driveway or that they're waiting for me. "This is my dad." I show them the picture.

"You look like him," Dee says.

"I thought so, too, but I wasn't sure if I was seeing what I wanted to see." Although I have my mother's dark hair and light brown skin, the shape of my face and eyes are all him. "I've always wondered who I looked like."

"Now you know," Nico says.

"Mateo, let's go check out Maria's pool, okay?" Dee says.

"Okay!"

She releases him from his booster seat, grabs the bag I packed for him before we left Nico's and takes him by the hand to lead him inside. I appreciate her giving me a minute to get myself together.

"This is *so* exciting," Nico says. "It's so cool to see you happy like this."

"For the longest time, nothing good ever happened in my life, and now I feel like there's something new every day. Well, except for Milo getting shot, that is."

"No one deserves good things more than you do."

"We all deserve it."

"I guess so, but some of us deserve it more, and you're the one who does. You've raised such a great kid almost completely on your own and put up with so much crap from your ex for years. You've seen Mateo through a terrifying illness and are helping him recover. You're a good, hardworking, honest, loving person, Sofia, and good things should happen to good people like you."

"Thank you for that and for coming with me to Minnesota. I know it's a lot to ask with everything else you've got going on and with Milo…"

"He'd want me to go with you guys." He reaches over to caress my face. "I'm glad I don't have to miss you for four days."

"I am, too."

"Wait for me." He gets out of the car and comes around to the passenger side. When he holds out his arms to me, I go to him, wrapping myself around him as he kisses me. "Ah, I needed that," he says a few minutes later.

"So did I." I kiss him again because I can, anytime I want. I'm never afraid to touch him or kiss him or playfully punch him, tell him to shut up when he's being outrageous or anything else that comes to mind. Everything about being with him is so much better than what I've experienced in the past. He's made me see my standards were set far too low.

"Let's go in before my family catches us making out in the driveway," he says before stealing one more kiss.

"Would they be surprised?"

"I doubt it."

NICO

The first thing we hear when we walk into Maria's house is the screaming laughter of Mateo and Austin's daughter, Everly, as they run through the huge house chasing each other. The two of them love to play together. I'm glad that Everly doesn't seem to see that Mateo struggles to keep up with her, even though he's two years older. Maybe that's because she's had her own health struggles, even if she probably doesn't remember them.

"They're so cute together," Austin says. "Can you have a beer, Nico?"

"I'm not driving for hours, so I can have one, and yes, the two of them are adorable."

"So are you and Sofia."

I glance at the man who will become my brother-in-law later this year. When I first heard Maria was seeing the star pitcher, I expected a head case. He's not that at all. "Thanks."

"You seem like a man who's in it to win it."

"I am. I love them both."

"I haven't known you long, but I understand that's a considerable change in your normal routine."

"Don't believe everything you hear."

"I believe every word of it," Austin says, laughing.

"Shut the fuck up."

That only makes him laugh harder, right as Mateo trips and falls on the tile floor.

I'm moving toward him before he crashes down, putting my beer on a table as I go. "You're all right, pal." I squat, bring him into my arms and hold him as he howls. I suspect he's embarrassed more than hurt. "You're fine."

Everly comes over and kneels next to us. "You're okay, Mateo." The adorable little girl runs her hand over his hair, I suspect the way Maria and Austin do when she gets hurt. "Let's ask if we can swim!"

Mateo perks up when she says that.

"Go ahead and get changed. I'll watch you guys." I help Mateo up and hold him for a second until he gets his bearings and runs off with Everly.

I get up off the floor, and Austin hands me my beer. "Good instincts. You were right there when you saw him fall. In my experience, that's either built in or it isn't."

I glance at him. "Are you still busting my balls?"

He grins. "Not this time. You did good."

"What happened?" Sofia asks when she comes from the kitchen with Maria.

"Mateo took a tumble, but Nico handled it like a pro." Austin puts his arm around Maria and kisses her cheek. "How are things in the kitchen?"

"Just about ready, thanks to some excellent help from my sister and your parents."

"They're the best."

"Yes, they are."

Something about Maria seems different, but I can't put my finger on what it is.

Sofia slides an arm around me. "Thanks for handling that."

"No problem."

"It's nice to have someone else looking out for him. I've never really had that before, except for Gladys, but she doesn't live with us."

"I love looking out for both of you."

"Our little boy is growing up," Austin says to Maria.

"I see that," she replies with a laugh.

"Shut up. I'm older than both of you."

"In years, maybe," Maria says. "In other ways, not so much."

"Are you going to let them talk to me this way?" I ask Sofia, who's helpless with laughter. "And quit your laughing. They're not funny."

"Yes, they are."

"No, they're not."

"We are too," Austin says. "Ask anyone."

Dee comes into the room. "Ask anyone what?"

"Whether Maria and I are funny when we're busting Nico's balls."

"Tell me more." Dee rubs her hands together gleefully. "No one deserves to have his balls busted more than Nico does."

"I'm taking my balls outside to watch the kids in the pool, so y'all can fuck right off."

"Me, too?" Sofia asks, gazing up at me with her most innocent look.

I put my arm around her. "Not you, but we'll discuss the matter of loyalty later."

"That'll be fun."

I absolutely adore this playful side of her, and seeing it slowly emerge as she becomes more comfortable with me feels like an achievement. We spend more than an hour seated on the pool deck with our feet in the water, watching over Mateo and Everly as they chase each other around in the pool.

I laugh as Mateo dodges Everly's attempts to dunk him. "They're so cute."

"I love that she sees nothing but a good friend when she looks at him."

"I was thinking about that earlier, and I thought maybe it's because she's had her own health struggles."

"Maybe. It's hard to believe both those angels had cancer."

"And they beat it. That's the important part."

"Yes, it is. I worry about it coming back, though. Jason said there's a twenty percent chance of that."

"That's the worst kind of worry. My mom faces a long road of regular scans and tests to make sure her cancer hasn't recurred."

"It's terrifying. Jason connected me with a social worker at the hospital who talked to me about how to manage the fear. She said to celebrate every good day and try not to think too far into the future."

"That's good advice."

"I think about it anytime I feel the fear coming back."

"You can talk to me about it whenever you feel afraid."

She leans her head on my shoulder. "Thank you."

"I'm here for all of it—the good, the bad, the ugly."

"Hopefully, we've had all the ugly we're going to have for a while."

"God, I hope so."

CHAPTER 23

MARIA

I'm so nervous, I can barely breathe. Austin came up with this idea before Milo was shot. We chose a Monday night when the restaurant would be closed and then debated whether to go forward with everything we planned after the shooting. I asked Milo if he'd ever forgive me if I got married without him there. After I told him the reason why we were moving things up, he told me not to be silly and to get it done while Austin's brothers are in town for the New Year's holiday. He also said he can't wait to be an uncle to my new little one.

It doesn't feel right to be doing this without my little brother there with us, but with Austin set to begin intensive workouts before spring training starts next month and his beloved brothers in town for the last time before the season, it's sort of now or never. I arranged to FaceTime Milo with his favorite nurse, Gianna, helping me. Now all we need is my parents, grandmothers, aunts and uncles to get here so we can do this.

Turns out that spontaneously marrying one of the most celebrated pitchers of his generation comes with a few steps I never would've considered. For example, the Marlins' publicity arm has been notified and a statement prepared to release to the media as soon as we make it official.

I'm in our bedroom changing into the casual white dress I bought for the occasion. It has a halter top that I'm trying to tie in a knot when Austin comes up behind me.

"Allow me."

Happy to turn the task over to him, I watch in the mirror as he ties the knot for me.

He's wearing a light blue button-down shirt with the sleeves rolled up over tattooed forearms.

"Even after all this time," he says, "sometimes I look at you, and I can't believe you're real. That we're real. That it all happened the way it did."

I'm not surprised that his sweet words bring tears to my eyes. Everything does these days. "I look at you and wonder how I ever landed a man as hot and sweet and sexy and amazing as you are."

"You didn't land me. I landed you. You were the far bigger catch."

"Right," I say, laughing now. "As if you and your millions and your limelight and your fancy everything weren't the biggest of big catches."

"None of that shit means anything compared to what you've given me and Ev, and you know it."

I turn to face him, placing my hands on his chest. "I love you both so much. So, so much."

"We love you more."

"No way."

"Yes way."

Shaking my head, I go up on tiptoes to kiss him.

A knock on the door forces me to pull back when that's the last thing I want to do. Kissing him is my favorite thing. "Come in."

Dee, who, along with Carmen, is the only other person who knows what we're up to tonight, sticks her head in. "Everyone is here."

"We'll be out in a sec," I tell her.

She flashes a big, goofy grin before she leaves, closing the door.

"Are you ready?" I ask Austin.

"Only because I get to marry you. No one else would do."

"I should hope not."

His smile is one of the sexiest things about him. "Only you, babe, and you know that, too. You saved my little girl's life, and then you made mine complete. I get to marry my own personal Wonder Woman."

"And I get to marry my own personal Superman."

He kisses my forehead and then my lips. "A match made in heaven. Let's go make it official, shall we?"

"Yes, please."

Holding hands, we leave our bedroom and walk out to the massive great room that opens out to the pool deck. All the people we love best, including Austin's brothers, Asher and Carter, are there, along with the District Court judge Austin asked to preside over the ceremony. As a huge Marlins fan, Judge Donlon was thrilled to be asked.

"What's going on?" my mom asks, her shrewd gaze taking us in as only the mother of four can do.

"If everyone can join us outside, I'll tell you."

Austin picks up Everly, who has been dried, changed and brushed by Dee, and the three of us lead the way to the corner of the yard that overlooks the Intracoastal Waterway, where a spectacular sunset is unfolding.

"Do you have Milo?" I ask Dee.

She hands her phone to me. "Hey, little brother."

"Hey. All systems go?"

"Yep, it's showtime. Milo gave me permission to go forward with plans we made before everything happened." Holding the phone so Milo can see, I turn to the others. "So, it seems I'm an idiot, and we're pregnant."

A shout of excitement comes from the entire group. Mom and Dad hug us all, while Nona and Abuela hug each other.

"I knew it!" Abuela says.

I'm shocked to hear that. "You did not!"

"She told me the other day that you were pregnant and wondered if you knew yet," Nona says.

"How do you do that?" I ask Abuela, shocked.

She shrugs as she hugs me. "I know my kids."

"Daddy, I wondered if you might be willing to give me away."

"Of course," Dad says, looking a bit misty.

"Right now."

Their faces and that of Austin's parents register shock.

I hurry to explain things to them. "We're still going to have a big party at the end of Austin's season, but we wanted to be married before he leaves for spring training, and his brothers are here this week, so…"

The judge walks up to us, waving to the others. "Love your restaurant."

"Thank you," Vincent says, shaking his hand.

I reach out to my dad.

Giving me the sweetest smile, he takes my hand and lets me lead him back toward the pool deck so we can do this right. I grab the gorgeous bouquet of white roses and lilies I stashed earlier under the bar.

Austin's brothers join him next to the judge, with Dee and Carmen across from them. Using his phone, Austin cues the song we chose for me to walk in to, "God Only Knows" by the Beach Boys, which we found when we Googled the top 100 love songs of all time. Neither of us had heard it before, but we agreed it was perfect for us. As the song plays on the Bluetooth speakers he installed in the pool area, I love it even more than I did the first time I heard it.

My dad looks at me with his heart in his eyes. "My beautiful Maria. I'm so proud of you and the family you and Austin are creating together. He's a wonderful guy, and that we get a beautiful granddaughter, too, just makes it even better." He kisses my cheek. "I wish you a lifetime of happiness."

"Thank you, Daddy. Love you so much."

"Love you, too, sweet girl."

I take the arm he offers me, and we walk together toward the loves of my life while Dee captures the proceedings on her phone for Milo, and Jason records for us.

When Dad and I reach the others, he hugs me for a long moment before he releases me and turns to shake hands with Austin, who is holding Everly.

"Take care of my little girl," Dad says, sounding choked up.

"Always, Lo. You have my word."

Dad nods and goes to join Mom and the others gathered around us.

"Family and friends," Judge Donlon says, smiling. "It's a great honor to be asked to preside over this joyous occasion in which two people who were clearly meant to be together pledge their lives and love to each other. Austin and Maria shared their incredible love story with me, and I was so moved to learn they met because of beautiful Miss Everly, who owes her life to Maria."

"Rie!" Everly says, making us all laugh through our tears.

"That Austin and Maria found each other this way is just amazing, and it's my pleasure to help them take the next step on their journey. They've chosen to write their own vows, so I'll turn things over to Austin."

I give my bouquet to Dee while Austin hands Everly to his brother Ash.

As I face the man who will soon be my husband, I see no one else but him.

"I thought I was all set for this until I saw you coming in with your dad, and it kind of hit me in this tidal wave of emotions, going back to the day we got the terrible news about Everly's illness through to the miraculous day when your donation saved her life, and then six months later, when I first got the chance to finally thank you for your selflessness. You gave me back my daughter, and I loved you forever for that before I knew there were so many other reasons to love you. A year after the transplant, when we could finally talk to each other about anything and everything, in a matter of days, you became my favorite person to talk to. I waited for your emails and texts like a lovesick teenager."

A ripple of laughter goes through the group, even as more than a few of them wipe away tears.

"I wanted to know everything about you, and the more I learned, the more I loved your big heart, your huge, crazy family and your amazing career taking care of people who need it so badly. All I wanted was to find a way to be part of your life for as long as I possibly could. And that was before I got to meet you in person."

That generates more laughter.

"Our first night together was the single best night of my life, right up there with the day Ev was born. Nothing in this world will ever compare to knowing, without a shadow of a doubt, that you were the one for me. I knew it before I met you. I knew it for sure that first night, and every day since then has just been further confirmation that there is simply no one else in this world who can compete with Maria Giordino. You've given my daughter the most incredible mother she ever could've asked to have, and we both know how lucky we are. I'm the luckiest guy, and Ev is the luckiest girl who ever lived, because we get to spend the rest of our lives loving you and being loved by you."

Jeez Louise.

Dee hands me a tissue I badly need. He's wrecked me.

"I, Austin Jacobs, take you, Maria Giordino, to be my wedded wife. To love and honor you for the rest of my life, come what may. I'm here for it."

"That was beautiful, Austin," the judge says. "Maria?"

"Am I expected to actually say something after that?"

Everyone cracks up.

"Just skip to the part that makes it official," Austin says, smiling.

"I will, but first, I want to say that you and Everly have made my life complete. I can't imagine a day without the two of you. I think all the time about those first few days we were finally allowed to really talk to each other, and if you were like a lovesick teenager, I can't imagine what I was like. I couldn't wait to hear from you either. Sometimes I still can't believe how fast it happened, but the part I like the best is how we were already in love with each other before we met in person."

"Best thing ever," he says, releasing my right hand to brush the tears off my face.

"Can we have Everly back for this next part?" I ask him.

He turns to retrieve her from his brother.

"Hi, Pooh."

"Rie! Married!"

"I know! I'm so excited to not only marry your daddy, but to adopt you. Do you remember what that means?"

"You'll be my mommy forever."

"That's right, and I will love you and take care of you and protect you and swim with you and do anything else you want to do together. I am so, so happy that I get to have you as my daughter."

She leans toward me, and I wrap my arms around her sturdy little body, thankful every day for her good health. "Love you, Pooh."

"Love my Rie!"

Laughing and crying and happier than I've ever been, I hand her back to Austin, who extends his free hand to me. Looking at them both, I say, "I, Maria Giordino, take you, Austin and Everly Jacobs, to be my husband and daughter. I promise to make our family the most important thing in my life for as long as I live. I love you both to the moon and back a million times."

"That's a lot," Everly says gravely.

She is the cutest thing ever. "It's a whole lot."

"Do we have rings?" the judge asks.

Austin juggles Everly to retrieve them from his pocket and hands his to me.

"Maria?" the judge says.

"Everly, you first." I take her hand and slide the tiny gold ring I bought for her onto her finger. It won't fit her for long, but I plan to put it on a chain when she outgrows it. "Everly, I give you this ring as a sign of my love and devotion to you. I'll always love you, and being your mom is the greatest honor of my life."

"Thank you, Rie."

Austin didn't know about that part, and it destroys him. He frantically wipes tears from his face as he shakes his head. "Well played, love."

Smiling, I say, "You deserve that after what you did to me." I take his hand. "With this ring, I thee wed. I love you forever."

He slides a diamond band that matches my engagement ring onto my left hand. "With this ring, I thee wed. I love you to infinity and beyond."

"Buzz Lightyear!" Everly says, starting another round of laughter.

"With the power vested in me by the State of Florida and Buzz Lightyear, I declare you husband and wife. Austin, you may kiss your bride."

He leans Everly in to kiss my cheek before he puts her down, places his hands on my face and gives me the softest, sweetest kiss.

"Ladies and gentlemen, I give you Austin, Maria and Everly Jacobs!" The judge leads an enthusiastic round of applause.

We accept hugs and congratulations from everyone, and then Dee brings the phone to me. "Milo wants to say something."

"Everyone, shut up," Nico says. "Milo has the floor."

"Hey, guys, that was awesome. Welcome to the family, Austin and Everly. And congrats, Maria. No one deserves this happy ending more than you do. Love you."

"Love you, too, Mi. I'm sorry it worked out this way."

"No worries. It was just like being there."

"We'll be in to see you tomorrow."

"I'll be here."

"See you then." I hand the phone back to Dee and accept a hug from my new mother-in-law.

"Congratulations, honey," Deidre says. "Jeff and I love you as much as Austin does."

"Thank you so much. I feel so lucky to be part of the Jacobs family."

"We're the lucky ones. From the minute you came into our lives, you've blessed us in every possible way."

We hug again, and when we pull back, we're laughing as we wipe away tears.

"Those had better be happy tears," Austin says when he joins us, putting his arm around me.

"They are," I assure him.

He wanted to hire caterers, but I wouldn't hear of that. Saturday night, before all hell broke loose with Milo, I cooked a feast that I now set out for our family, including lasagna, chicken parm, chicken marsala, antipasto, Caesar salad and garlic bread. Dee and Carmen help me put everything out on the long table we set up earlier on the patio.

Austin switches on the outdoor speakers and the lights we strung over the pool area.

"It's perfect," he says. "Absolutely perfect."

"It's all I need. Maybe we should skip the second one. I doubt we could top this."

"I'd be fine with skipping the big production. You're right. This was absolutely perfect, and you want to know why?"

"Well, *yeah*."

Laughing, he says, "Because you're my *wife* now."

"And you're my *husband*."

Our guests start chanting, "Kiss, kiss, kiss."

Naturally, we're happy to oblige them.

No question, this is the best day of my life, and I suspect it's only going to get better from here.

CHAPTER 24

MILO

"*T*hat was amazing," Gianna says after she ends the FaceTime call with Dee.

She got a little misty during the ceremony, discreetly wiping at tears as she held the phone for me.

"Your new brother-in-law is Austin Jacobs! That's so cool."

"He's a good guy."

"And a great pitcher. I can't wait to see him in action this year."

I've already decided she's my dream girl, but if she also loves baseball, I won't be responsible for my actions. "You're a baseball fan?"

"*Huge* baseball fan. I have season tickets to the Marlins and go to as many games as I can. Everyone is super excited about Austin joining the team."

Is it possible to fall in love when you can barely move? Asking for a friend. No, wait, that's not true. I'm asking for myself. "Thanks for helping with the call and all that."

"We couldn't let you miss your sister's wedding."

"I guess they had it all planned before I ended up in here. His brothers were going to be here for only a couple of days." I'm bummed to be missing the family fun, but being able to talk to Gianna makes it better.

"Your family seems cool," she says as she cleans the pins that hold the halo in place and then applies antibiotic ointment.

"They are."

"And *big*."

"Don't make me laugh, but yes, there're a lot of us. And what you've seen here this week is only a fraction. I have other cousins who don't live here."

"Jeez. That must make for a heck of a family reunion."

"It can get pretty crazy. You said you don't have much family?"

"Just my two younger brothers and me. My parents were only children, so no cousins. They died in an accident about four years ago, and my brothers live in California now, so it's just me here."

"I'm so sorry you lost your parents that way."

"Thanks. It was awful, as you can imagine. And my younger brothers weren't too keen on having their nineteen-year-old sister telling them what to do. It was a rough few years until they both went away to school, and I sort of got my life back.

"It was good of you to step up for them."

"It was horrible for all of us, but we survived it. Somehow."

"I couldn't help but notice the wedding made you a little teary-eyed."

"It was so sweet. The two of them are obviously perfect for each other."

"They are. You ought to hear the story of how they met."

"Oh, I know about it. I was there for the ceremony honoring Maria when the Marlins played the Orioles. It's such a great story, the way she saved his little girl, and then they fell in love." She subtly swipes at a tear again as she checks the catheter tubing.

Nothing says *sexy* like, *Hey, babe, can you fix my catheter?* Despite that unsettling thought, I'm undeterred as I try to keep her talking to me. "Are you okay?"

She gives a little shrug. "Weddings are triggering for me."

"Oh God. I'm sorry. I didn't know that when I asked you to help with the call."

"No worries. It's just that my fiancé sort of jilted me. On our wedding day."

"What? Seriously? I'm so sorry, Gianna. Clearly, he was a fool."

Her small smile doesn't quite reach her warm, expressive eyes. "I agree."

"How long ago did that happen?"

"Just over a year now."

"I'm really sorry that happened to you."

"Me, too." The sadness I see in her eyes kills me. "The thing that still bugs me more than anything is if he didn't want to get married, why did he wait until that day to tell me? I mean, we had a church full of people and a reception paid for. Why did he let it get to the point where I'd be humiliated in front of everyone we know, especially when he knew how hard it was for me to even have a wedding without my parents there?"

"I don't know why anyone would do something like that. What did he say?"

"That he woke up that morning feeling certain we shouldn't get married. He said he couldn't explain where the feeling had come from, but it was so strong, he couldn't ignore it."

I'm outraged for her. "And he couldn't have had that feeling *before* you put on the white dress and showed up to the church full of people?"

"Apparently not."

"He's an asshole for doing that."

"So I've been told by everyone in my life. It's taken me a while to let go of the life I thought I was going to have with him. That's a work in progress."

"No one should have to go through something like that. I'm sorry you did."

"Aw, thanks. It's life, you know?"

"No, it's not. It's cruel and unnecessary and cowardly to let something go that far if it's not what you want. You deserved much better than that."

"Thank you."

I keep waiting for her to say she has to check on other patients, but she's not in the usual rush today. "Do you have other patients?"

"No, just you. The ICU is unusually quiet today."

I love being her one and only. *Easy, Milo. You're her only patient. Not her one and only.* My goal is all about keeping her talking.

"How'd you end up getting shot in the neck, anyway?" she asks.

"It was a case of mistaken identity. The shooters thought I was my brother."

"What'd he do?"

"Started dating the soon-to-be ex-wife of one of them."

"That's it?"

"That's it. My brother owns a car service, and he was freaking out because they've been threatening her—and him—and he was afraid to leave her side while she was at work at the family's restaurant."

"Best food ever, by the way."

"I agree. There's nothing better. Anyway, I volunteered to take his rides, they thought I was him, and they shot me."

"That's *insane.* All because he was dating the shooter's ex-wife. People are loco."

"Yep."

"You got really, *really* lucky. I hope you know that. I heard the doctors talking that one millimeter different, and you're either dead or a quadriplegic."

I swallow hard when I hear that. I mean, I knew it was bad, but I hadn't heard it was that close a call.

"And you got lucky because Dr. Northrup was here and could operate. People treat him like a god around here."

"He's married to my cousin Carmen."

"I know. He's an incredible surgeon."

"He is. Do you know Dr. Wyatt Blake?"

"Of course. He's another rock star in this place."

"He's engaged to my sister Dee."

"I saw them here together yesterday. The women in your life sure know how to pick them, huh?"

I haven't given that much thought, but it's true. "I guess so."

"Having Dr. Northrup operate on you probably saved your life and your mobility."

"I feel very fortunate that it wasn't worse. When they asked me to wiggle my fingers and toes, I had no idea how much was riding on that at the time."

"There was a lot of relief when you could do that. Your brother... Nico, right?"

"Yeah, that's him."

"I saw him sobbing like a baby after he saw you for the first time after the surgery. I felt so badly for him."

"He blames himself for me being here. Sofia does, too. That's his girlfriend."

"It's not like they shot you."

"Try telling them that."

"I suppose it's only natural they'd feel guilty. It'll take some time, but they'll get past that, especially when they see you on the road to a full recovery."

"I hope so. Sofia and her son, Mateo, have been great for Nico. He's different since they came along."

"How so?"

"He was a world-class player until he met her. He hasn't so much as glanced at another woman since the first time he saw her."

"Wow. I love that. Sounds like he's found the one."

"I think so, but then this had to happen. I just hope it hasn't effed up things for them, you know?"

"I'm sure they've struggled with it, but are they still together?"

"As far as I know."

"Then they're probably working through it, which is a good test of their bond."

"I hate to be the one testing their bond. I like her for him. She's fantastic, and her son is great, too."

"Just like they're not the ones who shot you, you're not the one who tested their relationship. All the blame goes to the shooters."

"True."

"Did they get them?"

"Yeah, they're locked up. The shooting was caught on video surveillance the cops had in the area."

"Another lucky break. It may not seem like it from where you're sitting now, but Lady Luck has been on your side lately."

As much as I can, I look directly at her, hoping to convey much more than my agreement with her statement. "In more ways than one."

NICO

Watching Maria marry Austin has filled me with a powerful feeling of yearning to have what they do. Well, I can't swing the freaking mansion where they live, but my place isn't bad. It has everything Sofia and I need to make a life together, including the pool Mateo loves. As soon as her divorce is final, I'm going to ask her to marry me.

I let that thought settle for a moment, waiting for something in me to fight back against an idea that would've been comical before I met her. Marriage was for other people. Not me.

But there's no fight back. There's just resolve to make it happen as soon as possible.

As I watch her talk and laugh with my sisters and cousin, I'm thrilled that my family already loves her as much as I do. Even after everything that happened this week, they haven't missed a beat with her and were quick to reassure her that no one blames her for what her ex did. They not only talked the talk, but they've followed through with action, making her feel as welcome as she was before the shooting.

I'm watching her so closely that I notice when her entire demeanor changes after she checks her phone. I get up from the barstool and go to her while making note of Wyatt and Dee pushing Everly and Mateo on the swings. "What's wrong?"

"I got a text from Joaquín's mother. He's asking to see me."

"No way. You don't have to do that, Sofia."

"I know, but he says it's important."

Everything in me rises in protest of her seeing the animal who nearly killed my brother. But the last thing I want to do is behave with her the way he would have by taking away her ability to make her own decisions. "What do you want to do?"

"Not see him. Ever again."

"Then you shouldn't."

"What in the world could he possibly need to tell me at this point, after he nearly murdered my boyfriend's brother?" After a beat, she adds, "Why are you smiling?"

"You called me your boyfriend."

"Nico! Focus."

I put my hands on her hips and bring her in close to me, kissing the top of her head and breathing in the distinctive scent of her hair, the scent of my love. "I'm focusing on the most important thing here, and you calling me your boyfriend is a big deal. You want to know why?"

"Um, sure. Why is that?"

"Because I've never had a girlfriend before."

"That's not true. You've had *all* the girlfriends."

"There have been girls, yes, and women, yes. But never one I would call an official *girlfriend* until now."

"You're thirty-two years old, Nico."

"I'm aware."

"It's weird that you've never had a girlfriend before."

"I never wanted one before I met you. Now that's all I want, but only if it's you, of course."

The withering look she gives me is the one women have been giving men since the beginning of time, and I love it. I love her, and I need her to know that again. Right now. Leaning even closer to her, I whisper in her ear, "You're the only one I've ever loved."

"Nico," she says on a long exhale. "How do you do this to me?"

"What am I doing?"

"You know!"

Laughing, I hug her tightly. "You do what you need to with him. I'll support whatever you decide."

"You won't be mad if I see him?"

"Not if you feel it's something you need to do."

"I think maybe I'll go, for Mateo. Only for him."

"Okay."

She pulls back to look up at me. "This is not how it goes for me. I was ready for you to be mad."

"I'm not going to get mad. Would I like to kill him for what he did to Milo? Yep, but I'd never do that, because he's also Mateo's father. Rather, I'll look forward to seeing him convicted and put away for a long time while I have the honor of raising his son. If you'll allow me to, that is."

She goes completely still, and her face loses all expression.

That's not the reaction I was hoping for.

"Say something."

"You…"

"I want to raise Mateo. I want to marry you. I want to have more babies and a life and everything that goes with that, and I want it with you and him. I want it all, Sofia." So much for waiting for her to be officially divorced before I propose to her.

"But I'm the first girlfriend you've ever had!"

"And hopefully the last."

"Nobody marries their first girlfriend."

"Some people do. And they live happily ever after."

"You should really think about this."

"I have. It's all I've thought about almost since the day we first met."

"Stop." She tries to get free of me, and I let her go out of deference to what she's been through in the past, not because I want to let her go. "Don't say things like that."

To Dee, I say, "You got him?" I point to Mateo.

She gives me a thumbs-up.

I follow Sofia inside.

She goes straight to the main-floor bathroom and tries to close the door, but I'm right behind her and go in with her and shut the door.

"I want to be alone."

"Why? So you can try to figure out what kind of game I'm

238

HOW MUCH I WANT

playing here? Let me make it clear—I'm playing the game of *life*, Sofia. My life, your life, Mateo's. I want us to be a *family*."

To my great horror, she begins to cry. These aren't the elated tears my sister shed during her wedding. No, these are more of the heartbroken variety. "Talk to me, sweetheart. Why are you so upset?" I notice her hands are shaking, and she's more upset than I've ever seen her, even after Milo was shot.

"I... After everything with Joaquín and what it took me to get free of him... I promised myself I'd never get married again so I'd never be legally bound to a man who could control me the way he did."

I ache over what that son of a bitch put her through. "I get that, and I understand why you'd make yourself that kind of promise after the way he treated you. But I'm not him. I just want to make you and Mateo happy and keep you safe and give you the best possible life and family I can. I'd never want to control you or tell you what to do or keep you from doing things that make you happy. Whatever you want, that's what I want, too."

"And I love you so much for that."

"But?"

"It's hard for me to explain this to you because you haven't been through what I have."

"Will you try?" I want more than anything to understand her at the deepest possible level.

"I, um, when I was with him, I had nothing. No job, no money, no say in anything, no control over any aspect of my life. He was in charge of everything. I took care of Mateo, and that was my role. That and being available anytime he wanted sex. Other than that, I was nothing. I was just there."

"It would never be like that with us. You said yourself everything is different with me."

"It is, but..."

I frame her face with my hands and compel her to look at me. "Whatever it is, just say it, and we'll figure it out."

"You'd want us to live at your house."

"Well, yeah, I mean, unless you hate it."

"Of course I don't hate it. It's a beautiful home. But it's *yours*."

All at once, I get what she's saying. "We can buy something that's *ours*."

"That would be stupid when you have a perfectly good house that you already own. It's just that I'm afraid of going back to a place where I have no say over my own life."

"I know they're just words, but I swear on *my* life that will never happen to you if you're with me. Ever."

"I want more than anything to believe in you and us, but I've learned to be careful giving someone else the legal power to control me."

"I understand. Let me think about it, okay? I'm sure we can figure out something that'll make you feel comfortable."

"Maybe we could just live together or something. Why do we have to get married?"

"I guess we don't have to, but I'd kind of like to. At some point."

"Have you always pictured yourself married?"

"No, never," I say with a laugh. "I had zero interest in marriage until I found someone I couldn't live without."

She smiles and runs her hands over my chest on the way to curling them around my neck. "After everything with him, I wasn't looking for this, for you."

"I wasn't looking for it either, but then there you were, looking so sexy in your waitress uniform, and I had to know you."

We hold each other for a long time, until someone knocks on the bathroom door, forcing us to let go. For now, anyway.

I open the door to my cousin Dom.

"Are you guys doing it in there?"

"No, we're not doing it, so shut up."

"If you say so."

I push him out of the way and lead Sofia back to the party while thinking about the things she said. She goes to check on Mateo while I seek out a beer at the bar. I take the seat next to my dad.

"Where'd you disappear to?" he asks, pushing the dominoes on the bar toward me for a game.

I go through the rote motions of placing tiles, but my heart isn't in it. "I was inside talking to Sofia."

"Everything all right?"

"I think so. We were talking about getting married."

Dad's eyes go wide with surprise and delight. "Is that right? Well, that's excellent news, son. She's a lovely young woman."

"Yes, she is, but she's been through some tough shit, you know?"

"Having seen what her ex-husband is capable of, I can only imagine what she's been through," Dad says, sipping from a cocktail glass of rum as he ponders his next move with the dominoes.

"It was probably far worse than we think."

"I have no doubt."

"I need to give her some sort of assurance that it'll never be like that with me. I mean, I've told her I have no desire to control her or keep her from pursuing her dreams, but those are just words."

"You need a grand gesture."

"I know, and I was thinking… What would it take to make her a co-owner of my house?"

Dad looks at me, unblinking, for several seconds. "Are you sure about that, Nico? That's a risky move."

"Not if it would give her the security she needs to feel comfortable."

"I want you to think long and hard about this, son. She'd own *half* your house."

"I know, and that's the point." The more I think about this idea, the more I like it. "Could Mom help me with the paperwork?"

"She could, but I'm not sure about this, Nico."

"Why not? Didn't Austin and Maria buy this place together even though he paid for it?"

"Yes, I suppose they did, but—"

"No buts, Dad. If Sofia and I had been married when I bought the house, we would've bought it together. This is just adding her after the fact."

Dad gives me a small, satisfied smile.

"What?"

"You. That's what. I wondered if I'd ever see the day."

"What day?" I ask, exasperated.

"The day when you'd lose your heart to someone. And now that it's happened, I couldn't be happier about who you've chosen or how you're trying to make her comfortable in your life. Even though it's a risky move, I appreciate the reasons you want to do it."

"The house means nothing to me compared to her and Mateo."

"Then you're doing it for all the right reasons. Talk to your mother. She can draft it up for you. And while we're talking about this stuff, you should know that I have my grandmother's engagement ring if you'd like to give it to Sofia."

"Really?"

"Yeah. I've been saving it for you but figured it would probably go to Milo when it didn't seem like you wanted to get married."

"Wow. I had no idea."

"Because you've never come close to getting married, so why would you need to know about the ring? You should come by and look at it and make sure you like it for her."

"I'll do that. Thank you, Dad."

"You're welcome." He takes another sip of his drink and places another tile. "This week has shown us that we never know what's coming, and we need to live for the moment. This moment, right now, it's all there is, and if she's the one for you, then you're a lucky man."

"I know I am, and I want to give her all the comfort and security she's never had."

"That makes her very lucky, too."

"We both are, and we know it."

"Let me know if there's anything I can do for you."

For the first time in years, I kiss my dad on the cheek. "You've already given me everything I could ever need."

"Love you, son."

"Love you, too."

CHAPTER 25

SOFIA

*A*gainst my better judgment, I agree to see Joaquín, but only
because he's Mateo's father. I can't think of a single other
reason to waste a couple of hours I'll never get back. Nico is upset
about it, but he's keeping his thoughts to himself and letting me
decide on my own how to handle Joaquín's request, which I deeply
appreciate.

Elena set me up with an attorney she knows to go in with me.
I'm due to meet him outside the city jail at ten, and when I'm ready
to go, I find Nico in the room he uses as an office, working on his
laptop.

"I'm, ah, going now. I'll be back right after."

"Okay," he says, giving me a wary glance. "Drive carefully."

"I will." I start to walk away, but I can't leave it this way with
him. "Nico."

He looks up again, his expression guarded.

"I'm sorry you're upset that I'm doing this."

"I'll be fine if you are. Be careful, Sofia. I'm worried this is a
setup."

"They know by now how much trouble they're in. They'd be crazy to add to it."

He has nothing to say to that.

"I'll be careful. I promise. I love you."

"I love you, too."

I hate the tension that's arisen between us over the last few days, since I decided I'd see Joaquín before we leave on our trip tomorrow. Today was the soonest we could make it happen, so Nico and I have had to sit in this uncomfortable place while we worked and took care of Mateo and visited Milo. His mom is in her last week of treatment for breast cancer, so I made dinner for his parents yesterday, and we took it there while Mateo was at school.

Nico disappeared into the office with his mother for half an hour while I talked to his dad. After they came out, he wouldn't tell me what they talked about, which has only added to my stress.

He said we'd talk about it after Minnesota.

Because it's winter there, I had to buy some warmer clothes and coats for Mateo and me, which was not in my budget. Everything feels so unsettled, and my stomach hurts most of the time when I think about seeing Joaquín, flying to Minnesota, seeing my father for the first time, meeting my half siblings…

Not to mention all the complicated feelings I have for Nico and worrying about Milo. It's no wonder my head is spinning.

A few weeks ago, I heard Dee use that expression and asked her what it meant. Now it's one of my favorites. My head spins a lot.

I park at the city jail on Northwest 13th Street, use an app on my phone to pay for parking and meet with William, the attorney Elena hooked me up with who's going in with me. She thought it would help me to navigate the jail to go with someone who knows his way around.

He shakes my hand. "Nice to meet you. Right this way."

By the time we're seated in a waiting room, my hands are trembling from the experience of entering the jail, producing identification, walking through a series of locked doors and ending up in a room right out of a movie, with seats in front of glass with old-style phones to use for talking to the prisoner.

William stands about six feet from me by the door, there if I need him.

We wait ten minutes before Joaquín appears, wearing an orange jumpsuit. His hands and feet are shackled. He looks pale and possibly scared as he waits for the guard to unlock his hands. The dark hair that's usually kept stylish with pomade is a greasy mess, as if he's been pulling on it and hasn't showered for days.

When he sits in the chair and reaches for the phone, I do the same, nearly dropping it because I'm so nervous. He speaks to me in Spanish. "No estaba seguro de que vendrías." *I wasn't sure you'd come.*

"Vine por Mateo." *I came for Mateo.*

"You need to tell them it wasn't me, that I never could've done something like this."

I'm stunned that he would say that. "They have video."

"They can't see who was in the car, just that it was Diego's car. They can't prove I was in the car."

"You shot an innocent young man."

"I shot the guy you're banging."

I'm outraged on behalf of Milo—and Nico. "It wasn't. It was his brother, who has nothing to do with any of this."

He shrugs, as if that information doesn't mean a thing to him. It probably doesn't. "If you tell them it wasn't me, that'll matter."

"Why would I do that when someone I care about was nearly killed?"

His dark eyes turn hard in a heartbeat, and the old, familiar fear comes back in a wave of memories I wish I could forget. "You'll do it if you know what's good for you."

"Is that a threat, Joaquín? Are you going to get someone to finish what you started? Are you going to murder the mother of your child or some other innocent person because I don't want you anymore?"

The look he gives me indicates he'd love to see me dead. "If you tell them I wouldn't do this, maybe your son won't have to grow up without his father."

245

"Oh, he'll have a father, but it won't be someone who'd try to kill an innocent man because his wife dumped him."

"You can't just replace me."

"Yes, I can. You're in prison, where you belong and where you're going to be for a long time because you *did* do it. I can't help you. I won't help you."

"All it would take from me is one word to my boys, and you and your fancy Giordino boyfriend are dead. Is that what you want for Mateo?"

"Aren't you in enough trouble already?"

"What do I care? They're charging me with attempted murder. What's one or two more?"

I stare at him in complete amazement that he'd look me in the eye and threaten to have me—and Nico—killed. "When did this happen to you? When did you become capable of killing people?"

"It happened when my wife fell out of love with me."

"No, it happened long before that, and it's *why* I fell out of love with you. Because you became someone I don't recognize. I can't help you. I won't help you." I put the phone down and get up, walking away even as he screams at me to come back.

Even though I'm shaking as old traumas resurface, I keep moving toward the door where William waits for me. "He's asking me to vouch for him and to say there's no way he would've tried to kill anyone, and if I don't, he's going to kill me and my new boyfriend."

"Wait. He actually *said* that?"

"He did."

"You need to notify the police."

I was afraid he would say that. Sighing, I nod in agreement. "Sergeant Miguel Silva is who we've spoken with before." I text Nico and ask for his number.

He sends it without comment or question.

I put through the call to Miguel, and when he answers, I tell him who I am and what happened.

"Jeez, these guys never learn, do they? I'll get the paperwork started to file additional charges. Are you working tonight?"

246

"I am, and Nico is, too."

"I'll notify Patrol and have some officers assigned to you both for a few days."

"We're leaving tomorrow morning for the weekend. We'll be back Monday."

"Got it. That's good. Hopefully, his attorney will advise him to shut his mouth."

"Nico will be in a car at work tonight."

"We'll keep eyes on him. Try not to worry."

Right. Try not to worry when Joaquín threatened his life. I understand how lucky we are that Milo wasn't killed or paralyzed. We might not get lucky a second time.

These are the thoughts in my mind as a police officer follows me to Mateo's school and then to Nico's home.

Gladys is in the kitchen, pouring herself a glass of tea, when we come in.

Mateo drops his backpack and goes to give her a hug. "I want to swim."

"We will," Gladys says, "but first you need to unpack your bag."

He reluctantly goes to get the backpack, removes his lunch box and hands it to me along with the papers that come home every day. "Now can I swim?"

"Go get changed," I tell him.

"What happened?" Gladys asks after Mateo rushes from the room.

"He wanted me to tell the police there's no way he could've shot Milo, and when I said I wouldn't do that, he said one word from him to his boys and Nico and I are dead."

Gladys gasps. "Dear God."

"The police are aware and are watching. But I feel sick."

"Over what?" Nico asks when he comes into the room.

Gladys squeezes my arm. "I'll go check on Mateo."

When we're alone, I force myself to look at Nico and tell him what happened at the jail.

His expression never changes as he hears his life has been threatened—again.

"I was thinking that we should take a break until, you know—"

"Stop."

"But, Nico—"

"No, Sofia. We're not going to let them drive us apart. That's what he wants. He knows he's in deep shit, and he's still trying to control you even from jail. Don't let him do that."

"He meant it, though. You weren't there. You didn't see how he said it."

"We can't let him do this to us. It's what he wants. He has no power in there, and he knows it. The only power he has is to fill you with fear."

"It worked. I'm afraid."

"What did Miguel say?"

"More charges will be filed."

"That's good."

"And they're putting officers on both of us. I told him we're due to leave town for the weekend tomorrow, and Miguel said that would give them time to track down his friends."

My phone rings with a call from Miguel.

"Hello?"

"Sofia, this is Sergeant Silva again. I wanted to tell you that we've notified the prosecutor of Joaquín's threats this morning, and they're asking the judge to limit his access to phone calls and visitors considering the threats."

"Oh, that's good news," I say on a long exhale.

"Now, that's not to say he can't get word to his friends through other people in the jail, but it would make it much more difficult."

"Thank you so much. I feel better knowing that might happen."

"I'll let you know the minute we hear from the judge and will keep eyes on you and Nico in the meantime. You'll be back from your trip on Monday night?"

"Yes."

"Can you send me your flight information? We'll have officers meet you."

"I'll text it to you."

"Thank you."

"No, thank you. I'm thankful for your help, and I'm so sorry he's doing this."

"You have nothing to apologize for, Sofia. I wish I could say this is the first time I've seen something like this, but sadly, it happens far too often in domestic situations."

"Thank you again for everything."

"No problem. I'll keep you posted."

"Okay."

We end the call, and I'm left feeling completely numb, the way I used to after Joaquín threatened or hurt me.

"What'd he say?" Nico asks.

I update him on the prosecutor asking the judge to limit Joaquín's access to visitors and phone calls. "He said he'll let me know what the judge decides. I also need to text him the information about our trip."

"I'll take care of that."

"Oh, okay. Thanks."

He puts his arms around me. "I know it might not seem like it now, but everything is going to be okay."

"How can you be so sure? You're going to be in your car at work tonight. They know now they got the wrong guy the first time. It might not take an order from Joaquín for someone to decide they should finish the job he started."

"If they have an ounce of sense, they're all scared shitless by the charges Joaquín and Diego are facing. They won't come near me."

"You can't know that!"

"No, I can't, but I suspect that recent events have them running scared. They're hearing that Joaquín and Diego are looking at years in prison. That's going to matter to them." When he sees I'm unconvinced, he adds, "Think about it, Sofia. Why would they go to jail, possibly for the rest of their lives, because their friend or cousin is jealous of his ex-wife's new boyfriend?"

When he puts it that way, I start to feel a tiny bit better.

"With Joaquín and Diego in jail, they're probably fighting over who they're taking orders from now that they're out of the picture."

"That's probably true. They were the ones in charge."

"I bet we're the least of their concerns. They're too busy trying to figure out what Joaquín and Diego had going on so they can take advantage of their absence. People are loyal first and foremost to *themselves*, babe. You can probably bet that Joaquín wasn't just trying to intimidate you. He was probably pulling that crap on a lot of people who are now happy to see him locked up indefinitely."

"I heard from one of the other wives that they've been fighting a lot."

"See? There you go. They're going to be worried about their own families, not his."

I blow out a deep breath. "He scared me."

"I want to kill him for that."

"Please don't do that. I need you here with me."

"That's the only place I want to be."

We're still standing in the kitchen with our arms around each other when Gladys and Mateo return. He's wearing his swimsuit and arm floaties. He stops short when he sees us hugging.

"Ew, were you kissing?"

Nico laughs as he releases me. "We were about to, but then you showed up."

"Gross."

"You won't always think so, pal. How about another swimming lesson before I go to work?"

"Yes!"

I give Mateo a pointed look. "What do you say to Nico?"

"Thank you, Nico."

"My pleasure, buddy."

Nico sneaks me a kiss. "Text me when you get to work, or I'll worry."

"I will."

"Text me nonstop all night, or I'll worry."

"I will."

We smile at each other and steal another kiss.

"Love you," he whispers. "Can't wait for tomorrow. It's going to be so fun, and who needs to get out of town more than we do right now?"

"No one. I love you, too. Thank you for being there for me."

"Always. Mateo, give your mom a hug. She's going to work."

He comes over and gives me the fastest hug possible.

"You can do better than that," Nico says. "Hug her like you mean it."

Sighing, Mateo hugs me again, as tight as he possibly can.

"Love you, boo."

"Love you, too, Mama."

"Be good for Nico and Gladys."

"I will."

I watch as they go outside, the man I love and the little boy who is my world.

"He's a good man," Gladys says.

"Yes, he is."

If anything happens to that good man because of me, I'll die. It's that simple.

CHAPTER 26

NICO

*A*fter a visit at the hospital with Milo, who seems much better today, I'm on edge all night, waiting for Joaquín to make good on his promises, despite what I said to her. At every red light, I find myself glancing at the cars next to me, looking for someone who'd rather see me dead than with Sofia. Between multiple trips to the airport and a run to a Key Biscayne hotel, I cruise past the restaurant. I'm not even sure what I'm looking for, but I'm happy to see a police car parked outside each time I go by.

I put through a call to Miguel.

"Hey, man, how you doing?"

"Pretty good considering my life has been threatened."

"That guy is an idiot. The prosecutor is adding two more felony charges to what he's already looking at. He's handing them their case."

"Any word from the judge?"

"Just now. He's halted all visitation and phone calls for Joaquín and assigned him to the SHU—a special housing unit that takes him out of the general population, so there's no chance he can get his orders out via other prisoners."

"Oh, that's great news. Sofia will be so relieved. She said she'd heard there's been some infighting among his friends."

"We've heard that, too."

"So, they might have other worries besides whether Joaquín's ex-wife has a new boyfriend."

"That's the hope, but we're not taking any chances after what was done to Milo. We'll have cops on you guys until you leave town tomorrow and then when you get back. Joaquín and Diego are due to be arraigned tomorrow on the original charges, and the new charges for Joaquín."

"I'm glad we're getting out of here for a few days."

"What's in Minnesota, anyway?"

"The father Sofia has never met."

"Oh, damn."

"Yeah, she's excited and nervous."

"I'll bet. Well, try to enjoy yourselves."

"Will my family be safe while I'm gone? I worry that if Joaquín already put out the word and they can't find me, they'll go for someone else."

"We've got eyes on all his known associates and officers watching the restaurant, your parents' home, the entrance to your neighborhood and Sofia's building. We're sort of hoping they're stupid enough to show up in one of those places."

My heart aches at the thought of any of my family members in danger because of me. It's unbearable.

"It's going to be fine, Nico. Go on your trip and don't worry. We're not picking up on any sign of them receiving orders from Joaquín, and with him in the SHU, he's on lockdown for the time being anyway."

"Thanks for everything, Miguel."

"You got it. Will you update Sofia about the judge's orders? That'll save me a call."

"I will. No problem."

"Thanks. Have a great trip. I'll keep you posted on any developments."

"I owe you big, man."

"Just doing my job."

When I end the call with him, I leave a message for Sofia, telling her about the judge's orders so she'll get the news as soon as her shift ends. My last run of the night is an airport pickup with a drop-off in Brickell. With my passenger delivered, I head straight for the restaurant, hoping to catch Sofia before she leaves so I can follow her home.

I'm relieved to see her car still in the lot when I pull in. I get out of my car and take a long look around, my heart beating faster than usual. As I head inside through the back door, it occurs to me that anyone could walk in that door with a gun and change our lives forever. I've never had such a thought in this place that's been a second home to me all my life. I hate Joaquín and his threats for making me have it now.

I run into my uncle Vincent outside the kitchen. "Hey," he says, amusement dancing in his eyes. "Fancy meeting you here."

"Whatever. You know why I'm here. How is she?" I called him earlier to inform him about the threats Joaquín made, and he vowed to keep a close eye on Sofia and everyone else.

"We had a busy night, which gave her little time to think about anything other than work."

"That's good. She needed that."

"We all did."

"We're both sorry to have brought this to your door."

He waves away my apology with an impatient gesture. "You didn't do anything and neither did she, so don't take the blame. The only thing that matters is we're all safe, and Milo is on the road to recovery." He squeezes my shoulder. "You look like you're about to blow. Go make yourself a drink and take a chill pill before you have a stroke or something."

I laugh at his hip lingo. "A drink sounds good. Thanks, Vin."

"Anything for you, my friend."

I go behind the bar, which is usually Vincent's territory, and make myself a Tanqueray and tonic with a twist of lime and take it with me when I go to find Sofia.

She's on the Cuban side, talking to customers who've lingered over dessert and coffee. She hasn't noticed me yet, so I stop to watch her laughing and talking as if she doesn't have a care in the world when I know she's riddled with anxiety. I can't wait for her to be rid of that awful fear and to be free of the man who put it there.

As she turns away from the table, she sees me there, and her face lights up with a smile.

I move toward her, full of all-new understanding of why so many of the guys I grew up with have shackled themselves to one woman for a lifetime. That understanding eluded me before her. Now all I want is a lifetime with her.

She hugs me, and I wrap my free arm around her.

"I'm very happy to see you," she says.

"Likewise, my love."

"Tonight was *long*."

"Very long. All I could think about was getting back to you. How much longer are you going to be here?"

"I can leave now. I cashed out my last table and finished my side work a while ago."

"Let's leave your car here and go home together. We can pick it up when we get back from Minnesota."

"Are you sure Vincent won't mind if we do that?"

"He won't mind. I'll let him know."

"I need to grab Mateo's booster seat out of the car so we can take that with us."

"I'll meet you at the back door." I sip from my drink as I go in search of Vincent and find him with Nona at the Italian-side hostess stand. "Hey, do you guys care if we leave Sofia's car here while we're gone?"

"Not at all. Just leave the keys with me in case we need to move it."

"Will do."

Sofia joins us with her purse and keys handy.

I finish my drink, put the glass on a bus tray and take the keys from her. "I'll get Mateo's seat and come back for you. Uncle V wants to keep the keys in case they need to move it."

"Thank you, Vincent and Livia. Thank you for everything this week. I'll never forget your incredible kindness."

"We love you and Mateo, and we're so happy for you that you finally get to meet your father," Nona says. "We hope the trip is everything you want it to be."

Sofia hugs her, and when she pulls back, both women are blinking back tears. "You all… You saved my life and Mateo's. We owe you everything. Thank you for showing me what it means to be part of a family."

"You're stuck with us, sweetheart," Vin says with a warm smile. "Have a wonderful time with your father. Send us pictures."

"I will."

I grab the booster, put it in my truck and go back inside to give Vin the keys. "We'll see you Tuesday."

"Safe travels." He gives me a quick hug. "Be safe."

"You, too," I say with a look for him.

He nods. "We'll be fine. Don't worry."

If only it was that simple, I think as I drive us home.

"I don't think I've ever been happier to see anyone than I was to see you come in tonight," Sofia says. "I was a mess all night worrying about you out there."

"Did you get the message I left you on your phone?"

"Not yet. I haven't checked it."

"The judge agreed to no visitors or phone calls and put him in a special unit that makes it so he can't have someone else do his dirty work for him. It's temporary, but it should show him what happens when he threatens people's lives from jail."

"Oh my God, that's such a *relief.*"

"It doesn't mean someone won't take matters into their own hands, but it greatly reduces the chance of him giving an order that one of his friends or family members feels like they have to follow."

She loudly exhales a deep breath and then laughs. "I wonder what he's thinking all by himself in the special unit, cut off from his ability to have us killed."

"I hope he's thinking he made a very big mistake threatening you."

"Do you realize this is the first time I've felt like I won in a situation with him? He always wins. Whatever he wants, he gets. He even got joint custody *with a criminal record*. I fought that so hard, and somehow, he *still* got one night a week with Mateo. I had to turn my son over to a criminal one night a week. I hardly slept the nights Mateo was with him out of fear of what he might see or hear."

"Well, you won this time. You fought back, and now he's paying the price for threatening you, and he knows it was you who put him in that unit."

"Doesn't that make him more dangerous to me?"

"I think the judge will leave him there long enough that he gets the message about what's going to happen if he threatens people. I'm sure the judge will also have a few words for him at his arraignment tomorrow."

"I'd sort of like to see that."

"We'll get a full report afterward. We have better things to do tomorrow, such as meeting your dad and siblings for the first time."

"I can't believe that's really happening."

"I'm so excited for you. I can't imagine how you must feel."

"This entire month has been... What's the word for it when something is so strange..."

"Surreal?"

"Yes! That's it. Surreal. Everything with you and Milo and now meeting my father and just, well, everything."

"Most of it is good stuff. As upsetting as it was for Milo to be hurt, he's going to be fine, and that's all that matters. He's doing so much better, so we can count that as a good thing, too."

"I'm afraid to relax. Whenever I do, something else happens."

"I think it might be safe to relax, sweetheart. Everything will be better now. He's out of your life—and Mateo's—and you're getting to meet your father and his family. Life is going to get much sweeter for you going forward."

"You forgot the most important thing." She turns in her seat to face me. "This. Us. You're the sweetest thing in my sweet new life, Nico. I hope you know that."

"I want to be that and everything else to you."

"You are. Of course you are."

"You tried to break up with me earlier," I say in a teasing tone.

"That was because I was trying to keep you safe!"

"Don't do that again."

"I didn't want to do it the first time. That was the last thing I wanted, but the thought of you being in danger is terrifying to me."

"Likewise, my love. Keeping you and Mateo safe is my top priority."

"Keeping you and Mateo safe is my top priority."

"You forgot to include yourself."

"So did you."

"If something happens to you guys..." My throat closes at the thought of it. It's unfathomable.

She reaches for my hand and holds it with both of hers. "You've become... everything."

"Same for me with you. Every single thing." At a stoplight, we share a smile and a kiss. "I had no idea it was possible to feel like this."

"Me either. I thought I'd been in love before, but I haven't. Not like I am with you."

"I've never come close to this. I was waiting for you."

When we get home, Gladys is asleep on the sofa.

Sofia covers her with a blanket and shuts off the TV before we check on Mateo. His little suitcase is packed and ready for the trip. He's asleep with his arm hanging off the bed. Sofia resituates him and covers him with practiced ease, as if she's done the same thing a million times before.

We cross the hall to my room—or is it ours now?

"We need to pack," she says.

"I don't want to." I slide my arms around her from behind. "There are so many better things we can do."

"Later. First, we pack."

"You're no fun."

"Yes, I am, but our flight is early, and we need to do it now. My dad told me it's very cold in Minnesota, so Gladys brought some warmer clothes from my place to add to what I bought. Do you have a winter coat?"

Groaning, I follow her into my walk-in closet. "Yes, I have a winter coat." Once again, I wrap my arms around her. "Are you going to keep me warm in Minnesota?"

Laughing, she shakes me off and gets busy packing. "The sooner you get done, the faster we go to bed."

I've never packed so fast in my life. Jeans. Sweaters. Boots. Underwear. Done.

"You forgot your toothbrush," Sofia says as she meticulously folds every item before placing it into her suitcase.

"I'll need it in the morning. I won't forget it. Don't worry." I give her ponytail a gentle tug. "Come to bed. I need to hold you."

Smiling up at me, she says, "Your grandmother is right about you—and so am I. You're the devil."

"She never said I'm the devil. She said I'm a button pusher."

"You're a *devil*. For sure."

I reach for her and hoist her over my shoulder, spinning her around and making her scream with laughter. As I lower her to the bed, the door swings open and smacks against the wall.

"Stop!" Mateo cries. "Don't hurt her!"

I release Sofia so she can go to him. "He wasn't hurting me. I was laughing."

"I heard you scream," he says, his voice hitching on a sob that breaks my heart.

"I was laughing. I swear. Nico would never hurt me. Would you, Nico?"

"Never. I love your mama so much. All I want is to make her happy and make her laugh. She was laughing, Mateo. I swear to God."

He breaks down into heartbroken sobs that make me want to smash things as I imagine what he's seen and heard in the past that makes him fear the worst.

Sofia holds him until he calms.

"Will you come see me for a minute?" I ask the little boy.

He hesitates, but only for a second.

I lift him onto my lap. "I want you to know something really important, okay?"

He nods.

"I love you as much as I love your mom, and I promise you, man to man, that I will never do anything to hurt either of you. All I want is for you both to be happy, okay?"

"Okay."

"If I ever do anything to make you afraid, I want you to tell me, okay?"

"I will."

I kiss the top of his head and hug him tightly before releasing him to go back to bed with his mom.

I hear her talking to him before she returns to my room and sits next to me on the edge of the bed. "I'm sorry about that."

"Please don't be. I'd always want him to come to your rescue if he thought you were being hurt."

"I hate that he has reason to be worried about that. You were great with him. Thank you for that."

"I'd never, ever touch either of you with anything other than love on my mind. I swear on the lives of everyone I love, and that's a lot of people. You never need to be afraid of me that way. I'll spend the rest of my life proving that to you and Mateo."

"I know, Nico. I already know that, and now he does, too."

When I put my arm around her, she rests her head on my shoulder.

"Let's get some sleep. Tomorrow is going to be an exciting day for you."

We crawl into bed and snuggle up to each other in the middle. With our arms and legs intertwined, I decide that sleeping wrapped up in Sofia is better than the best sex I ever had before her.

I intend to continue showing her—and her son—how a real man treats the woman he loves.

CHAPTER 27

SOFIA

*M*ateo is subdued in the morning after the incident during the night. Before she leaves, I explain to Gladys what happened, and she assures him that he doesn't have to worry about that with Nico. He hugs and kisses Gladys before Nico has one of his guys drive her home.

Another car comes for us and drops us at Departures at MIA.

I'm so thankful to have Nico with me. He knows how to navigate the airport chaos and has us checked in and on our way to airport security within minutes. Mateo takes it all in, and while he hasn't had much to say to either of us this morning, he seems excited about the trip.

Nico is great with him, pointing out things he doesn't want my son to miss, such as the conveyer belt at security or the X-ray machine that Mateo initially balks at entering. Right away, I realize it reminds him of things he's experienced at the hospital.

"It doesn't hurt at all," I tell him. "Watch, Nico will go first."

He stands in the machine with his legs spread and his arms up while Mateo barely breathes as he stares at him.

"Mateo's turn," I say, nudging him forward. "Just do what Nico did. I swear it doesn't hurt."

Mateo goes into the machine and awkwardly positions himself into place.

"Don't move," the TSA agent says.

I hold my breath in the seconds it takes for the machine to complete the scan.

"All done," the agent says.

Nico receives Mateo while I go through the scanner.

After we clear security, we stop for breakfast at a restaurant on the concourse. That's a word I learned today when I heard Nico say it.

By the time we board the plane an hour later, I've almost forgotten to be nervous about flying for the first time.

Nico tells the flight crew that it's mine and Mateo's first flight, and the pilot comes out to give Mateo a wings pin. My son is thrilled with the wings and the attention from the pilot, who invites him to see the cockpit while the other passengers are boarding.

It's all so exciting, and at the end of the three-hour-and-twenty-minute flight, I'll meet my father for the first time. My excitement dies the second the plane speeds down the runway and lifts into the sky.

Nico sat in the middle seat so Mateo could look out, but that's the last thing I want to do.

"Look," Nico says. "You can see all of Miami."

"No, thanks."

He covers my freezing, clutched hands with his warm one. "You should look, Sofia. It's amazing to see everything from up here. There's nothing to be afraid of."

I force my eyes open and glance to my right, where I can see the beach below. I can't help but lean over Nico for a closer look. He's right. It is amazing. Until the plane hits a bump, and I nearly die of a heart attack.

His arm around me keeps me still as he chuckles at my reaction. "It's fine. It's like a car hitting a pothole."

Ugh, I'm never going to survive this. I'm wound so tightly, I feel like I might explode.

When the stewardess comes to take a drink order, Nico asks for Bloody Marys for us and a Sprite for Mateo. "The vodka will help," he assures me.

He's right. After a few sips of the cocktail, I do feel calmer.

Mateo is loving everything about this, especially having Sprite in the morning.

Nico is endlessly patient with him, answering all his questions and pointing to things out the window. There's a monitor on the back of the seat in front of us that shows the progression of our flight, which Mateo finds fascinating. When he starts to get itchy, Nico sets him up with his headphones and the movie *Cars*, which Mateo loves.

"You're so good with him. Thank you."

"He's great. I love being with him. I just hate that he thought I could hurt you."

"And I hate that he's programmed to expect the worst of the men in his life."

"I'm going to show him something better. I'll lead by example."

"Knowing the men who raised you, that makes Mateo a very lucky boy."

"Even if something were to go down between us, which *isn't* going to happen, I'd still be there for him. You have my word on that."

"Love you for that and a million other reasons."

"Love you, too, for two million reasons."

As I lay my head on his shoulder, I realize I do that a lot. Rest my head on his strong shoulder, knowing he's as solid and reliable as he seems. Maybe he's been "toxic" to other women. But for me and my son, he's just what we need.

At some point, I must've dozed off, because I come to suddenly when the plane touches down with a jolt.

"That's just the landing," Nico says. "There's going to be a loud roar, but that's the pilots slowing the plane."

I'm glad he told me that because the roar would've terrified me.

"That was so fun, Mama. I can't wait to fly again!"

"We'll fly home on Monday. That's in three days."

"Yay!"

While we wait for our turn to get off the plane, Nico puts Mateo's backpack on his little shoulders and holds his hand.

I'm relieved to see Mateo acting comfortable with him after last night. I felt so bad for Nico, who's been nothing but kind and generous to us. But sadly, I understand all too well why Mateo was afraid. I hope that over time, he'll forget the way his father used to scream and yell and sometimes hit me when he was in one of his rages.

That seems like a long time ago now, but the scars still run deep in both of us.

We walk toward baggage claim, where I'm supposed to meet my father. I'm suddenly full of nerves. What if he doesn't like me or takes one look at Mateo and sees nothing but his limitations? What if—

"Stop spinning." Nico gives my shoulder a squeeze. "He's going to love you both. How could he not?"

"Now you can see inside my mind, too?"

"I know you, and you worry too much."

"For good reason!"

"Maybe, but you've got nothing to worry about here. He was so eager to meet you guys, he sent tickets for *this* week. Not next week. *This* week. It's going to be fine. I know it."

"Thank you for saying what I needed to hear."

"Just relax and enjoy every minute."

With him by my side, holding the hand of my little boy, I'm able to let go of the tight knot of stress I've carried with me for so long, I barely recall life without it. It's been like a constant ache in my chest. I'm not sure if it's being away from Miami, getting to meet my dad or being with Nico, but I feel better than I have, well, ever.

I suspect most of that is because of Nico's steady, loving presence. When he tells me everything is going to be okay, I believe him.

We take the escalator down to the baggage claim area, and I recognize my father instantly. He's holding a sign that says Sofia, Mateo and Nico! The exclamation mark indicates he's as excited to meet me as I am to meet him.

As we move toward him, I notice there's more gray in his hair than there was in the picture he sent me, but even from ten feet away, I see the same resemblance I spotted in the photo. I look like him. There's no denying it.

And then he's hugging me, and I'm hugging him like it's the most natural thing in the world to be hugging this man who gave me life.

When we pull apart, we're both crying as we stare at each other.

"You look just like my sister," he says, seeming as amazed as I feel.

"I think I look like you."

"You do. She and I are twins. The pictures of her when she was your age... Well, you'll see."

"This is Nico and my son, Mateo. Mateo, honey, this is Jon, your grandfather. Can you say hello?"

"Hi," Mateo says with a shy smile.

"Grandfather," Jon says with a laugh as he shakes hands with Nico and Mateo. "That's gonna take me a minute." After Nico grabs our bags and Mateo's booster seat, Jon leads us to a parking garage where he's parked a black SUV. We get Mateo settled in the backseat and strapped into his booster.

"Take the front." Nico uses his chin to point to Mateo. "I've got him."

"Thank you." I get in the front seat next to my father. My *father*! The biggest missing piece in my life has been located, and he seems great. That's such a relief and a sorrow at the same time when I think about what my life might've been like if he'd been in it from the start.

But today is no time for revisiting a painful past. Today is for making new memories with the three "men" who are my future.

At least I hope so.

NICO

Watching Sofia with her new family is one of the most incredible experiences of my life. They're super friendly and welcoming, even Jon's wife, Kathy, who would've had good reason to be wary of this sudden appearance by a daughter and grandson. Sofia has two half sisters—Lily, who is thirteen, and Morgan, who is eighteen —and two half brothers—Tyler, fifteen, and Luke, eleven. They all seem like sweet kids. They're fascinated with Sofia and Mateo, who has made them aunts and uncles.

Jon brings out pictures of himself and his twin sister, Jessica, from when they were younger. He's right that the resemblance between Sofia and her aunt is uncanny. She gets her darker skin tone and coloring from her mother, but the rest is all Jon and Jessica.

"She lives in Wisconsin, so you won't get to meet her this time," Jon says, "but she's looking forward to seeing you soon."

"Do you have other siblings?"

"We had an older brother, Joe, who died in an accident when we were kids."

"Oh no. That's so sad."

"It was rough." Jon hands her a photo of his late brother. "We idolized him. Followed him around like little puppies."

"I'm very sorry you lost him."

"Thank you."

Jon and Kathy work together to produce a roast beef dinner with baked potatoes, green beans and salad. The food is delicious, and the conversation is easy, considering we all just met today.

Their home is a split-level with bedrooms upstairs and down. They offer us separate rooms or one together.

"We can all stay together," Sofia says. "Mateo might want me in the night if he wakes up."

"Sounds good," Kathy says. "Lily and Morgan, make up the bed and air mattress in Morgan's room, please."

"Thanks for letting us use your room," Sofia says to Morgan, who has reddish-blonde hair and freckles across her nose.

"No problem. Come on, Lily."

"Put some towels out, too," Kathy calls after them. "I tell them this is the reason I had kids, so I can get them to do things for me. They become very useful as they get older."

"That's good to know," Sofia says, seeming to soak up every detail of this visit like a sponge.

My phone chimes with a text. "It's from Miguel."

I hand the phone to Sofia so she can read it. *The judge ripped Joaquín a new one in court today and put the fear of God in him about how much trouble he's already in, and if he wants to make it worse, he'll keep threatening people. He'll have two weeks in solitary confinement to think about his behavior going forward.*

"What does this mean?" She points to the phrase *ripped him a new one.*

I grin and lean over to whisper in her ear, "Ripped him a new asshole."

"Oh!" She laughs even as she cringes. "I'm sorry I asked, but that sounds painful."

"That was the goal."

"And this? What does that mean?" She points to *solitary confinement.*

"He'll be in a cell by himself." I squeeze her hand to convey my relief that Joaquín got what he deserved in court. I glance at Mateo and then at Jon and Kathy. "We'll fill you in later."

"Mateo," Kathy says, "why don't you come with me, and let's see if we can find some dessert?"

He gets up to take her hand like he's known her all his life and goes with her to the kitchen.

"You've all been so sweet," Sofia says. "Thank you so much for everything."

Jon shakes his head, his expression full of regret. "I had no idea, Sofia, or you would've met me long before now."

"That's good to know. I guess all we can do is make the best of it going forward."

"And we will. For sure. About your mother..."

"She's not really in my life."

"I'm sorry to hear that."

Sofia gives a small shrug. "It's for the best. She isn't supportive of me."

Jon's deep sigh says so much. "Tomorrow, I'll show you around." With a smile, he adds, "Maybe I can convince you guys to move to the Twin Cities area."

The thought of that hits me like a lightning bolt of fear that strikes out of nowhere. Will she want to move up here to live closer to her new family? Who could blame her for wanting that? What will I do if she does?

That possibility never occurred to me before Jon suggested it.

We tuck Mateo into bed on an air mattress in the room the three of us are sharing, and then we join Jon and Kathy for a nightcap in the living room. Their kids have gone to bed, so it's just the four of us. Jon lit a fire in the fireplace that sends a cozy glow over the room.

"Is it always this cold here?" Sofia asks.

"From about November to May," Jon says. "You get used to it."

"I'm not sure I ever would after growing up in Mexico and Miami."

"Same," I say. "Our blood is too thin for this weather." I thank God it's so cold here. Maybe that will keep her from wanting to move, even with all the pluses she'd gain by living here.

We fill Jon and Kathy in on what's been going on with Joaquín and what happened today in court.

"Good Lord," Kathy says. "I'm so sorry you've been through such an ordeal."

"Thank you," Sofia says, "but he's where he belongs, and I'm trying not to think about him anymore. Our divorce will be final any day now."

"And your brother, Nico," Jon says. "He's all right?"

"On his way to a full recovery, thank God."

"What does Mateo know?"

"Not much," Sofia says. "He doesn't like going to his dad's house, so he hasn't asked for him. We're hoping it stays that way for a while longer. Eventually, I suppose I'll have to tell him the truth."

"We can worry about that when the time comes," I say, squeezing her hand.

Sofia can't stop yawning, so we encourage her to go to bed.

Jon gets up to hug her. "Thank you again for coming all this way."

"Thank you for having us."

"It's a pleasure."

"I'll be up in a few," I tell her, hoping for a minute to talk to Jon alone.

"I'm out, too," Kathy says. "Is there anything I can get you?"

"No, we're fine," Sofia says. "Thank you for your hospitality."

She gives me an uncertain look, as if to ask if she said the right word.

I smile at her and give her a thumbs-up.

They leave the room together.

Jon gets up to put another log on the fire and then holds up his glass. "One more?"

"Sure, thanks."

He pours me a generous amount of whiskey and the same for himself. Smiling as he hands me the glass, he says, "This is how you stay warm during the winter in Minnesota."

"I can see how it'd be helpful."

"Sofia mentioned that Mateo has been sick?"

Nodding, I say, "He had a cancerous brain tumor removed more than a year ago. He's doing well, but still working to come back from that."

"Wow. Was that the end of it? The surgery?"

"He had radiation, and the doctors are hopeful that he's beaten it. He's had a lot of therapy, but they said it's going to take time to fully recover. He's been swimming in the pool at my house, and we can already see him getting stronger."

"I can't believe how much she's been through."

"There's so much more than that. It's not my story to tell you, but just know there's more."

"I can see that you care for her very much. Have you been together long?"

"Not that long officially, but friends for quite some time. I love her and Mateo very much. In fact, I hope to ask her to marry me soon."

"That's wonderful. Congratulations."

"Thanks."

"I guess it's a pipe dream to hope you guys might move here."

"I own a home and a business in Miami. I wouldn't be able to move."

"So, I shouldn't push too hard for that, huh?"

"I want Sofia to be happy. If she'd be happier here where all of you are—the only family she's ever really had until mine adopted her—then I'd sell everything to be with her and Mateo."

"But home is Miami for both of you."

"Yeah."

"Then my daughter and I will have to find a way to see a lot of each other. We can FaceTime and talk on the phone and get to know each other the newfangled way. Whatever it takes."

"I think she's very lucky to have found you and your family. It'll make all the difference to her to know you're here and that you care."

"I do care. Hearing from her was such a shock, but once that wore off, it was just curiosity and concern and so many other emotions."

"I can't imagine what that must've been like for you."

"My wife said we need to see it as a blessing. Two more people to love."

"That's a nice way to look at it."

"She's right. It's not Sofia's fault this was handled the way it was—or mine. All we can do is make the best of it. And that's what we'll do."

"If I were to ask your daughter to marry me, sir, would I have your blessing?"

Jon laughs. "I hear daughters these days want their fathers to say that the only blessing they need is that of the prospective bride. But you seem like a nice young man, Nico, and you obviously love them both. You'd have my blessing, for what it's worth."

"I think it'll be worth a lot to a woman who's never had a father to look out for her."

CHAPTER 28

SOFIA

*T*his weekend is right out of a dream. My new family is funny and sweet and kind. They remind me a lot of Nico's family. Jon's sister, Jessica, is so excited to meet us that she decides to drive four hours on Saturday to come to his home with her husband and three teenage children. I not only have a father for the first time in my life, but I also have siblings and cousins, a stepmother, an aunt and uncle. It's overwhelming, but in the best possible way.

Jon and Kathy offer to watch Mateo on Sunday night so Nico and I can have a date.

After hearing about Giordino's and our confession that it's made us restaurant snobs, they recommend a place that comes highly recommended in downtown Minneapolis, called P.S. Steak.

Nico drives Jon's truck into the city, while making jokes about crashing my father's truck. "Do you think he'd forgive us?"

"He seems so nice. I'm sure he would. But let's try not to let that happen."

"I'm a professional driver, love. You're in good hands, and at least it's not snowing."

"Have you ever driven in snow?"

"Nope."

"That must be so scary."

"Not if you do it all the time."

"I'd never get used to that."

"If you moved here, you mean?"

I whip my head around to look at him. "I'm not moving here. We live in Miami."

"I wouldn't blame you if you wanted to after finding such a wonderful family here."

"They are wonderful, and this has been the best weekend of my life, but my home, *our* home, is in Miami. You're in Miami. Your family. My job. Our life."

"I'm kind of relieved to hear you say that. Ever since Jon mentioned it the other night, I've been a little worried that you might want to move."

"I don't. As much as I want to know them, my whole life is in Miami."

"Not anymore."

I nod to concede that point. "I'm so looking forward to more good times with them, but I'm not going to move here. On top of all the other reasons, it's freezing."

"Only in the winter."

"Which lasts six months! I'd die." I glance over at him. "I hate that you were worried about that."

"I want you to be happy. If being here makes you happy, we'd figure it out. Somehow."

"You say that when you have a home and a business and a big life in Miami."

"That big life would look very lonely if you and Mateo weren't there anymore."

"I wouldn't leave you, Nico. Not after everything we've been through and shared, and... I just... I wouldn't."

He smiles at me. "That's good to know."

The steak house, located in an elegant historic building in

downtown, has chandeliers, gorgeous moldings and comfortable leather seats in the booths.

"This might just be good enough," Nico says with a grin.

"It's not Giordino's, but somehow, we'll make do."

We check our coats, and Nico waits for me to be seated before he sits across from me.

I'm wearing a black wrap dress that Morgan loaned me when I said I hadn't brought anything to wear on a date. I have a sister to borrow clothes from. She asked if she could visit me in Miami on her spring break, and we're already making plans.

"What're you thinking about? You look so happy."

"I'm thinking about having a sister to borrow clothes from and how she wants to visit me on her spring break."

"Happiness looks nice on you—and so does Morgan's dress."

"Thank you for encouraging me to look for my dad. I never would've done it if you hadn't given me a push."

"I'm so glad it's worked out this way. You deserve to have a wonderful, supportive family."

"I'm thankful for them, but I already had that before I met my dad and his family. Your family has been the first one I ever really had, and you all mean so much to me. The way you all forgave me for what happened to Milo—"

"There was nothing to forgive," he says. "You were as horrified by that as we were."

"Still… It could've changed everything, and it didn't."

"That's because we love you. I love you."

"I love you, too. All of you, but you most of all."

"And here I thought you'd say Nona and Abuela were your favorites."

"They're right after you in second place."

We order drinks and steak for dinner as well as the crab toast appetizer. It's all delicious. Not just the food, but the company, too.

"This is our first real date," I tell him.

"We're long overdue."

"We had to come to Minnesota to get a night off together."

"It won't always be this way. Soon enough, I'll be able to hire someone to take the night shifts for me, and we'll have more time together."

"Not if I'm still working nights."

"I think you should try to go to school, if you still want to, that is."

"I wish I could, but it's just not feasible. I can't afford it."

"If you and Mateo lived with me, you could." He holds up a hand. "Before you say no, hear me out." Standing, he comes to sit next to me, turning so he's facing me. "I know how important it is to you to never again find yourself in a position like you were before." He pulls a paper from his pocket and unfolds it before handing it to me. "That's why I asked my mom to draw this up."

I quickly scan the page but can't make sense of what appears to be a legal document. "What is it?"

"It's a deed to half of my house."

I nearly die of shock. "*What?* Nico. No." I try to push the paper back into his hands, but he won't take it.

"You're hearing me out, remember?"

I can barely breathe, let alone listen.

"If we had met sooner and gotten married, we would've bought the house together."

"You know how I feel about getting married again."

"I do, but I love you, Sofia, and Mateo. I want to live with you and love you and take care of you both. I want you to be able to decorate our house and finally make it a home. I want you to go to school and do anything you want. But more than anything, I want you to have the security you've never had before, and by making you the co-owner of our house, if anything ever happens to us, which it won't, you'd have a financial cushion. I have some debt on the house that I used to start my business, but I'm paying that down every month. All of this to say, will you please marry me and spend your life with me and let me spend mine with you and Mateo and the other kids we'll have together?" He takes my hand and kisses the back of it. "I want everything with you, if you'll have me."

I use my napkin to wipe the tears off my face. He's totally overwhelmed me with everything he said, which proves he *sees* me and understands me like no one else ever has.

"I should also add that I asked your dad for his blessing, and he said it was up to you, but he approves of me for you."

"Anyone would. You're amazing."

"I've never been more amazing than I am with you. You and Mateo... You guys make me want to be the best version of myself so I deserve you."

"I said I'd never get married again after... Well, you know."

"Yes, I do, and I'm hoping you'll reconsider, because I've never wanted anyone to be my wife before, and now no one else will do. It has to be you. And Mateo. Maybe I could adopt him at some point if his father is out of the picture indefinitely."

"You're making it very hard for me to say anything other than..." I take a deep breath and let it out.

"Jump, sweet Sofia. I'll always catch you. Always."

"Yes."

He hugs me so tightly, it almost hurts, but in the best possible way. When he pulls back, we're both in tears.

"Thank you," he says, kissing me softly.

"Thank *you*. For everything."

"Wait! I forgot the best part." He reaches into his pocket and withdraws a ring that he slides onto my finger. "This belonged to my great-grandmother, and my dad saved it for me. He joked that he thought I was never going to need it, but as soon as he saw me with you, he decided to have it cleaned. He said he had a feeling you might be the one for me, and he was right."

The ring is a gorgeous round diamond in a nest of brown stones.

"Those are tiger's-eye stones. My great-grandfather supposedly told my great-grandmother the color reminded him of her eyes. They remind me of yours, too, which means you're meant for me."

"It's the most beautiful ring I've ever seen, and that it was your great-grandmother's means so much to me."

"I'm glad you like it."

"I love it, but there's one thing..."

"What's that?"

I push the paper across the table to him. "As much as I appreciate the gesture, I won't accept this."

"Why?"

"That house is yours. I wouldn't feel right."

"What if we sold it and bought something else together?"

"That would be foolish. Your house is beautiful. It has everything we'll ever need and then some."

He shrugs. "Either you accept this," he says, pushing the paper back to me, "or we sell it and buy something together."

"You're being stubborn."

"I want my wife to feel safe and secure—in every possible way, including financially. I respect what it took you to leave him and get your own place and start over. That must've been so hard for you, but you did it, and you made a beautiful home for yourself and Mateo. If the need ever arises again for you to start over, I want you to always know you could, while hoping you'll never want or need to."

Every word he says goes straight to my heart. This man. This wonderful, beautiful, sweet, caring man...

"You really want to do this?" I ask him.

"I really do. I want it for you."

"I want everyone who's aware of this to know I don't want it."

"So noted, and only my parents know. I'll tell them you fought back."

"Please do. I'm not here because of what you have. I'm here because of *who you are*. I love who you are."

"I love who you are." He kisses my neck and makes me giggle. "Every single bit of you."

A throat clearing behind Nico has him spinning to face the waiter.

"Will there be anything else, sir?"

"Yes, please," Nico says. "We need champagne to celebrate our engagement."

"Congratulations to both of you."

277

"Thank you," Nico says. "And something chocolate for my fiancée. She loves chocolate."

"Who doesn't love chocolate?" the waiter says. "I'll be right back."

Nico turns back to me. "You're still going to marry me, right?"

"Yes, I am."

"When?"

"Uh, I don't know."

"Soon. I want to marry you soon. I want you to look into going back to school. I want to swim with Mateo every day and have babies and go on vacations with my family and have holidays together and come here to visit your dad and the rest of your family—and have them visit Miami. I want it all, and I want it right now—with you."

"How soon are we talking?"

"Spring?"

"That's pretty soon."

"Unless you want a big, fancy deal."

I shake my head. "I'd love something like Maria and Austin did. Small and intimate. But with your family, it's never *small*."

"Not to mention your family, too."

"That's right. I have a family."

"I bet Maria and Austin would lend us their pool deck to do the same sort of thing they did. If you're down for that."

"I'm down for it." I place my hand on his face, still trying to believe he's mine to keep forever. "I'm down for all of it."

EPILOGUE

NICO

We have the quietest sex of our lives in her sister's bed, with Mateo asleep on the air mattress on the floor.

"I feel dirty for doing that in your sister's bed," I whisper to her afterward.

"Stop. Don't even say it. We're going straight to hell."

I cup her breast and play with her nipple. "But what a way to go."

She shivers and presses into me, as if she's already thinking about round two.

After we sent a text with our news and a photo of Sofia wearing the ring to my family, the congratulations came flooding in. Everyone is thrilled for us, which makes me so happy. I could never have married someone they don't love as much as I do.

I never could've married anyone but her.

Raising my head from her shoulder, I look down at her. "Thank you for saying yes."

"Thank you for asking and for everything else you did, too."

"We're going to have the best life together."

"I can't wait for all of it."

"Me, too, love."

MILO

I'm sick of being in the hospital, sick of being stuck in bed, sick of the itching around the screws that hold the damn halo in place. And don't get me started on the freaking catheter. That's the worst. Even though I hate almost everything about being here, there's one bright, shining light amid all the misery.

I count the hours each day until she comes on duty at three p.m.

Her days off are the worst, with nothing to look forward to, other than the visits with my wonderful family members. They bring me so much food that I can share it with everyone on the floor.

Gianna told me they've also been keeping the nurses fed, which has made me the most popular patient on the ward.

That's what my family does best. They feed people, and it doesn't surprise me that they're doing what they do while I'm in here.

It's five minutes to three, and the clock is moving backward, or so it seems to me as I watch mindless TV and wait for *her*.

I think a lot about what her fiancé did to her, and it makes me so mad on her behalf. Why would anyone wait until the absolute last minute to decide he didn't want to get married? And was the man insane? She's stunning and sweet and sexy and caring. Who does he think he's going to find that's better than her?

I've decided his insanity is my good fortune.

When she comes in, the first thing I notice is the smile she's always wearing when she enters the room. Her silky dark hair is up in a ponytail that puts her pretty face on full display. I could look at that face for hours and never get tired of the view.

"Hi there. I heard you were up and walking today. That's awesome!"

"It was all kinds of fun, let me tell you. Especially with this ridiculous catheter along for the ride."

"I have good news for you. Dr. Northrup put in orders to remove it, so we can do that right away if you're game."

"You mean... *You* would remove it?"

"Yep."

I'm not at all sure how I feel about that. "I, uh..."

"I do it all the time. It's no big deal."

"I'm offended on behalf of my junk. In my opinion, it is a *very* big deal."

She snorts with laughter. "Why do all men think the penis is the center of the universe?"

"Because it is literally the center of our universe, and this isn't how I was hoping you'd get your first look at mine."

She leans on the bed rail, seeming intrigued. "Oh, no? What'd you have in mind?"

"Well, I figured I'd at least buy you dinner first."

Her left brow rises in an arch look. "Are you flirting with me, Mr. Giordino?"

"What if I am?"

"Well, I would say you're a courageous man, flirting with a woman like me who's sworn off all men forever."

"Don't do that."

"Oh, it's already done. I signed a contract that declares me single for life."

"I'm going to need you to break that contract so you can go out with me the second I'm out of here."

"The same second?"

"The very same second."

"Hmmm. I'll have to get back to you about that."

"Don't make me wait too long. Thinking about going out with you is the only thing keeping me sane in here."

"The only thing?"

I look her dead in the eyes. "The. Only. Thing."

"Are you always this blunt when you want to go out with someone?"

"I'm never this blunt with anyone, and I've never wanted to go out with anyone more than I want to go out with you."

"Milo," she says with a nervous laugh. "What meds did they give you today?"

"I'm off everything but the antibiotic." I cover her hand with mine, hoping she'll be okay with that. "I mean it, Gianna. I want to see you after this."

"I think I'd like to see you, too, as long as, you know… I'm kind of a mess still from, you know…"

"You're not a mess. You're the furthest thing from a mess."

"Maybe on the outside, but on the inside…" She shrugs. "Not so great."

"How about we see what we can do to fix that?"

She looks at me for a long time, so long that I start to worry she's going to turn me down. "I think I'd like that."

I'm so relieved, I'm nearly light-headed with it. I'm not sure when she became so important to me, but I'm starting to think getting shot may turn out to be the best thing that ever happened, as crazy as that seems.

"Now, about that catheter…"

"Can't we get someone else to do it?"

"I'm it. So, man up, and let's get it done."

"Will it hurt?" I ask around a huge lump of fear that's suddenly lodged in my throat.

"Like hell."

"*Really?*" I ask in a high squeak of a voice.

Laughing, she says, "Really. But you'll be fine. I promise. Shall we get it over with?"

I want to run and hide, but I'm not allowed to run. "If we must…"

Read Milo and Gianna's story, *How Much I Need*, coming Valentine's Day 2023! Turn the page to read *Nochebuena*, A Miami Nights novella.

Thank you for reading *How Much I Want*! I hope you loved Nico and Sofia's story as well as catching up with the rest of the

Giordino family. I love writing this series and enjoy every minute I spend with these characters. I wrote this one while I was in South Florida this past winter, and it was so fun to be living in the area while I was writing the book. I've told you before that Fort Lauderdale and Miami hold a special place in my heart, with many fun family memories there, which makes writing this series extra special for me.

Join the How Much I Want Reader Group at *www.facebook.com/groups/howmuchiwant/* to discuss Nico and Sofia's story with spoilers allowed. And make sure you're a member of the Miami Nights Series group at *www.facebook.com/groups/MiamiNightsSeries* to be the first to hear about new books and other series news.

A special thank you to Erica Bettin, who I met in Fort Lauderdale and had a wonderful conversation with about the challenges of learning English as a native Spanish speaker. I so appreciate her insight and wisdom. As always, Dr. Sarah Hewitt, family nurse practitioner, was helpful with the medical details, and Captain Russell Hayes, retired, Newport, RI, Police Department, helped with the criminal/law enforcement elements of this story.

As always, a huge thanks to the home team of Julie Cupp, Lisa Cafferty, Jean Mello, Nikki Haley and Ashley Lopez, who do so much to help keep everything running smoothly behind the scenes, especially when I was in Florida for two months and we had to do a lot of punting!

My editors, Linda Ingmanson and Joyce Lamb, are always there for me when I need them, and I so appreciate their many contributions. Anne Woodall, Kara Conrad and Tracey Suppo are my primary beta readers, and I love getting their feedback on every new book. Gwen Neff helps me keep the details straight on all these series I have going, and she's been such a valuable addition to my team.

Thank you to my Miami beta readers: Dinorah Shoban, Stephanie Behill and Angelica Maya. Check out Dinorah's recipe for coquito, or Spanish eggnog, below.

And finally, to my amazing, devoted, loyal readers—I appreciate you all so much. I hope you love this latest trip to Miami! Turn the page to read *Nochebuena*, the holiday novella from late 2021 that comes BEFORE *How Much I Want i*n the series timeline.

Xoxo

Marie

Dinorah's coquito recipe

- 1 (12 oz) can evaporated milk
- 1 (14 oz) can sweetened condensed milk
- 2 cups (1 15 oz can) cream of coconut (like Coco López)
- ¼ tsp cinnamon
- ⅛ tsp nutmeg
- 1 tsp vanilla
- 1 ½ cups white rum
- cinnamon sticks for garnish

I suggest 1 1/2 cups of white rum. If that sounds like too much, start with 1 cup and add more to taste. I like to add just enough rum that it's prickly on the back of your throat and warms you on the inside. It will be one of the few drinks you'll have that is cold that warms you up. Just be careful because the flavor of the rum gets stronger the longer the drink "marinates."

Another reason I choose to make my coquito without egg yolks is that it extends its shelf life. Coquito should last in your refrigerator for 4-6 months. If your coquito has a little fat cap at the top, that is completely normal. That is just the coconut milk fat separating, which is normal. Give your coquito a poke and a good shake, and you are good to go.

NOCHEBUENA

A MIAMI NIGHTS NOVELLA

CHAPTER 1

MARIA

"*I have to get home.* There's no way I can miss Nochebuena, the biggest and best night of the year in our family." Literally translated, *Nochebuena* means *good night*, and it's how the Cuban community celebrates Christmas Eve. Abuela pulls out all the stops to put on a feast of such epic proportions, we can't move for days afterward. We look forward to it all year, and missing not only the party itself, but the day-long prep with my grandmothers, mother, aunts, sister and cousins is inconceivable to me.

Austin has had the patience of a saint as we grapple with weather delays on the way home from ten days in Hawaii, where we attended the wedding of one of his Miami Marlins teammates while enjoying the vacation of a lifetime.

Our honeymoon is going to have to work awfully hard to top this trip, which was perfect until we landed at LAX and learned we probably can't get to Miami today due to a massive storm in the middle of the country. Tomorrow, which is Christmas Eve, is looking iffy, too.

He reaches for my hand and draws me down into the seat next

to him. "Weather delays mean rough air, and you don't like rough air any more than I do. I know it sucks to be stranded, especially at Christmas, but I'd rather spend the holiday in this airport than fly through that crap."

He's right. I know he is, especially since I totally freaked out on the flight to Hawaii when we flew through thirty minutes of pretty intense turbulence over the Pacific. I had visions of crashing into the ocean that had me on the verge of hyperventilating for the full half hour that the plane bounced through the sky.

I sag into the chair, feeling defeated.

"At least we have each other, right?" he asks with the cute grin that turns my insides to mush every time it's directed my way, which is often.

My gorgeous man is even more so than usual after ten days of sunshine turned his skin a dark tan and made his blond hair even lighter. He's unfairly beautiful, and I notice women looking at him everywhere we go. However, he never looks at anyone but me, which is one of many ways that loving him makes me a very lucky girl.

"What about poor Everly?" I ask of his three-year-old daughter, home with his parents and counting the days until Daddy and Rie get back from Hawaii. "We can't miss Christmas with her." I want to wail at the thought of missing our first Christmas as a family.

"Even if we can't get there, she'll still have a wonderful day thanks to everything we did to prepare before we left, and we'll make it up to her with a trip to Disney or something when we get home." He puts his arm around me and draws my head onto his shoulder. "What is it that Nona always says? We can plan everything except the weather."

"That's Abuela's saying."

"I knew it was one of them, the sources of more valuable wisdom than anyone I've ever met. They'd tell you the same thing I am—sit tight with your wonderful fiancé and stay safe for Christmas. What else can we do?"

"Nothing, I guess." I can't believe this is happening. I've been counting down to the first Nochebuena with Austin, Everly and

Austin's parents as part of my family. I couldn't wait for them to experience the magnificence that is Christmas Eve with the Giordinos.

"I wanted to be there for Dee tomorrow, too. Wyatt is having his annual cardiac checkup, and she's losing it." My sister's fiancé is a seventeen-year heart transplant survivor. With the average life expectancy after transplant right around eleven years, the annual checkups are a source of tremendous stress to everyone who loves Dr. Wyatt Blake, especially my sister, who is enduring it for the first time after falling for him this year.

"Why's he having that done on Christmas Eve?"

"I guess it's the one day no one wants to schedule surgery, so it's a lighter day for him."

Wyatt has parlayed his personal experiences into a successful career as a cardiothoracic surgeon.

Austin runs his fingers through my hair, which he knows soothes me when I'm wound up about something. "Can I ask a weird question?"

"Sure."

"Why does your family celebrate Nochebuena? You guys aren't even Cuban."

That's true. I'm not, but my cousin Carmen is, and her Cuban grandmother belongs to all of us, regardless of whether we're related by blood. That's how it works in our family. Christmas Eve has always belonged to Abuela, and it always will. I lift my head off Austin's shoulder to look him in the eye. "Baby, on Nochebuena, we're all Cuban."

CHAPTER 2

DEE

I tell myself to calm the hell down, but myself isn't listening. Wyatt is fine and has told me repeatedly there's no reason to worry about a routine cardiac checkup. Try telling that to my blood pressure, which must be sky-high as I've counted down to Christmas Eve and the only thing that truly matters to me on a day that's usually full of family, food and fun. I'm the one who's going to end up with a life-threatening cardiac condition unless I can find a way to chill.

Easier said than done.

I need him to be okay.

That is all I need to be okay myself, and it's all I want for Christmas.

I'm so brittle with anxiety that I fear one wrong look from someone will break me, which is why I'm going with Wyatt to the hospital rather than helping with Nochebuena preparations tomorrow.

I've never once, in my entire life, missed that time with the women in my family, but I've also never had to deal with the possibility of losing the man I love to the heart condition that's been at the center of his life since he was eight and diagnosed with cardiomyopathy.

Wyatt tried to save me from days like tomorrow by attempting to talk me out of loving him. He failed miserably at that, thank goodness. Every other day I've spent with him has been pure bliss. Today—and tomorrow—are the only days on which his situation has invaded our happily ever after. I tell myself I can get through two days of hell to have the rest of the time with him, but I have to be honest. The worry is more debilitating than I expected it to be when I decided to fight for the life I want with him.

I'm so upset, I feel sick, which I'm going to have to hide from him when he comes to bed after a shower. I hear the water turn off and steel myself to be my usual chipper self when I'm with the man of my dreams. And everything about our life together is a dream come true.

Except for this one thing—the specter of his uncertain health that hangs over days like today when we're forced to confront his reality. The rest of the time we do a pretty good job of pretending like we have nothing to worry about.

He jokes about having outlived his warranty.

I don't think that's funny, but I laugh so he doesn't think I'm fretting over him.

He doesn't like when I do that.

I'm wound tighter than a drum tonight, and there's no way I'm going to be able to hide that from him. I need to remember this for next year and have my doctor fiancé prescribe me a sedative that'll knock me out for two full days so I can wake up when it's over to hear he's fine. What do you suppose the ethics of something like that would be?

Before I can think of something I can do—immediately—to diffuse my stress, he's coming out of the bathroom, naked as the day he was born with the gorgeous, elaborate chest tattoo that hides his surgical scars on full display.

"I love that freaking Peloton," he announces. "Best workout I've ever had. Makes me sweat my balls off."

I hate that freaking Peloton and hold my breath every minute he's on it, pushing himself to extremes that cannot be good for his transplanted heart. Okay, I admit it, living with a man who's outlived his warranty is harder than I thought it would be.

"Don't sweat your balls off. I need them for procreation." I try for a flip, nothing-on-my-mind tone that I think I pull off rather convincingly, since he laughs at my comment.

Here's the truth—he was right, and I was wrong. But even knowing how hard it is to live with his potential medical challenges, I wouldn't change a thing about days that end this way, with him curling that hot, muscular, perfectly healthy body around mine and setting me on fire with needs I never knew I had until Dr. Wyatt Blake showed me.

"What's wrong?" he asks, zeroing right in on the fact that my muscles are so tense they must feel like concrete to him.

"Nothing. What could be wrong two days before Christmas?"

He raises a dark brow that manages to call me out on my bullshit without him having to say a word. "You promised me you wouldn't do this."

"What am I doing?"

"Freaking out over what will be a perfectly routine annual check of the ticker."

"I'm not freaking out about that."

"Yes, you are."

"No, I'm worried about how Abuela assigned the sweet plantains and yuca to me for the first time ever, and I want to get them right. She'll never let me hear the end of it if the plantains aren't sweet enough."

"You did a trial run last week, and I ate every bite of what you made. I think you've got this, babe."

"You're hardly an impartial customer. You like everything I make for you."

"Yes, I do." He kisses the end of my nose and then my lips. "And your family will, too, so how about you stop feeding me sweet-plantain bullshit and tell me the truth about how you're having a thermonuclear meltdown about this checkup I'm having tomorrow?"

"No, I'm not!" That my voice is a full octave higher than my usual tone doesn't do much to make my case.

His soft laughter echoes off the walls of our huge bedroom in the house we bought to live happily ever after together. Except that won't be possible unless he's here with me for a very long time. "Let's see what we can do to make you nice and relaxed so you can get some sleep."

After months of nights just like this, he knows exactly how to kiss and touch me until I'm not thinking about anything other than how I can get more of his special brand of magic. His tongue is soft, persuasive and insistent when it encircles my nipple, making it stand up with attention and interest in what might come next.

Sometimes that might be teeth, other times it might be gentle suction that's almost enough on its own to take me right over the edge into orgasm. He's that good. Tonight, seeming to realize they're needed, he brings out the big guns and has me quivering like a bowl full of jelly under him in no time at all.

What, me worry? Ha, who has the brain cells for that when Wyatt Blake has your legs on his shoulders and his face buried in your hoo-ha? Not me, that's for sure. He's found the natural sedative I needed in the form of multiple orgasms—and that's before we get to the main event.

And you wonder why I was willing to risk epic heartbreak to have this with him?

"Dee."

His voice pulls me out of my head to open my eyes, blinking his gorgeous face into focus.

He's propped above me, watching over me with blue eyes gone fierce with love.

When he looks at me that way, he can have anything he wants.

"Are you with me?" he asks as he begins to press his hard cock into me.

"I'm with you."

"I want you to repeat after me. Are you ready?"

He expects me to speak when he's stretching me to my absolute limit? I lick my lips and nod.

"I, Dee Giordino…"

"I, um, Dee Giordino…"

"Do solemnly swear to stop worrying about Wyatt Blake…"

I don't want to say those words, so I shake my head.

"Say it."

Begrudgingly, I say the words.

"Because he swears to God on a stack of Bibles there's nothing to worry about. If something was wrong, he would know it."

My chin quivers as I battle emotions that want to suck me into a spiral from which I might never recover.

"Do you hear me, babe?" he asks in a soft but urgent tone. "I would *know* if there was something wrong. There's nothing wrong, and they aren't going to find anything tomorrow. You got me?"

I want so badly to believe that.

"Delores…"

He's pulling out the biggest of guns now—in more ways than one as he withdraws completely from me.

I grasp his muscular ass cheeks and try to put him back where I want him. "Why did you stop?"

"Because you're not hearing me."

"I am!"

"Then why are you still all tense, and not in a good way?"

"Can't help it. I love you, so I worry."

"We had a deal about this. You promised if I let you fall in love with me, you wouldn't be stressed all the time."

"Haha, *let* me fall in love with you… As if I had any choice. I think I loved you the first time you turned those potent blue eyes my way at Carmen and Jason's wedding and smiled."

"That was all I had to do?" he asks with a small grin.

"I was that easy."

"You were so beautiful that day in your bridesmaid gown." He kisses me sweetly as he enters me once again, making me gasp from the pressure and the pleasure. "So happy for your cousin getting a second chance at love."

"She deserves it."

"She does, and so do you. I promised you I'd give you everything, and I intend to keep that promise. But you need to keep *your* promise to trust me that I'll tell you if there's anything to worry about. Right now, today, there's nothing. I swear it, Dee." He kisses me again, deeper this time, rubbing his tongue against mine before he retreats. He never stops moving in me, firing up my body even as he touches my soul with his heartfelt words. "My heart has never been in better shape than since I found you."

Swoon.

"But you have stop making yourself sick over me. What good will it do if I live to be a cranky old man, and you worry yourself into an early grave over me?"

He does make a good point.

His hands slide beneath me to grasp my ass as he picks up the pace. For several minutes, there're no words, only sharp gasps and deep sighs of pleasure as we reach the peak together in a loud crescendo that makes me thankful we don't have neighbors close by.

Wyatt comes down on top of me and wraps his arms around me.

I hold on tight to my one true love.

"Do you feel any better?" he asks after a long silence.

"I feel sublime, as I always do when I get to be with you like this."

Bending his neck, he plants a kiss on my chest. "What about on the inside, where your freak-o-meter has been running on overtime?"

"I'm trying to find ways to cope with the worries."

"And how's that going?"

"Good days. Bad days. The day before your annual checkup? Not so great."

"I think we need therapy about this."

"You do? Really?"

"Yes, I do. I'm used to living with the uncertainty of it all, but you're not, and you need some coping skills beyond my ability to sex you into relaxation."

"Don't underestimate your potent capabilities." I smile at him. "I feel better than I have all day."

"Which is great, but since I can't keep you in bed for days at a time—although we really ought to do that sometime—we need extra help with this. Would you be willing to go?"

"If you think it would help, of course I would."

"I do think it would help. I had a ton of therapy when I was younger and first dealing with my precarious health situation. It made a big difference for me. I want that for you, too."

"I'm sorry if I've done a poor job of hiding my worries from you."

"I don't want you to hide *anything* from me, Dee, especially worries about me. I'll ask around about a good therapist and get us in there in January, okay?"

"Okay."

"And in the meantime, you're going to help with the Nochebuena preparations tomorrow while I do my thing at the hospital."

"No, I want to go with you."

He kisses the words right off my lips. "You're going to be with your family like you are on Christmas Eve every year. There's nothing you can do for me but lose an entire day sitting in waiting rooms. You won't even get to see me."

"But I'll be *near* you."

"There's nothing you can do, sweetheart, but shiver in overly chilled waiting rooms. You're already cold all the time. That'll make for a miserable day for you when you could be having fun with your girls. I promise I'll come straight to Abuela's the second I get out of there."

I think about that for a second. "You're sure there's nothing I can do if I go with you?"

"One thousand percent positive."

"All right, then," I say on a long sigh. "I'll do it your way, but I'd better be the first to know if there's anything wrong."

"There won't be anything wrong, and you'll always be the first to know everything."

"I guess I can live with that if it means I get to live with you."

"That's my girl," he says with another sweet kiss as he gathers me in close to him. "Now get some sleep. You've got a pig to roast tomorrow."

CHAPTER 3

CARMEN

*T*he smell of the roasting pig is making me want to vomit, but that's not surprising since every smell makes me sick lately, or so it seems. I'm constantly swallowing bile as my stomach churns relentlessly. No one told me pregnancy was going to be this difficult. Sure, I've heard stories about morning sickness, but it's the all-day sickness that's killing me. And after a miscarriage earlier in the year that no one knows I had, I've held off on telling people about this pregnancy for fear of having to take it all back if this one doesn't take either.

"What's wrong with you?" my mom, Vivian, asks me when we're in Abuela's hot, crowded kitchen with the other women in our family, less my cousin Maria, who's stuck in LA.

"What? Nothing."

She raises a dark brow that lets me know she sees right through my bullshit. As the only child of a woman who suffered *nine* miscarriages before she had me, trust me when I tell you that not only does she see through my bullshit, sometimes I feel like she can also read my mind. "Are you fighting with your sexy neurosurgeon?"

"No, I'm not fighting with Jason."

"Well, then, what is it? This is your favorite day of the year, and you look like you'd rather be anywhere else."

Before I can come up with a reply she'll accept, she takes me by the arm and all but perp-walks me outside, thankfully to the front of the house and not the back where the pig is roasting in the above-ground Caja China that Abuela bought years ago for Nochebuena. It replaced the hole in the ground where the pig used to be roasted.

My cousins Nico, Milo and Dom, all of whom are actually from the Italian side of the family, were recruited yesterday to go with Abuela to choose the pig. They were also in charge of cleaning and preparing it for roasting. I can't think about that process, or I'll lose the meager contents of my stomach. "Tell me what's wrong so whatever it is won't ruin both our days."

"Nothing is wrong, Mami. It's actually something good."

Again with the eyebrow.

"We were waiting to tell you—"

She lets out a shriek that the entire neighborhood probably hears and wraps me in a hug so tight she nearly squeezes the puke right out of me.

"Mami! Stop your screaming before someone calls the cops!"

"A woman is allowed to scream when she finds out she's going to be a grandmother, and why in the world didn't you tell me before now?" With her hands on my shoulders, she holds me back so she can give me a full inspection. "What's the problem?"

"No problem other than feeling like I'm going to die every minute of every day."

She winces. "I was like that with you, too, but not with any of the others. That's how I knew you were going to stick."

That information renders me nearly speechless. "Really?" I ask in a higher-than-usual tone.

"Yep. I swear I subsisted for months on wafer crackers and ginger ale."

"That's what I've been eating, too."

"And the smells!" She makes a revolted face.

"Oh my God! The worst. The pig is taking me over the edge."

"Then let's get you out of here for now."

"I can't leave." Just that quickly, I'm battling tears, which is another thing that's been ridiculous lately. Jason laughs at how I cry over *everything*. "I'll miss all the fun."

"No, you won't. You can come back later when everything is cooked, and the scents won't be so pungent."

"We don't want people to know yet, Mami. I'm not even three months. I want to wait awhile longer."

"I won't say anything."

Now it's my turn to give her the famous eyebrow.

"I won't! I swear. I certainly understand about being superstitious. After the fourth time, we didn't tell anyone."

She's so rarely referred to her difficult road to motherhood, preferring instead to focus on the joy she found in finally having me.

"I have no idea how you managed to get through that *nine* times."

"It was brutal, but I wanted you *so* badly that I kept trying, and you, my precious girl, made all the struggle worth it from the second you took your first breath." She sweeps my hair back off my shoulders. "And now you're going to make me an abuela." Fanning her face, she fails to stem a flood of tears.

I hug her. "I've been *dying* to tell you."

"I'm so glad you did and that we have this sweet secret. There's nothing you could give me for Christmas that I'd love more than this."

"I had a feeling."

"Go home, rest up and come back later to enjoy the party. If you're anything like me, everything is better later in the day."

"Yes, it is. What'll I tell everyone?"

"I'll tell them you have a terrible headache, and you wanted to go home and lie down so you can be here for tonight."

"Thank you. The pig took me over the top."

"I had the same issue the year I was expecting you. I couldn't come to Nochebuena at all that year."

"I can't imagine it without you there."

"I cried all night, and Daddy was right there with me the whole time, telling me I'd have a lifetime of holiday celebrations, and missing one wasn't going to kill me." She laughs in a low, husky tone as she rolls her eyes at her own foolishness. "I was *so* dramatic then."

I bite my lip to keep from telling her she's never outgrown her flair for the dramatic.

"Oh, stop it! I can *hear* what you're trying not to say!"

We lose it laughing. It's the best laugh I've had in weeks, and we end up clinging to each other as we wipe away the good kind of tears. We've had more than our share of the not-so-good kind, especially after I lost my first husband when we were twenty-four. "Will I be able to read my child's mind the way you read mine?"

"God, I hope so. You never could keep anything from me, and it seems you still can't."

I give her a saucy, defiant look. "You didn't know I was pregnant for a whole month."

"I suspected you were."

"You did not!"

"Ask Daddy! I told him your cheeks were fuller, and you had a glow to you."

"My cheeks are full of puke, and the glow has to be a gorgeous shade of green. Jason says he's afraid to hug me lately out of fear I might spontaneously puke."

"My poor baby. It's so dreadful, but so, so worth it. You're the best thing to ever happen to me, and this baby will be that for you, too."

"Thank you, Mami. I'm sure it'll all be fine once I get past this lovely stage. I think I'll take you up on the offer to make up a headache for me so I can go home for a while. Would you mind grabbing my purse and keys off the counter? I can't go back in there." What normally makes my mouth water in anticipation of holiday feasting is having the opposite effect today.

"Wait right here. I'll be back."

While she goes inside to retrieve my stuff, I focus on breathing in through my nose and out through my mouth. I'm not sure why that helps suppress the nausea, but it does, and I'll take what I can get. My phone chimes with a text to me and Dee from Maria.

There may be hope. Austin and several of his teammates are chartering a plane to get us back to Miami! She includes the praying hands emoji.

Oh, thank goodness! It wouldn't be Nochebuena without you!

What she said, Dee adds. *What's your ETA?*

Hoping by six. The plan is to fly south to avoid the weather in the Plains. Gulp. I'm scared.

They wouldn't do it if it wasn't safe, I tell her. *Try not to worry. We're so glad you're coming. Keep us posted!*

Will do.

Mami returns with my purse and keys. "I told the others about your headache, and they said to feel better and get back here for the fun later."

"I will. Thank you for this. I just heard from Maria. Austin and his teammates are chartering a plane."

"That's great news. We were just saying she has to be having a meltdown over possibly missing Nochebuena."

"She is."

"Now get yourself off to nap. Whatever you need, Mamacita, whenever you need it, you tell your Mami, and it shall be."

Hugging her, I blink back ridiculous tears. "What would I ever do without you?"

"Your life would be too boring to bear without me."

"I hope I never find out."

"Text me if you need anything."

"I'll be fine. Jason is taking a half day today, so he may even be home when I get there."

"Tell him I said to take good care of my baby and her baby."

"I will, but he's been amazing, of course."

"I have no doubt."

She's still standing outside the house to wave when I drive away. I wonder if she's going to go back inside and tell the others I'm pregnant, but then I decide she won't do that. After what she endured, she knows why this is a secret that needs to be kept until we're sure. And if she does tell people? Oh well, it's not like they won't find out eventually.

I never told any of them about the miscarriage I suffered in August. I didn't even know I was pregnant when I was already losing it. The whole thing was sad and traumatic. I made the choice to keep it between my husband and me because we were both too raw to have my entire family descend upon us, wanting to help.

There was nothing anyone could do, and as long as Jason and I had each other, we got through it. My doctor told me to expect it might take a while to conceive again, so we were surprised when it happened quickly. But I'm still superstitious and slightly worried that history might repeat itself. How did my mother go through that *nine* times? How and where did she find the wherewithal to keep trying after an ordeal like that?

After having it happen once to me, I have all-new respect for the fact that she stuck with it long enough to get to me. It's interesting that, until it happened to me, the concept of nine miscarriages was just words to me. I had no earthly idea of how devastating an ordeal a miscarriage is.

I spent days sobbing in my husband's arms, thinking the world had ended, which, with hindsight, I blame on the hormonal overload.

Jason was a freaking saint through the whole thing. He never left my side until he absolutely had to go to work, because, you know… brain surgeon. People needed him, so I had to let him go. But I took three days out of work, waiting until I was certain I could get through the day without hysterics before I went back to my job in the Miami-Dade General Hospital's public relations department.

But I was sad for a long time afterward and shocked to find out I was pregnant again so soon. Now, I'm anxious—and nauseated— all the time. What my mother said about being nauseated only with me gives me comfort. Maybe feeling like shit is actually a good sign.

When I arrive at our place in Brickell, I take the elevator to the seventh floor and am about to put my key in the door when it opens to reveal my husband dressed in running clothes.

"Oh, hey," he says, surprised to see me. "You're home." He takes a closer look. "What's wrong?"

"Couldn't handle the smell of the pig roasting."

"Aw, poor baby." He puts an arm around me and guides me into our gorgeous condo, which is even more so decorated for the holidays. I absolutely love our view of Biscayne Bay and never get tired of watching the activity on the water.

We sit together on the sofa, Jason with his arms around me and my head on his chest.

"What can I get you?"

"This is helping."

"I got plenty of that anytime you need it."

After being widowed so young, I'd gotten used to soldiering through life's challenges on my own. Doing it with Jason is so much better. "Did you hear from your mom? Is her flight all set for the morning?"

"It is. She'll be here by noon. She and my brother are going to my grandmother's tonight. Speaking of my grandmother, I had a nice chat with Mimi on the way home. She says to say hi to you."

"Glad you got to talk to her." I stifle a yawn. My eyes are so heavy, you'd think I didn't sleep for ten hours last night.

"Let's put you down for a nap so you'll feel up to going later. It's not Christmas for you without Nochebuena, so we gotta get you there."

I take the hand he offers me and let him help me up. "Not sure I can do it. The pig took me over the top, and that's never happened before."

"You've never been pregnant for Nochebuena before."

"True. What if I don't feel up to going back? People will know something's up. I told my mom—"

His brows rise so high they nearly touch his hairline. He certainly knows by now the way news travels in my family—at the speed of light times a million. "You did? I thought you didn't want to tell anyone yet."

"She was worried, and I didn't want her to be."

"Will she keep a lid on it?"

"I think so. She understands better than anyone why we'd want to sit on it for a while."

"I keep thinking about them going through what we did *nine* times."

"I know," I say with a sigh as I settle on the bed.

Jason lies down next to me and pulls a throw blanket over me.

"You were going for a run."

"I'd much rather snuggle with you."

"Not that I'd ever say no to that, but if you don't run before tonight's epic feed, you'll be miserable."

"I keep forgetting how this feed is even more epic than Sunday brunch."

"This feed makes Sunday brunch look minor league, and it lasts for *hours*."

"I remember from last year. I couldn't move for days after."

"Exactly. Go run so you won't hate yourself later."

"First I need a kiss to hold me over." He tips my chin up to receive a soft, sweet kiss. "Will you be okay?"

"I will. I promise. I just want to sleep."

"Should I wake you to go back to Abuela's?"

"By four thirty at the latest."

"Will do. Sleep tight. I love my gorgeous baby mama."

"She loves you, too, and promises to forgive you for doing this to her in ten to fifteen years."

His laughter makes me smile even as my eyes close. I can't keep them open for another second. That's the last thing I recall before he's kissing me awake hours later. The first thing I notice is how good he smells.

"Wake up, my sleeping beauty."

"Don't wanna."

"You can't miss Nochebuena."

I give myself another second before I force my eyes open to view the face of my adorable husband. This is our second Christmas together, and I continue to be amazed by how fast the time goes by. After I was widowed when my police officer husband was killed on the job, time seemed to come to a complete stop. Now it seems like the days fly by so fast I can barely keep up.

"What're you thinking about?" He kisses the spot between my brows. "You're doing that thing you do when something's on your mind."

"Just thinking about Tony and you and life and how amazing and painful it all is."

"You must miss him even more at this time of year."

"I do. He loved Nochebuena and was the one who went with Abuela to get the pig every year. That was their special outing together."

"That's so sweet."

"Thank you for helping me keep him close."

"He's part of you, and I love every part of you."

I raise my hand to his freshly shaven face and draw him into a kiss. "Let's get going so we don't miss any of the fun."

"Ready when you are."

CHAPTER 4

ABUELA

*N*ochebuena is my favorite day of the year, but I might be getting too old for the work that goes into it. Don't get me wrong—I have outstanding help from my daughter, Vivian, and our wonderful extended family, but it takes weeks of preparations and planning to pull off this Christmas Eve spectacular. Every year, I swear I'm going to turn it over to a younger member of the family, and every year, I end up committing to one more time.

"Where do you want the avocado and tomato salad?" my sweet, special gentleman friend, Alfredo Muñoz, asks.

"Garage fridge, please, and then remind me it's there later when I can't remember where I put it?"

"You got it, mi amor."

I want to sigh every time he calls me that. *My love.* They say there's no fool like an old fool, and I'm the biggest of old fools, because that man makes my knees weak every single day with the way he looks at me and speaks to me and treats me like I'm the most precious thing in the entire world to him.

I have a *boyfriend* at seventy-six.

The notion is so funny as to be laughable.

Livia Giordino, Vivian's mother-in-law, my best friend and favorite sparring partner, comes in from the garage, carrying the huge arroz con leche, or rice pudding, that she makes every year after I showed my Italian friend the secret years ago.

"Did you remember the extra sugar?" I ask her, as I do every time she makes it, because pushing her buttons is so much fun.

She gives me her trademarked withering look. "I make it better than you do."

"No way."

"Yes way."

I could fight all day with her and never get tired of it, but today I don't have the time—or the energy—to go ten rounds with her. "I saved room for it in the kitchen fridge. Thanks for making it every year. We all look forward to it." See? We can be nice to each other once in a while. Blame it on the holidays that put us all in a festive mood.

"Thank you for hosting and letting the Italians in. We appreciate it."

"What is it we always say? Everyone is Cuban on Nochebuena."

One of my greatest pleasures is seeing my grandchildren—and Livia's—enjoying the traditions we brought to Miami from our homeland more than sixty years ago now. My mother, siblings and I fled with the clothes on our backs after my father was executed in the days leading up to the revolution. I vividly remember the last Nochebuena we celebrated at home in Havana and how stark our first Christmas Eve in Miami was by comparison.

But the exile community opened its arms to us, and by the second Christmas, we were once again embracing our traditions. No matter how many years pass, however, I've never forgotten that first Christmas in Miami. I think that's why I carry on with hosting Nochebuena, even if I'm ready to hand it off to the next generation.

One more year…

Alfredo returns from the garage, carrying the buñuelos, or yuca doughnuts, made by Elena, mother to Nico, Maria, Dee and Milo.

Elena follows him in. "Maria texted that they're still scheduled to land at six. Austin's parents are going to bring Everly to meet them here."

"I'm so glad she'll make it in time." Our sweet Maria adores Nochebuena and looks forward to it all year. I adore the way our Italian family members embrace my Cuban heritage on this special day.

"The bakery was absolutely mobbed," Elena adds. "I'm glad we ordered ahead. Lorenzo is bringing the Cuban bread and pastelitos." She's married to my son-in-law Vincent's brother, but we're all one big happy family. I wouldn't have it any other way, especially on Nochebuena.

"Excellent." It's all coming together.

Alfredo puts the buñuelos on the counter and comes over to me.

I smile up at the handsome man who has become so special to me over these last few months. "Thank you for all the help."

"My pleasure, but you look tired. I want you to sit for a bit and put your feet up. You need to pace yourself."

A few months ago, I would've scowled at any man who tried to tell me what to do. Decades of widowhood made me fiercely independent, but Alfredo wants only what's best for me, which is why I allow him to take me by the hand and lead me into the front parlor that's always ready for guests.

For four years, he asked me to have dinner with him every Saturday night at Giordino's, the Cuban-Italian restaurant Vivian and her husband, Vincent, own and run with my help and Livia's— and now Dee, the new general manager. Every week for four years, I declined Alfredo's kind offer. Until I finally said yes, which was the best thing I've done for myself in years.

When we're seated together on the sofa, still holding hands, he turns to face me. "You're running yourself ragged."

"I do that once a year."

"You do it every day, but today more than the others. What a production this is!"

"You have Nochebuena in your family, too."

"We do, but yours is spectacular by anyone's standards."

"What's that English saying the kids like so much? Go big or go home?"

"Ah, yes, one of my favorites. Speaking of going big or going home… I've been thinking about you and me and our special friendship as we count down to the holidays and the new year."

"What about it?" I ask warily.

"Don't give me that look," he says, smiling. "It's all good things. Such as whether I might convince you to marry me one of these days."

"Marry you?"

"You told me to speak English to you, right? That you want to learn?"

"Yes, Sofia and I are learning together," I say of the young woman our family has "adopted" since Jason saved her young son's life.

"So you understand what the word 'marry' means."

"As I have been married in the past, I do understand."

"Excellent."

"I don't want to get married again."

He frowns. "Why not?"

"Because."

"That's not an answer, Marlene."

"It's the only answer I have, Alfredo. I like things the way they are. We have a nice time together. Why does it have to be more than that?"

"Because I love you, and I want to be with you all the time and not just some of the time."

I knew he cared for me, but to hear him come right out and say he loves me and wants to be with me all the time comes as a surprise. Well, sort of a surprise… It hasn't been so long since I lost my husband that I don't understand the difference between friendship and romance. My time with Alfredo is most definitely the latter. I just learned that term—latter—in English class last week. There's former and latter. While I enjoy my friendship with Alfredo, it is indeed a romance.

"And I'm a fool," Alfredo says, "because today is certainly not the day to have this conversation when you're preparing for the biggest party of the year. My apologizes, sweetheart. We shall revisit this at a more appropriate time."

He's so dear and so kind and so... well, everything, that I reach for his hand and cradle it between both of mine. "Will you give me some time to think about your kind offer?"

"Of course. Take all the time you need. I'm not going anywhere. I just... I want you to know that the time we've spent together is the best time I've had since I lost my dear wife. You are so very special to me."

"And you are special to me. Very special indeed."

"It's enough for now to know that." He leans in to give me a kiss on the cheek. "Have you eaten anything since breakfast?"

I think about that for a minute. "I can't say that I have."

"I'll go find you a snack. Be right back."

After he goes, my mind races with thoughts I never expected to have again. *Marriage.* My goodness, the man is full of surprises!

Livia comes into the room. "There you are." She's as tall as I am petite, and while my hair has gone snow-white, hers is still dark with streaks of silver running through it.

"Alfredo made me take a break."

She sits next to me and puts her feet up on my coffee table, as at home here as she is in her own home. I wouldn't have it any other way. "He's a good man."

"Yes, he is." Lowering my voice, I tell her, "He wants to get married."

"That's no surprise."

"It was to me!"

"Because you're stupid that way. Can't see the forest for the trees when you're standing in the middle of them."

"Can we talk about the ways you're muy estúpida?"

"We're talking about you right now. That man is hopelessly devoted to you, and of course he wants to marry you."

"We're old, Livia!"

"So what?"

"What in the world am I going to do with a *husband* at my age?"

"Are you so demented that you really need me to tell you that?"

I scowl at her, which only makes her laugh. The bitch. That's one of my favorite English words. "There hasn't been anyone since my Jorge passed." I lost my husband suddenly a lifetime ago, when we were forty-two. "I'm not sure I could do... *that*... with someone else." Jorge was my one and only, my one true love.

"You could."

"What makes you so sure?"

"I see a man who adores you and would do everything he could to make you comfortable."

"I can't picture it, no matter how hard I try."

"So, you have thought about it..."

She makes me want to smack her, which of course she knows.

"I wish I could find a nice man like Alfredo."

That shocks me. "You *do*?"

"Yes, I do. I'm tired of being alone. Aren't you tired of it?"

"No," I say, glancing at the doorway. I wouldn't want Alfredo to overhear us.

"You want to hear a secret?"

Siempre. "Always."

"I have a crush on my flight instructor." Ever since Vincent decided the four of us needed lives outside of work, Livia has been fulfilling a lifelong dream of becoming a pilot.

"How old is he?"

"Sixty."

"That's fifteen years younger than you!"

"Believe it or not, I was able to do that math myself. And besides, it doesn't matter. I like him. He likes me, and if he asks me out, I'm going to say yes."

"You'd be a cradle-robbing cougar."

"I liked you better before your English was so good."

That makes me laugh harder than I have in days. I'm still laughing when Alfredo returns with a bowl and a glass of iced tea with lemon, just the way I like it.

"I never know if I'm going to find you two laughing or locked in mortal combat."

"It's a minute-to-minute thing," Livia says, standing to give him her spot on the sofa.

"Don't get up on my account," Alfredo says.

"I need to go check on the boys and the pig. I heard Domenic is taking regular samples," she says of her grandson, who's home from New York City, "and with his appetite, there won't be anything left for the rest of us if he's not stopped."

"Get right on that, then," I tell her, well aware of Domenic's ferocious appetite. Although not even he could put a dent in the gigantic pig roasting in the backyard.

"Sofia was putting the finishing touches on the moro," Alfredo says of the black beans and rice that are a Nochebuena staple. "She wanted you to try it."

The smell has my mouth watering as I take the steaming bowl from him. As I take the first bite, flavor explodes on my tongue. "Oh yes, that's muy bueno."

"Your protégé is coming right along."

"Yes, she is."

"Lovely Sofia has blossomed under your tutelage and Livia's this year."

"She's a wonderful young woman, and we're thrilled to have her as part of our family."

"I think you're a wonderful woman with the way you made her and her son part of your lives. You have no idea what you've done for her."

"She's a very special person and so is her little Mateo. We're the lucky ones."

"And you wonder why I love you."

"Actually, I don't. I'm very lovable."

His laughter rocks his entire body. "Yes, you are."

"I want you to know... I appreciate having you in my life, and I'm very happy I finally said yes to you after all those years of you asking me to join you for dinner."

"But?"

"No buts. Just that. I will think about what you asked me."

He leans in and kisses me. "You make me very happy, mi amor."

I use another of my new vocabulary words to sum things up. "Likewise."

CHAPTER 5

SOFIA

I'm keeping careful watch over the moro after Marlene taught me how quickly the rice and beans can become mushy. After I turn down the heat on the gas stove, I stir the huge pot to keep the rice from sticking to the bottom of the pan. Marlene taught me it's a delicate balancing act. I had to look up the meaning of that expression and learned it means to carefully manage two or more things. Today, I'm managing the rice and beans and the attention of a man who makes my heart race when he looks at me the way he does.

Nico Giordino.

His sisters and cousin have warned me away from him.

Maria says he's toxic with women. I had to look up the meaning of the word *toxic*, too. I found out that means his behavior would add negativity and upset to my life, which is the last thing I need after what I've gone through with Mateo's father.

Speak of the devil... That's another phrase I learned from Livia. Anytime I hear something I don't understand, I ask for the meaning. Since the medical emergency that brought me to Dr. Jason Northrup and the Giordino family, I'm determined to learn as

315

much English as I can. While I was blessed with wonderful translators who helped me navigate the medical maze, I decided that I need a basic understanding of English, too.

Marlene, who committed to learning English after her first trip "home" to Cuba since the revolution made her realize that Miami is now her home, has been my partner in learning English. While we will always be proud native Spanish speakers, we're pleased with what we've learned so far at our ESL classes.

Back to the devil… He's due any minute to deliver our son to me for Nochebuena and Christmas morning.

Joaquín Diaz was my childhood sweetheart, who somewhere along the way fell into the wrong crowd, got himself into trouble with drugs and petty crime and made my life a living hell for years with intense emotional abuse that later became physical. I've finally broken free of him, thanks in no small part to Marlene and Livia, who heard about our plight when Mateo was sick, offered me a job with benefits and quite simply saved my life—and my son's. Thanks to them and a friend who's a lawyer, I've filed for divorce and received a protective order that requires Joaquín to stay five hundred feet from me. The only exception to the order is when we hand off our son between visits.

Sometimes I still can't believe it's come to a need for official protection from the man I loved for most of my life.

"Sofia," Nico's cousin Domenic says. "Someone's asking for you outside."

I experience a moment of pure joy at the thought of seeing my little boy that's quickly followed by the dread of having to see his father. After washing my hands, I ask Dee to keep an eye on the moro for me and go out through the garage to greet my son.

He's doing a lot better than he was, but he's still got a long way to go in his recovery from brain surgery to remove a cancerous tumor. Thankfully, Jason got it all, and he recommended a course of radiation that's now completed. But the damage to his fine motor skills, another English term that has become familiar to me, was significant, thus the ongoing physical and occupational therapy.

Nico pulls up in his father's truck as I emerge from the garage into bright South Florida sunshine. Marlene sent him to pick up the keg from a nearby liquor store. He approaches Joaquín's old red sedan, which is parked in the driveway. "I'll take him," he says to Joaquín.

I stand back and allow Nico to intervene on my behalf, not willing to admit what a relief it is to have him deal with Joaquín so I don't have to.

"I need to speak to my wife," Joaquín says in Spanish as he tightens his hold on Mateo.

"She's not your wife any longer," Nico reminds him, also in Spanish, as he reaches for my son.

"Back off, dude."

I step forward before the two of them get physical. I wouldn't put it past either of them. "It's okay, Nico. I've got this."

Glaring at Joaquín, Nico takes a step back but stays nearby. Just in case.

I take Mateo from Joaquín and hold him close. He smells like cigarette smoke, which enrages me. How can Joaquín smoke around him—or allow anyone else to—after what he's been through? "What do you need?"

"I want you to come home for Christmas," he says in Spanish. "Where you belong."

"I'm sorry, that's not possible," I reply in English.

His scowl turns a face I once found handsome ugly. "You're so fancy now, you can't even speak your own language?"

"I'll see you on the twenty-seventh." I turn away from him to carry Mateo inside. He's looking forward to swimming in Marlene's pool before the party begins later this afternoon.

"Don't take another step," Nico says to Joaquín.

I continue on as if I didn't hear that. I trust Nico to make sure Joaquín doesn't follow us inside. But the minute I'm safely in the house, I rush to the front window to look out to make sure the situation isn't escalating. Mateo snuggles into my embrace, seeming relieved, as he always is, to be back with me. I cringe to think about what goes on when he's alone with Joaquín, but the court requires one overnight a week with his father.

The two men are exchanging words, but that's all it is.

After Joaquín makes an obscene gesture at him, Nico walks away, his fists rolled tightly by his sides. My heart races at the sight of him, angry on my behalf. Why does that mean so much to me? Maybe it's because for years no one was ever angry on my behalf while Joaquín was bullying me into doing everything his way.

Nico comes to find me in Marlene's dining room where the huge table is covered with serving dishes and other party items.

"Gracias," I say to him. "Lo siento." When I'm upset, I revert to my native language.

"Don't thank me or apologize to me," he says in a harsh tone that's not directed at me.

How do I know that? I couldn't say other than he has never been anything other than sweet to me, but Joaquín can make the sweetest person angry in a matter of seconds. I never saw that side of him until after we were married.

"I don't like the way that guy acts as if you still belong to him."

"He knows I don't."

Nico puts his hands on his hips, frustration apparent in his pose and expression. "Does he?"

"If he doesn't, that's not my fault. What else can I do besides file for divorce?"

"I hate the idea of you guys not being safe," he says, softly so as not to alarm Mateo.

"We're safe," I say, but the waver in my voice tells the true story. I never feel truly safe except for when I'm at work, surrounded by people like him who care about me. And Nico doesn't even work at Giordino's. He's just there a lot, especially when I'm working.

"I wish…" He stops himself and shakes his head.

"What do you wish?"

"We should talk about that sometime when we're not surrounded by people during a holiday."

My heart is beating so fast I wonder if I'm going to pass out, or something equally embarrassing, in front of the man who has become a close friend over the last few months. What does he want to talk about?

"I'm going to contact a friend of mine who's a cop and ask him to send cars by here later, just in case your ex decides to come back and start trouble."

I swallow hard at the thought of my ex-husband causing trouble for the family that's been so good to us. "You really think that's necessary?"

"I do."

"Maybe Mateo and I should just go. If we're not here, then no one will bother your family."

"You're safer here than you'd be anywhere else. The people here would kill for you."

"Would they?"

"They would."

"All of them, or just you?"

"All of them, but especially me."

"And why is that?"

"That's the thing we should maybe talk about when my entire family isn't about to arrive for Nochebuena."

The look he gives me when he says those words steals the breath from my lungs. Nico Giordino is the sexiest man on the planet, and I'll fight anyone who says otherwise. Right in that moment, I don't care that his own sisters and cousin think he's toxic toward women.

I just want more of him and the way he makes me feel.

CHAPTER 6

MARIA

I feel like I'm going to hyperventilate if we don't get to Abuela's soon. The flight from LA that took us to the southernmost part of Texas to avoid the storms in the Plains, seemed endless, even if it was "only" six hours. I can't wait to see Everly.

Austin and I bonded a year after I donated the bone marrow that saved Everly's life. With her mother not in the picture, she's now as much my daughter as she is his, and I've been counting down to my first Christmas with both of them.

We've finally landed in Miami and are trudging through the terminal with several of Austin's teammates and their wives or girl-friends, all of whom are as eager to get home as I am. Some of them have kids and were afraid they were going to miss Christmas with them.

As they head to the parking garage where we left our cars, Austin stops me. "We're going that way." He points to the left of the garage.

"What do you mean? We parked over there."

"Just come with me," he says, taking my hand as we say goodbye to the others. One of them is having a New Year's Eve party that we're looking forward to. Austin has fit right in with his new Marlins teammates, and their significant others have been welcoming to me, as well.

Because I'd follow him anywhere, I let him lead me away from where we left his BMW SUV. I don't get why he'd want to delay seeing Everly any longer than we already have. I'm about to ask that question when he stops next to a white Mercedes G-Class SUV parked at the curb. It has a gigantic red bow on top. A man I've never met is standing next to it. Austin greets him with a handshake.

"Thanks again for this," Austin says to him.

"My pleasure."

"Uh, what's this?" I ask Austin in a low tone that can't be overheard by the other man.

"It's your new ride," he says, grinning widely. "Merry Christmas."

I stare at the gorgeous vehicle, recalling how I said the one his teammate had gotten for his wife was cool. But that didn't mean I wanted one for myself.

"Say something," he says, his smile fading.

"It's really nice, Austin." My stomach begins to ache. "Thank you."

He tips his head to look at me more closely. "Why do you not seem happy?"

"I, uh... Tell me you didn't get rid of the Honda." I've had my silver Honda Civic for years, and I love that car.

"Not yet," he says, seeming baffled. "But we won't have any problem selling it."

"I can't sell that car."

"What's going on here, Maria?"

I eye the G-Wagon, which is what his teammate called theirs. "Could we maybe discuss this in private?" In addition to the man who apparently delivered the new vehicle, people are swirling all around us, hustling to get to where they're going for the holidays.

It's only a matter of minutes before someone recognizes the Marlins' famous new pitcher.

"Sure." He gives the man a hundred-dollar bill he had ready for him. "Merry Christmas."

"Same to you, and if I might add, I'm a huge fan. Go Marlins."

"Thanks, man." Austin accepts the bro-shake-back-slap guys do these days and then holds the passenger door for me.

The new-car smell is the first thing I notice.

Austin takes the bow off the top, stashes it in the back and gets into the driver's side.

"What about the BMW?"

"We'll get it tomorrow." He looks over at me. "I should've asked if you wanted to drive."

"No, you can. I'd be afraid to drive a car this expensive."

"The car is *yours*, Maria. Of course you're going to drive it. And why do you want to keep the Honda if you have this?"

"I can't drive this to the clinic where I work with people who don't have enough to eat, Austin."

He releases a deep sigh. "You said you liked the one Lolo got for Elle."

"I do, but that doesn't mean I expected you to get one for me."

"I wanted to do something cool for you for Christmas. I thought you'd love it."

"Anyone would love this car, Austin."

"Anyone but my fiancée, you mean."

My stomach aches in earnest now. "Please don't be hurt. You're so amazingly generous, and you know how much I appreciate that, but this car is not me." And it sort of pains me that he didn't already know that. How could he not know?

He surprises me when he pulls over just outside the airport and puts the SUV in Park before turning to me. "We give a ton of money to charity. I've fully funded the new clinic."

"And I love you so much for that. You'll never know what that means to me."

"I do know what it means to you, because I know you. I know

what matters to you. As long as we're taking care of those less
fortunate, aren't we allowed to enjoy a few luxuries?"

"We live in the most beautiful home I've ever seen and just had
ten magical days in Hawaii. Our life is one big luxury."

"So, what's one more?"

"I don't want to hurt your feelings. You obviously went to some
trouble to arrange a nice surprise for me, and I don't want to
ruin it."

"You're not hurting my feelings. I just thought you'd need a bigger
car for when we started adding to our family, and this thing is a beast. I
want my family in something super safe, because the way people drive
around here freaks me out. I pity the fool who hits you in this thing."

"It does seem rather rugged."

"It has amazing safety ratings."

"I am a safety girl."

"See? I knew that. Please don't be thinking I don't get you,
because I do."

I reach for his hand and curl mine around it. "It's a really nice
surprise. Thank you."

"You're welcome."

"But I can keep the Honda for driving to work?"

He rolls his eyes. "If you must."

"I must."

Leaning across the center console, he says, "Kiss me."

So I kiss him because there's almost nothing else I'd rather do at
any given moment.

"If you're not happy, I'm not happy," he says. "If you decide you
don't want to keep the G-Wagon, we won't keep it. It's no big deal."

"It's a big deal that you want me to drive the safest car you could
find."

"Keeping you and Ev and any other kids we have safe is the only
thing I care about."

He's still grappling with the trauma of seeing his beloved
daughter through a near-fatal illness, and knowing that makes me
understand one of the primary reasons he wants me to have this

particular vehicle. "Then I'll drive it with pleasure to everywhere but the clinic because it brings you peace of mind."

"Thank you."

"I love you."

"I love you more," he says as he pulls back into traffic and hits the gas to get us to Abuela's.

"No way."

"Yes way."

"I can't wait to see Everly."

"I know. This is the longest I've been away from her for anything other than work."

We debated taking her with us to Hawaii, but after a rocky transition, she's gotten into a good routine in Miami with a preschool she loves and new friends. She spends so much time with Austin's parents, who live with us, that we decided it would be better for her to stay in her routine. Not to mention, it was the first time we've truly had to ourselves since we became a couple. Even though we FaceTimed with her every day, we still missed her like crazy.

I'm almost bouncing in my seat by the time we pull up to Abuela's, which is mobbed with cars. We end up parking two blocks down the street and are walking to the house when we see Wyatt approaching from the other direction. I've been so caught up in getting home to Everly that I almost forgot about his big annual checkup today.

"How'd it go?" I ask him before we even say hello.

My sister is happier with him than she's ever been in her life, and the thought of anything happening to him is simply unbearable —even if we all know he's living on borrowed time.

He gives a thumbs-up. "All good. Got my inspection sticker renewed for another year."

"Oh, thank God." I hug him tightly. "Thank God."

"Awww, you guys love me."

"Yes, we do."

Dee comes running out of the house, stopping short six feet from him. "You were supposed to text me!"

"I got done early so I came right here. All good under the hood, baby."

She lets out a cry and runs for him.

He wraps his arms around her and lifts her off her feet.

"Put me down! Your heart!"

"Is in perfect shape, especially since it found you."

He puts her down and kisses her as Austin gives my hand a tug toward the house. "Let's give them a minute."

"Thank God he's okay."

"You said it."

"They've only been together a short time, and I already can't imagine her without him."

"Me either. They're a great couple."

We enter into chaos in Abuela's kitchen. Every woman in my family, or so it seems, is overseeing some part of the feast, but the only "woman" I want to see is the little one who's wrapped herself so deeply around my heart that it's like she's always been there.

"So glad you made it," my mom, Elena, says when she hugs me and then Austin.

"Us, too," I reply.

My mom is wearing a stylish wig after battling stage three breast cancer. She finishes treatment in January, and we're all counting the days until that nightmare is behind us. That was another reason why I couldn't bear to miss Christmas in Miami this year.

"Where's our princess?" Austin asks.

"In the pool with your dad. She can't wait to see you guys."

I clap my hands with glee as I accept hugs from Abuela and Nona. "We can't wait to see her."

We greet a million other family members, or so it seems, on the way outside where the scent of roasting meat fills the air and makes my mouth water. I was too wound up to eat on the plane, and I'm starving.

Everly sees us coming and lets out a blood-curdling shriek that startles her poor grandfather. Austin's dad recovers quickly, lifting her out of the pool so she can run to us, soaking wet. But ask us if we care as we engage in a tight group hug.

"Rie! Swim!"

I'm laughing through tears as I breathe in the sweet scent of her blonde hair, which is plastered to her head. She has cute little earplugs, since she contracted an ear infection from too much swimming.

"Daddy's here, too," Austin says as he kisses her whole face.

"Daddy! Swim! Now!"

"Give us one minute to catch our breath and get changed, and then we'll swim," Austin tells her.

She's already squirming to get loose so she can return to her favorite thing.

Austin puts her down, and she rushes to her grandfather, who holds out his arms to catch her when she jumps fearlessly into the pool.

"Business as usual around here," I tell him.

"Did she grow like six inches while we were gone, or does it just seem like that to me?"

"Not quite six inches, but she does seem taller."

We accept hugs from the entire family. I'm thrilled to see my cousin Domenic and other cousins and friends who've gathered for our favorite night of the year. Abuela has gone all out as usual, and the musical group that comes every year is already playing all our favorite Cuban songs. My cousin Carmen looks a little odd, which immediately has me wondering what's up with her.

"Nothing," she says when I ask her that. "I'm just feeling a little off."

I gasp. "Are you preggo?"

"No, no, nothing like that."

"You're a terrible liar. You always have been."

"Don't say anything, please?" she asks, her eyes filling. "I'm not ready."

I hug her as tightly as I have in ages, so happy for her, even if she looks like she's about to puke. "My lips are sealed."

I'm so relieved to be here, among my people with the new

people I fell in love with this year, ready to celebrate and enjoy this sacred night of family and gratitude. We eat like the good Cubans we all are on this special occasion, devouring the ton of food Abuela and the others made—but leaving more than enough for the lazy day of leftovers we'll enjoy tomorrow.

For hours, we dance, sing and laugh with cousins and friends. We drink beer from the keg and gorge on desserts, such as arroz con leche, flan, buñuelos, natilla (a custard dessert) and turon (a semisweet and nutty delicacy). If you asked me to pick my favorite, I wouldn't be able to, so I have a taste of everything. At eleven fifteen, we walk the short distance to Midnight Mass at the parish Abuela has belonged to since the sixties.

Austin's parents took Everly home to bed, and we promised to tuck her in again when we get home after Mass.

I love the music most of all—"O Come, All Ye Faithful," "Silent Night," "The First Noel," "Joy to the World," "O Holy Night" and "Ave Maria." Tears fill my eyes as my heart overflows with joy and gratitude.

A year ago on Nochebuena, I couldn't have imagined how my life was about to change or that a year later, I'd be engaged to the most wonderful man and preparing to adopt his beautiful daughter. Everly and I will always share a special bond, one that is literally bone-deep.

I give thanks to God for bringing them and Austin's family into my life and pray that we have many happy years together. I pray for Wyatt's continued good health, for my mother's recovery, for Carmen and Jason and the baby they're expecting, for Carmen's late husband, Tony, and his family, for my dad, brothers, sister, grandmothers, aunts, uncles and precious cousins. I'm blessed beyond measure, and I know it.

"Are you okay?" Austin whispers.

"I'm so happy. So, so happy, to be here with you and my entire family and to get to go home to Everly. Everything is perfect."

Smiling, he says, "Feliz Navidad, mi amor."

"Feliz Navidad."

ALSO BY MARIE FORCE

Contemporary Romances Available from Marie Force

The Miami Nights Series

Book 1: How Much I Feel (*Carmen & Jason*)

Book 2: How Much I Care (*Maria & Austin*)

Book 3: How Much I Love (*Dee & Wyatt*)

Nochebuena, A Miami Nights Novella

Book 4: How Much I Want (*Nico & Sofia*)

Book 5: How Much I Need (*Milo & Gianna, Coming Feb. 2023*)

The Wild Widows Series—a Fatal Series Spin-Off

Book 1: Someone Like You

Book 2: Someone to Hold

The Gansett Island Series

Book 1: Maid for Love (*Mac & Maddie*)

Book 2: Fool for Love (*Joe & Janey*)

Book 3: Ready for Love (*Luke & Sydney*)

Book 4: Falling for Love (*Grant & Stephanie*)

Book 5: Hoping for Love (*Evan & Grace*)

Book 6: Season for Love (*Owen & Laura*)

Book 7: Longing for Love (*Blaine & Tiffany*)

Book 8: Waiting for Love (*Adam & Abby*)

Book 9: Time for Love (*David & Daisy*)

Book 10: Meant for Love (*Jenny & Alex*)

Book 10.5: Chance for Love, *A Gansett Island Novella* (*Jared & Lizzie*)

Book 11: Gansett After Dark (*Owen & Laura*)

Book 12: Kisses After Dark (*Shane & Katie*)

Book 13: Love After Dark (*Paul & Hope*)

Book 14: Celebration After Dark (*Big Mac & Linda*)

Book 15: Desire After Dark (*Slim & Erin*)

Book 16: Light After Dark (*Mallory & Quinn*)

Book 17: Victoria & Shannon (Episode 1)

Book 18: Kevin & Chelsea (Episode 2)

A Gansett Island Christmas Novella

Book 19: Mine After Dark (*Riley & Nikki*)

Book 20: Yours After Dark (*Finn & Chloe*)

Book 21: Trouble After Dark (*Deacon & Julia*)

Book 22: Rescue After Dark (*Mason & Jordan*)

Book 23: Blackout After Dark (*Full Cast*)

Book 24: Temptation After Dark (*Gigi & Cooper*)

Book 25: Resilience After Dark (*Jace & Cindy*)

The Green Mountain Series

Book 1: All You Need Is Love (*Will & Cameron*)

Book 2: I Want to Hold Your Hand (*Nolan & Hannah*)

Book 3: I Saw Her Standing There (*Colton & Lucy*)

Book 4: And I Love Her (*Hunter & Megan*)

Novella: You'll Be Mine (*Will & Cam's Wedding*)

Book 5: It's Only Love (*Gavin & Ella*)

Book 6: Ain't She Sweet (*Tyler & Charlotte*)

Single Titles

Five Years Gone

One Year Home

Sex Machine

Sex God

Georgia on My Mind

True North

The Fall

The Wreck

Love at First Flight

Everyone Loves a Hero

Line of Scrimmage

Romantic Suspense Novels Available from Marie Force

The Fatal Series

One Night With You, *A Fatal Series Prequel Novella*

Book 1: Fatal Affair

Book 2: Fatal Justice

Book 3: Fatal Consequences

Book 3.5: Fatal Destiny, *the Wedding Novella*

Book 4: Fatal Flaw

Book 5: Fatal Deception

Book 6: Fatal Mistake

Book 7: Fatal Jeopardy

Book 8: Fatal Scandal

Book 9: Fatal Frenzy

Book 10: Fatal Identity

Book 11: Fatal Threat

Book 12: Fatal Chaos

Book 13: Fatal Invasion

Historical Romance Available from Marie Force

ABOUT THE AUTHOR

Marie Force is the *New York Times* best-selling author of contemporary romance, romantic suspense and erotic romance. Her series include Fatal, First Family, Gansett Island, Butler Vermont, Quantum, Treading Water, Miami Nights and Wild Widows.
Her books have sold more than 10 million copies worldwide, have been translated into more than a dozen languages and have appeared on the *New York Times* best-seller more than 30 times. She is also a *USA Today* and #1 *Wall Street Journal* bestseller, as well as a Spiegel bestseller in Germany.

Her goals in life are simple—to finish raising two happy, healthy, productive young adults, to keep writing books for as long as she possibly can and to never be on a flight that makes the news.

Join Marie's mailing list on her website at *marieforce.com* for news about new books and upcoming appearances in your area. Follow her on Facebook at *www.Facebook.com/MarieForceAuthor*, Instagram at *www.instagram.com/marieforceauthor/* and TikTok at *https://www.tiktok.com/@marieforceauthor?.* Contact Marie at *marie@marieforce.com*.

Made in the USA
Monee, IL
23 May 2022

96899205R00199